Because of Us

NINA ARADA

Copyright © 2022 by Nina Arada

All rights reserved

No part of this book may be used or reproduced in any form or by any means, electronic or mechanical, including photocopying, recording, or by any information storage and retrieval system without prior written consent of the author except where permitted by law or for the use of brief quotations in a book review.

The characters and events depicted in this book are fictitious. Any similarity to real persons, living or dead, is coincidental and not intended by the author.

Published by Nina Norwalt

Edited by Elaine York / Allusion Publishing

Cover Design by Okay Creations

Hot Air Balloon Art by Shannon Payne @spayne.illustrations

❧ Created with Vellum

content warning

This book contains potentially triggering content including sexual violence, death, alcohol abuse, and anxiety. Please take this into consideration and feel free to reach out with questions or concerns. For anyone suffering or seeking help, please contact the National Sexual Assault Hotline at 1.800.656.HOPE available 24 hours a day, 7 days a week.

To that little girl filled with all the insecurities, just wait, because in the end, you burn the brightest.

playlist

"Popular" **Nada Surf**
"ocean eyes" **Billie Eilish**
"IV. Sweatpants" **Childish Gambino**
"goosebumps" **Travis Scott**
"Happier Than Ever" **Billie Eilish**
"Tear in My Heart" **twenty one pilots**
"First Breath After Coma" **Explosions in the Sky**
"Sweet Dreams (Are Made of This)" **Marilyn Manson**
"Stitches" **Shawn Mendes**
"Lua" **Bright Eyes**
"Kamikaze" **MØ**
"Lost on You" **Lewis Capaldi**
"Blood Bank" **Bon Iver**

Be sure to check out the QR code after the story for a full playlist of songs that accompany and inspired Because of Us.

prologue

WORDS.

Famous quotes. Poems. Lyrics. Novels. Fairy tales.

I've always been fascinated with words and how they can be pieced together. They explain feelings I don't know how to put into words myself, and bring understanding to what I've yet to feel. As a little girl, I craved the words from the books I'd read and the songs I'd listen to. I would doodle them into notebooks, turning them into art. And as a woman, I had them carved into my skin as a completely different form of art.

These words would guide me through some of the toughest moments of my life and heal me in a way I couldn't comprehend.

At times, the words would follow me when I just wanted to leave them behind. And I'm glad they did because more times than I'd like to admit, those very words were all I had.

chapter one

last day of sophomore year, 2013

josie

THE SUN IS HARDLY out to play but I'm wide awake. I woke up eighteen minutes before my alarm this morning and just stared out the window, rubbing the soft material of my childhood blanket with thoughts of the upcoming summer.

"Joe!" I hear my mom shouting in the hall, acting as my brother's personal alarm clock. He answers her with a grunt, followed by, "Why don't you yell out 'Josie, despiértate!' like you do me?" His impersonation of my mom's voice and thick Spanish accent is spot on.

"Well, because she uses her phone as an alarm—unlike you—and not her mother," my dad pipes in.

I sigh and get out of bed, wandering into my closet for a last-day-of-school outfit. It's May and we live in Florida, so jeans and my favorite gray hoodie with a floral design sketched in black on the front doesn't make sense, but it's happening. It's like a security blanket.

Plus, last day means I'm just taking a few exams and probably watching *Remember the Titans* for the millionth time.

Once I'm ready, I greet my parents and grab a banana for the road, following my brother out to the car. *Our* car. This morning, during those eighteen minutes that I was waiting for my alarm to go off, I thought about starting my first shift at my new job at the local ice cream shop this weekend... a job where I plan to save most of my earnings so I can finally have my own vehicle. Joe, my twin, I should add, and I share my mom's old Honda Civic, but our dad says as soon as we can put aside two grand, we can get another car. If I don't have to fight Joe over who gets the car every weekend, I'll be happy. I don't even care what kind of car it is if I'm the one who contributes most of the money, or if I'm the one who ends up with this ancient thing on wheels that requires a pencil wedged underneath the stereo to keep it in place, allowing it to play music. I just want my own ride. My freedom.

Let me present to you Exhibit A on why I'm obsessed with having my own car: here I am now in the backseat of the car that's half *mine* sitting and waiting in front of Leah Peters's house. Imagine Leah as...the leader of a group of *Heathers*—because that's who she is. Now, imagine her as my brother's plaything—because that's what she is, too. I'd hate to use the phrase girlfriend, but it isn't that serious between them like she wishes it was. Most mornings you can find her and her minions striking up a convo with Joe and Wes, my brother's best friend, before class. She twirls her hair while her posse hangs onto her every word, puffing their chests out. They giggle and I roll my eyes. For the last two weeks (basically since my brother started hooking up with her), I've gotten an even earlier dose of her gum-smacking because we've picked her up from her house to give her a ride to school. Insert eyeroll.

Honestly, she and her friends annoy me much less than they did before. Unlike two years ago, I'd stand there, green with envy, as I watched them talk up my brother and his best friend. I would have done anything for their perfect blonde locks or even Leah's boobs. But alas, here I am, still, with my boring, brown frizzy hair pulled back into a ponytail. I can literally feel the flyaways creating a disgusting halo around my head. Let's not even talk about my chest, or lack thereof. My mom had to return the bras she welcomed me home with last weekend when she came back from visiting my aunt. Apparently, I'm not the size B they think or wish I was. I'd have to save a few bucks, invest in a flat iron, and do lots of praying to the boob gods if I want to look anything like the Heathers. But I. Don't. Care. I wanted to be them back then, and now that I know who they are under those padded bras and bleached-out manes, I'm okay being me. My boring self. And kind. I'm a kind person.

Okay, maybe not so much to the Heathers.

I don't understand what they get from being so rude to people, specifically those who don't look like carbon copies of Leah Peters and her crew.

Don't get me wrong, being more popular wouldn't be such a bad thing. Having more friends would be fun.

But I want people to like me for me, not because I'm fake or because I got drunk at the Prom afterparty (and showed everyone my boobs, Leah!), or because of my brother.

There's my downfall. Joe. His real name is Jose. *I wonder how popular he'd be if he went by that?* Anyway, Joe plays football, skips sixth period more times than he attends it, and he brings booze to the parties through one of our cousins who's over twenty-one and doesn't care. I'm pretty sure Joe pays him like twenty bucks or something. There's just something about him being the "cool" twin that hides me in the background when it comes to our peers.

I hear Leah, then I smell her before I even see her. Her choice of perfume wouldn't be so bad if it weren't so damn strong. She plops into the front passenger seat, all clinking jewelry and giggles and perfume and teeth, greeting my brother with a loud, wet kiss on his cheek.

"Hiiii! Last day in that hell hole!" she sings. "Now we are officially juniors!"

She turns to look at me and gives me a fake smile. I slit my eyes and press my lips together, throwing back an even faker one.

She rolls her eyes and grips Joe's bicep. "I'm so excited for the end-of-the-year party tonight! You're still taking me, right, babe?" Leah looks up, longing for him to drive her there, and anywhere, full speed into a future with four kids, a dog, and an infinity pool with a jacuzzi off to the side. *Gross, Joe, please don't marry this chick or anyone else like her.*

"Yeah, girl. We won't miss it," my brother answers her.

I tune whatever else he has to say to her out and grab my phone from my backpack after I feel the vibration from a text come in.

Cora: Almost here?
Me: Like 10 more mins. Otw to pick up Wes. We had to pick up you-know-who again.
Cora: Oh, gross. When will ur bro see that I'm the one he needs?
Me: Ok, stop. THAT'S GROSS.
Cora: Yeah, yeah, yeahhh, sister! Ha! Don't forget my book.
Me: Dean Holder comin' in hot!
Cora: *winky face*

Cora Bennett, my lifeline. We've been best friends since kindergarten when we would sit outside her apartment building and sell our watercolor paintings, fifty cents apiece. I think we made two bucks that summer thanks to random family members stopping by. Most of our teenage summers have been spent sipping Frappuccinos and chewing on biscotti while we sit across from each other in the teen romance aisles of the local bookstore. We'd spend our allowances on books with charming covers and dreamy book-boyfriends, then trade them to one another full of highlighted words and crammed notes along the edges of the pages. Now, we'll be stepping into this summer together, sharing the hopes of first (real) boyfriends, first parties, and hopefully a first kiss for me. Cora already experienced that one when she dated that dud with the squirrel as a pet for two weeks freshman year. Needless to say, she didn't have much insight on the whole process since it was a one-and-done thing.

I lock the phone and place it in my lap, screen down trying not to look out the window at Wes as he walks up to our approaching car. But my eyes fail me the second he opens the door to the backseat and steps in.

I see him: backward hat, football jersey, and ocean-colored eyes.

Then I smell him: I don't know what it is, but it's a scent I could pick up a mile away. It's all *him*.

Finally, I hear him, "Hey, Josie." I swear his voice gets deeper every time I hear it, and this morning it goes straight into my veins, stimulating my whole being more than a shot of Cuban coffee could do at this hour. He tips his head down at me as he sits in the backseat, my backpack separating us, and he throws his on the floorboard in front of him. He straightens his leg and pulls his phone out of his pocket. I look away, not wanting to seem nosey. I know he's not huge on social media, but he and Joe are forever talking about anything and everything football due to their obsession with Fantasy Football.

I swear these guys eat, sleep, dream, and piss football. ESPN is constantly on at home if it's not my parents watching the news. Joe and Wes both made the varsity team this year which is big for only being sophomores. I think it's a fun game and I get it for the most part, but I don't know how they get so much out of it.

At least with my books, I'm living a completely different life with every story and every flip of the page.

"Ughh," he grunts and slams his fist on the seat between us, just missing my bag and causing me to jolt in my seat.

He looks at me and does a double take. "Sorry, didn't mean to scare you," he says, sporting the most adorable smirk I've ever seen as he leans forward onto the center console, cupping the headrest in front of me, switching his attention to my brother. "Can you believe they traded another running back this morning?" *Ah, as promised, football talk.*

His scent and the vein that's making a name for itself on his arm are overwhelming my senses. Over the next few minutes, he slowly leans back into his seat again. Their conversation is all tight ends and running backs and I'm bored to tears with it. While they drone on, I wonder if my new job will allow me to have free ice cream at every shift because that could be dangerous.

"Hey, do you need a ride to work tomorrow, too?" My brother asks Wes from the driver's seat, interrupting Leah's attempt at football talk and eyeing Wes in the rearview mirror.

Wes adjusts his hat as he answers with an exhale, "Yeah, if it's cool. It's the one night a month my Grams needs the car for bingo night. If you can't, no worries, the bus will just get me there like a half hour early."

"Nah, I got you," Joe replies.

"Bingo? That actually sounds like fun," I chime in, imagining Cora and me in our seventies in floral dresses, big ol' hats, and doused in Leah's perfume.

Speak of the devil, she comes in with her two cents, "Of course, you want to play bingo. I'm sure you and your lame friend would fit right in clutching your books and hiding granny panties under all that." She motions toward my outfit.

Joe laughs *with* her, and Wes gives me a sad smile back here that they can't see. My cheeks redden with embarrassment, and I choose to ignore her and avoid all eye contact with Wes. I pull out my headphones and put them in my ears, attempting to drown out Leah and all the sunshine and positivity that she brings everywhere she goes.

Once we get to the school, I'm quick to get out of the car and leave them behind. I find Cora and hand her the book she's borrowing from me. She can tell something's off with my mood, but I tell her I didn't sleep well. As we walk to class, which is in the same vicinity as where my fellow passengers go, my phone vibrates with a text. I don't recognize the number and I look around. Cora is chugging from her water bottle, Joe's got an arm around the megabitch's shoulders, and he's laughing with Wes. All my other classmates are loud in conversation on a high of the last day of school.

Unknown: Let your smile change the world, but don't let the world change your smile.
(Anonymous)

chapter two

present day, 2022

josie

MY QUADS BURN as I squat and alphabetize the books on the bottom shelf. I'm not complaining. This is the best task they've given me at this job. I knew it would be dangerous when I applied at a bookstore for a part-time gig to earn some income before I start my true career, and I was right, I've already spent more than half of what my first paycheck will be on some beautiful paperbacks. Loose Leafs sits on the corner of a busy intersection in downtown Tampa and has a cute café with tall glass walls letting passersby look into the two-story library. The greenery and aesthetically pleasing décor make it feel like I'm not actually working.

We got an influx of new books to go on the extra shelves the owner ordered, and I've been itching to get to the romance part of this mess. With that being said, *goodbye, entire paycheck*! But that's not a big deal as I'm this close to starting my big-girl job, and staying with my parents saves me a buck, too. Sadly, the current status on that sitch: over it.

Cassie, hums over with another cart full of books. "Ahhh," she sighs, "Aren't they all so pretty?"

"I know. It's bad. I want them. All," I say with a chuckle.

"Tell me about it. If I bring home any more books, I think Brandon will have a stroke. But we are moving in together, which means a smaller rent bill and a bigger library," she says, looking off to the side, daydreaming.

"Wait. I thought you guys already lived together?" I stack the last of the Paranormal Romance and stand up to grab the label to stick on the Contemporary Romance shelf.

"We do. We're just gonna move into the same bedroom and try to get another roommate," she explains. "I met Brandon through a mutual friend. I moved in when he and his friend needed another roommate. We started dating a few months after I became the third roommate, and now I can't even remember the last time I slept in my own bed."

"That's a great idea, and a smart way to save some money. I'm more than ready to leave my parents. It's been a couple months since I've been back, and my mom has officially become a smotherer. Free rent is nice, though."

It's been almost seven years since I left my hometown of Tampa and moved four hours south. I'm back now, and in so many ways my hometown has changed, but in other ways it's exactly as it was before. More traffic and buildings, but the same old man selling dollar bags of the most delicious churros out of a little truck outside the Spanish market.

At home is a different story, though. Because of Joe. Not having him there is different. It's quiet and cleaner, and my mom spends all her time and energy on me. Anything she does lately is done with me in mind. *I have to get sparkling water for Josie. Make sure to park on the street so Josie can use the garage. Let's take Josie to that new Mexican restaurant. Don't forget to make her chocolate chip pancakes in the morning.* I missed my parents, but damn, I need my space. I'm also twenty-five now, not twelve.

"Aww! She just misses you, I'm sure!"

"No. Just, no. It's too much." I whine dramatically, using my hands to cover my face. I peek between my fingers before I admit, "I literally never have one item of clothing in my laundry basket because she does laundry every day. And I can never find anything because she cleans up my room."

"Josie, you're kidding. I wish Brandon would do my clothes and pick up after me. I'd even give him more blowies for that!" She flips her blonde hair and lets out a laugh, complete with a snort. Cassie is constantly laughing at herself, and I love it, it fits her personality perfectly. She's sunshine with legs and eyes the color of a blue sky.

"Eww!" I cringe as I throw the backing of the label I stuck onto the bookshelf at her, but it doesn't go very far and ends up caught in my hair. I'm fishing the thin piece of paper out of my hair when she shrieks, scaring the hell out of me.

"Move in with us!" She almost yells it.

"Huh?" I question her, looking around to make sure we aren't disturbing any customers.

She shoves my arm playfully and I almost fall against the bookshelf. She must frequent the gym. "Seriously, you can move into our apartment. You'll get along great with Brandon and his friend, Miller. Plus, it's less than five minutes away," she looks to the side and taps her chin with her perfectly manicured nails. "You'll still have to drive over the bridge if you get that job in St. Pete you want, but it would be so fun!" Her excitement grows with every fact she spits at me. I can see her now, barging into my room with a green face mask plastered on, clutching snacks and wine, ready for a Netflix binge night. "Your mom will probably have to cough up some quarters for your laundry... but say you'll think about it!"

I laugh as I pull the cart farther down the aisle, "Yes, yes. I will," I tell her as she starts to bounce away silently clapping, she must remember where we're at.

"Hey!" I call out to her before her head pops back into view. "When do you need an answer?"

"We've been talking about it for a little while now, but knowing I have someone reliable like you and some eye candy," she rolls her eyes and adds, "Brandon and Miller will be more than patient."

I smile at her, "Alright. I'll text you later."

My mood starts to mirror Cassie's as I imagine a bedroom with my own Pinterest-inspired décor and coming home to a laundry basket strewn with my dirty clothes. It's weird, I know, but I need my independence back. I've practically been on my own for a while now and it's weird living with my parents again. I will miss my mom's cooking, though, because I can't cook for shit. I try, but it doesn't compare to her dishes. But that's okay, I'll come home for regular visits and food.

My manager, Scotty, pokes his head into the aisle and lets me know I can take my fifteen-minute break. I thank him for the heads up and park the cart out of the way at the end of the bookcase. I stop at the café and grab an iced coffee before I step out to take a seat on a bench. The sun feels good on my face, and after a few minutes of just sitting here doing nothing and enjoying the peace, I grab my phone and unconsciously tap on the colorful camera icon to check out the latest Instagram stories. I find myself not in the mood to see everyone's Instagram-worthy perfect lives and tap right through them. Swiping out of Instagram, I go to my messages to let Cora know about my possible new place.

> **Me:** Hey! So, I might have a new place!
> **Cora:** Really?! That was quick! Where at?
> **Me:** Off Dale Mabry, smack dab in the middle of the city. My friend is moving into the same room as her bf so her room will be open now.
> **Cora:** Fun! I'm glad you're happy at home. There are days I miss it there.
> **Me:** Yeah, it's weird being back.
> **Cora:** Yeah, I'll visit soon. And we will have a blast! We can make some money outside your new place.
> **Me:** Hookin' or selling our paintings?

Cora: Both, duh!
Me: LOL

Cora and I were inseparable for years. This isn't the first time I've returned home, the first time I left Tampa was the summer before junior year of high school. I went to live with my aunt, so our time together turned into random holidays and whatever weekends our families were willing to trek between Coral Springs and Tampa to reunite us. After high school, Cora moved to Las Vegas with her dad to attend UNLV, and we really lost our time together. Thanks to technology, we've never gone a day without chatting. Whether it's through phone calls, texts, or one of the many social media apps, take your pick.

I pull up my "weekly word," as I like to refer to them, and let the words sink in. These texts come in most weeks, and when they do, it's on a Monday morning. It's been years since the first one on that last day of tenth grade. I've replied several times, sometimes with secrets, other times just angry and cursing, but my texts always fail to send, highlighted with a red "x".

Mon. July 23, 9:00 AM
Weekly Word: He looked at her the way all women want to be looked at by a man. (F. Scott Fitzgerald)

Mon. August 6, 9:02 AM
Weekly Word: I wonder what I look like in your eyes. (Anonymous)

Mon. August 20, 9:07 AM
Weekly Word: We are all fools in love. (Jane Austen)

Today, 9:01 AM
Weekly Word: It scares me how perfect you are. You could never see it, either. I'm terrified that you still don't. (Me)

The last text pisses me off. I don't even close the app before I lock my phone and shove it in my pocket; out of my sight but still within arms reach. I've blocked the mystery number numerous times, but that only lasts until Sunday night when I unblock because I need the next random quote or song lyric or confession more than I'd like to admit.

chapter three

present day, 2022

wes

CHILDISH GAMBINO BLASTS out of my headphones, sweat dripping down my calves as I sit on the metal bench in the locker room and chug my post-workout drink. I weight-trained for about an hour, then ran on the treadmill for eight miles. I usually shower in the locker room, but an ice bath in my tub is what I need after this week. I had a full schedule and picked up some extra clients when one of our trainers called out yesterday.

I'm living the dream doing what I love as a personal trainer at Pump House and when I'm not training my clients, I'm training myself by taking a load off my boss's plate and learning the ropes on how to run a successful gym. And weightlifting. Always weightlifting. But that's the real dream: owning my own gym. This is my home. The exercise is therapeutic for me, and helping my clients reach their goals and conquer their dreams, there's just something about it. Everyone tells me I need to bring a cot in here and move in. I'm really starting to believe them.

The music fades out some and comes back after the message tone dings. I pull my headphones out and lock them in their case, throwing them into my duffle bag before I grab my phone again to check the message.

Grams: Don't forget my watermelon tomorrow.

A smile creeps on my lips and I shake my head. Tomorrow is Friday, my day off and I'm picking up groceries for my grandma. It's the least I can do for the mother figure in my life. And for a dozen good ass cookies. Legit, best cookies ever.

Me: Don't forget my snickerdoodles.

I grab my duffle and keys from my locker, walk out onto the main floor and wipe my face with the towel that hangs off my shoulder when I do a double-take at the dime-piece that's kickboxing on the other side of the room. She's in a pair of tight black shorts that stop right under her ass with a black sports bra covered by a loose mint tank top. I couldn't care less about what colors a girl's wearing, but it makes her skin look delectable from here. Unconsciously, I bring a fist up to my mouth and bite down, craning my neck to get a better view. She's tan and fit and my dick wants to jump out of my shorts and take a look himself. She's training with Bobby, and I make a mental note to ask him about—

Holy shit.

It's her.

My heart rate picks up after being down a beat or two, and I can't remember where I am or what I'm doing or what year it is. *Hell, who's the damn president?* Because Josephine Fucking Rodriguez is smashing the shit out of a punching bag. Her hair is up in a messy bun that falls a little every time she swings a punch or kicks. I scratch my head and look around to see if anyone has witnessed the coma I just slipped into. Everyone is in fucking la-la land and they're on crack if they don't notice the angel who's whooping ass on the other side of the room. This shit can't be real.

I mean, I knew she was in town. Her parents told me she was moving back now that she'd graduated with her master's degree. I haven't visited them in a while now, mostly due to fear of how she'll react when she sees me, not because I don't want to see her. But the last thing I expected was to see her at the gym, let alone *my* gym. My legs hold me in place. I want to go to her, but she hates me. She has to. I don't think I'm ready for her to slug me with that right hook. Or kick me in the balls, which may be her preference.

I finally find the strength to walk away and promise myself that this won't be the last time I see her, but not without glancing her way three-hundred times before I reach my truck.

I dry myself off after fifteen minutes in an ice bath. My muscles are sore, and I know they'll thank me later for the cold soak, although it did nothing to clear my brain. I feel drunk with the sight of Josie on my mind, still in shock. It's been seven years since I laid eyes on her, and shit, she's more enticing than I remember. Back then she spent minimal time on her hair and makeup, or anything that had to do with her appearance. Obviously, she wasn't done up for her workout today, but her matching outfit and toned body proves self-care and confidence have moved up on her list of priorities. Seeing her looking like a badass kickboxing was hot, but I'm sure she's still sweet ol' Josie. I'll have to call her dad and see how she's doing before I show up for a surprise visit. I could see that her punch has improved after watching her train. I once saw her punch Joe when he locked all the bathrooms in the house when she had to pee. She ended up popping a squat in their backyard and coming in right after with a legit fist to his gut. It was pretty epic.

It's official because this girl has crawled into my mind and might as well get comfortable. I have a feeling she's not gonna leave for a while. I need to know everything about her. I knew she moved here looking for a new job, but I want to know more *about her*. What's she like now, seven fucking years later? Why did she choose to become a counselor? Does she still play with her hair while she's lost in a book? Is she single? Does she still hate me?

More importantly, does she remember that summer like I do?

I knew what she'd look like, well, sort of. Her Facebook page is private, but I look her up every now and then to check out her profile picture. Last time I checked, it was a picture of her and Cora. Josie had her eyes closed with her hair in a messy ponytail and wore a huge smile with Cora kissing her cheek. I know she had a boyfriend because she's had more than one picture of the same douchebag on there. I assume that's over but I'm not so sure and I won't ask her parents. But damn, I didn't realize how good time had been to her until now. Her toned legs, ass like a... *stop, Wes.*

I'm itching to call Bobby and ask for every detail of their session and find out how long he's been training her exactly. I feel the need to threaten him within an inch of his life if he so much as looks at her funny. I want to convince him to come up with an emergency and have me fill in for their next session. I'd love to see her face when I walk up to the counter to tell her she'd be training with me.

It's August and I live in Florida, AKA the sun's asshole, so I get dressed in a tank top and shorts and throw on a baseball cap. Tonight, our Fantasy Football league has a draft set up and I've got all my picks ready. I listen to football podcasts when I drive, and pay extra money for cable during this time of the year just to catch the games. I live and breathe football, and it makes me feel close to Joe again. Years ago, football season meant I'd spend every Sunday at the Rodriguez residence with Joe's mom keeping our appetites in check. She'd make us classic recipes and try out new ones on us, too. Joe, his dad, and I wouldn't move from the couch. We'd get pissed at bad calls and get loud when our favorite players scored. We'd study plays that we could perform in our own high school football games. And I'll never forget how I'd sneak glances at Josie coming in and out of her room before she left the summer after tenth grade. But I always made sure to keep an eye on the game, I was too much of a chicken-shit to ever get caught by her twin or her dad. I've gotten better over the years without Joe, but I still struggle with the memories…and seeing Josie today just brought it all back to the forefront. The sight of her in my gym of all gyms, when I least expected to see her, has my brain all scrambled up. I can barely think straight and have no clue how I'm going to draft a dream team in this state. I walk out my door silently praying for at least the third pick in the draft.

chapter four
present day, 2022

josie

I COLLAPSE into the driver's seat of my car. That workout was intense but fun and I try to exercise at least three times a week. A counselor once suggested it to relieve stress and I'm not gonna lie, it works. I'll even suggest it to my future clients, or patients, whatever you want to call them.

I haven't done kickboxing in a while, but my new trainer, Bobby, said it would be fun to get into again. It's not a bad idea because the job I'm interviewing for in the next few weeks has some later in the evening appointments. You always think you're invincible until you're walking to your car alone in the dark.

I shoot Cassie a text to send me her address. I didn't have any plans after my workout, and she begged me to come over and check out her place. I don't think she's completely moved out of her room, but she insists I check it out ASAP. The first thing I plan to do as her roommate is raid her kitchen to find the culprit of her sunshiny attitude. I'll bet her fridge is stocked with Red Bulls or some sugary drink. I wouldn't doubt if her bathroom mirror has some sticker wishing her a lovely day or maybe even one reminding her to smile. Although, she'd never forget to do that. I've come to crave the positivity she emits. We've only just met, but Cassie and I became instant friends during our first shift together. On our break that day, we grabbed lunch at a pizza place nearby. She looked at me with her big blue eyes and asked me to tell her everything about myself. I told her I couldn't do that. Before I came up with an excuse as to why I'm not an open book, she shrugged her shoulders and told me everything about herself instead. *Everything.* The girl can talk. I like her and it's good I found her so soon. I need something constant and distracting in my life if I want to make it work in this city.

According to Siri, I've reached my destination. I park in front of building C as Cassie instructed and take a quick whiff of myself. Not bad, but I still spritz myself with a coconut spray, just in case.

I walk up the stairs and find her door: 211. I knock and take a step back, admiring her doormat. The word "welcome" runs across it in black cursive. She must've picked it out because I can't see a guy picking out that mat. Honestly, I can't imagine a guy buying a welcome mat at all.

"Hiiii! Come in, come in," she sings, holding a glass of wine and giving me a side-hug.

I'm standoffish as I warn her, "Oh, I'm all sweaty from the gym."

She waves me off. "You're fine, this is Brandon," she says as she moves out of the way, gesturing toward her boyfriend and closing the door behind me. Brandon towers over his petite blonde girlfriend. He's got dark, medium-length hair with blue eyes that complement a charming smile.

Brandon runs his hand through his hair before he rolls his eyes at his girlfriend's excitement and shakes my hand. "Hey, glad to meet you. Cassie's been excited for you to come check the place out. I think she was scared we'd get another dude in here and didn't want to be outnumbered."

She uses the back of her hand to shield her mouth and whispers loud enough for us to hear, "It's a constant sausage fest. I'd prefer more tits and less dick around here."

He chuckles and stretches his arms up before putting an arm around her shoulders. "Now, why do you think I'm moving you into my bedroom?" He wags his eyebrows then kisses her temple, obviously enamored with her. Seems to be exactly the kind of guy Cassie needs. From first impression, at least. She blushes and pushes him off to grab my hand and pull me to her former bedroom. My eyes widen at her aggressiveness, and I throw a wave back at Brandon, "Nice to meet you!"

The apartment is clean and gives you that cozy feeling, already a plus. She shows me around the bedroom I'd be staying in. The walls are bare, and the size isn't great, aside from the walk-in closet, but it's perfect for me. Cassie insists on me using her bed and dresser she no longer needs, which is ideal because I don't have any furniture. We walk back out into the common area while she tells me about the pool and a local taco place they order takeout from weekly. The kitchen looks brand new, and there's a dining room table with stacks of mail and a couple of laptops. A gray, U-shaped couch is peppered with pillows and throws of all shades of teal. It surrounds a huge TV, and I can already picture Netflix marathons in the living room. She says there's a lot of football watching in this place, which isn't a surprise when you have male roommates.

I nod as Cassie points everything out, and admits to being the interior decorator here, which I'd assumed. We step out onto the balcony, and she shows me the relaxing view. It overlooks the main road, full of rush-hour traffic, but you can't miss the gorgeous sun setting between the palm trees that line the median of the street. It's the perfect representation of Tampa and gives me the same sense of *home* that I felt my first night back when my mom poked her head in my room to notify me dinner was ready. I instantly remembered her interrupting my angsty teen novels to let me know the food I'd been smelling the last few hours was ready all those years ago.

"So, what do you think? And we talked it over, we'll split the rent at a price that leaves some extra money that we can put toward stuff we all share, like detergent and TP and stuff."

It sounds like I'm in college for the first time. When I

did start college, I was staying with my aunt Leila where I've lived since high school, and never experienced living with a roommate or any of this. I want movie nights and girls' nights and, heck, even I can enjoy football. Lord knows I know the basics. My brother and his friends took football to another level. My heart rate picks up when old feelings start coursing through my veins at the flashbacks of football Sundays in my childhood home and Friday night games. I all but throw a right hook at memories of the boy who stole my heart, then lit it on fire, creeping in my mind so I can clear my head and give Cassie real feedback on her place.

"I really like it. I want to say let me think about it, but honestly, I love it."

She is watching me with her eyes wide, waiting for an answer. "So..?"

"So, the location is great. And I'll be able to save some money. I do want to make it clear that I'll be preparing to get my own place one day. Is that okay?"

"Yeah, the lease just renewed a few months ago and the guys are pretty chill and good with communication on stuff like that. We know this isn't forever for any of us."

"Okay, cool." I nod my head. "Yeah, I can see myself living here."

"Yeah? Yes! YES! I've never had a girl roommate! Yay!" She throws her fists in the air and runs in place before she almost knocks me over with a hug.

She lets go of me and begins to drag me back to the living room like

I'm her little Raggedy Ann. "Let's go tell the guys. And you've gotta meet Wes. Be careful, he's easy on the eyes, if you know what I mean." She winks at me.

The name immediately makes my stomach drop. I'm speechless as I try to gather all the pieces of my brain that just blew up and made a mess in my head. Just at that very moment, I hear a deep voice call out from the other side of the apartment. A voice I still often hear in my dreams.

Panicking, I state, "I thought you said his name was Mill--"

And it hits me, coupled with his voice. Miller. As in, *Wes* Miller.

"Oh, yeah. I don't know, it's a guy thing. Sometimes they call him by his last name."

"Hey, Brandy, baby! You ready? I can't wait to see how early you pick your quarterback, dumbass."

He's picking up his hat and turning it backward as he emerges from out of the hallway…and the last seven years of my life escape me. I feel like a teenager again. My heart is beating out of my chest, and there's a strong possibility I could pass out right now. Wesley Miller is a mere fifteen feet away from me right now. He stops dead in his tracks and our eyes are glued to each other.

"You're lucky you're the only person he's allowed to ditch me for! Wes, this is Josie, AKA your new roommate. And no touching, she's a good one!" Her introduction is a blur. All I can see is an older, more sexier version of my childhood crush who turned into my boyfriend for just a moment there. The boyfriend who stole my heart years ago before he left it there shattered and in a million pieces. It took me so long to get it back together, and I'm now realizing I've still got some pieces missing. It's like he's already trying to take it back, incomplete and broken, before we've even said a word to each other.

I want to look away, but I can't. This man is not the boy I grew up with. Well, he is. He's just an adult version of him. He's wearing a tank top that shows off his tan arms, that and the fact that he must spend as much time at the gym as he does at the tattoo parlor. He's got his signature backward cap on, and damn it if I don't feel the smile that's crept up on his bearded face all the way down into my core. He doesn't have a full beard, but he definitely hasn't shaved in a few weeks. Fifteen-year-old Josie just died at the sight of him. Twenty-five-year-old Josie is failing herself. I swore I'd see Wes and be able to put our past behind me, but seeing him here in the flesh with his devastating smile, I'm all but ready to see him in a new light.

I find the courage to break eye contact and shoot a smile at Cassie, but I can't help but look back at him half a second later. His eyes are all over me. I feel his gaze burning up and down my body, tracing the sweat that's already dried up from my workout. I don't want to get into our history with Cassie just yet, so I chime in before he has a chance to.

"Hi, nice to meet you," I hold my hand out to shake his. He tilts his head in confusion but decides to play along.

"Nice to meet you, too, Josie." his smile is still there, and my name hangs in the air. Seeing him, knowing that we are going to be roommates, it's all too much. I can hardly breathe in this place. I have to go. I turn toward Cassie and ask her when I can officially move in. I swear she says tomorrow, but I'm too busy picturing Wes and his massive hands exploring my body, reaching more area of my skin at once than it ever did before. I have to literally shake the image out of my head as I practically run out of there.

My hands grip the steering wheel. *What the fuck just happened?* I never planned on seeing Wes again. Well, I knew I would eventually run into him at some point. And I'm willing to bet my parents still talk to him, but they'd never admit it to me. I didn't expect to see him *now*. This is something I'd hoped to be prepared for. And why did my body react like that? It was hard to breathe and I got all shaky. It's been seven whole years, I wouldn't think those feelings could possibly come back so fast and so intense. Hell, I started imagining those new and improved arms lifting me up like they used to as I'd wrap my legs around his waist. But now he seems like a completely different Wes. And I am a completely different Josie thanks to hours upon hours of therapy and healing myself. Nothing and no one could have prepared me for this.

For seeing Wes and knowing that I'd be seeing him everyday now.

God help me.

chapter five

last day of sophomore year, 2013

josie

BLACK BEANS SIMMER on the stove and it smells delicious. My stomach growls at the thought of grubbing on rice, beans, and whatever meat my mom picked for today in less than an hour. She walks into the kitchen in her oversized shirt and black bicycle shorts to check on dinner, and smiles when she sees me sitting at the bar.

"Hey, mami, you're home early. How was your last day?" she asks.

"Cora dropped me off before she went to babysit. And my day? Eh. Nothing special. I'm one of three kids who showed up to the last period of the day. I don't know how the others get away with skipping so much all year long." I hop off the barstool and pinch a piece of meat she started shredding, popping it in my mouth, but not before she swats at my hand and raises an eyebrow, "Mija, I still need to fry it again. It's almost ready."

I climb back onto the barstool and pull my planner out of my bag. The school year is done, but my love for my planner stays. Nothing brings me joy like organizing my life, taking notes, and doodling all the words that flutter through my mind. It's filled with colorful lyrics and book quotes written all throughout the worn pages. My mom always says she wishes I'd organize the rest of my life like I do my planner.

Mom pours herself a cup of iced tea and tells me about the sales she saw at the mall today. My mom, the little bargain shopper. She's got the luxury of staying home while my dad works for the local electric company, which his been his job since he graduated high school. We're not wealthy, but I know my family's comfortable. My dad provides for us what he can, yet he teaches us to work for what we want, too.

"Sooo," she coos, "your dad said to wait for the next holiday, but I'm not waiting 'til Christmas! Is he crazy? And I couldn't pass up the deal." She disappears into the dining room and comes back with a JCPenney bag. She's giddy about whatever this is. Then, it hits me. I jump out of my seat.

"A straightener. You got me a hair straightener?!" Now I'm the giddy one. She hands it over. "And it's Paul Mitchell? Mom!" I grab it and run my fingers over the smooth packaging. "For my little brain," she says, using her nickname for me since I bring home the grades she never did. She kisses the crown of my head and continues, "It was on sale, and I had a coupon on top of that. I could've gone and put it away for the holidays, but I wanted you to have it now."

I hug and thank her. My aunt Leila flat-ironed my hair when she last visited, and I'm positive my dad was gagging at how vain I became that night. My hair was so smooth and weightless. I couldn't stop touching it. And I felt hot. It made me look older and prettier. Like I had makeup on when I didn't. I wasn't desperate to have it, but now I do, and I can't wait to put it to good use. Maybe I'll tame these curls for my first day at the ice cream shop.

"Broooo. I wish–I wish you could've seen your face," I hear my brother's laugh booming from the front door. Wes's laugh joins in, "I thought my leg was gonna break. It was like bending the wrong way for a second! E-brake on that POS, dude. E-brake!" You can barely understand the words through the guffaws coming from them. They walk into the kitchen shaking their heads, calming down from their laughing fit when they see us.

"Hey, Ma," Joe greets my mom with a kiss on the cheek. It's a Hispanic thing.

"Mama's making food!" Wes calls out. He also greets her with a kiss on the cheek. He's not Hispanic, but he's practically family.

I get comfortable in the barstool again and put my new toy to the side. Promising myself that I'll be rewarded with straight hair after I get caught up with my planner. I watch the guys check out the food. Then, I fall out of my seat when Wes covers the pot of beans and proceeds to flip his hat backward, pat his stomach, and smile at me with a wink. Okay, I didn't fall out of my seat, but I swear I almost did. His eyes are locked on mine, and his teeth are perfect, and the butterflies in my stomach are running amok in there. I return the smile and quickly look away. I glance at my planner and decide to put my hair up in a bun; I've got to do something with my hands because the nervous energy is buzzing through me.

"So, Ma. Dinner looks great and I know it will be because you're... like... the best cook ever. Duh," Joe explains in his best impression of a teenage girl.

"Ay, Dios! Spit it out, mijo. What do you want?" My mom interrupts him. I giggle at her reaction to his attempt at sweet-talking her. Joe looks at me, his eyes shooting daggers.

"So... there's this party tonight. It's Dylan's end-of-the-year party. He is expecting Wes and me to go."

"Nope. No," she replies, shaking her head.

I giggle again. More daggers.

Joe throws his hands down and sucks on his teeth. He is officially a toddler, ready to throw a fit.

"Jose, you almost failed your Spanish exam last week! Spanish! Papi, I spoke to you and Josie solely in Spanish for the first few years of your life. I don't understand how you almost fail. And you said you even studied for it with that nice girl." She checks the rice cooker and looks at him in bewilderment.

This is news to me. Ha! Serves him right. That weekend I had plans to go to a movie with Cora and some other girls. The story was that he was coming with us because our parents don't trust us outside of the house if we're apart. It's more like they don't think *I* can take care of myself, because they let him do whatever he wants. Totally not fair and one-hundred-percent sexist.

Anyway, I couldn't get a hold of him so we could come home together, and I had to make up a story for him. We ended up giving different stories, and I got in trouble for lying. He didn't get in trouble, though, because my parents believed his stupid story about studying at the library when I—and everyone else at Plant High School—knew that he just went to hook up with Leah Peters. I don't even think he knows where the library is.

I must be completely absorbed in my mom's and brother's conversation because it isn't until his scent reaches my nostrils that I realize Wes has pulled back the barstool neighboring mine and made himself at home. His leg resting inches from me.

"Mom," Joe grunts. "You know I don't know how to write in Spanish. It's very different."

"Oh, please, Joe."

I look over at Wes to see his reaction to the banter between my mom and brother, but his eyes are peering into my planner. I realize I'm absentmindedly tracing over the words I've been doodling throughout the day. The words go across a sun with a tiny smile and float through the clouds.

Let your smile change the world, but don't let the world change your smile.

I immediately lift my fingers from the page. He then

reaches over and points at the spot on Tuesday that says *Algebra Exam* next to the circled *94*.

"You got a ninety-four?" His eyes lock onto mine again.

"Yeah, what'd you get?" He could tell me he failed and I'd congratulate him.

"Eighty-six, I hate parabolas. But good for you!" He puts his hand up, palm facing me.

I high-five him.

"Wes! Stay with the program here." Joe pulls Wes's attention away from me.

Wes clears his throat before he utters his own plea, "Isabel, please let us go to the party. I can drive us now that I've got my license. Being that we just got on the varsity team, everyone's gonna be looking for us there." His puppy eyes make an appearance, and if my mom can deny that look, then she is a savage because I'd walk straight into traffic if those eyes asked me to.

"Okay." *Okay?* "On one condition," she proposes.

"Anything," my desperate brother begs.

"You take Josie."

chapter six

present day, 2022

wes

I PULL into the parking lot of my favorite smoothie joint.

"Are you at that shake place yet?" My grandmother's voice comes through my truck's speakers.

"Yes, Grams. I'm here."

"Okay, good. I hate it when you kids talk and drive."

"Grams, I told you. I have you on Bluetooth so I hear you through the speakers," I explain to her for the millionth time.

"Wesley, I don't know what that means."

"Alright, lady. I'm gonna go now. I'll see you next Friday with your food."

"Okay. And you watch your tone with me, boy. Calling me lady. I wiped that ass at one time," she threatens.

I laugh, "Okay. Love you."

"Love you, baby boy. Be careful." The beep sounds when I end the call.

I call my Grams at least twice a week. If she doesn't hear from me after a few days, she assumes I died or went missing. Growing up, she was all I had. After my first semester at the local community college, I realized that school wasn't for me, and decided to drop out and get my personal training certification. Grams agreed it was a good idea for me since she saw how uninterested I was with school and how I struggled. She also realized how obsessed I was with working out and learning everything I could about the body and food and being healthy. She came up with the idea for me to save money until I could hold my own, and then she would get herself into an assisted living facility. This way her "baby boy could be a normal grandson and not have to care for his Grams all the time." I fought her hard on that for a while. But we made the decision that I would get her groceries and adjust my schedule if she needed a ride to a doctor's appointment.

That semester in college was the toughest time of my life, and I think she knew I needed a healthy social life.

I walk into Extreme Juice and stand in line. I usually train on Saturday nights, but I decided to take the night off. After today's last training session with a client, I did my own workout and left.

I'm hoping to hang out at home tonight. Maybe run into the new tenant. *Maybe.* It's been over two weeks since Josie came to check out our place. Cassie told her she was welcome to move in ASAP, but apparently, she's been busy and hasn't had the time. I don't believe it for a second. I'm willing to bet she's avoiding me.

"Hey, Wes," Leah Peters greets me, hair wrapped in a bun at the back of her company hat. Leah has worked here since high school. Now she's the manager, but during her first couple years here, they had every right to fire her. I doubt she knew then that working for a smoothie joint would be what saved her life.

"Hey, Leah. I'll have the usual. Plus, an order of the Raging Red Bull," I order and flash a smile. A zap of post-workout energy zips through me and I manifest gaining a new roommate tonight by ordering an extra smoothie.

She nods as she punches my order in. "Haven't seen you at the register in a while," I state. She's usually in the back working the books or making food orders.

"I know, we are understaffed this week. That's why you haven't seen me at the gym either, but I have been working out, just later in the evening."

"Nice! You never cease to amaze me, girl. You still making it to meetings?" I don't say "AA" meetings to ensure her privacy. It's been a bumpy road for the *it* girl of my graduating class, but she's been doing well for a while now.

"Yeah," she admits as she wipes the sweat at her temple. "I haven't been making it to my usual meeting, but I make sure to attend one on a different day of the week."

"That's awesome, Leah. We still good for next week?" I call out as I walk away from the register to the stand where my drinks will be served.

"Tuesday morning, bright and early," she answers with a small smile before taking the next customer's order.

I follow my wheatgrass shot with an orange wedge and take my smoothies, making sure to nod at Leah on my way out the door.

Her door is closed. It has been the whole time since I got home a half hour ago. Brandon told me he helped Josie bring up four trips worth of boxes, and instantly my jealousy ensued. I was hoping I would be the one to help move her in, but she never gave Cassie a clear move-in day or time. My level of jealousy was more than it should have been for a girl I'm not supposed to know. I'm not really sure why she wants it to be that way. So, now Brandon thinks I've got the hots for her. *No shit.* I just cocked an eyebrow at him and stormed back into my room like the twelve-year-old that I am.

Brandon and Cassie left for the store to pick up snacks and drinks for tomorrow. It's the first football Sunday of the year, and I'm stoked. This year we get to watch it on an even bigger screen that I bought with my winnings from last year's fantasy league.

After pacing the space between the couch and her door for over five minutes, I finally grow the balls to knock. I almost bolt back to my room like I'm playing ding dong ditch or something. Maybe I can act like I dropped something in the kitchen, and I never actually knocked? I'm about to throw myself on the floor and play dead when she opens the door, her bright brown eyes looking up at me. *Fuck.* Each time I see her hurts more than the last time.

"Hi," it comes out rough so I clear my throat and try again, "Hey, Josie." I rub the back of my neck, a nervous habit that's started in the last few moments. "I, uh, got you a Raging Red Bull." I hold the smoothie between us like it's no big deal.

Her eyes light up, "You remember that?"

I remember everything, Josie.

"I took a gamble as I knew it was between this one or one they don't make anymore." *Lie.*

She takes the drink from my hand and turns back into her room, walking away from me but still replying to my lame attempt at greeting her. "Thanks for the smoothie, Wes." She turns around to face me and points her drink my way. "Or is it Miller now?"

I reach up and grab the doorframe with both hands, unsure what to do with myself as I rock back and forth and answer her, "Most of the guys on my Fantasy Football league all refer to each other by last name." She nods in silent understanding.

"So, you're back."

"I am," she says, taking a sip of the drink and letting out a small moan that makes my dick twitch. She puts the smoothie down on her desk, then starts arranging everything on it. A calendar, pens, a framed photo of her and Cora, and a stack of books. It's Cassie's old desk, which matches the rest of the bedroom furniture. I remember putting it together with Brandon. Took us five hours.

I look around at the mess in here and I couldn't imagine it any other way. Isabel, her mom, always had the house immaculate, but when you walked into Joe or Josie's room it was like a bomb went off in there.

"You're working with Cassie at the bookstore?"

"Yep." *Okay.*

"Soo…" I suck at this.

"Actually," she shoots her attention to me, stopping my awkwardness. And I'm all ears. "What's the WiFi password?" She walks over to her bed and opens her MacBook, sitting cross-legged.

"Oh, yeah," I respond, thankful I can help with something. But all I really want to do is carry heavy shit around for her. God, I'm an asshole.

"It's bigmac. All lowercase," I explain.

She scoffs, "Really, big mac? And what's the network? Is it…Two Guys One Modem?" Her eyebrows drawn together.

I laugh, "That was before Cassie moved in."

She scrunches her nose as she types in the password.

"What?" I ask, wanting to know what's going on in that beautiful head of hers. Yet, there's a part of me that doesn't want to know because she's scaring the shit out of me just being in her proximity again.

"Why'd you make the password Big Mac?"

Oh. "I was eating one when I came up with it."

"I see you haven't changed, still a kid at heart," she says with a sigh and a slight eye roll. It's a solid punch to the gut, and all sorts of feelings zip through my body, ending at the tips of my toes.

Guilt for the way I treated her.

Shock that she's acknowledged our past. *Twice.*

Terrified that she'll never let me back in.

Hope that she will.

"I'd like to say I have." I watch her as I wait for her reaction while I'm still haphazardly swinging at the door.

"Oh, yeah?" She finishes typing and looks up at me for half a second before she is up and grabbing her smoothie.

"Look, Josie, I know we have a rocky past, and ever since Joe–"

She interrupts me, "Nope. No, let's not do this, Wes." Bowing her head down, she balances her smoothie in her lap and presses her fingers to her temples, closing her eyes. "I get it, you live here and Tampa is smaller than I ever imagined, but I'm not ready." She looks up at me again, "I almost changed my mind."

"Changed your mind about what?"

"About accepting the offer to stay here. But I know this is something I've got to deal with. I just couldn't stand to live with my parents anymore. They are great, but I'm going nuts there. Let me get settled with my new job and save up some more money, and I promise I'll be out of here by the spring."

That is the last thing I expected to hear today. But, seriously, what else did I expect? Once upon a time, I broke this girl's already broken heart. What did I think a smoothie and shining some light on old memories was gonna get me? Her in my lap? Fat chance.

"Don't do that, Josie. You don't have to go. It's a nice place and we all get along here." I slowly walk the few steps to sit on the foot of her bed. She looks at me with her eyes so big it makes her presence seem overwhelming. I don't even know where to begin. "Josie," I hold her gaze, "I'm sorry."

Her eyes brim with tears and my chest feels like it's been ripped open. She's in pain, and I want nothing more than to hurt whoever did this to her. But I can't do that. Because it's me. I'd be annihilating myself.

I can't bear to see her like this. Subconsciously, my hands go up to her face, "Baby, don't cry–"

She smacks my hands away and gets up to her feet, the smoothie rolling out of her lap in front of me. She steps back and says with a shaky voice, "No! It's a little too late for an apology, Wes."

"Don't do this, Josie. How exactly was I supposed to reach you if you blocked my number?"

She mocks me, "Oh, no. No, no." She wags her finger at me, "You cannot turn this around on me. You know damn well I have no fault here, so don't try me with that. Get out of my room, Wes."

"Josie, I'm sorry. Let's start off with a clean slate." She takes a step back with each step I take forward, so I keep myself rooted to where I am. "We can't live in the same place like this. We can put this behind–"

She interrupts me, and I'm thankful Brandon and Cassie are MIA because they would reconsider the succubus tenant they let in with her sudden roaring,

"GET THE HELL OUT OF MY ROOM!" She covers her face and lets out a sob. I'd do anything—anything in this fucking world—for her to let me comfort her. Her pain is contagious and I can't stand to see her this way.

She looks as though she's about to shove me, but just hovers her hands over my chest before she curls them into fists and drops them to her sides. She inhales, then audibly exhales, before she says, "I swear I will make it bearable for us to live here, but I'm not going to just up and forgive you right now. So, if you'd please leave," she says as the tears run down her face, "and do not call me baby. Ever. Again."

Fuck.

chapter seven

evening of the last day of sophomore year, 2013

wes

I PULL up to the curb in front of the Rodriguez home and text Joe that I'm here. I rub my sweaty hands on my jeans and pull down the sun visor to take a quick peek and make sure I don't have anything in my teeth. I shut the visor, keeping an eye on the front door of the house. Tonight's party will be the same as all the others: mostly upper-classmen hanging out, drinking and smoking. Joe will probably have his cousin bring more booze which, to me, comes off shady as hell. But who am I to judge… to each their own as long as no one gets hurt.

Since Joe and I made it on the varsity football team as sophomores, we get more attention than we used to, and I don't hate it. We're pumped for tonight, but what I'm most looking forward to is Josie joining us for this party. Isabel, Joe's mom, forbade Joe from coming out to this party unless we brought his twin with us.

Joe and his sister are constantly bickering, and he

doesn't really treat her the best in front of our friends. I don't care for it, but in the end, it's his sister and I don't feel comfortable telling him how to treat her. Plus, I can't risk him having any inkling that I might have the hots for her. You know, bro code and all.

    I'd be lying if I said I didn't have a crush on my best friend's sister. I'm not sure what it is about her. We sort of have an unspoken bond. I think she feels it, but I'm not really sure. There's something there when we make eye contact. Something I've never experienced with any other girl. We've known each other since we were kids, and I always thought she was cute even though it's obvious she doesn't see herself in that light. I might even be attracted to that, too. Confidence is sexy but what about teaching someone that they are beautiful? Showing someone this whole side to themselves they've never noticed. I'd be down for that lesson with Josie.

    I snap out of my thoughts the second I hear the door open. She walks out in front of him rolling her eyes.

    "I'm just sayin'," Joe explains, "don't embarrass us tonight. It's a big night for me and big man over there." He points to me on their way over shouting, "What up, forty-three!"

    I smile and shake my head. I almost do a double take as my eyes sweep over Josie as I take in her outfit: a black long-sleeve top with jean overalls but it's a skirt, not shorts overall, complete with classic black and white Chuck Taylors. Hm, didn't know skirt overalls existed. But I ain't complaining. And her hair is straight, something I've never seen. Josie has big, long curly hair that hangs just halfway down her back and now it's swaying right above her ass, it looks silky and smooth and neverending. *Shit.* Tonight's gonna be a tad more difficult than I expected. Honestly, this is probably the most effort I've seen Josie put into her appearance.

Huh. Maybe she does see it.

The car shifts as Joe gets into the front passenger seat and she climbs in the backseat, a completely different backseat than it was earlier. I stopped by the gas station to clean it out before I got here, tossing a million empty plastic water bottles. Or shall I say, *recycled* them.

I nod at her through the rearview mirror and pull into drive as I greet them, "Y'all ready for tonight? It's gonna be a rager," I say the latter in a sarcastic tone.

"Whatever. You guys can do whatever, I'm going to meet Karen," he says, settling into his seat.

Josie pulls herself between us over the center console, "You do know her name is Kiera, right? And what about Leah the Mega Bitch?"

I laugh, "Oh, God. This is Melissa all over again."

Joe groans and covers his face with both hands.

"What? Who's Melissa?" Josie asks, looking between us.

I look over at Joe, then at Josie, and she stops her gaze at my mouth. I lick my lips, then explain with a grin, "So, Melissa Waters was..." I pause before I continue, "well, let's just say she was inspecting something in your brother's pants and..." I grip the steering wheel, unable to control my laughter.

This earns me a shove from Joe before he finishes the story, "This girl was going down on me—it was my first time, might I add," he says, index finger in the air.

51

"Only time," I cough out. I can see Josie gagging from the corner of my eye.

He shoves me again and continues, "And I said, 'Wow, Melanie, you're really, really good at this.'"

Josie covers her mouth, "You did not. You called her by the wrong name! Please tell me she hit you or bit you or something."

Both Joe and I cringe at the idea of biting.

"She slapped me and pushed my ass out of her car, and I had to beg forty-three over here to come pick me up from the park that night," he responds, pointing his thumb at me.

I'm coming down from my laughing fit when Josie lowers herself in the back seat and explains, "I would bite a guy who called me the wrong name while I... did that."

"Over my dead body you'd be doing *that* anytime soon," Joe says nonchalantly.

I peek at her in the rearview mirror and she rolls her eyes, again.

See what I mean? They bicker, all the time. Joe turns up the music, then turns it back down before he replies to her unanswered question, "I told Leah I needed to slow down with her because I'm not ready for anything serious. She yapped on the phone like that Charlie Brown teacher. But I had to, she was turning into a stage five clinger. I'm not lying to her. Laying out the truth. Also, I wanna see what Karen finds in my pants."

"Kiera!" Josie and I shout together.

josie

We pull into a neighborhood lined with parked cars up and down both sides of the street. Wes parks a couple blocks away, and as we walk down the street, I pull my phone out of my pocket to find texts from Cora. I'm hoping she's here and telling me where we can meet up.

> **Cora:** Hey, so sry! The kid I'm babysitting just puked his face off AND his parents are running late. I don't think I can make it!!!
> **Cora:** I was so pumped for this party too! Our 1st REAL one! Wahhhhh!

My belly immediately starts to tumble with nerves. When my mom mentioned I had to go to this party with the boys, I was pissed. I hate being a babysitter for my brother and, aside from Wes, I don't really care for Joe's friends. But once I was venting to Cora about it, she convinced me that I was being dumb and that she'd join me and we could enjoy our first true party together. Last time we went to a party it was eighth grade and we all ended up watching *Harry Potter*. Not a bad time, but not a party. And now her babysitting gig just fudged the bucket.

I reply to her text, letting her know not to worry about it and that there's always the next party. I imagine a summer full of parties and bonfires, memories we'll never forget. We're walking up the sidewalk to the house when Joe stops and waits for me to catch up.

"Don't take drinks from anyone but me or Wes. Again, don't embarrass us." He holds up a finger for each rule. "And, have fun, Prudence." He ruffles my hair and I smack his hand away, running my fingers through my silky hair again. I will kill him if he ruins my perfect, straight locks. It took me over an hour to flat iron this mane.

I should tell him not to embarrass *me,* but instead I tell him, "Don't worry, I won't unveil how much of an idiot you are to your super cool friends." Then I leave them outside and go toward the house. I'm not stupid, I'm not gonna drink here for the first time. With a bunch of people I don't know. Cora and I promised each other we would get drunk together for the first time. That way we can both witness how we would act while drunk. Bonding as best friends should.

I walk up the steps of a bungalow home that resembles a forest with huge plants scattered around the porch. And a pink door? Cute. I grasp the doorknob and turn it, opening the door to a scene out of the movies. High schoolers are littered around, most my grade level or the now-seniors. Majority of them are holding red Solo cups, some have their own sticker-covered water bottles full of who-knows-what. I walk down the hallway that leads into an open living room and kitchen separated by an island lined with stools. There's a barely there scent that reminds me of a skunk, not sure what that's about. Thankfully, I see some girls from my art class huddled up in the kitchen and walk over to them.

Jessica looks up at me and then does a double take. "Hey, Josie! I didn't know you'd be here." Her BFF, Amanda, looks over at me and smiles. "Hey, girl!" I hug each of them and tell them about how I got roped into attending this shindig.

"Oh, it's no biggie. I mean, yeah, there's a lot of people and drinking and stuff, but this isn't some Project X shit," Jessica explains.

Amanda pipes in, "Yeah, there's like zero chance the cops will show up." Aaaand now I'm worried the cops are going to raid the place.

Jessica offers me beer from the keg, but I decline it and grab a bottle of water instead. We get caught up in a conversation about the new Leonardo DiCaprio movie coming out this summer, when I look over and see Joe sandwiched between Wes and Kiera on a couch. When I focus on Wes, I catch him looking at me. He tips his water bottle at me, and I mirror the gesture with a tight-lipped smile. I bring my attention back to Jessica and Amanda, but I can feel him coming over. By the time I look up, Wes is next to me and greets the girls with a nod.

"You good?"

"Yeah, I am. Thanks," I reply, unsure why I'm so nervous. I've known this guy for years, but we just always have this weird barrier between us when my brother is around.

"Do you want me to make you a drink or anything?

A beer from the keg? I'm not drinking, so don't worry about me driving us home."

"No, I'm perfectly fine with my water." I shake the bottle for show. I nod toward my brother. "Looks like he found Karen, huh?"

He chuckles. "Yeah, looks that way. Wonder what she'll find in his pants."

"Probably tighty-whities and hopefully not an STD," I say with a gag.

"Wow, I would have never come up with those assumptions," he states with a chuckle and positions himself to lean against the island. I didn't even notice that the girls had walked away. I want to call them back to join us because I have no idea how to converse with this guy. I could bring up Algebra, or if he likes his position on the football team. I could ask about his Grams, or the name of that cologne he always wears. Maybe I'll ask what color he considers his eyes to be at the DMV because they aren't blue and they're not quite green either. I wonder how many hats–

"Are you excited to start working at the ice cream shop?" He pulls me out of my thoughts. *Thank God.*

"Yeah, I am, actually. My first shift is tomorrow. Did you find yourself a summer gig?"

He takes a swig of his water and twists the cap back on, wiping his mouth with the back of his hand and nodding, "Yeah, I'm going to be a lifeguard at the Y." Of course, he's going to be a lifeguard. I suddenly imagine myself in need of CPR. *Don't make things weird, Josie.*

"That'll be fun. You can work on your tan." And

then I lightly punch his arm. Now would be a good time for a sinkhole to just swallow me up, please.

Wes snickers, and as he's about to reply, Leah shows up and wraps her hands around Wes's left bicep.

"Hey," he says awkwardly as he tries to pry her fingers off of him.

She gives me a nasty look, and then raises herself on her tiptoes to whisper something in his ear.

That's my cue. As soon as he brings his gaze back to me, I give a small wave and start to walk away. I think I hear him call my name, but I ignore it. Who knows what she said to him, but more than likely it was something I'd never have the balls to say. Wes is so out of my league, and I'm not even sure why I got excited at all when he came over to talk to me. My brother practically begged me to stay away from him and Wes, so that's what I'm going to do.

chapter eight

present day, 2022

wes

"YOU FUCKER! CATCH THE DAMN BALL!" Bobby shouts.

"Interception! Interception!" Brandon jumps off the couch, throwing his hands up. Then he gets in Bobby's face. "Thanks for the extra points, baby!"

They're playing each other this week in our fantasy league.

Welcome to football season. My favorite time of year. Assholes yelling and never-ending shit talking. I get up to grab a drink. Brandon catches me out of the corner of his eye and shouts over the couch, "Beer me!"

Cassie's in the kitchen making her guacamole dip. I stick my finger in to get an early sample taste.

"Jerk! I'm not done. And no one knows where your nasty hands have been! Outta here!" she shoos me out of her way.

I grab my water and his beer and set them on the

counter. I pop his open with a bottle opener, my eyes on *her* door the whole time. I saw Josie go in and out of the apartment earlier. I want to brag that I got a smile, but I wouldn't even call it a smile. It was more of an *'Oh, God. There he is, just fake a smile and move on,'* kinda thing.

I know I fucked up. One encounter is not going to settle all the history we have. It's been so long, but she's still obviously hurt, and rightly so. It was seven years ago, we were just out of high school and we both were dealing with everything that happened. I didn't make the best choices. I had no fucking clue what I was doing. I know I'd make better choices *now*, but that's not going to fix anything, is it?

Typically, I'm on a high from all the first Sunday of football excitement, and it might seem like I'm here for it today, but my nerves have me on another level. I've wanted nothing but to check on her today, but since I value my life, I've kept to myself. If she decides to hang out, am I supposed to ignore her, or does she want me to acknowledge her? I feel like there's no right answer here. My mind is spinning to a point where I can't truly enjoy a day I look forward to every year.

"Bobby, want a drink?" I offer as I hand Brandon his over the back of the couch.

"Not now, dude. My quarterback is throwing like a girl and it's pissing me off," he whines.

"Hey! You've never seen me throw, so watch your mouth," Cassie threatens.

"Quit your yappin' and finish that dip, girl. I'm starving." Cassie loves to hate my sexist jokes. I would never seriously ask a woman why she isn't in the kitchen, but with Cassie I can't not do it. It's too fun. Plus, she knows I respect all females.

She narrows her eyes at me. I put my hands up in surrender, "I'm kidding, I'm kidding. Please, you're the best guac maker in the whole wide world."

"Yeah, I am. So, shut up and go watch your game." She holds up a knife and points to the living room. With my hands still up, one gripping a water bottle, I back into the living room.

"Bro, your girl don't play," I advise Brandon.

"You look for it. What you should do is quit looking toward Josie's room and pay attention to your team. You're going down. Connor's gonna get here soon with a damn boner for Tom Brady."

"What? Shit." I sigh and open up the fantasy football app on my phone. He's right, I am losing now. But I'm only projected to lose by less than ten points, so I've still got faith.

We're all going over our players and who we benched and why when I hear Cassie giggling. I turn around to look in the kitchen and I have to do a double take. Josie's emerged from her dungeon. And apparently, she left all her clothes in there because I swear, she isn't wearing any. She's got on a loose, long tank top with one of those bra things underneath. It's similar to what she had on at Pump House, but this bra is yellow and lacy. I want to rip it off. With my teeth. Even just tug at it.

Brandon snaps his fingers in my view. I jerk my head back and cock an eyebrow at him. He points his beer bottle to the TV.

"What are you, *her dad*?" What does he care if I look at her?

"No, but she's our new roommate and my girl's friend, so let's not make it awkward when she's only been here two days."

Yeah, yeah, yeah. I nod at him in understanding.

Even though my eyes aren't on her, my mind won't fucking get off her.

The girls keep giggling and I want to turn around and see so bad my jaw hurts from clenching it.

A knock sounds at the door and I about pull a damn hamstring jumping up so quickly to get the door. The guys look at me like I'm on crack because really, who gets so excited about opening the door other than a child or a dog?

I stride over to the door and glance at her. She's looking so I nod and greet her, "Hey, Josie. Welcome to football Sunday." I flash her a toothy smile and continue to the door. I catch her lips barely lift at the ends in response before continuing my trek to the front door.

I open the door to Connor holding up some homemade dish, and he uses his free hand to smack my stomach in greeting, "What's up, sexy beast? How's your ass feeling because I'm waxing that shit!" He follows it with a guttural laugh.

Passing me, he walks into the kitchen and starts to uncover whatever he made when he sees her. *Dammit.*

He looks up and raises both brawny arms, hands to the skies, "Sweet Jesus! You have answered my prayers!"

Just as fast as I got off that couch, my jealousy arrives at football Sunday. Connor is a good guy. He's friends with Brandon, and we've been in the same fantasy league for a few years now. We all hang out during the off-season, too. But here's the thing, Connor has a charm the ladies can't deny. He sports a golden man-bun and a beard. He likes to cook, and he's always climbing shit, too, rocks and mountains and whatever's taller than he is, and for whatever reason, the girls love that about him. But if I remember correctly, Josie's different. She doesn't like all that attention and cockiness out in the open. Unless she's changed, she isn't your typical girl. I'll just sit back, get comfortable, and watch him make an ass out of himself.

She's looking at him like the idiot that he is.

Cassie jumps in, "Connor, this is Josie. She's our new roommate. Josie, this is Connor, Brandon's friend." Josie smiles at him.

I swear he is devouring her with his eyes. "Girl, are you a time traveler? Because I swear I've seen you in my future."

The girls laugh and the caveman in me jumps in with my two cents.

"Ay, she's new around here, man. Don't embarrass her, have some respect," I spit out.

She looks at me with raised eyebrows.

He turns to me, "Wesley, did you miss your eye appointment? Don't tell me her 'being new around here' is keeping you from trying with this beauty," he says, using his fingers as air quotes.

I shake my head and throw daggers with my eyes in his direction.

"I can speak for myself, thank you very much," she

pipes up. My head shoots over to look at her. She's glaring at me, then she turns to Connor and reaches for his hair, "Impressive man-bun!"

The fuck? I was wrong, I don't know this girl anymore. Shy Josie has left the building.

Connor puts a hand on his chest and lets out his deep rumble of a laugh again. "I like this girl! Welcome to the club, beautiful." He puts his hand up to high-five her and she goes with it.

"I know, right! I love it," Cassie reaches up and also gets a feel of his golden locks. I look at the three of them like they're high. Since when did the long-hair look become okay for guys?

"Wanna see the best part?" Connor asks the girls. Then he reaches back and lets his hair down. "Ready?" he asks.

We wait.

He gathers his hair, smoothing it against his scalp a few times, switching hands with each stroke. I look at the girls and they might as well be drooling with a pair of hearts for eyes. He ties it into a bun and the girls are blushing. For real? They are goo-goo, ga-ga because he can do something that they do multiple times a day.

"Fuck this. I'm not gonna sit here and watch you play Fabio." I shake my head and go back into the testosterone-filled room, thankful Josie hasn't ripped my head off for my virile behavior.

A few minutes later, Connor joins us for the game. We're all cursing and high-fiving. He nudges my arm, "Fuck, she's hot, right. What's up with you? Getting all butt-hurt in there," he asks, intrigued.

"I don't know, man. I talked to her yesterday. She seems shy and shit, so I wanted to stand up for her." *Lie.* I'm an asshole who wants her all to himself.

"She didn't seem shy to me," he admits. It's the truth, I've never met a creature more intimidating.

And that change in her behavior scares the shit out of me.

At half-time, we go into the kitchen and serve ourselves. There's Cassie's guacamole, chips, fruit, and chili. Before Josie went back into her room, she finally noticed Bobby, my coworker/her personal trainer, and talked about how it's "such a small world." *Tell me a-fucking-bout it.*

During the third quarter, I hear her come out of her room again and decide instantly that I'm still hungry. Cassie's on the couch cuddled up against Brandon, so it's just me and Josie when I turn around from the fridge. And now, all my blood is rushing to my dick. For real, I have to face the fridge again and adjust myself. Josie is the only girl in the world who can make my cock spasm by just glancing at her. Since I was on the other side of the island earlier, I didn't catch her ripped jean shorts. *Goddamn.* She's looking down at her phone, hair in a messy bun and I get the urge to sniff it. God, I'm a creep.

Ah, fuck it. Who cares, right? I kinda want to rile her up anyway.

Slowly, I head over to her and stand behind her,

hand on the knob of the silverware drawer she's blocking. Her familiar coconutty scent shoots straight into my brain, and if I wasn't already sporting a semi, that would've done it. She tenses up when she realizes where I'm at. I bring my mouth down to her ear, "Why aren't you watching the game with us?" It's almost a whisper.

She audibly gulps, "I was just finishing up organizing my room."

"Did you finish it?" I'm still in her bubble.

"Finish what?" Huh, this is working better than I'd expected.

"Your room." I chuckle.

"Oh, Yeah."

I look down at her lips. I've kissed many lips, but no pair compares to those. They're soft and perfect and parted right now. I break my stare and bring my attention down to the counter. "Well, come watch it with us, silly," I tell her playfully, then pat her twice on the hip to move over before I open the drawer, grab a spoon, fix myself a second bowl of chili, and walk away.

josie

He made a bowl of chili and walked out of the kitchen as if he wasn't just invading my space and whispering and nudging and... sniffing? Did he sniff me?

I can still feel his warm breath on my neck. *I can do*

this. I can act normal around a guy I dated way back then. Except he's not just any guy. He's *the* guy. He's the exception, the one who has kept me up at night more often than I care to admit. He's the one my mom has learned to stop bringing up in casual conversations because I simply can't handle it. He's the one who brings me back to square one. Back to a time where I didn't leave my bed, to a time where the only people I would talk to were Cora and my aunt Leila. But that was a long time ago.

I can do this.

I take a deep breath and head into the living room with my plate of fruit and chips. I sit on the floor by the couch Cassie and Brandon are occupying.

Everyone's having a good time and the guys seem to like the fact that us girls are getting into it. I catch Wes's eyes glancing toward me every few minutes and try with every cell of my being to ignore it.

Cassie cracks me up. She keeps asking questions that even I know, and the guys can't help but roll their eyes. They even shush her when she pipes up at the wrong time. An interception is thrown with only a few minutes left and she decides to ask how many points a touchdown is worth.

Earlier, when I walked out and realized I was surrounded by several guys I don't know, I freaked out a little. Clearly, a few guys here in the middle of the day with friends I trust are more than likely harmless, but I went into fight or flight mode. I went straight to my room to sort out my thoughts for a minute. It was while I was sitting on my bed looking around at my minimalistic, boho-inspired room that a framed print on the wall caught my eye. The cardstock I framed years ago has nude colors throughout it and in a pretty black script reads, *Let your smile change the world but don't let the world change your smile.* It was my first weekly word and put the moment into perspective. We live in beautiful world with too many ugly corners within it. And although I found myself in one of those corners all those years ago, I can't let that type of ugly define moments like these.

It's been almost a decade, and counseling and time have helped tremendously in my healing journey, but that does not erase what happened. I still have these moments where I freak out a little bit. But those words, sent at the moment I needed to see them the most, encouraged me to come back out here. And now getting to know these guys, and see their friendship and dynamic with each other and how they mess with Cassie, it feels right to be here. I feel even more comfortable hanging out with these strangers. Plus, Brandon would never let anything happen to her, just like I know Wes would protect me, too.

I usually don't root for a team, but I start to enjoy myself as the other team gets close to the end zone on a tie game with less than a minute left on the clock. Everyone's on the edge of their seats. Then, the quarterback sees an opening during the last possible play for the game and makes a run for it, scoring a beautiful touchdown. The room comes to life with all of us cheering.

I throw my hands in the air and look over at Wes who fist pumps a few times with a huge Cheshire grin on his face. His eyes move down to me, then settle on my side where I sport my favorite tattoo, and I swear his eyes almost pop out of his head. His face turns red and he throws a hand to his mouth and starts violently coughing into it. As the cheering dies down, everyone's attention is on him.

He's bent over, hardly breathing when he straightens up and points to his throat and mutters, "Went down the wrong pipe." He sounds like an old man. I know my ink in that spot usually gets a reaction, especially from guys, but I've never witnessed a reaction like that.

Guys really like the sight of a little side-boob, I guess.

chapter nine

night of the last day of sophomore year, 2013

josie

THE PARTY HASN'T BEEN horrible, and I find myself outside in the backyard with a bunch of classmates whom I've known for years but have barely spoken to. A few kids stand out to me, like Drew Scott from biology and Sarah Meadows from writing, but I choose to sit next to Jessica and Amanda. There's a variety of chairs surrounding a fire. I sit on a small makeshift bench made of pallet wood. We chat about summer plans and which classes we want to take next year. Each of us enjoying the end of one era as we look forward to the beginning of a new one.

I look around and see that Drew has his eyes on me. He's laid back in a black camping chair, a beer bottle in hand, and he nods at me. Drew is cute in the shaggy hair, random-hole-in-his-jeans, lazy way. We sat next to each other all year and he's always been friendly. Our small talk usually started with him asking for a pencil and randomly recommending music I've never heard of.

There's a hum of chatter and it grows as more people come outside, including my wasted brother, his friends, and the *Heathers*. Where did Kiera go? I would much prefer her presence.

Seats are filled and spilling with people when someone shouts, "Let's play a game!"

Rebecca, one of Leah's minions, suggests we play "Spin and Dare" which I've never heard of and definitely not participating in. My brother mumbles asking what the game's all about. It's explained as a Spin the Bottle meets Truth or Dare. The dares come from a bowl of written down and folded-up dares. I haven't played either game since I was a kid and there is no way in hell I'll play this mashed-up version. The introverts like me can't even choose 'truth' if they wanted to.

A raggedy notebook, a few pens, and an empty bottle of vodka appear in no time, and the hum has died down some as people are busy coming up with dares. I look over at Wes laughing at my idiot brother who has locked his phone from entering the wrong password one too many times. I hope he doesn't drink much more because I'll be the one answering to my parents as to why the golden boy is off his rocker.

An announcement that the game is ready to begin has me slowly getting up off the bench just as Amanda grabs me by my wrist and pulls me back down, promising it'll be fun. My shaky knees and belly cramps are telling me this will be the opposite of fun. Yet she won't let me go.

Because of Us

The first spin lands on a girl who I think was in my PE class last year. She reaches into the bowl and reads her dare out loud, "You've been naughty, you're in time-out on someone's lap for the next two spins." She immediately responds to the dare, "Well, that's easy," and sits on her boyfriend's lap, kissing him as soon as she's settled. If I had picked that one, I definitely would have sat on Jessica or Amanda's lap.

The girl gets back up off her boyfriend to spin the bottle, then sits back down. *Please don't land on me. Please don't land on me. Please don't land on me.* It lands on Jessica, two spots over from me. She gets up, mumbling that she's not kissing anyone she doesn't want to.

"Cop a feel on the person to the left of you," she says, giggling.

Everyone joins in laughter because it's no secret Jessica and Amanda are besties. She walks over to Amanda with grabby hands and palms both of Amanda's boobs, shakes them, and even motorboats her all while laughing hysterically. The guys watch them in awe—with a tinge of wishful thinking.

"Next!" Rebecca shouts, surely jealous that the attention isn't on her and her friends.

Jessica spins the bottle and I watch it, holding my breath, when it lands on Wes and we lock eyes right away. After one, two, three seconds, he breaks our stare and gets out of his seat, flipping his hat backward before he grabs the bowl and starts mixing his hand in there. I don't know why, but he has a toothpick sticking out of his mouth, rolling it around in thought while he picks a

73

dare. Like where did he get that? The sight of him gives me goosebumps.

He clears his throat before reading the dare, "Take your shirt off and leave it off for the remainder of the game. Hm. That's it?" He looks around and shrugs. Wes turns to me and tosses his hat in my lap before he makes a show of reaching back and pulling his shirt off over his head. Maybe it's not a show to everyone, but it sure as hell is to me, and my mouth goes dry as I stare at him in awe. He shoves the shirt into the back of his pants so it's hanging out and reaches down to get his hat back, smirking at me as he does so before going back to his seat. Shirtless and now it's me looking on with a tinge of wishful thinking.

Lord, if you're listening, when I die... I'd like to be reincarnated into that toothpick. Thank you so much.

A few rounds go by, and I've witnessed a moron run and jump over the fire, two girls French kiss (the guys went wild with this one), someone's horrible rapping of "Row, Row, Row Your Boat," and now I'm watching my brother attempt to drunk breakdance, and I can't lie, this isn't half bad. I've been laughing between my mini-panic attacks hoping the bottle doesn't choose me as its next victim. Watching Joe make an ass out of himself has me dying of laughter, and reminds me of when we were kids. He's on his knees, ass up, and can't catch his breath from laughing, and Wes is in tears.

I don't even notice the fact that the empty bottle of Tito's has been spun and is now pointing at me until a few people call out my name. I take a deep breath, composing myself, and taking my time before I make my way to the bowl. I give myself a quick internal pep-talk because I am finally, sort of enjoying myself. This can be fun like it has been for everyone else. My brother watches me as he stands up and shakes his head, laughing, "Let's see how this goes."

I'm unfolding the little piece of paper and I can feel my face redden. My brother stands up and almost trips in the three steps it takes to get to me.

He takes the dare from my hands and reads it to himself, but it's definitely loud enough for most to hear, "Make your best 'O' face while looking someone in the eye." He scoffs, "That's bullshit. She ain't doing it." Shaking his head, he throws it off to the side while everyone whispers and giggles and...

this

is

my

nightmare.

He picks up another dare, but is interrupted when Leah gets up and takes the bowl from him.

"Let's just skip her. She probably doesn't even know what an 'O' face means and no one's going to want to kiss her."

My eyes burn and I hold in my tears with all of my being. I wipe my eyes before the tears fall, pat my front and back pockets, making sure I have my phone on me, and as soon as I feel it secured in my pocket, I pull it out and start walking away. I hear Amanda call after me, and even Wes, but my quick glance back shows my brother holding him back, telling him to leave me alone.

I'll never forget the hopeless look on Wes's face, or the sound of the mean girls cackling at me.

I round the side of the house and find a gate with a latch but no lock. I unlatch it and close it back up in hopes that no one will follow me. The second I'm alone in the front yard, I let out the biggest breath and begin pacing back and forth, counting to ten, then backward to one. Over and over. That girl has no reason to be such a bitch to me, and would it take so much for my brother to defend me? Not only was it embarrassing to not even know where to begin with that dare, but my brother's protection of my sex-life and *not* my feelings is humiliating.

I sit on the curb, hands shaking, holding my phone to my chest. I can't wait to be out of this place. My aunt Leila is the first person I think of. I pull up her contact on my phone and send her a message.

Me: I can't wait for my vacation with you. I hate this place.

Leila is only eight years older than me and has always been my rock. I plan to stay with her for two weeks this summer, and it can't get here fast enough. She always gives the best advice, and I'm sure right now she would tell me to just ignore everything that happened at the fire. She'd tell me that I am enough, along with all the reasons why. She makes everything brighter and clearer, and I need that so bad right now.

The squeaky gate interrupts my thoughts and I try to wipe my eyes as best as I can. I hear the gate shut and footsteps getting louder behind me. I'm sure it's Wes. My brother finally let him chase after me. He's probably going to take me home and then come back for Joe.

I look over and see a pair of beaten-up Vans. *Not Wes.* Before I crane my neck to see who it is, Drew comes up next to me.

"Leah's a bitch," he states.

I laugh and wipe my eyes, nodding my head and agreeing with him.

"Your brother's also an ass."

"Another fact," I chuckle.

Sniffling and wiping my eyes again with the heel of both palms, I admit, "I knew coming here was a bad idea. I don't do parties."

"Yeah, they are usually pretty lame. I just didn't have anything else to do."

"Did you come with anyone?"

He pulls a cigarette out of a pack that appeared out of nowhere and lights it, taking a hit before answering, "Yeah, I've got some friends in there, but I drove separately in case I wanted to dip out early."

He offers me the cigarette and I shake my head, "It wasn't so bad for a second, but I don't know. I'm just not cut out for all this socializing. I would have been happy at home with a book. My mom made me come with my brother to keep an eye on him."

Cigarette in his mouth, his eyebrows shoot up and he takes another puff before he confesses that his mom thinks he's working at his movie theater job.

The smell of smoke is nauseating, but his presence is comforting. We make small talk. He tells me about his job and that he's been working there for a few months now.

"What's your favorite and least favorite part of your career as a movie theater attendant?" I say the last part all prim and proper as if the position is more prestigious than it really is.

He chuckles before answering, "I like that when I clean the theater I can listen to my headphones and be in my own world, and I hate making the popcorn. I'm traumatized because on my first day I burnt it and the fire department had to come check everything out. The place smelled awful forever."

"You're kidding? Oh my gosh. You're serious. On your first day?!"

"Yep, it was embarrassing as fuck, but I thought it had like a timer that went off. Apparently not." He smiles at me and his eyes are twinkling in the moonlight.

I started the night wondering if I would talk to a guy here tonight. My mind is always on Wes whenever he's around, and when he came up to me in the house, my expectations went through the roof, like maybe something would finally happen between us. Like maybe my lifelong dream of Wes being my first kiss was within arms' reach. Then Leah squashed that like she does everything else. I sit here and listen to Drew's deep chuckle, and watch the smoke that leaves his mouth every now and then, and I wonder, what if it's him? I would have never expected it, but that's how life goes, right?

"Let me give you a ride outta here."

My heart rate increases, and I know it's because I'm nervous.

As if he can tell what he's asking, he puts his hands up in surrender, "I only had one beer, scout's honor." He holds up two fingers, and I tell him it's fine and that yes, he can take me home.

We walk to his Jeep Wrangler where he opens the passenger door for me and helps me get in. As he walks around the front of the car, my phone vibrates in my hand. I lock my phone as soon as I read the text and don't reply. I have one goal in mind and that is to leave this party, my brother, Leah, and Wes—along with all the dreams of mine Wes holds onto—behind.

Joe: It's Wes. Tell me you're okay and you didn't leave.

chapter ten

present day, 2022

josie

IT'S Monday morning and I'm trading out my flip flops for heels in the driver's seat of my car. I just pulled up to a building in an area of several business-y, tall buildings. An interview for my first real adult job is in fifteen minutes and, I'm not sure how some do it, but I'd rather walk barefoot through hot coals than wear heels while driving.

A few weeks before I moved back home, I started applying for jobs. Having a title of Licensed Clinical Social Worker means that I help people with their mental health as well as other aspects of their life. In school, and with internships, I'd worked with couples and families, kids, and even older people and military families. Some were in rehab facilities. I've even worked with prison inmates before.

This job, in particular, is a private practice. It's

owned by psychologist (meaning the doc went to school for four more years than I did), and has several counselors and social workers under his supervision who are seeing clients privately. I'd prefer to work somewhere more community based, but regular people need therapy, too. I, personally, believe everyone needs therapy.

I walk into the lobby, the heels echoing my every step. The directory confirms that I need to ride the elevator to the sixth floor. I walk into the elevator after it dings open and lean my head back against the wall, reflecting on what my life has been like these last few weeks. I've got a part-time job and working on getting my big girl job, a place to live (albeit with particularly tatted and jacked, unexpected, and annoying company), and I'm meeting new people.

I video-chatted with Leila last night and caught her up. She's proud of me, as always, but it was nice to unwind with her. She's like my own personal therapist. Pointing out the good in being more independent, AKA choosing to live on my own and not mooch off my parents, even though they'd never see it that way. Boundaries are hard for my family, and I had to start creating them right away. And pointing out the bad in freaking out on Wes and trying to push him away while choosing to still live in his apartment. She was always team Wes. She feels he needs a second chance, or at least a chance to explain after all this time. Leila knows he suffered, too.

Okay, fine, so Wes isn't annoying per se, he's just throwing a wrench in my plans, and if there's something

I've learned about myself, it's that I've got to be in control. Whether it's the flavor I choose to put in my coffee (white mocha + toffee nut, thanks), or what school is scrolled across the top of my diploma, I like to be the one to hold the power in that decision.

When Wesley Miller is around, control is the last thing I can grasp onto.

And that's hard for me to deal with.

The ding pulls me out of my thoughts. That was a long six floors.

I find the door to the suite of the office and, right away, I hear the white noise machines in the corners of the waiting room that keep the voices that may be overheard from the appointments that are in session. Thirsty plants hang from the ceiling, and several pamphlets with happy models line the wall.

I walk up to the front desk where a girl is on the phone scheduling an appointment. She wears a big smile, but obnoxiously chews gum, holding up a finger, signaling me to wait.

Once she's off the phone and ready for me, I explain that I'm here for an interview with her boss. She then prompts me to take a seat in the waiting room. Thankfully, it's empty, and I pull my phone out to check unread text messages.

Today, 9:04 AM
Weekly Word: Never love anybody who treats you like you're ordinary. (Oscar Wilde)

Today, 9:58 AM
Cora: I miss you. I met a guy and my mind is still on Joe. How do you do it? I don't know how he's been gone for all these years now. It feels like yesterday.
Cora: Remember when Wes stole that bag of chocolate-covered pretzels for you and you almost broke his nose?

I pull up the first text knowing I will need to give more time and attention to Cora's texts later.

Almost ten years and I've saved every single quote from my 'weekly word.' Every time a quote comes through, it determines how my day, and sometimes how my week, will go. It isn't always a quote, sometimes it's song lyrics. Either way, the words feed my soul. The Mondays that come and go without a message always seem different, those are the days where I can feel the Monday Blues everyone talks about.

I don't know who it is. I'm not even sure I want to know. I don't want them to stop. I crave the messages. I'll never forget when I upgraded my phone once and they tried to change my number, I threw a fit until they handed me my new phone with the same number and threw in a brand-new case at no extra charge.

Over the years I always suspected that it was Cora, but she's denied it every time. I once thought it was Joe and Wes working together. It would have totally been like them to trick me with a secret admirer, but the texts still come, so it's obviously not them. I've learned to not worry about *who* it is anymore, and just try to embrace the words instead.

I take a deep breath before I reread Cora's texts slower this time to really take them in. She does this, she falls into this funk every few months. She handles our past better than I ever have, but when these moments come up, I call her, and we have a two-hour conversation about anything and nothing. It usually helps. It helps me, at least.

I reply to her and plan a talk for tonight after I get home. Some FaceTime and wine. Sometimes we chat about all of our currents: books, TV shows, what song we can't stop listening to. And other nights we reminisce and cry like blubbering fools over a time we'll never get back. Being that she brought up the time I elbowed Wes in the face on accident because I was so excited he got me my favorite snack, I know tonight will be the latter.

"Josie?"

I look up to find Dr. Jane Francis. I recognize her from some articles she's been featured in, and my old professor knew her (hence, how I got the interview).

"Hi, yes…" I shake the hand she's held out to me. "Thanks so much for this opportunity."

"Of course, no problem. Come on back and let's get started."

That night, I'm on the way home with a new job under my belt and wine, cheese, grapes, and a couple of cupcake-smelling candles in my passenger seat. Billie Eilish spills out of my speakers as I continue my drive under the starlit sky.

Shortly after my interview, I worked a shift with Cassie where we got to celebrate the news of my new job with coffee during our break, and I was able to present Scotty with my new schedule. My new job will have me sharing an office with another counselor, working opposite schedules until my clientele builds. So, for now, I'll be in on Mondays, Wednesdays, and Thursdays, leaving the rest of the week open for Loose Leafs if I want. Scotty says he can work with me, which is nice, but if it becomes too much, he understands I'll be putting my notice in.

I'm giddy and seeing life in a new light now that I am officially Josie Rodriguez, LCSW. The moon is out and my windows are down. A cool breeze whips my hair around, and driving through these streets at night brings more memories of *that summer* and random late drives just like the one Cora remembered today. She knows that I moved into Wes's apartment, but that's about it. She's been hounding me for more details on the matter. We've been so busy, I haven't been able to catch her up, but when I dropped the bomb on her, she couldn't believe it and told me it would probably be in my best interest not to move in. *Too late now.*

I turn the key into the front door of the apartment and quietly walk in. My steps and bags echo down the hallway, but I see that the apartment is dimly lit by the light underneath the microwave in the kitchen, and some light shines from the gaps at the bottom of my roommate's doors. I quickly go into my room and shut myself inside, dropping all my belongings onto my desk and chair. I switch my lamp on and change into plaid cotton shorts and a tank top. Grabbing my laptop out of my bag, I get a foot away from my bed when my heart gets stuck in my throat. A bag of chocolate-covered pretzels sits under a sticky note scribbled in a handwriting I'd never forget: *Congrats on your new job. (Cassie's not the best at keeping secrets, btw.) I'm not asking for forgiveness, I don't deserve it. But please don't break my nose for these, I've seen your right hook and know this time you'll be successful at it.*

Ten minutes later, I answer Cora's FaceTime request with my tear-soaked face holding up a bag of Flipz.

She shakes her head, "Typical Wes Miller."

Sniffling and wiping my tears like the emotional mess that I am, I explain, "He left it in my room with a note congratulating me on my new job and brought up the same thing you talked about today."

"Wow. First off, congrats!" She cheers her wine glass to the camera, inspiring me to grab my wine from the bag and pop the top. I take a swig, forgoing a glass. "How weird that he and I both thought of that today. I must have put it out there into the universe."

"For sure, so weird." I exhale and just smile at her. "I can't believe I have a big girl job. Just like you," I say with a wink.

"A hotel manager is hardly a big girl job."

I make a face that says *seriously?*

"Okay, okay, it is. It just doesn't feel like it is when Bennett is attached to my name."

Cora's dad, Sam Bennett, is well known in the hotel world, and although Cora fell into his footsteps, she's always felt like she's spoiled in the industry due to everyone being scared of her dad. I always tell her that it's because of how good she is at the job, and not just because she's the daughter of the Hotel Mogul.

"Here we go. Tell me about this guy you mentioned." I reach over and grab a tissue to dab my nose.

"No, no. Don't deflect. Tell me about living with fucking Wes Miller," she sighs and makes a show, clasping her hands up to her chest. "Is he still as dreamy as ever?"

I nod with a closed-mouth smile.

"I bet he went nuts when he saw you."

I cover my eyes, unable to hide the blush. "I pretended not to know him."

"What! How do you do that? The guy was your first real boyfriend. I know it didn't last long, but geez, he only ate you out about forty times that summer like you were a goddamn summer special buffet! He'd recognize you if you weren't wearing pants. That's for sure."

I try to turn down the volume on my laptop and can't hold in my laugh. "Oh my gosh, Cora, stop!" My giggles get the best of me, but I try to keep them down.

"I'm just saying. Do you think his dick has gotten bigger since then?" she asks while looking away and tapping her chin.

"Oh, God, who knows, but he is definitely bigger.

Get this, he works as a personal trainer, and it shows. He's jacked. And tatted up. I thought he would never get a tattoo."

"That's a good way to get it going again between you two. Play a little... *I'll show you mine if you show me yours.*" Her eyebrows bounce around.

"I will hang up on you, Cora Bennett."

"Okay, okay. Sorry," she giggles. "But really, how do you pretend you don't know him?"

"It's because of Cassie. I don't think I'm ready for her and her boyfriend to know our past. We definitely recognized each other. I thought I was gonna pass out. But I acted like I was meeting him for the first time and booked it out of there. I did have a private convo with him the day I moved in." I let out a fake laugh before continuing. "Well, more like I went off on him."

"Why?" she asks, genuinely invested in my reunion.

"Because he basically wanted to apologize and start off with a clean slate."

"Ouch."

"Yeah. But that passed and we were pretty civil during a football game here the other day. Ugh, he smelled so good. The same."

"I bet. That's nice. I still have these weird moments where I swear I smell Joe."

"Yeah?"

"Yeah."

I don't want to talk about Joe right now. I love him, he's my brother, but we have let his death, not *him* as I've learned with lots of therapy, hold us back from so much. For years the guilt ate me up.

"So, like I said in my text, I met this guy." She smiles, then scrunches her nose.

"Okay. What's his name? What does he do for work? Celebrity look-alike?"

"His name is Mitch. He works security for the casino at my hotel. And I'd probably cast Jacob Elordi to play him."

"Holy shit, really?"

"No, but that dude can get it."

We laugh, and when she catches her breath she explains more, "No, really, he does have a little air of that guy, but not as tall. He's stayed at the hotel a few times overnight for work. I set him up with a room and he kept coming to see me. We went on a date and we had a good time. But I don't know, we'll see."

"Sounds like you're not really into him, I'm sorry."

"It's okay. Honestly, I'm so busy right now, the last thing I need is a man. How do you like your new place?"

"It's nice! You'd love Cassie. She's a character. At first she'll probably be a bit much for you, but I know she'd grow on you."

"Well, I'm glad you met a new friend and she got you this place."

"I know. I couldn't live with my parents forever. Plus, living with them would make it harder for me to leave if shit hits the fan."

"Shit will not hit the fan, babe. Be positive. Put that shit into the universe," she says with her arms out and eyes closed.

If only it were that easy. The reason it's taken me so

long to come back is because I'm scared. My hometown holds so many memories I never want to forget. But it also holds my deepest, darkest nightmares.

Moments I'll spend my whole life trying to forget.

But deep down I know that I'll never be able to forget.

chapter eleven

night of the last day of sophomore year, 2013

josie

DREW PULLS into the road with a fluidity to his driving. He uses the blinker and looks over toward me, flashing a smile in my direction. He has a playlist of various artists I've never heard of playing low in the background, shedding light on the awkward silence that falls between us.

I tell him the cross streets by my house before asking if he's taken his SAT yet. I plan to take mine for the first time this summer, giving me a chance to take it another time or two before I apply to colleges. A bunch of students have already tested this year, though, and I just wondered if he was one of them.

"Nah. My dad owns a landscaping company and I'm sure that's what I'll do after graduating."

"Oh, cool. Is that what you want to do?"

"I don't really care what I do, as long as I can make some cash. I'm sure my dad will pay me well, and I'll probably just bullshit in the office like my older brother does."

I cringe at the thought of his older brother. Teddy Scott is nasty. He was a senior when we were freshmen. He always looked like he needed a shower and was rude and a bully to most kids. Not surprised that Teddy just bullshits around for his career. Fits him well. But I didn't peg Drew to dream for that after high school. I figured he didn't know what he wanted to do—like most of us—but I thought he would at least aspire for something more than that.

"Are you close to Teddy?"

"Sometimes, he can be a real douche, but we get along okay." He looks over to me and continues, "Alright, so enough about me. What's up with you? What are your summer plans? Have you taken the SAT? And tell me, what's up with this straight hair? I'm diggin' it," his spiel ends with him reaching over and touching my hair.

His words and his gesture bring warmth to my cheeks. I feel like I've never heard him put a string of that many words together and I can't believe he noticed my hair. While I was straightening it, I wondered if Wes would like it, but I figured most guys wouldn't pay any attention to. The fact that Drew noticed has woken the butterflies in my belly.

Wearing a smile, I answer him, "Thank you. Yeah, my, uh…" I run my fingers through my hair, "my mom got me a straightener, and tonight was my first time using it. I haven't signed up yet but plan to take my SAT this summer sometime. And this weekend I start my summer job at a new ice cream parlor downtown."

He nods as I talk and shifts his position some while keeping his left hand on the steering wheel. His right hand lands on my leg and he says, "Well, you should definitely keep the hair straightener because you're smokin' tonight."

The second he touches me, I silently gasp. That is not what I was expecting. And what did he say? *I'm smokin'?* I look at him wide-eyed and he winks at me in response. My nerves are eating away at me, and I don't know how I should be feeling. Drew's always been so nice to me, and although I've always had a small attraction to him, I would have never imagined he saw me as anything other than the girl with an open mind for music who lets him borrow school supplies.

He lifts his hand from my thigh long enough to turn the volume up, then puts it right back where it was, and now my hands are sweating. The music gets into my head. Can I see myself dating someone like Drew? What kind of boyfriend would he be and what kind of girlfriend would I be? Would my parents approve of him? What would Joe think? Wes? I'm not sure if they even know Drew or what they think of him. I fantasize that Wes would be pissed and threaten to beat him up if he mistreats me, but for all I know he probably wouldn't give a shit.

We pull into my neighborhood, and despite my nerves and shaky voice, I give him directions to my house. I'm confused when he takes a right where I tell him to take a left.

He gives my leg a squeeze before asking, "There's a small park here, right?"

"Yeah, there's a basketball court and some picnic tables."

"Let's chill some more before I drop you off."

"Oh, okay." I'm surprised he didn't mention his plans sooner, but I figure it's not even eleven yet, and I'm good as long as I get home by midnight. I don't even want to think about what to tell my parents about Joe and why we're coming home separately again. *Hi, Mom and Dad. Oh, Joe? He just let his girlfriend talk crap about me in front of everyone. I'm all good. I had another boy bring me home.* Boy, would they get a kick out of that.

Drew parks and we get out of his Jeep to sit at the picnic tables overlooking the courts. He sits on the table, and I take a seat on the bench just below him to his left. He pulls out a cigarette and lights it before we fall into a conversation about our classmates. I know who his friends Justin and Tony are, but I've never talked to them. He knows Cora and refers to her as my friend with the "big tits," which he isn't wrong about, but I didn't expect him to say that. Drew is definitely unpredictable outside the classroom.

"So, I assume you're not talking to anybody, huh? Unless you're with that Miller guy..." He stubs out his cigarette on the table.

"Wes? No, he's just my brother's best friend." Nervously, I use my nail to pick at the wood of the bench before I answer him, "No, I'm not talking to anyone. You?"

"No," he answers. "And if I was, I'd be a shit boyfriend right now."

"Why's that?" I ask, knowing full well it's because we're alone on a Friday night, and he rescued me from that party.

He reaches over and moves a lock of hair behind my ear, "Because a good boyfriend wouldn't be sitting here with another girl, thinking the things I am thinking."

Okaaay, this is new for me. I'm horrible at flirting.

"Well, good thing you're not taken then." I say it with a shaky voice because *holy shit, is he about to kiss me?* The way he's watching me makes my world stop.

Drew moves down to sit next to me and puts his hand on my thigh again. "I wonder if we will have any classes together junior year?" he says with his eyes gazing into mine. "Will you still let me borrow a pencil?" Then, he gets closer and whispers in my ear, "Maybe I can cheat off your paper?"

My heart is beating a million miles a minute as his hand starts to creep higher. I'm glad I shaved my legs before I left the house today. And he smells like cigarettes, a scent I've always hated. But for some reason his aroma is doing weird things to my head.

He goes on, "Maybe we can have study dates, just the two of us."

Next thing I know, I stop his hand as it's gotten to where his fingers are grazing the hem of my skirt and I turn my face toward him. His face is inches from mine, and his smoky breath comes out of him as I inhale them with shallow breaths. His grip on my leg tightens right before his lips press into mine. Two chaste kisses are followed by his tongue pushing into my mouth. It's sloppier than I imagined it would be.

It's actually nothing like I imagined my first kiss would be like. His free hand grips the back of my head, and combined with the grasp he's got on my thigh, it's more aggressive than I expected. I lap my tongue against his in hopes I'm doing it right.

The second his hand creeps higher, I bring my hands up to his chest and slowly push him off with a giggle.

He bites his bottom lip, admitting, "I've been wanting to do that all night. Since you sat near the bonfire."

"Really?" I look down and away, embarrassed. I've never gotten this attention from a boy before. I dreamt of moments like this with Wes, but he never once made me feel wanted. Sometimes I felt like the only girl in the room, but with Joe around, I know Wes would die and give up his football jersey before ever making a move on me.

"What do you mean 'really?' This skirt had all the guys at Dylan's party checking you out. Now tell me for real, what's up with you and that Miller guy. He was watching you like a creep tonight. Y'all fuckin' around behind your brother's back or what?"

"What?" I ask, rearing my head back in shock. "Me and Wes? I already told you, I swear there is nothing going on there."

"Alright, alright. I'm just saying, I saw what I saw, and either he wants up this skirt," he says, fingering the hem. "Or he was reminiscing about a time when he was already there."

Something about Drew is off. This isn't like him, and even though some stuff he's saying I've wanted to hear for some time now, I'm ready to go home.

"I think I'm ready to go home," I say out loud.

He startles me when he practically hops off the picnic bench, mumbling to himself words I can't make out. I contemplate walking home by myself because he's making me uncomfortable. I don't know if he is nervous and actually likes me, or what is going on with him. On foot I'm fifteen minutes from home, and it's close to midnight, so I'll ride the short drive home with him.

"Is everything okay? Do you mind taking me home?"

He's gripping the back of his neck and his eyes cut to me. "Yeah, Josie. I can take you home." He's short with his response but turns around and heads to his Jeep. I follow him, pulling my phone out of my pocket. 11:23 PM and no other texts from Wes but there are three missed calls. I shouldn't be upset with him, but he also shouldn't let my brother boss him around all the time. I lock the phone and stick it back in my pocket, choosing to ignore Wes for now. I look up to see Drew holding the door open for me, but avoiding eye contact and looking past me.

Once I'm in the crook of the door, I feel his hands grip my hips from behind and a nervous laugh falls from my lips. I place my hands on his to remove them, but before I can turn to look at him, his lips are on my neck, and I pull my head forward and away from him. His grasp on me tightens and I can feel him pushing up against my ass.

"Drew, what are you doing? You're hurting me," I cry. Unsure of his aggressive hold on me and why he's doing this.

"If you'd hold still, baby, I promise I can make you feel good," he says as his right hand gets a firmer grip on my side, and his other hand fingers through my hair, pushing it to the side, giving him more access to my neck. He kisses and sucks and my breath catches. I don't like this at all. I don't understand why he's being like this and I just want to leave.

I go into fight mode and attempt to turn around and push him off me when his hand at my neck pushes my head down so fast, it hits the center console, and he brings my right hand up by my head, holding it there. My left hand is trapped under me, and although Drew isn't big, almost scrawny in comparison to my brother and his teammates, his force on me is stronger than I would've expected. I can barely catch my breath, and I focus on breathing in through my nose and out of my mouth as the fear is making me feel like I'm going to pass out...and that's when I hear it.

Zipping.

No, no, no, no, no, no.

"Drew, please stop. I'm begging you. Why are you doing this?" The tears prick at my eyes, and I try to kick back at him, but he pushes my head down again, using my right hand that he still has in his hold, and he uses his other hand to hike my skirt up. The more my kicks and squirming do nothing to help me, I slowly feel myself go numb all over.

He uses his knee to spread my legs, and I swear I use

all the strength in the world to keep them from opening. My legs finally give out and I'm crying out unintelligible words until the fight in me is gone and I let him take what he wants.

He rips my underwear.

I hear him spit into his hand.

The stinging and sheer force of his actions pulls a scream out of me that somehow makes me feel like it's just me alone in the world. Me and this monster disguised as a boy.

He grunts and mutters unintelligible phrases and the bile rises up into my throat.

I try to focus on the round keyhole in the glove compartment as that's where my line of sight is as he continues to hold me down, but my vision is filled with tears as he drives into me over and over and over and over again. I start to feel this night will never end. My face is hot and the tears fall onto his Jeep's seat like a waterfall. I bite down on my arm to try and bring the attention there, and attempt to forget the awfulness that's truly going on. I hate myself for not being strong enough to fight.

He grips my shoulder in one hand, and my hip in the other, and takes and takes and takes what's now become his.

Almost instantly, the fullness is gone, and I assume he finishes what he started on the ground. His panting sounds far away as he pulls my skirt back down like the motherfucking gentleman he is. The entire scene is surreal. I decline his offer to take me home and stand there pitiful and broken, the shell of a teenage girl, as he takes off in his Jeep. While I face the fifteen-minute walk home in the condition that I'm in.

I feel dead and empty.

I feel pathetic for not being able to push him off. For not kicking harder or yelling louder. I'm exhausted and sick to my stomach. And angry. God, am I angry. This guy just stole my innocence like it was nothing, when less than an hour earlier I actually wondered what it would be like to date him.

Somehow I make it home before midnight, my parents, thankfully, already in bed. So I won't have to explain why Joe isn't here, why my hair is a mess, and why there are tears streaming down my face.

And in the morning I won't need to explain my sudden desire to leave and live with Leila, or why I'm in "such a pissy mood" as Joe says.

Nope, no explanations will be necessary as I run and hide.

chapter twelve

present day, 2022

josie

ACCORDING TO MY IPHONE, I have less than twenty minutes to get on the road before I'm late for work. Other therapists run late on their clients without batting an eye, not me. I don't typically run late, but Cassie's phone didn't charge last night, resulting in her missing her alarm and most definitely running late now. So we are taking turns using the bathroom we share to get ready. The apartment has two bathrooms, one guest bathroom that I share with Cassie and Brandon, and then one in the master suite. The master suite in which I have yet to go into and am currently trying to avoid at the moment. They mentioned before that he's the main one on the lease and that's why he has the bigger room and private bath. I'm not complaining, I couldn't imagine having to share the bathroom with him.

"Seriously, Josie?" Cassie says, leaning over the sink,

inches from the mirror curling her eyelashes. "He's probably asleep and I'm already late, you're not. Please, it would help me out so much. He probably won't even wake up. It's just Miller."

I roll my eyes and walk away, mumbling to myself, "It's just Miller," only to find myself pacing outside of Wes's bedroom door. We've been avoiding each other the last couple weeks. Okay, maybe *I'm* the one doing the avoiding, and I've been pretty successful at it til now. I never mentioned anything about the pretzels to him, didn't even thank him, mainly I didn't know what to say. So I just avoided him at all costs.

Brandon and Cassie switched cars today, God knows why, and he forgot to leave her with his keys, so she needs the spare, which happens to be in Wes's nightstand, of all places. I'm about to walk back over and argue with Cassie a little more, but I can see her holding her curling iron in one hand, and she's leaning over sideways strapping on a shoe with her other hand.

I shake my hands out, then run my fingers through my hair and pull it into a ponytail. I don't have much time anyway. I need to just go in there, grab the keys, and leave.

The door isn't completely shut, and it opens more when I softly rap my knuckles against it. Stepping into his room, the scent takes over my senses as if I were being put under a spell. It brings back memories of being in Joe's backseat with Wes. And being in Wes's backseat with Wes, for that matter. I shake the wayward thoughts from my head.

I tip-toe farther into the room, and if I thought the smell knocked me off my feet, the sight of him really does me in. The room is immaculate, not surprising as I know Wes can't handle a mess, but his bed is a chaotic shamble of gray sheets, pillows, and inky limbs. He's face down, one leg covered by the sheet, and the other covered in tattoos. The entire bottom half of his exposed leg is full of ink. I want to take a closer look at the intricate black art, but I know the clock is ticking.

A quick peek won't hurt.

I take two quiet steps toward his bed before I'm leaning over with wide eyes. The back of his calf shows football laces stitched down the center and surrounded by floral designs. I spot a butterfly with the script *Grams* running through it and what is probably his grandmother's birth year just below it. It's when I notice the books floating throughout the flowers that I decide I should stop while I'm ahead. Now is not the time to get caught up in the meaning of the tattoos Wes probably uses as a form of therapy.

I force my eyes to roam up and over his plump ass that is secure in a pair of bright briefs covered in cartoon-y melting pizza slices. This guy and his love for food. He always worked out like it was his job. Funny since it is now, and then he would make sure that his cheat meals were worth the extra fatty, greasy calories. I can remember him teaching me the proper push-up, and then licking ice cream off my lips the same day. His boxers grip onto him below a sculpted back that is smooth and tan as my eyes roam over the arm that is holding onto his pillow while the other arm is hidden underneath.

Somehow, I tear my eyes away from him in order to get back to my mission: the nightstand. It has a lamp, a clock, his wallet, keys, and phone. I peek over at him as I get down on my haunches and pull open the drawer. It sticks, causing me to use more force, and then a loud clunking sound startles him awake.

"The fuck!" Wes turns to face me, confused and startled with squinted eyes and messy hair. "Josie? What are you doing?"

I give him a nervous smile and whisper, "I'm sorry! I was just getting Brandon's spare key for Cassie." I look in the open nightstand and I see a small notebook, some old phones, some receipts, and several condoms which stop me in my tracks, but I don't let my mind think about Wes' sex life. I move stuff around looking for the key fob, wanting to get out of here as fast as possible. I'm not even caring if I'm late anymore, just needing out of his space.

He leans over and his scent overwhelms me, I can even feel the heat radiating off of him. "Here," he says with his gruff morning voice and hands me the key.

"Thanks," I say, making eye contact, then quickly breaking it and standing back up. He rubs his face and puts his head back down before lifting it to ask, "What time is it, anyway?"

I pull my phone out of my back pocket. "It's eight-twelve." I take in the view of him laid out again as I leave the room, only to hear him mumble, "Don't stare at my ass, Josie, I'm not a piece of meat."

I scoff at him, "I was not!" He did not see me unless he's got eyes in the back of his head.

"Yeah, okay. Drive safe to work, you peeping Tom."

I throw a quick thanks at him and choose not to acknowledge the latter part of his comment. I find myself smiling to myself as I walk back to Cassie to hand her the key.

I hide my smile before I walk into her room where she's throwing stuff in her bag.

"You're a lifesaver, thanks!" She has no idea the mental journey that little task was for me.

"Okay, I'm outta here before I'm late, too."

"Yeah, have a good day! Oh hey, join us for drinks later. You get off work around six, right? You can meet us at the bar right after."

"Yes, I think my last client is at five. Send me the deets." I don't give a clear yes or no answer yet because I'm not sure if I'll be up for drinks or if I'll be too exhausted to go out. The last few weeks working two jobs has me passed out the second my head hits the pillow.

I get in my car and out on the road in good time. My day gets better when the person in front of me in the drive-thru decides they want to perform an act of kindness and pay for my drink. I pay it forward by doing the same to the person behind me because that's the right thing to do. Arriving to work right on time with a little pep in my step, unsure if it's from the coffee or the half-naked guy I saw this morning, I decide maybe I will go out for drinks later. I have to step out of my room and stop being the little hermit

I've been these last few weeks. After all, I deserve to have fun.

I sit down at my desk and my phone buzzes right before I put it away.

Weekly Word: Life is a balance of holding on and letting go. (Rumi)

wes

I run my finger over the condensation on my glass of water while Brandon and Cassie bicker about toothpaste. Yes, toothpaste.

"Your teeth are perfect, babe, and white toothpaste is going to keep them nice and clean and white and healthy."

"I know, Brandon," she says his name and you can tell she's rolling her eyes without even looking at her. "But the charcoal kind makes them even more white and pearly." She follows her point with a cheesy smile. She'd be perfect for a Crest Whitestrips commercial. Or maybe even a commercial for... black toothpaste?

"This really a thing?" I bravely ask.

"Yes!" they answer in unison.

"And it leaves a mess that Cassie doesn't feel the need to clean up."

"Oh my God, I will get to it. Maybe around the same time that you figure out we have a hamper." She gives him a fake smile.

Yikes.

Their banter constantly reminds me that I'm lucky to be single.

Then *she* shows up and I mentally take that back. Josie's standing at the table with a smile that doesn't reach her eyes, wearing ripped jeans, a white tank top, and strappy heels that leave my mouth dry.

"Josie! Thank you!" Brandon calls out, relieved. "Okay. What are your thoughts on the black toothpaste?"

She pulls her seat out and clinks her purse over the table, a confused look on her face. "What black tooth– Oh! Is that what the speckles are from? They're like all over the sink and mirror. I wondered what that was." She does this cute little giggle, and my dick wakes up and raises his hand as if someone's taking the class role —*present!*

"Thank you!" Brandon shouts and slams his hand on the table as if Josie has just settled the Great Charcoal Toothpaste Debate, startling myself and the girls.

"Whatever," Cassie sighs with another eye roll, then changes her tune. "How was work today, Josie?"

She starts to answer that she's had a good day when she is interrupted by the waitress. Josie orders a sour beer and turns her attention back to the table, making eye contact with me a few times. They don't last more than a second each, but I welcome the attention.

"After this morning's chaos," she says, narrowing

her eyes at Cassie, "the Starbucks I went to had one of those pay-it-forward things going on, so that was cool. Well, then the secretary at my job–"

Cassie interrupts her, "You mean *your* secretary?"

She presses her lips and thinks about it before continuing. "I mean, yeah, I guess she is my secretary. Anywho, she left early and didn't tell me, so I had to check out the last person on my own, which I have no clue how to do. But they were nice enough while I muddled through it."

The waitress brings her beer and she takes a sip right away after thanking the server. "Oh!" she exclaims, "Next Monday I have my first full schedule! Like start at nine, break for an hour at lunch, and last client at five. Isn't that cool?"

She's smiling for real now and damn, it feels like they just pumped some extra oxygen in here. She always did that, shifted the mood to something lighter and brighter. Something I can't explain. I don't know how she does it, or if anyone else feels it, but I've never felt this from anyone other than her. I have to literally shake off this heady feeling. Last thing I need is her getting upset if our roommates figure out that something else is going on. Or that something else *went on* because she's definitely not letting on to any of our history.

She zips up her little purse and places it in her lap before she points at no one in particular and says, "It's weird being an adult, but I'm diggin' it." She looks at each of us, then brings her focus back to me and eyes my water. "No beer for you?"

I stare at her for a few seconds before I take a breath and give her something she isn't expecting, "I don't drink."

"Really?" Her eyes are the size of saucers.

"Yeah, I've been sober for a while now."

It kills me. She can sense that this is something big. She doesn't know the whole story, but she has to know it's got to do with our past.

I grind my molars and hate the fact that this is a thing at all. She remembers the Wes who would have a good time, beer in hand. Loud and touchy. We'd do some partying and we'd go to bed. Always ending the night holding my girl, a hand on her hip and her taste on my lips. Best summer of my life.

I was always responsible with my drinking...until I wasn't. It was a short yet deep stint I had with alcohol during the darkest months of my life where I just wanted to forget and go numb. I didn't want to deal with all the guilt that consumed and drowned me from the inside out. I would end up drowning myself every day in booze. I'd fall asleep holding on to a beer, and wake up grabbing a cold one before I even checked the time. Finally, I ran into someone just as broken as I was, and we helped heal each other. I know better now. I just lost a little control then.

"I'm sorry, I--" Josie starts to apologize before I interrupt her.

"No worries, babe." I wink at her, then turn my attention to Brandon and give him a slug on the arm, "Come on, I want to whoop your ass at the shuffleboard table."

Brandon and I get up and walk around the table to head to our game, but before I walk away, I have to reassure her that her questioning my drinking was okay and didn't rattle me. I can't just walk away from that revelation like nothing. I bend over, hand on her shoulder, and whisper, "We have a lot to talk about, but know that I'm okay."

chapter thirteen

present day, 2022

josie

CASSIE IS TALKING my ear off about some makeup she ordered online, but my mind is not on mascara and concealer, it's on the guy playing shuffleboard on the other side of the room. He keeps looking at me, and I wish he didn't know that I've been catching every glimpse he throws my way, but it's no secret I'm stealing glances, too. My control is withering away as I finish up my third beer. Not the best idea, but I need liquid courage if I'm going to handle Wes tonight.

I used to know Wes so well. He'd clear his throat when he was nervous and play with his hair—or mine—when he was tired. A certain lazy smirk told me he was horny. Now I know nothing about him, let alone have the ability to read him. He said he'd never get a tattoo, but he's got enough that probably tell a story I'm not sure I'm ready to hear. And, he doesn't drink? I have so many questions, but at the same time, I don't want to open that can of worms. I decide to put my thoughts aside to try to be a good friend and actually pay attention to Cassie.

"Yeah, I got a steal, girl. So glad I grabbed that CC cream," she says.

"So, now I'm not supposed to use BB cream anymore and I have to switch to CC cream? I don't understand makeup."

She laughs at me as if what I said was a joke. Then she looks around and leans in closer to me. "What are your thoughts on Wes? Yeah, I've never seen him drink," she says, waving her hand like it's no big deal, and continues. "He doesn't care that anyone else drinks. He says he was on a bender for a while there when he started college, but he never goes into much detail. I have no idea why. I think he lost a friend or girlfriend or something."

Or something.

She shrugs and takes a swig of her beer, looking at me. "Is he your type?"

I choke on my beer and have to wipe the dribble off my chin. "I mean, he's not ugly." I don't know what else to say. *Uh, you mean the guy I crushed on for years, then one summer we fell in love and I gave him my everything and he broke my heart during the worst time of my life. Yeah, no. Not my type.*

"Not ugly? Are we talking about the same guy?" She laughs. "Of course, he's not ugly. He's hot as hell. He's super sweet. And he's only brought home a few girls and they usually–"

I cut her off because the last thing I want to hear is

all about the girls Wes brings home to put those condoms to use that he has stored in his nightstand. "I don't need to know the details," I say with a smile, "I mean, yeah, he's hot and all, but I just don't think I'm looking for anyone right now."

"Who's hot?" Brandon asks as he comes up behind us and wraps his arms around Cassie from behind, whispering in her ear.

Wes sits on my other side and looks at me with the remnants of a smirk on his face. Cassie giggles and pushes Brandon off of her.

I stand up and announce I'll be right back. I need another drink. Okay, so maybe I don't *need* another drink, I just can't with Wes suffocating me. That's dramatic, I know, but the longer we actually hang out, the harder it is for me to look away and ignore him, and it makes it hard to breathe.

I walk over to the bar, focusing on walking straight. I'm not drunk, but I'm definitely feeling the alcohol weighing me down. I check my phone while I wait for the bartender to notice me, only to see the weather app warning about possible flooding. No surprise there, it always rains here, and it always floods the streets.

"I rarely see a hot girl rockin' curls like this." A random guy comes up next to me and shoves his hand my hair. I rear back and mean mug him. He's got blonde hair combed over, a pastel polo, and a sweaty upper lip that really grosses me out.

"Thanks?" I say it in a bitchy tone and face the bar again.

He doesn't back away and keeps talking, "I'm Chad. What's your name, beautiful?"

"Not beautiful," I mumble, but hope he hears it.

He chuckles, then leans in closer to me and says, "Let me get you a drink."

"I can manage to get myself a drink, thanks." I swear if he sniffs my hair, I will punch this preppy boy. I typically don't react in such a hostile manner with strangers but I can tell he's drunk from the scent he's giving off, and the more he leans over, the more I feel like he's going to face-plant. A part of me feels the familiar weight in my stomach from the nerves of this douchebag getting handsy, but the other part of me knows that I can handle myself in the situation thanks to kickboxing and other self-defense courses I've taken over the years. Although, that is questionable considering my current state. I have more faith in the fact that my friends are less than twenty feet away.

The second I'm about to elbow Chad as he's got a hold of my waist, I'm spun away from him, finding myself tucked into the crook of Wes's arm. With a set jaw and a voice so deep it rattles me from the inside out, Wes pulls me in closer and tells Chad, "I think you should find your frat buddies and get the fuck out of here."

I swear the heat went up in here all of a sudden. Being pulled into his side, I feel like I've been warped back to when I was eighteen and in my bed with Wes. He'd wrap his arms around my giggling self while trying to keep me quiet so no one would hear us. The guy can cuddle.

Chad's laugh cuts into my reminiscing and he throws his hands up in surrender. "Hey, I just saw a pretty lady and I wanted to compliment her with a drink."

"No need. I'll take it from here. And when a woman tells you no in more than one way, she fucking means no."

"Alright, alright, man. It's all good." Chad starts to walk backward away from us, waving as he did so.

"Don't look at her, don't even think about her," Wes calls out, pointing to him.

"He's gone now, so you can calm down," I explain to Wes and peel his arm off of me.

"Calm down? That asshole was literally touching you!"

The bartender finally gives me his attention and I hold up a finger and shout over the noise, "One shot of vodka, your cheapest." I wonder if my drinking affects Wes at all but I push the concern aside and bring my attention back to him. "I can handle myself. I'm a kickboxer," I say with pride, then do a quick punch into his abs. The jab startles him and pulls a laugh out of me.

"You think you're cute, huh?" He nods his head at me, then lowers himself so we are eye level, and admits, "I know you kickbox. I saw you at the gym the same day you came to check the apartment out. And a few times since. With Bobby."

"You saw me, or he told you?" I ask, wondering how he saw me, and *OMG, I hope I didn't look like a hot mess.*

He moves back some, giving me more space to

breathe, and leans against the bar. "That's my gym. Well, not *my* gym but I work there."

I do remember learning that they work together from that football Sunday, but I didn't know Wes had seen me a the gym. The bartender places the shot in front of me, and before I can pay, Wes does.

I eyeball the clear liquid before downing it, knowing this is my last drink for the night because Wes is telling me about wanting to own a gym, and I should pay attention to this important stuff, but the lines outside the corners of his lips have my attention at the moment.

"That's kinda cool, you're gonna own a gym," is the response I come up with because now I'm distracted with the tattoos that mark his arm. I haven't been up close to them like this. I make out a beachy scene and the state of Florida filled with flowers. It's pretty and I wonder what it all means to him.

"I'm not going to… yet. Are you really this drunk right now, babe?"

My eyes shoot to his and he chuckles an apology.

"Let's go back to Cassie and Brandon," I say, clutching my purse and turning away from the bar.

Wes grabs my elbow and says, "They left."

"They left?"

"Yeah, and I, um," he says as he scratches his chin with his thumb. "I told them I'd give you a ride home."

"Ha, no." I laugh to myself. I can't believe this. I can't get in a car with this guy. That's too much.

"Oh, Josie, come on. What, are you gonna get? An Uber?"

"Yes." It comes out more like, *duh!*

He scoffs. "Seriously. No. Come on, it's a fifteen-minute drive and it's pouring out. We can pick up your car tomorrow."

"No, I Uber'd here. My car is at the apartment. I was planning to drink. Well, not as much as I did, but I didn't wanna drive. I can leave how I arrived here. Thank you very much." I walk to the exit while Wes tries to keep up with me. We step outside into the dark, humid night and stand under an awning. I pull my phone out and open up the Uber app, but before I start setting up my ride, Wes grabs the phone out of my hand, tips his hat at me, and says, "Be right back!" before he takes off running in the rain to his car.

Wesley Miller! I should've known he would pull this. He better get me Taco Bell.

A big black truck pulls up and he climbs out of the driver's side and walks around to me holding a blanket up to shield me from the rain. I roll my eyes because, of course, he has to be a gentleman. And then, I go along with him because, what the hell else am I supposed to do? He helps me climb into the passenger seat, and as soon as he gets back in the driver's seat, just as he's taking off his wet hat and throwing it on the dash, I say, "You better get me Taco Bell."

"Yes, ma'am," he obliges.

Nina Arada

The windshield wipers squeak back and forth and I'm content scarfing down a burrito supreme while Wes drives us home.

I'm trying really hard to act like this doesn't affect me at all. I'm trying really hard not to punch him in the face for being… well, for being him. But most of all, I'm trying really hard not to straddle the fuck out of his face. I mean, I can't do that with him driving and all, especially in the rain, for that matter, but aside from this burrito, all the things I want to do to him are taking over my mind.

I can't believe he's right here. Driving me home, to where we both live. He's bigger than I remember. Wes was always athletic, always lean and muscular, but this is something else. The muscles rope up his arms, and his left arm, which I can't quite make out the details from here in the dark, is completely covered in dark ink with hints of color here and there. Guess him wanting to own a gym one day makes sense with how he's ripped.

He keeps glancing over, watching me with wonder. The way he used to. The way that would confuse the heck out of me. He would smile and wink at me when my brother wasn't watching. He would strike up random conversations and ask how I was doing. Minutes later he'd join Joe in redirecting me to the band geeks during lunch. They did it all the time, and I wasn't even in band, so those kids would look at me like I was crazy. There was also that time they laughed along with the *Heathers* when they asked me if I dressed myself in the dark that morning. I don't think Joe ever realized that it hurt me that bad, but it did. Popularity came easy to him. To me, not so much.

Then Wes did a three-sixty *that summer*. The summer after graduation. Both he and Joe took Cora and me in as if we were different people. And we were, at least I was. In the earlier years of high school, I was quiet and timid and so self-conscious. I could go back and smack some sense into myself.

But all I needed was a couple years away, living with my Aunt Leila. She taught me to love myself and respect myself and ignore the haters. So, when I came back after graduating, that's what I did. I put on my hater blockers and things were different. Joe and Cora started dating, at first to my dismay. And I fell in love with Wes. *My God, did I ever.* I thought I was in love with him in my younger, pubescent years, but no. *That summer* changed everything. We spent night after night together. Me in his football jersey, him in my arms. It was my favorite summer, one for the books. And it was over in the blink of an eye.

"Why'd you become a social worker?" he interrupts my thoughts.

My eyes dart to his.

"You don't have to answer." He thinks he struck a nerve. He kind of did, but he doesn't have to know that.

"No, it's fine. Umm, I don't know, I guess I just want to help people. I've seen mental health counselors in the past, and I believe in it. I worked for a mental health office in Coral Springs as a receptionist. It may be my comfort zone, but I love it. Being healthy isn't just exercising and finishing your veggies. The mind needs more love than most people think." He nods as if he knows exactly what I'm talking about. I crumble up my burrito wrapper and burp. An unexpected burp, I should add.

My hands fly to my mouth and he starts laughing. "Oh my God, how embarrassing. I'm sorry." I can feel my face heat up, but he just smiles at me and looks back at the road. This man's face. It's like nothing I've ever seen. I want to reach over and touch it.

"How long have you been into kickboxing?" The question almost startles me. Thankfully, his questions and that burrito are sobering me up, because with my mind going down the road it's been on since I got into his truck, I can't be acting on the thoughts I'm having.

"What is this, twenty questions? I used to do it a while ago. I just started again. I'm surprised you didn't come over to criticize my moves all these times you've supposedly seen me." I know for sure I was a sweaty mess.

"I would never criticize you and you know that, Josie." His voice is deep and smooth, and I can almost feel the words come out of his mouth and surround me. I thought he'd be different, thought he'd have a darker, harder shell. Hurt and jaded from losing Joe, but he's the same and I don't know how to handle that.

He glances my way again, and this time adds a gaze down my body. I feel a zing go straight to my core.

"Tell me about your boyfriend."

"I don't have one." I feel like he knows that. I'm sure he gets the four-one-one from the mouth of the south, AKA my mom.

He presses his lips together and nods. He seems content with my answer.

"Anymore," I add in just to mess with him. Although, it's true. I'm still in touch with Wyatt. We were on-again, off-again for a few years.

His eyebrows jump to his hairline, "Anymore?" He changes his position and gets more comfortable, leaning his elbow on his door like he's ready for storytime.

"No, sir. We are not about to get into this." I'll update him on my life, but we are not going to Boyfriendland. Not happening. Just like I don't want updates on Girlfriendville. Both should and will be permanently closed for construction.

He gets back into his previous position, "That's fine. You don't have to tell me about him." Then he mumbles to himself, but I hear him clear as day, "As long as I never have to meet the douchebag."

"You know what, Wesley?" His eyes go wide at his full first name. "You're not allowed. You can't come around here rescuing me from other guys." *It's too late.* "You can't get all pissed off that I have an ex-boyfriend."

He's focused on the road, slowing down over the speed bumps in the parking lot of our apartment complex, and I can see his jaw ticking, the street lamps illuminating his face.

My body is completely turned toward him. "What? Did you want me to stay single forever? You can't get pissed at every guy who comes around for me. You're gonna sit here and tell me you never had a girlfriend?"

"I didn't," he says it so serious and low, I almost don't hear it.

"Of course, you haven't." I shake my head. He parks the truck and looks down. My eyes are practically burning a hole in his head. I turn and open the door to get out of the truck. He's quick, because by the time I close the door and turn around, he's right there standing at the back of the truck watching me.

I walk toward him, feeling a light sprinkle of rain on my arms and my cheeks. I point at him, then to my chest, and in my semi-drunken moment, I spill it all. "You. Broke. My. Heart. During the most difficult time in my life. And now you're upset that I moved on. You can't be serious." I look at him in disbelief.

A few steps closer and I see he's got tears in his eyes. "Fuck!" He yells and slams a fist on the top of his truck bed. He closes his eyes and lifts his face up to the sky, bringing a hand up to his mouth. I let him gather his thoughts. It's official, after that revelation to him, I'm sober as hell now.

Still facing up, he says, "I'm sorry." Then he turns to me. "I don't want you to forgive me. I can't have that. But, let me show you that I've changed, that it was a mistake and that I can be the man you deserve to have."

I'm speechless. I want to say something. But the words are stuck in my throat and I feel the tears well up in my eyes. He steps closer to me, leaving us inches apart. His hand comes up to my cheek and I close my eyes, allowing a tear to escape. He rubs it away with his thumb. I want to fall into him. Have him hold me and heal me, and I know in my heart he can be the man I deserve. But it scares the shit out of me to give myself over to him again.

I open my eyes and he's watching me with his bottom lip pulled under his top teeth. I want to kiss him *and* forgive him, unlike his request. It's drizzling and we're standing in this dark parking lot, his hand on my face, and I didn't even realize I'm holding myself up with a hand gripping one of his biceps. It's a movie script scene in need of a kiss to complete it.

I close my eyes. "You knew where I went."

His head tilts to the side in confusion. "What?"

"Why didn't you come and find me, Wes? I waited years for you, and you never showed up."

His eyes look back and forth into mine. "I did."

I rear my head back and he drops his hands to his sides. "You did?"

"I did. And you were with him."

chapter fourteen

that summer, 2015

josie

SOMEONE I THOUGHT I could trust to drive me home, someone who violated my innocence, is what pushed me out of Tampa.

I didn't return for two years.

In those two years, I saw my parents for some holidays, or when they would drive Cora over for a visit. Coral Springs is just a few hours away so they'd make it when they could. They didn't understand why I left. But it was evident that I wanted nothing to do with the city I never thought I'd leave behind. I can't blame them, I told them I was humiliated at the party and didn't want to come face to face with my classmates again.

Typical parents probably wouldn't let their teenage daughter up and move hours away, but my parents trusted me. I was always a good girl. Hell, the main reason I went to that party was because my mom would only allow my brother to go if I joined him. And they trusted Leila and my relationship with her. Leila was going through her own rough patch, so although they asked me numerous times to come home, it was no secret that Leila needed me, too.

I saw Joe when he joined us for that first Thanksgiving after I left, but it ended with us fighting. I hugged him and cried when he arrived, and he instantly knew the party wasn't the reason for my departure. Had the party been the reason, then he would have been a part of why I left and I wouldn't have greeted him with open arms. He pulled me aside that night after a nice Cuban-inspired Thanksgiving dinner of black beans, white rice, and pork and asked me to be honest with him. I wouldn't. I cried and pushed him away and refused to tell him what happened to me. My stomach turned when he asked who drove me home, but I kept the secret to myself. I didn't think he could handle it. I didn't think *I* could handle it if he knew the truth. He never came back to Coral Springs after that.

Thankfully, Leila brought me back to life by the end of that first year. She and Cora are the only ones who know what happened. Well, them and the monster.

I made some friends in the second year, thankfully, and I finally found the courage to go back to Tampa after graduating. I promised my parents I'd return with them after my graduation. It was my end goal.

Time had passed quickly in those two years but I'd grown in many ways. I was ready to face the world and put the demons behind me.

The greenery of the trees go by in a blur as I take in the familiarity of my city in the backseat of my dad's

SUV. All sorts of memories flood my mind as we approach a place I never thought I'd go years without seeing. I'm filled with courage and bravery and hope for new beginnings. It's a heady feeling, really. But I realize I'm heading right back into the demon's fire when I see the sign that says Welcome to Hillsborough County.

wes

"My mom's making yellow rice and chicken, isn't that your favorite?" Joe asks as he turns down the street to his house. We just finished up graduation rehearsal since tomorrow we finally fucking graduate high school. Joe invited me over for dinner, and since Grams is at bingo night anyway, I said why not?

"Yeah, man. I swear your mom cooks with crack."

"Tell me about it. My future wife will have competition. Anyway, she says she has a surprise for me. I have no idea what it is," he explains.

"You sure I can come? I don't want to interrupt anything special that she has planned."

"Are you serious, dude? You're family."

He pulls into the driveway and we head into the house. A house that has been like my own. The Rodriguez family has always been more than welcoming to me. Isabel and Mario, they're the parents I never had. My mom only comes around when she wants money from Grams, and I've never met my dad. Couldn't even tell you his name.

"Oh, he's here! He's here! Oh, and you brought Wes, qué bueno!" Isabel smacks a loud kiss on Joe's cheek, then one on mine, and drags Joe into the dining room by his hand.

Mario is sitting at the table. I tip my head at him… and then I see *her*. It literally feels like someone punched me in the gut as a chill comes over me. She's got her hair dark and long as always, with calmer waves, and fuck, I want to reach out and touch it. She looks between me and Joe, and then keeps her eyes focused on him, wearing that same smile. It's been too long since I've seen it.

"Josie? Are you serious?" Joe says in shock, and I think I hear his voice crack. He looks back and forth between her and me, and points to Cora who is sitting at the table, too. "Did you take a jet here?" Cora laughs at him as he almost trips, walking around the table to hug Josie.

We don't discuss it much, but ever since Josie left that party a couple years ago after being humiliated, she and her brother stopped talking aside from a Thanksgiving blowout. She never came back to Tampa, and when their parents would go visit her, Joe never went with them.

Tears stream down Josie's face while her brother hugs the life out of her. She looks up at me, and I don't want to embarrass her, so I look away and over at Cora, giving her a small wave.

They separate themselves and Josie wipes the tears from her eyes and steps toward me.

"Hey, Wes," she says, going in for a hug.

"Hey, girl, don't leave us for that long again. You got this guy over here bent out of shape," I say, referring to her brother who is showing a side of himself I've never seen. I wrap my arms around her and kiss the top of her head as it comes up to my chin. Her hair smells like coconuts, and things seem to shift in the world. I've never actually held her like this before. Quick hugs or cheek-kisses are a norm in this house, but holding her like this, it's unfamiliar. I don't want to let her go.

We part and she looks up at me. Shit. Eighteen looks good on Josie Rodriguez. I have to force myself to keep my eyes away from the small amount of cleavage she's revealing to the world. Her straight white teeth smile up at me, and the second we lose all physical contact it feels colder in this tiny dining room.

There's commotion in the background from the excitement of Josie being back. She and I are still holding eye contact when Mario calls out from the head of the table, "Okay, okay. Everyone, calm down. Sit down. Let's eat. Your mother has been cooking all day…and crying, might I add. We've got all of our kids here and we are blessed." He looks over at Isabel and smiles at her.

Everyone settles down. Isabel sits at the one end of the table across from Mario. I sit next to Joe, Cora's across from me, and Josie's across from her brother.

The hum in the room quiets down while everyone starts eating, and Josie is asked of her summer plans.

"Umm," she says, finishing her bite and taking a drink before she continues. "I don't really know. Just getting back into the groove of things here before I start at USF. Catching up with this babe." She leans over and pulls Cora into a side hug. Cora giggles and Josie continues, "I'll look for a summer gig next week. I've got money saved up from the job I had in Coral Springs, but I want to save more so I don't have to work when school starts up."

Mario chimes in, "That's smart, mija, but you can probably work a part-time job when school starts so you're still bringing a little something in."

Both Joe and Josie roll their eyes. Their dad is into investing and saving every dime he makes. Although, in recent years he's taken Isabel on more cruise vacations. I guess the savings are paying off.

"We'll see, Dad," Josie says, clearly bothered. Then she turns to Cora and says, "Hey, let's go to Target tonight before they close so I can grab a few things."

Before Cora can answer, Joe practically bounces in his seat. "We can take you!" He exclaims, motioning between us. "Wes and I have no plans…we can take you two and I'll get you a book or whatever you're into these days."

We all kinda stare at Joe as if he's grown another head. "What?" He looks around. "Look, Josie." He pleads for her attention. "We haven't been on the best terms in a long time, but you're my twin and I love you and we are gonna enjoy this last summer before college. Wes and I will make sure it's unforgettable." He looks at me, waiting for my input.

"Yeah, you won't regret coming back," I add in.

"Oh, look at them, papi, they are all getting along better than ever!" Isabel says to her husband with a dreamy look on her face.

Joe takes a heaping bite of rice, and with a full mouth points his fork at Josie and says, "Only if Cora's along for the ride." Then he sends a wink to Cora.

"Great," Josie says, rolling her eyes but showing a hint of a smile.

Either Josie is oblivious as to how she's walking through Target, or she's trying to embarrass me in public. She's leaning her arms on the handle of the store cart with her ass in the air, swaying side to side with each step. I may have to come up with an excuse for us to separate from the girls because I'm definitely chubbing right now. I look over and see Joe ogling Cora's ass. I'm not mad because 1) she's not my girl and 2) it keeps him from noticing my eyes on his sister.

"We are going to the girls' aisle so..." Josie coos, "how about y'all go check out video games or try on clothes for each other or whatever you guys do here," she says, giggling the last part out. *Thank God*, it's like she read my mind.

Cora laughs with her, then shoots her arm out and grabs Josie's shoulder. "Or..." she says with a mischievous look on her face. "Why don't you two go find something for each of us, and we'll pick out a little something for you guys. Fifteen-dollar limit." She wiggles her eyebrows as she looks at all of us to gauge our reactions, but her focus lingers on Joe. He looks like his jaw is about to hit the floor, and Josie smacks Cora in the arm.

"Quit flirting with my brother, gross!"

"Shh! We're just having fun." Cora brings her eyes to Joe again and bites her bottom lip. This is gonna be interesting.

Josie grabs Cora by the arm, dragging her away, then shoots a glance over her shoulder as they walk away. "Make sure you guys pick good gifts for us." Her eyes remain lingering on mine a second longer than necessary.

"My phone just died! I'm gonna have Wes text you!" Joe shouts next to me.

He tells me her number and I send her the standard: **Hi, it's Wes :)**

"Your sister's gonna kick your ass if you play her friend."

"I'm not stupid. I'll make it clear what's going on, but I know Cora's had a thing for me for a while. I can't lie, she's hot, and she was always more confident when my sister was around. She's usually more shy and shit when we see each other at school."

He rubs his hands together. "What the hell do we get these girls?"

"Fuck if I know. You know them both better than I do."

We walk through the store going in and out of the

aisles before we finally have both of our gifts. Well, first Joe picked out a red lacy thong that I had to talk him out of giving Cora, but now he says he'll save it for another time. I picked out a book with a flowery cover that was in the romance section, along with chocolate-covered pretzels for Josie because I know she loves these lovey-dovey books, and Flipz are her favorite. For Cora's real gift, Joe picked out a sun hat that has "Hello, Sunshine" etched on it and a gold anklet. I'm impressed with his choices, although I swear, he has a foot fetish now after he spent almost twenty minutes searching for the perfect anklet.

My phone buzzes with a text from Josie: **We're all done and waiting outside.**

josie

Cora's cackle can be heard from the other end of the parking lot. I glare at her while she eats gummy worms and sits inside her cart living her best life. Yes, *in* the cart. And she's laughing at me trying to climb into mine, because unlike her journey into the cart, which included me pushing her ass in there, I'm positive I'm going to bust mine.

"Here," she says, sitting up with candy hanging out of her mouth. She holds onto my cart and I fling myself in.

"I swear these things seem bigger from the outside," I groan while I settle in.

I'm going through my bags so I can separate what I got Wes from my stuff. At first I had no idea what to get him, then I saw a green hat that says "KALE" across the front and figured it was good because he always wears hats, and Cora says that now he's super healthy and into sports and fitness. Not surprised because the boys always played some sport, and Wes has always kept himself fit. I look over at Cora scrolling through her phone.

"Will you just show me what you got my brother?"

"Yes. But promise you won't get mad."

"Ughh," I groan. "Fine. I'm scared now."

She looks in the bag and brings it to her chest, looking at me straight on, snickering to herself. When I see it, I can't believe my eyes. She bought lingerie.

"Are you kidding?!"

"Hey! You can't get mad!" She's giggling, then her face goes serious. "You know I've always crushed on your brother. It's our last summer. Let's have a good time."

"You're right, but..." I hesitate, then continue, "I just don't want you to get hurt. You know how Joe is."

"Exactly. I know how he is. I know not to expect more."

"How nasty. That's my brother." I point at her. "I want no details of anything that goes on between you two. Anything!"

"Enough about me, did you see Wes and his face when he first saw you?"

"No, what was it like?" What is she talking about? I *need* to know what she's talking about.

"What are you weirdos doing?" Joe says, while both of the guys shake their heads as they walk out of the store. Wes smiles brightly, and damn if it doesn't go straight to my core.

Not that I have time to fixate on that feeling because just as I recognize it for what it is, Cora calls out like a maniac, "Cart race, cart race! We're gonna kick your ass!" And with her hands held high in the air, Wes goes for my cart as Joe goes for Cora's and we're off.

chapter fifteen

that summer, 2015

josie

YOU COULDN'T SMACK the smile off my face if you tried. I crawl into my bed, fresh-faced and in a tank top and shorts reminiscing over every moment of tonight.

After we distributed gifts, which Cora thought would be a better idea to open once we were home and alone, we raced in the shopping carts and, I swear, I can't tell you the last time I laughed like that. My belly ached and my cheeks hurt, but we successfully started off our summer with a bang.

Cora insisted my brother push her and Wes push me. I was nervous, but the second Wes leaned into the cart from behind me and whispered in my ear, "Let's make this a ride you'll never forget," I realized the goosebumps that traveled up my arms weren't from my nerves.

The guys pushed us all over the parking lot, and we laughed and screamed, and I thought my heart would fly out of my chest because I didn't think they'd actually push us *that* fast.

The moon shone above us and the humidity left us coated in thin layers of sweat, but we didn't care.

We switched with the guys. Watching them climb into the carts was entertainment enough for the night. Wes suggested we stand farther apart so we wouldn't crash. What he didn't expect was that once we were laughing and half way down the parking lot, we'd pick up speed and my steering leaned a little to the left, cutting into Cora and Joe's path. Joe started yelling at her to turn when she almost hit a parking block, so she swerved right into my cart causing Joe's head to bump into Wes's face.

Tears pricked my eyes as I laughed. I felt guilty for laughing, but the guilt only consumed me when I noticed Wes was bleeding. His eyebrow was busted, and that's when he started laughing and blaming Cora's bad driving and Joe's big head.

By then, the nighttime security asked us to leave the premises as Target was closed. Joe drove us for a long time that night, taking longer routes and driving over bridges. Joe was smoking cigarettes, and the smell was nauseating, triggering memories that I tried best to keep distant, but failed to do all night. The cart racing was a nice distraction but while we were shopping around Target, I couldn't kick the sickening feeling that I could run into Drew. I made sure that Cora was within a few feet of me the entire time.

But then during the car ride, I'd look over at Wes, who was sitting in the back seat with me after Cora called shotgun, and it was like his presence was stronger than the smoke and the memories of the monsters that haunt me.

More than once I'd look over at him and he'd have his elbow resting out of the window, hand up to his mouth—eyes on me. The streetlights would go in and out over his face, showing me a look of need and hunger, and that look would send a shiver through my body. His chain, and an earring that I did not remember him having would gleam and shine from the moonlight. Not once did he turn away, but as soon as he'd come to and see that I caught his stare, he'd shoot me a smile that told me things that I know he couldn't say in present company.

The music was blaring, and with the breeze from the windows being down, I held onto my hair on one side. I was looking at the clear sky and the water we were driving over when I felt Wes touch my hand. I looked down at his pinky hugging mine, and when I looked up at him he leaned over as if to tell me something. He had to yell over the noise, and all I could make out was, "I have so much I want to say right now!"

I looked up at him, confused, and yelled, "What!"

When I leaned my ear to him again, he said, "I'm just glad you're back!" He looked at me and called out again, "This is fun!"

I smiled back and I noticed that there was something different about him. We had always had a connection, but it was always frayed with my brother around. Joe was obviously still around, but I'm not sure if Cora being his distraction allowed Wes to open up because his gaze lingered a little longer, and his attention to me seemed like there was more there just under the surface.

I can't explain it, but it's almost as if he couldn't risk the chance of letting me slip through his fingers again.

We dropped off Cora, then Wes, and then I jumped in the front seat. Joe and I didn't talk, but as we sat at a long light he reached over and pulled me into a side hug and kissed the top of my head. I never imagined this would be my first night back. Had I known, would I have come back sooner? Could I have gone back to that school after what happened?

Maybe waiting til now to return was the right thing to do. Instead of wondering, I'd take this night and hope that this was just a small glimpse of our summer.

A knock on the door snaps me out of my thoughts. "Josie?" My mom peeks in, then leans against the doorway. "Did you all have a good time? Get everything you need?"

"Yes, we actually had a lot of fun. And yes, I think I'm all set."

"That's good, mami. Your dad's going to make café con leche and chocolate chip pancakes in the morning before we go to your brother's graduation." I beam at the thought of my favorite breakfast, then instantly push away the nagging thoughts of seeing my past classmates at graduation. I'd skip it if it were up to me, but I know it would break my mom's heart. She walks into my room and kisses my cheek, wishing me a good night and leaves, closing the door behind her.

I have so many memories of sitting on this bed and having nightly check-ins with my mom, and even more serious conversations here, surrounded by purple walls and floral touches she'd creep in whenever she could. There's always going to be a part of me that feels guilty for leaving my family after that night. I felt I had no other choice at that moment, I wanted nothing more than to crawl into my adolescence and forget. The best I could do was get away and start fresh because as bad as I wanted my youth back, he took it from me. And tonight? Tonight was the first time I felt young again.

Wild and free.

I reach over to undo the Target bag and find my favorite snack and a book that I love. I run my fingers over the pink flowers that form a texture to the cover of the paperback. Funny, I actually owned this book, but left it with my aunt Leila as she loved it, too, and I wanted her to keep it.

I get up, run over to Joe's room, and knock on the door, but it's already open and he shoves something under his pillow, definitely caught doing something.

"Hey, what's up," he asks.

With a smirk, I respond, "Just wanted to say thanks for the book and pretzels."

"Oh, that was all Wes. I was busy looking for an anklet for Cora. You think she'd wear an anklet?"

"Yeah, she would. She'd also wear the underwear you just hid."

He throws his head back howling out a laugh. "I like your friend, Josie."

"Yeah, and you better not break her heart."

"I won't. Now, get out so I can send her a pic of me in this."

"You're an idiot!" I laugh, and then we exchange goodnights.

I return to my room and send Wes a photo of myself holding the book up to where it covers my face below my eyes and say, **How do you know my favorite book, creeper?**

Seconds later my phone vibrates.

Wes: Lucky guess?
Wes: How do you know I love KALE?

He attaches a photo of himself wearing the hat and a smirk that goes straight between my thighs.

Josie: I hear you're a health freak.
Wes: Among other kinds of freaks, I'd say so.
Josie: Oh, God. You've really been hanging out w my bro too much.
Wes: Did you have fun tonight?
Josie: I did. You?
Wes: Yeah. My eyebrow hurts.
Josie: OMG! I'm so sorry, but that was hilarious.
Wes: Glad you found it funny.
Josie: LOL, you need a nurse to take care of you?
Wes: Depends on the nurse…

Freaking out is an understatement. I put the phone down, sit up and tie my hair into a messy bun and wring my hands out. I decide I can be brave. The last couple years haven't been easy in the dating department. It's hard to trust guys I don't really know. But when it comes to Wes, I've known him for as long as I can remember. I trust him. Right as I decide to finally send out a message, his comes through at the same time.

Wes: JK LOL
Josie: I mean, I do have a sexy nurse costume from a party.

Within seconds, a FaceTime call from Wes flashes on my phone. My heart feels like it's going to fall out of my ass. I check myself out in the selfie on the screen before I take a deep breath and answer.

"Bullshit. I call bullshit," he says, then flips his hat backward.

I laugh and start to talk lower because I don't want to be loud and bring attention to my parents or Joe. "I'm serious. There was an end-of-the-year costume party last year, and it was the easiest costume to pick since it was out of season." His eyes are huge as I explain like he can't believe it.

"Pic or it's a lie."

"Actually, I do have one, hold on." I maneuver my way through the phone and send him the photo. I had my hair big and curly with a little nursing cap sitting in it, and the red and white outfit was super short with white stockings coming down into a pair of white Chuck Taylors. I'm squished in between a group of girls, all giving a similar cheeky smile.

I wonder if he notices that I stand out. I'm the only one in actual stockings rather than fishnets. I skipped the heels for sneakers. My cleavage is out, but I spent the night trying to cover it up. It's the one and only party I went to, and I made sure to stay with my friends the entire night. I even made them go into the bathroom with me.

The phone doesn't allow me to see his reaction, but I hear him cough a few times. I know I'm not as sexy as my friends in the photo, but it's still more revealing than he's ever seen me. I'm dying as I wait for his response to it. He reappears on the screen and rubs a hand up and down his face and says, "Yeah, it's good."

"Yeah, it's good?" I scoff.

"I'm not at liberty to tell you what I really think of that little outfit, Nurse Josie."

I let out a cackle, then slap my hand over my mouth trying to stifle my laugh. I don't notice I have my phone face down on my chest until Wes says, "I'm sorry I got you something you've already read." I pick the phone back up to see him lazily staring back at me.

"No, seriously I don't have it. I mean, I did. But I left it with my aunt because she just loved it so much. So, I was planning on getting it again. It's perfect. Thank you."

"What's it about?"

I laugh. "You don't want to know."

"Of course, I do. I bought it. And it's your favorite."

My eyes lock with his.

"It's beautiful, but it's sad. I don't want to be sad tonight."

"Okay, don't tell me what it's about," he says with a chuckle. "Tell me about you and what I've missed out on these last two years."

"Me?" I laugh nervously. *Aside from forcing myself to have friends and avoid every party I could aside from the one where I had a hundred panic attacks dressed as a sexy nurse?* "Umm, I really enjoyed living with Leila. And the area, Coral Springs, was nice. Smaller and less hectic than it is here. But if it ever got too slow and quiet for us, Miami was less than an hour away. Leila taught me some of my mom's recipes, which will be fun to make for her now that I'm back. We read a lot together. I'm honestly going to miss her a lot. Hmm…"

I sigh, trying to think of something else to tell him about myself before he interrupts me, "I'm sorry we made you leave. I should have stood up for you more. I was a coward. I didn't want to step on Joe's toes. But the truth is he should have defended you, his twin. And he didn't. But believe me when I tell you, Josie, he has changed."

"That's not it."

He tilts his head and asks, "What do you mean? What's not it?"

"I didn't leave because of you guys."

"Why did you leave?"

I bite the inside of my cheek and look around, then repeat, "I don't want to be sad tonight."

I can see the hurt and confusion in his eyes. He wants to take my pain away, and I'm willing to bet Wes would turn my pain into his own if he could.

"Okay!" I attempt to change the topic and adjust my position on the bed so that I'm lying on my side, propped up by my elbow, and I have the phone up on my nightstand. It falls forward a few times before it's set, and he's just looking back at me with his sexy smirk that I'm not sure I'll ever get tired of.

"Show me your… room, Wesley Miller!"

He shakes his head after rearing it back, "You're testing me, Josie. What do you want to see?" He flips the camera to show me around.

"What the heck?! Why is it so clean in there? I thought every teenage guy had a messy room and posters of women in bikinis."

"Nope, just trophies and jerseys and my desk. I like to keep it clean. My grams always made sure I kept it tidy growing up so, I don't know? I'm just used to it."

He flips the camera back to himself and mirrors my position on the bed. I can almost feel the warmth from his body lying next to me on my bed, in my room.

"Hmm. My mom cleaned our rooms for years."

"Yeah, she still does for Joe. Spoiled brats."

My jaw drops. "Take that back! We're just loved." And the second the words leave my lips is a second too late. Wes has never had a healthy relationship with his parents. Hence why he was raised by his grandmother who loves him more than anything. That's his true mother figure.

"Oh my God, I'm sorry, I didn't mean that."

"It's no biggie. You ever been to bingo?"

Huh? "What? Bingo?"

"Yeah, like at a casino."

"I'm confused."

He rolls his eyes. "I'm taking Grams tomorrow. I think you'd have a good time. Come with us."

"Well, I… I think Joe works tomorrow night."

"He does." I look at him like he's speaking a different language. "I want you, Josie, just you, to come out with my me and grandmother tomorrow. We'll go to the game at six, and afterwards, if she hits it big, she'll buy us burgers and shakes at Steak 'n Shake, and if she doesn't, I'll buy her and," he points to me before continuing, "you a burger and a shake. What do you say? Wanna come with me to bingo?"

I take a deep breath and fix my elbow so now my head is resting on my clasped hands, like I'm ready to sleep. It takes a lot for me not to reach out across the bed toward the phone, toward him, in case he's really here. Knowing he's not, I still smile at him and nod my head before I answer, "Yes."

chapter sixteen

present day, 2022

josie

PULLING my phone out from under my pillow, I check the time. 7:38 AM. I rub my eyes to find black eyeliner smeared all over my fingers. I didn't even remember to wash my face before I crashed last night.

Staring at my popcorn ceiling, I remember the conversation I had with Wes after the bar. I wondered for years if he'd ever come looking for me. There was no way I would've gone chasing him after what he did, but I always thought he'd come back and fight for me. I *knew* he would. I did the calculations in my head, and if he saw me with Wyatt, who was the only person I dated in Coral Springs, it could have been anytime after six months of me leaving. Wyatt and I didn't make it official for a few more months after that, but it was mostly for him, because as much as I hate to admit it, my mind was still stuck on Wes. And years later, I still wasn't over Wes. Poor Wyatt, never had a chance.

I groan and hide under the crook of my elbow. I could see the pain all over his face last night. What did he expect, though? That he could literally push me out of his life and that I would wait around. Sadly, I would have, and I did, but we would've just gone down a road of toxicity after that breakup, especially coupled with grieving Joe. Years passed before I realized that I needed to be away in order to deal with the profound feelings that were starting to swallow me whole.

After we came back into the apartment from the rain, we didn't say anything else and went our separate ways. I got up a few times debating if I should go talk to him before I finally gave myself a break. This is normal, what we went through was heavy. I've been gone long enough to know time helped me heal. It's obvious time helped Wes heal, too. But that doesn't mean that everything just disappeared.

The truth is we live together and we have some past stuff to sort out, but everything will be okay. *Everything will be okay.* I don't need to fix everything right now. I don't even need to have a full-on conversation and settle things the next time I see him. I'll take it slow. Step by step.

My phone vibrates, and once I wrestle it out from under the covers, I see that I have a text from Wes. I didn't realize he still had the same number.

Wes: Your key to the apartment is on the counter.
Found it in my truck.
Josie: Thx.

I drag myself out of bed and start my morning routine. I need to make it to my gym session at eight-thirty this morning. Bobby signed me up for extra sessions so I'm not just doing kickboxing. He even hooked me up with free workouts after we figured out we had mutual friends, one of them being my now roommate.

As I squeeze into my workout shorts, it dawns on me that I'm probably going to see Wes at Pump House. I check myself out in my full-length mirror and notice how puffy my face is from crying last night. I typically don't put on makeup for a workout, but a little moisturizer and foundation to clear my blotchy skin up won't be so bad. After looking over myself more times than necessary, I finally leave, swiping my keys that Wes found from the counter where he'd left them.

wes

I sit at the computer in my small office at Pump House, watching the circle spin in the middle of the screen while all of the updates complete. Sipping on my piping hot coffee that still has steam rising from the top of it, fixated on the calendar pinned to the corkboard behind my monitor, I didn't even realize that this Friday is Joe's birthday. Which means it's also Josie's birthday. *Fuck.* I have to figure out something to do for her that's not too much, but shows her I'm here and I'm not going anywhere. Show her that I'm gonna try to earn her trust back. Last night fucked me up. I can't remember the last time I fought tears that hard.

I'll never forget the day that I drove over three hours to beg her to take me back. To tell her the hell I'd been through and that I was changed and better and sober and hers. I was always hers. And dammit, I still am.

I debated if I should tell her about the time I drove up and saw her holding flowers and a balloon and kissing that guy. My stomach still turns at the memory of that. I saw her laugh, her fucking laugh that still does inexplicable things to me, and then she stood on her tippy toes and kissed the fucker. I know that's the guy she dated because as the years went by, she had more than one photo of them together as her profile pic on social media.

I wasn't going to tell her, but when she asked, I couldn't let her think I didn't go looking for her. Truth is I wanted to tear them apart and fight for her, and maybe I should have, but when I saw that laugh, her happiness radiated off of her. And if my girl was happy then I didn't want to take that from her. Josie may be one of the strongest women I've ever met, but the world never ceases throwing her curveballs, and I wasn't about to be another.

My cell phone buzzes on my desk louder than it should. I see Bobby's name and answer.

"Hey, what's up?"

"Dude, I just walked outside and I have a fuckin' flat. I'm putting a donut on it now, but my mechanic says he only has openings this morning. Do you mind rescheduling my morning and I'll be in this afternoon?"

"Yeah, that's fine. I don't have clients so I'll see if they'll see me, or if they prefer to reschedule, but no biggie. Keep me updated."

"Awesome. Thanks, man."

We hang up, and once my computer screen shows it's updated, I sign in and check a few emails before I down the rest of my coffee and head to the front desk for Bobby's schedule.

"Hey, Marla," I greet our front desk assistant. "Can you help me out with Bobby's morning schedule?" I explain the situation.

"Yeah, I'll call his clients. His first will be here any minute, though, but I'll reach out to the rest of them this morning." Then she grins and says, "Oh, look, here's his first client."

I look up to see Josie walking up as I stare at her wide-eyed. *Shit.* She's in those damn shorts again. Do we not have a dress code for those? They can't be legal for public use, let alone appropriate during a workout.

Before I speak up to explain Bobby's absence, Marla jumps in—I mean, it is her job. "Hey, Josie. Unfortunately, Bobby just called and said that he can't make it. You can either reschedule, but since you're already here, you're more than welcome to train with Wes."

Marla is all smiles and I'm about to give her a raise because how can Josie say no to her?

Josie is surprised and seems to be caught off guard. I'm about to chime in and reiterate that she can reschedule if she prefers, but she twists her face into an exaggerated smile and answers, "That's fine. I can work out with Wes. Why not?"

My eyebrows shoot up and I give her a nod. I'm impressed with her answer. I startle them with a loud clap before I rub my hands together. "Let's get started."

Aside from kickboxing classes, which I would not have been able to work on with her as I don't have the right training for it, she and Bobby have had two previous sessions together. I suggest she warm up on a cardio machine while I go check her file. Trainers keep files of their clients where we record what's been worked on and what the client wants to work on. I crack my neck and take a deep breath because today is lower body for Josie. The previous workouts have been upper body and core training. So, today I'm supposed to work on her legs and ass. *Great.*

I walk up to find her climbing off the elliptical after her fifteen-minute warm-up. There's a barely there layer of sweat on her chest, and I pull my eyes away from the rise and fall of that exposed area.

"So, according to Bobby's notes, today is lower body training. You ready?"

"Oh, yeah. We talked about that. He was gonna show me how to do a Russian squat or something?"

"A Romanian deadlift."

"Yeah," she points at me, "that! I don't even know what it's for."

"Glutes," I reply to her but my voice cracks. I signal her to follow me and walk us over to a different part of the gym with free weights and more room to show her some moves.

"What's it for? That special squat," she asks from behind where she's catching up to me.

I stop and take a step back, allowing someone to pass us and look down at her over my shoulder. "Your ass. You want a firmer ass?" My eyes locked on hers.

Her eyes widen. "Oh. Yes. I did request that." She tightens her ponytail and looks around nervously.

"Well, that'll do it."

I waste no time and go through several different exercises with her, including different types of lunges and squats. She impresses me with her box jumps, and as she finishes her last set I go and grab a thirty-pound bar for the deadlift she was asking about. I get her into position, feet hip-width apart and knees slightly bent. I show her how the bar is supposed to be held at her hips and then slid down her thighs without bending her knees farther. She's doing it correctly, except her ass needs to stick out more.

"Like this?"

"No." I reach my hand out to help her with the stance, then ask, "May I?"

She visibly swallows, then nods.

I stand behind her and instruct her to begin lowering the bar. Careful not to let her ass touch me, although my dick wants nothing more than to graze the beautiful curve, I grasp her hips and pull her back the little bit more she needs. Looking around because this is oh so inappropriate, I see that no one is really watching, everyone's in their own world.

"Like you're at the club backing your ass up with your friends," I huff.

It clicks and I roll my eyes, I should have said that in the beginning. It takes all the cells in my body, but I move out from behind her and watch her from the side.

"Like this?"

"Yep." I nod.

"Can I ask why you wear those shorts?"

"What do you mean?" She pants as she continues through the reps.

"Your ass is hanging out."

She damn near drops the bar two reps early and looks around, adjusting her shorts. "They are workout shorts, thank you very much," she whisper-shouts.

"Yeah, well, they aren't... never mind. It's none of my business," I whisper-shout back.

She throws me the fakest smile she can muster, "Exactly...it is none of your business."

"Okay, sorry."

"It's fine. I'm not the only girl wearing these here."

"I know." I deadpan. She's right but, damn, I'm gonna stick a sensor on those shorts so she can't go anywhere in them. I'd say that I'd burn them, but I don't hate them that bad.

"Alright, our last one will be some hip thrusters."

As she has for most of the session's moves, she knows exactly what to do, and just wants to make sure she is doing the move properly so as not to hurt herself. Not gonna lie, I've kept my cool the whole time...only coming close to losing it when I had to help her with the deadlifts. But now that she is literally thrusting in the air, I can't help but steer my mind headfirst, right into the gutter.

Memories of our first time hooking up in her bedroom and how she responded to my touch come to mind. I've never been with anyone who was that in sync with me in bed. It came naturally for us. It didn't take us long to figure out what we liked and didn't like and, boy, did we calculate everything we could under the covers.

"Am I doing it right?" She pants again and pulls me out of my memories.

"Yes, you're good."

This girl couldn't mess up a thrust if she wanted to… and now I'm going to have to go run ten miles to get rid of the pent-up energy that I have inside me after her workout.

Josie: I just wanted to say thanks for today's workout. It already hurts when I try to sit on the toilet.
Wes: You did good then. No prob. Thanks for not making it awkward. Marla at the front has a crush on me.
Josie: Shut up!
Wes: No, I think she's married with kids but damn, she's not blind.
Josie: Anyway, I'm grabbing Thai for dinner. I got Cassie and Brandon's order. You want some?
Wes: You know what I like ;)

Josie: OMG BYE

Josie: I give you an inch and you take a foot.

Wes: I'll give you a foot ;) ;)

Josie: You wish.

Wes: Tell me I'm wrong and you don't know what I like.

Josie: Garlic chicken with rice.

Josie: Extra veggies.

Wes: See.

chapter seventeen

that summer, 2015

josie

I APPLY my liquid matte lipstick like a pro. I'm no makeup guru, but I'm obsessed with this brownish-orange lip color, and it goes well with my skin tone. I'm zipping up my makeup bag when my bedroom door swings open, my brother sticking his head in like he's a damn giraffe.

"Excuse me?!" I shout, because *not cool*. He can't just bulldoze in here.

"Do you have my apron for work?"

"No, why would I have it? And seriously, would it kill you to knock on the door before you come in here like that?"

He rolls his eyes. "You would lock the door if you were changing or flicking your bean, or doing whatever the hell you do in private."

"Oh my God, gross!"

"Hey," he says with a nod. "Why you getting all pretty? Where are you going?"

"Movies with some of my new work friends." *Lie.*

"Oh, okay. Have fun. Be careful. I'm at work doing stock til like one in the morning." I know this because I've gone to great lengths to find out his schedule, which consists of sending the photo to myself that he takes of it and deleting the evidence while I also pray I don't find photos I don't want to see.

"Okay, have a good night at work," I say, sending him out of my room.

I don't enjoy lying to my brother, but it's become a new thing for me. Truth is, I'm finally going out with Wes tonight. Alone. Ever since we went to bingo with his grandma two weeks ago, we've been spending more time together. The problem is, we haven't been able to spend any of that time on our own.

I'll never forget how nervous I was when I arrived at their condo before bingo and he let me in. He fumbled going in for a hug when he greeted me, and then he asked if I wanted anything to drink. He was being a proper host but it was awkward since this was the first time we'd ever really spent time together without Joe around. The feeling didn't last as we were out the door in minutes, and his grams was a real hoot taking over the conversation. She actually did win a few hundred bucks, which they say is a usual occurrence for her, and she bought us burgers and shakes as promised.

I lost count of the number of times I caught Wes watching me sip my shake that night.

A few days later, I went over to his place where

Grams was over the moon to teach me how to bake her famous snickerdoodle cookies. Our greeting at the door was smoother this time, though it was still different to see him in person without my brother around. The fact that we both knew we were hiding our time together from Joe was like an elephant in the room. For whatever reason, our daily phone calls lacked the awkwardness that came up in person. Grams took over the show again, happy to bake. But I swear she could see right through us. It was her idea to send us to the grocery store probably knowing it would be the first time we were truly alone, but it wasn't for very long.

We had finally planned to go to the movies a few days after that in an attempt to have some privacy, but my brother hijacked that one when someone had to trade shifts with him at work leaving his schedule open. We picked up Cora, and the four of us went to watch the new *Jurassic Park* movie.

Then there was the lunch with my mom.

My dad and Joe were working, and I was under the impression that my mom was visiting a friend, but she pulled into the driveway right as Wes did and she was so excited to see us. She dragged us out to her favorite Mexican restaurant. She never even asked what Wes was doing at the house while my brother was at work. Being that she had a designated driver (me), she was two margaritas in when she started trying to convince Wes to ask me out. I wanted to hide under the table.

"Look at her, Wes. She is sexier than I was at her age. I couldn't pull off cleavage and my hair was as flat as this table," she explained, slapping the table. Wes and I looked at each other, then at her. "Aye, you know what I mean. It had no volume. But really," she turned to me, "why not try and date Wes?" she whispered as if he wasn't a foot away from us. "I mean, look at him." She pressed her lips and pointed a look his way.

I looked over at him and he leaned back in his chair, placed his hands behind his head and gave me the cheesiest smile I've ever seen. He loved every second of my mother acting a fool.

That day, when we got back home and my mom went inside, we floated around each other like two opposite sides of magnets that you tried to force together, but ultimately they never aligned. I could tell something was up and thought that maybe he wanted to kiss me. He kept grabbing the back of his neck, and his eyes wouldn't leave my mouth, to the point where I wondered if I had leftover queso dip on my face. Twenty minutes later after he left, a text came through, confirming my thoughts.

> **Wes:** I swear I'm going to kiss you one of these days, Josie. I hope you'll let me.

So, here I am getting ready for my first real date with him. I think. We never did specify this would be a date, but it's pretty obvious.

He should be here to pick me up any minute. My parents are out at dinner and Joe just left for work. I offered to meet him somewhere or even at his place, but he insisted on picking me up.

Before I get my shoes on, I hear a knock at the door. I

take a brisk walk to the front door, opening it to Wes's back. When he hears the door open, he turns around and gives me that smirk of his. He's sporting his signature backward hat and a subtle gold chain peeks out of the collar of his white tee. "Hey."

Nervous as hell, I reply with the same simple, "Hey."

Tripping over my words, I tell him to come in while I get my shoes on. I don't expect him to follow me all the way into my room, but he does. I grab my classic black and white Vans to pair them with my black skinny jeans that are torn at the knee, and an oversized top that matches my lipstick and falls off the shoulder some. The entire time I'm wondering if and when he will kiss me, and if I'll be bad at it. It won't be my first, but it'll be my first *with him*.

Once I'm ready, I stand in front of my full-length mirror out of habit. As I tell him I'm good to go, he goes to wrap his arms around me from behind and rest his chin on my shoulder. Before I can control my reaction, my body spasms. An obvious jolt that was caused from fear. He came from behind and it startled my system. Funny how your body and your subconscious psyche pick up these things before you actually do. Now I feel like he's going to think I'm scared of him and I'm not. I trust Wes. A lot. He could *never* be Drew.

He loosens his hold some and rears his head back.

"You okay? I didn't mean to startle you," his voice drips with concern.

Before he can take a step back, I grab his forearms and hold him still. Looking at his reflection in the mirror, I reassure him. "I didn't mean to jump. I just didn't expect you to come from behind like that."

"You sure?"

"Yes. I like this, this is okay." His scent envelops me along with his touch. He's never really held me...like this, at least. But I will admit, recently our hugs have lasted longer and longer with each goodbye.

"You can stop checking yourself out in the mirror, you look great."

I smile and thank him. My stomach is doing somersaults in there. You'd think that the more we hang out, the less nervous I'd be, but it's quite the opposite.

"I'm just glad you're not showing off all that cleavage your mom is so fond of."

I turn and look at him, unsure what he's getting at.

"Grams is in the car, and I don't want her to make a comment about your boobs and embarrass you."

"What? She's here?" I practically pout, irritated that we never get time on our own. I swear someone is out to get us.

He straightens himself out and grins at me, using a pointer finger to playfully nip at my nose. "I'm kidding. It's just us tonight." He takes the two steps to my bed and collapses on it before leaning back, balancing himself on his elbows. He nods his chin toward me, asking what I want to do tonight.

I place a hand on my hip and glare at him. "Not funny, that little joke you played there."

"I was just testing how bad you wanted to have me all to yourself, and now I know."

I shake my head at him. "Alright, Romeo, then why

are you asking me what I want to do? Shouldn't you have it all planned out?"

"I should...but I don't. I figured you could choose what we do, and I have to go with it. Then, next time, I'll pick and you gotta do what I want." He smirks at me.

"Okay, fine. So, you'll be down for whatever I come up with."

"Okay, maybe not *anything*."

I watch him, lying in my bed. Probably marking it with his scent. Something I have absolutely no problem with.

We could go to the movies, walk around downtown, or even grab dinner. I am hungry and want to avoid people, too. Joe works at Home Depot, so that's easy to avoid. And my parents are with friends who live on the other side of the city. I'm trying to think of something different and fun to do. I love the beach, but that's not original. I'm practically tapping my chin when he ceases my thoughts.

"What's going on in that pretty head of yours?"

"Thai. I want Thai food. And the bridge." I sit at the edge of my bed, then look over at him elated at the thought. "You know the Gandy bridge? I remember as a kid, my parents would take us there with my cousins and we would catch crabs!" I laugh, then continue, my face reddening when I realize my choice of words, "Okay, I don't want to catch crabs. But we can order the food to-go and go eat it in the bed of your truck and just look out at the water."

It dawns on me that I may be over excited. He's just

staring at me, gaze set on my mouth. I wipe the corners of my lips in case I went too far with the lipstick.

"It's lame, huh? We can do something else."

"No, no. It's cool, we can do that. I mean, I think some douchebags take their cars to those side beaches to race on the weekends, but it's a Tuesday night and," he explains, then pulls out his phone, checking the time, "if we leave now we can catch the sunset."

"Let's do it!" I'm giddy and feel like I'm acting like a child, but it's just nostalgic to me. Grabbing food from my favorite restaurant and going to this small beach we would frequent as a family when I was a kid. All with the boy I've dreamt about for years.

Wes gets up from the bed and stretches his arms up so high, I swear he could probably touch the ceiling. "Let me remind you, though, Grams isn't in the car, so if you want to change into a cleavage-enhancing top, the sun will wait for us."

I backhand his stomach, resulting in a sexy chuckle from him.

"Very funny."

chapter eighteen

that summer, 2015

wes

I'M DRIVING to the Thai restaurant while Josie places our to-go order.

"Yes, mild. And an order of garlic chicken with rice and extra veggies..." She says it as a question, looking at me. I nod, confirming my order. "And extra peanuts with the pad thai. Okay. Yes. Thank you." She hangs up, then turns to me and pinches my bicep.

"Ow! What was that for?"

"I'm just so excited. This is my favorite dish ever. Don't tell my mom but, I even love it more than her rice and beans."

I widen my eyes and look between her and the road. "Isabel would kill you."

"I know. But imagine, when I'm on death row for..." she thinks for a minute. "I don't know, I'll never be in that situation, but if I were, and they asked what I wanted for my last meal, this would be it."

"Wow." She has no idea how cute she is.

"Don't make fun. I'm serious. What's your last meal choice?"

"A McGangBang, fries, a Coke and an M&M McFlurry."

She doesn't respond so I look over at her. "What?"

"You're serious?"

"Yes."

"Why?"

I laugh. "Why? Because that meal has everything you need: a McChicken, a McDouble, ice cream, candy, a soda, and carbs. You can't go wrong."

"You can and you have. I hope you never face having to choose your last meal."

She settles herself back in the passenger seat and grabs my phone out of the cup holder between us. She taps my password in and goes to the music app, taking over the radio. That's where we're at in our relationship, we are finally acting normal around each other without Joe having to be present. She knows my password, doesn't ask to change the song, and makes herself at home in my truck, throwing her feet up on the dash.

My head spins with us and what we've got going on. I was nervous to send her that text the other day about wanting to kiss her, it's obvious we are into each other, but it's weird to finally hover over that line. She replied with a *maybe* and a winky face emoji. That's good enough for me.

I always had a crush on Josie and felt like I needed to protect her. Finally, Joe's pulled his head out of his ass and has treated her like he should treat his sister. I'm grateful she's back, although I still have no clue why she left in the first place. I thought for sure it was because of us and how we let people humiliate her at that stupid party, but she swears that isn't the case.

It's wrong sneaking around behind Joe's back but there's something about Josie that I can't stay away from. Aside from being fixated on her mouth—that sets off inappropriate thoughts in my brain—and her insane body, which I can't even let my mind wander off to right now or we would drive head-on into oncoming traffic, she's got so much other stuff going for her. She makes me laugh, and I love that she's positive and happy, although there's something else there that I crave to protect. But the way she lights up a room is my favorite thing about her. She wasn't this happy-go-lucky girl before but now that she is, it just adds to her. She constantly points out the bright side of a situation. Take tonight, for example. I told her we could do whatever and she chose to grab take out to eat from the back of my truck on a run-down beach. I don't think this place is going to be what she remembers or expects, but I will take her anywhere right now. She's searching for her adolescence, and I'm more than happy to help her find that.

We pick up the food and I drive us to the bridge. The sun is about to set, and when we pull off to the side onto the small, dingy beach, she sits up in her seat and looks around. There are a few families sitting around in camping chairs with their kids running around in bathing suits, playing in the sand. I can see the disappointment in her face, but I choose not to entertain it and try to make the best of what she was expecting here.

"I've got some blankets in the back, let me lay them in the bed." I've only got an old comforter and two sheets, no pillows or anything, but this will make do. I lay them out and make it as comfortable as I can. Josie climbs in and sets the food around us. I grab our bottled sodas and join her in the back of my truck. Aside from the little noises she makes with her first few bites that go straight to my dick, we're quiet as we eat. I grab her drink and unscrew the top off, holding it out to her. She thanks me and takes a few sips.

"So, did you make many friends in Coral Springs?"

"Yeah, a few. Leila and I lived in an apartment, but it was just outside a really nice neighborhood, so most of my friends were loaded. That was cool, riding in their fancy cars and hanging out in houses that were the types of properties we would vacation at growing up. But I mostly stayed in touch with Cora, no one took her place. Oh, and there's my *weekly word*," she mumbles that last bit before throwing out, "but I guess that's a one-way street." She shrugs while she plays with the rips at her knees.

"Huh?" I'm more than confused.

"Just this thing. I get these random texts and I have no idea who it's from. It's quotes. Sometimes song lyrics. I don't know, it's weird but I love it."

"And you don't know who it is?"

"Nope." I don't like this one bit. Who is this? A stranger? Some guy?

"Is it like an automated thing?"

"Maybe? I don't get them every week, but when I do, it's Monday mornings. I've replied but never get a response. I've always loved words, you know, quotes with deep meanings and stuff, so I thought maybe I signed up for something, but there's something about it that makes me think it may be someone I actually know."

"I don't know, Josie, what if it's some creep?"

She laughs and lifts her butt up to pull her phone out of her pocket. "Nah, they are harmless. I won't lie, it's creeped me out, but it's been going on for a couple years now."

She opens the text thread and hands it to me. "I thought it was you and Joe at one point, they are usually sweet or sad or funny. Never mean or anything."

I scroll through and read messages from the last couple weeks.

Mon. June 8, 9:09 AM
Weekly Word: Women are meant to be loved not understood. (Oscar Wilde)

Mon. June 22, 9:04 AM
Weekly Word: Wake up every morning with the thought that something wonderful is about to happen. (Anonymous)

Yesterday, 9:00 AM
Weekly Word: The person, be it gentleman or

lady, who has not pleasure in a good novel, must be intolerably stupid. (Jane Austen)

I chuckle at that last one, because this girl loves her books. "Huh. So, you have no idea who this is. I don't know," I scratch the side of my head and hand it back over. "What if it's dangerous?"

"Really, Wes? It's hardly dangerous. It's just my phone number, and they're always positive messages. Someone could do more damage on Instagram." That's true.

"Alright, but promise me you'll tell me if things with your wordy-word get weird."

"It's *weekly word*," she corrects me with a gorgeous ass grin on her face.

"Whatever, you know what I mean."

"Yes, I know."

"So," I peek out at the horizon and look back at her, "no boyfriends in Coral Springs?" I bite.

She smiles at me and shakes her head.

"What did you miss about being here?"

"My parents and Cora. Not so much Joe since we weren't that close, as you're aware of. They have all the same foods and stores as they do here for the most part."

"Except for the Thai food."

She laughs and agrees with me, "Except for the Thai food, yeah."

"Joe's still being better with you?"

"Yeah, he is." She has a dreamy look on her face. I know she and Joe have soft spots for each other, they were just harder to find before. "Well, today he barged into my room when I was putting on makeup asking if I took his dumb orange work apron."

I laugh at that. "Why did he think you'd have it?"

"Who knows. I wonder if he found it. I wouldn't doubt that he's worn it around Cora with nothing else on." She gags at that statement and starts putting our trash in the brown bag the food came in. I help her clean up and then set the bag in the corner of the bed, away from us. She scoots toward the rear window, sitting up against the back of the truck with her knees bent. I mirror her position.

"What's your thought on that?"

"On what?"

"On your brother and your best friend."

She sighs, "Ugh. I don't know. I just don't want him to hurt her, you know. But at the same time, Cora is a strong girl and she could probably easily do some no-strings-attached deal with a guy. I definitely could not."

That piques my interest. The last thing I'd want with Josie is no strings attached. If I went all in with Josie, that's what it would be—all in. I mean, it would be hard with her family, aside from her mom, but I don't know that I could have us just casually hooking up.

"Why couldn't you?"

"Ew, I don't know. I would feel like crap all the time. Like he'd be using me and I wouldn't be good enough for him to take out in public or show off to his family. I wouldn't be able to let myself fall for the guy. And who doesn't want to fall, you know?"

I'm fixated on her face and what she's saying. I

watch her do this thing she does all the time where she runs her fingers through her hair and flips it to the side when I notice she's waiting for a response from me.

"You, uh," I clear my throat, "you ever fallen before?" I ask her nervously as I run a finger up and down the side of my Coke bottle.

"No," she looks up at me. "I haven't. You?"

"No," I say with a small shake of my head, and I look around the small beach. The sun is almost gone, just a sliver peeking over the horizon.

She covers her face with her hands, and for a second I'm nervous she's crying or some shit, but she groans and says, "I'm so sorry. This place is a dump. Not what I was hoping for and nothing like what I remembered. Definitely not first date vibes." She slaps her hand over her mouth like she can't believe she just said that out loud.

"First date, huh? Is that what this is?" Her face is still covered by her hands and I slowly peel them away, one finger at a time. "Are you not enjoying yourself?"

Her hands fly off her face. "What? No! I am enjoying myself."

"I am, too. So, don't apologize that you asked to go to this nasty little beach."

She laughs and playfully smacks me on the arm.

We get quiet for a little bit there and I turn my head, leaning it against the back of the rear window of my truck. She looks over at me staring at her.

"He'd be stupid to not take you out in public or show you off to his family. And if he doesn't think you're enough, then he doesn't deserve you. This guy would be the definition of a fool."

Her head tilts and her eyes squint some as she asks, "Who?"

"The dumbass who would want you without any strings attached."

"Oh."

"You're more than enough. You get that, right, Josie?"

She bites her lip and nods at me. Her eyes go back and forth between my eyes and my mouth.

I bring my hand up and palm her cheek. Her lips part and I run my thumb back and forth across her bottom lip.

"You know, I tried to imagine how you may have changed over these last two years before you came back."

"Yeah?"

"Yeah. And I tried to imagine what tonight would be like. I've imagined this for a long time now. So many times. But I've never tried to imagine what your lips taste like."

She swallows before asking, "What do you mean?"

"I mean, I wouldn't be able to stand myself if I imagined them being any less than the reality, and at the same time, I know my imagination couldn't even try to measure up to what it would be like to kiss you."

Two short breaths pass and her mouth crashes onto mine. Our lips connect for a few seconds before I pull away and look at her. Our eyes lock, and it's as if we never ate our meal and our sudden hunger can only be fed by our mouths colliding. I kiss her again, bringing her bottom lip between mine. She tilts her head and gives more into the kiss. My hand moves to her thigh and now, I'm fucking scared. I don't typically take it slow with girls. Usually we're both here for one thing and one thing only, but this is Josephine Rodriguez and she terrifies me. I don't want to freak her out and pressure her, so I'm not moving my hand any farther and I'm going to let her set the pace.

I pull away and peck the corner of her mouth and go to kiss the other corner when she grabs my face with both hands and brings me back to the center. I feel her tongue invade my mouth—a welcome invasion, obviously—and when our tongues meet, I swear I feel it all the way down to my toes, as well as other places. She moans and starts to turn her body toward me. She's really setting the pace now and I'm all in.

The second we stop for air, I admit, "You have no idea how long I've wanted this." I move to her neck, kissing the soft skin that tastes like coconuts as she tilts her head to the side to give me better access.

"Me too. I have to say, I have definitely imagined this, but never in the bed of your truck..." she says it all breathy and sexy.

I chuckle against her skin, high off this moment. "I don't care where the fuck we are right now, baby."

I grab her chin and pull her back to me for more of her mouth. I've finally had a taste, and now I'm fucking addicted. She gasps before the kiss and then climbs onto my lap, straddling me.

Shit, shit, shit. She's gonna feel my hard-on. I grasp

her hips and try everything to keep her still, but my thumbs betray me and start rubbing her silky flesh that sits right above her jeans. Her hands cover my neck, and now she's grinding on me in a rhythm that matches the strokes of my thumbs. Once she starts moaning, I stop the kiss.

"I'm sorry." I gasp.

"Oh, gosh. No! I'm sorry," she starts lifting herself off me, but I tighten my hold on her to not let her up. "I must be moving too fast, I–"

I put a finger up to her lips to shut her up, "Josie, you're fine. Please, believe me. I'm enjoying myself, if it isn't obvious." I thrust my hips up to remind her that I'm *thoroughly* enjoying myself.

"Oh, okay. Umm, why did you stop then?" She picks at her nails, hands hanging between us, and looks up at me, her brown eyes peeking under her lashes.

"Because I want to take it slow with you. At least as slow as I can manage for now. If we keep this up, I'm going to embarrass myself."

She leans forward and giggles, resting her forehead on my shoulder.

"You scared me," she admits as she sits back up. "I thought I was a bad kisser or something."

"What?" I throw my head back laughing, then bring my focus back to her. "You couldn't be a bad kisser if you tried." I reach forward and kiss her again, her hands steadying on my shoulders.

"Does it bother you that we're sneaking around?" I ask her, hating that she lies to her family when she's with me.

"No."

"Do you want to tell them?"

"No," she laughs. "I kinda like having you all to myself, is that weird?"

"No." I move some hair that's falling forward behind her ear. "I'm all yours."

chapter nineteen

present day, 2022

wes

THE DISTANT SOUNDS of pots and pans being manhandled has me blinking awake. I grab my phone off the nightstand and check the time. 9:06 AM. It's Friday, my day off *and* Josie's birthday. I don't think she has plans, at least, according to Cassie she doesn't. I'm hoping to take over her morning and possibly steal her for lunch, too.

I get out of bed and pull on some basketball shorts before I stroll into my personal bathroom to take a leak and brush my teeth. I stop mid brush when I hear some yelling and then loud music. I finish up and rinse out my mouth, heading out of my room and recognizing the song as "Tear in My Heart" by Twenty One Pilots. When I open my door, the song booms even louder. *What the hell?*

I stop in my tracks as soon as I digest the view in front of me. I rub the scruff on my face as a reality check because God, I hope I'm not hallucinating right now. Josie has her back to me and is dancing around the kitchen. She's cracking eggs into a bowl and wears an oversized black shirt that hangs right under her ass. *Is she wearing anything under that shirt?* She shimmies around, and my dick is well aware of what's going on.

I pull the bar stool back so I can sit down and get comfortable for the show. I try to make noise because as much as I know she will sadly stop this little performance the second she knows I'm watching, I don't want to be a creep either. She doesn't notice the screech of the chair and continues jumping around like she's at their damn concert, singing to a wooden spatula. When she opens the cabinet and reaches up for a plate, I realize she has the damn shorts on. I swear my headstone will read: *Wesley Miller, death by short-shorts.*

I clear my throat, and this time she hears it over the music. She spins around, holding the plate up to her chest and marches to her phone to stop the music.

"What the hell, Wes?! You scared the shit out of me!"

"I didn't mean to scare you," I chuckle and she glares at me. "You woke me up with your little concert out here," I explain.

"I thought I was alone. Aren't you supposed to be working?" She turns back to the stove and turns it off before she piles her scrambled eggs onto her plate.

"It's Friday. I'm off on Fridays."

"Oh, well, I didn't mean to wake you."

"It's fine. I never sleep in this late. Plus, I was hoping to catch you this morning."

She holds her plate and takes a bite of her eggs before she says a garbled, "for what?"

"I have something for you. Hold up." I run into my room and come back with a pink gift bag. She's staring at me, particularly at my chest, still eating her breakfast when I hold it up to her.

"Come on, open it," I plead and hold the bag up to her.

She puts her plate aside and mumbles something about me not having to get her anything. I wish her a happy birthday as she pulls the tissue paper out.

She glances up at me and back in the bag, a shocked look on her face.

"Is it bad? Do you already have it?"

"No, it's great I haven't read it yet. It's actually on my TBR."

I have no clue what that means, I just grabbed whatever romance book sounded interesting to me. This one was about a second chance. I didn't even finish reading the blurb, that was all I had to know. She doesn't pull it out of the bag and pulls out the other gift.

"Perfect timing, they could come in handy now, huh?"

She scoffs at me, "Workout pants? Really, Wes?" She smacks me with the pants and I go to grab them but she pulls away.

"I can return them if–"

She cuts me off, "No. I want them."

She holds them up and inspects them.

"What are your plans today, birthday girl?"

"I'm going out to dinner with my parents. Before

that, I have to do some laundry and I have work to catch up on. Nothing exciting." She looks up at me.

"That's boring. Laundry and work on your birthday? Come on. Let me take you somewhere."

"Me?" She points to herself.

"Yes, you, girl. I know someone who would want to see you today."

josie

Breathe in. Breathe out. I repeat this mantra in the mirror a few times. I tried to say no to Wes, but he insisted I'll enjoy whatever it is he has planned. I wanted to just make sure and keep myself occupied today. Laundry and work would have done the job, but I was planning on getting myself a book, which is already done now, thanks to Wes. I also thought about going to a movie or something to keep busy. I would drag Cassie to spend the day with me, but she's working. Obviously, Cora lives in another state. And although there's no way to ignore the fact that my brother would be turning twenty-six with me, I don't want to dwell on him like I typically do on our special day. Had I made more plans with my parents, I know it would have been full of Joe talk, so I opted for just dinner instead. I don't mind talking about my brother, I just get nervous and don't want to go into a downward spiral.

So now Wes will be the one entertaining me.

I tie my hair up in a messy bun and leave a few curls framing my face. I almost put on the sundress I plan to wear for dinner, but opt on my favorite ripped jeans and a floral top that shows a bit of midriff instead. Considering he always freaks out whenever I show some leg.

He scared the shit out of me earlier, and who let him out of his room without a shirt on? *Geez.* He was all tattoos and a rocky road of hard yet soft skin. The one particular tattoo that caught my eye this time was the jersey with my brother's number on his pec. It took some strength to not reach out and touch him there. Touch the body that my fingers probably still remember. And why must he always gift me books? Ones that are perfect for me. I should turn the pants he got me into shorts. But I won't, those are Lululemons and probably cost more than half the clothes I own.

I apply some blush and mascara before I step out of my room to find Wes on the couch, scrolling through his phone. He looks up at me and does a double take at my outfit before he's up on his feet and ushering me out the door with a clear of his throat followed by a "Let's get going."

It's drizzly out, and the smell of wet trees lingers in the air. He helps me into his truck, and it reminds me of when he drove me home a week ago. The smell of him in here covers up the scent of the rain out there. My eyes skim over his jeans and hunter green shirt that stretches deliciously across his chest.

Really? Deliciously? Get a grip, Josie.

My eyes end their little journey on his smiling face.

"What? Why are you smiling like that?"

"I'm just glad you agreed. I expected to have to promise you Starbucks or something."

"Yes, well, I do expect coffee considering I didn't exactly get to make myself any before you rudely interrupted my moment this morning. Which, may I add, was a good time for me."

"That makes two of us."

I roll my eyes and ask him where he's taking me. He says it's a surprise and to sit tight. I feel like an eight-year-old with my huffing and puffing. I peer over at him and watch him flick the wipers on, then check his mirrors as he changes lanes. Why is it so hot when a man does the simple, mundane tasks of driving? Fourteen-year-olds can do it, for God's sake. But watching Wes drive me around, the muscles in his forearms ticking here and there send a zing to my nipples, and now I'm rubbing my legs together for some sort of relief.

I reach over to adjust the air vents and he looks over at me.

"Hot?"

"Yeah, just a little." I feel like I'm fifty and having a hot flash.

He drives me through the Starbucks drive-thru and tells me that he usually has dinner with my parents on this day. I didn't know that. I knew he kept in touch with them, but they never told me about an annual dinner.

"Your dad invited me tonight, but I decided I didn't want to intrude. I'm happy to steal you for some of the day."

"You can come tonight." *Whoa, did I just say that out loud?*

He looks at me for one second, then another before focusing back on the road.

"Do you plan to visit his grave?"

"No. I mean, I will. But not today. Every year I'd try to avoid anything I can with Joe. I'd wish I could sleep through the day and completely skip it, but I know it's not healthy. It's not what he would want, you know?" Wes nods in understanding. "This is the first time since we lost him that I've chosen to enjoy the day, like he would have. So, cheers to twenty-six and no tears!" I laugh and hold my coffee up, pushing down the guilt that typically consumes me on this day. His eyes crease at the sides as he smiles and holds his coffee up to mine.

"A day for dancing and…old friends." Old friends?

I look up to see we are pulling into an assisted living facility. Where the hell are we going? Am I going to serve food to old people?

He parks, and once we're out of his truck, he guides me up to the second floor and knocks on the door, looking over at me with a sparkle in his eye and it hits me. His grams. Now I'm giddy with excitement because I love this woman.

The door opens and I hear her raspy voice. I don't think she's smoked since Wes was a kid, but it sounds like she never quit.

"Alright, Arnold. I'll see you at trivia on Thursday," she calls out as an older gentleman with a flat cap and some strong cologne steps out, nodding at me and Wes.

"Oh, Wesley!" She pulls him in for a hug and then sees me, and dammit if my eyes don't water.

"Josephine! What on earth are you doing here?"

I giggle and step into her arms for a hug. It's one of those good hugs, so much more than just a greeting. I hold in my tears and accept the love she always has to give.

"Oh, you kids are just making my day! Come in, come in."

"Grams, what's up with you and Arnold," Wes asks, wiggling his eyebrows at her.

She swats him on the arm. "Oh, Wes, please. Arnold probably couldn't get it up if I were hanging sideways from a pole."

Wes makes a disgusted face and I almost spit out my coffee.

"What? You asked," she says with a shrug.

"Anyway. I brought your old friend Josie here to see you because it's her birthday."

"And you couldn't warn me? I would have gotten something for her," she cries with another swat at him. "Happy birthday, sweetie. I didn't know you were in town. Hell, I didn't even know you two still talked." They lock eyes and I swear they are having a whole conversation without saying a word.

I interrupt the silent exchange, "I just came back a couple months ago. I was staying with my parents until my friend said she had a room open. I had no idea the room was in Wes's apartment."

"Is that so?"

"Mm-hmm," I confirm. She's still looking at Wes in a way I don't understand.

That summer we were together, we spent as much time at their small condo as we did at my parents. She would live in the kitchen, often teaching me different recipes, or kicking me out of her way. I had no problem with the latter as I'd find myself snuggled up to Wes, either on the couch or on his twin bed.

She knew it all. And never once judged us for anything. My grandparents passed away when I was younger and I don't remember them much so she was very much like a grandmother to me. For that short time, at least. She knew when we were sneaking around, and I know she knew we were having sex. She'd always make off-hand comments about making sure we were safe.

And I can only assume she was there during Wes's grieving for Joe.

And for me.

Wes breaks the silence and starts talking about the weather and some extra tasks he's been working on at the gym. He explains how he has less clients lately but more work to do behind the scenes.

She listens to him and nods her head, but she keeps looking at me. I smile at her and she returns a smile back at me, but it doesn't reach her eyes.

We catch up. I tell her some about my life with my aunt down south and how I just started a new job as a counselor. Wes listens with her to every word I have to say.

"A counselor? That's great, sweetie. I always knew

you'd make something of yourself. Lord knows we are all in a different world now with these phones and wee-fee–"

"WiFi," Wes coughs into his fist as he corrects her. I swat him on the arm this time and she nods at me in appreciation.

"Oh, whatever, Wesley. *Wi-Fi*. Either way, we are all much smarter but still need someone to talk to about what's going on in here," she taps her head.

The discussion takes a turn and is no longer about me. He tells her that he will still visit her just as much, but he wants to start ordering her groceries to be delivered. She doesn't trust it.

"They don't know how to pick the right avocados," she argues.

"Aaaand, that's our cue to go, Grams. Love you." He hugs and kisses her, and when she reaches for me, she holds me at a length where she can whisper in my ear.

"Please make sure he takes care of himself. I don't think he'd survive it a second time." When she pulls away, she's got tears in her eyes.

When Wes broke my heart all those years ago, I went through hell, but I never thought about the fact that he probably did, too.

chapter twenty

present day, 2022

josie

WE CLIMB BACK into Wes's truck after catching up with his grams. The sun is back out and you wouldn't have even known it rained if it weren't for the small puddles that are quickly drying up. I have no idea where he's driving us to now, but I can't form the words to ask because all I can do is think about what Grams said. What exactly happened to Wes when I ran away from all the heartbreak? For the second time.

"What's this?" Wes asks as his finger barely touches my side, ceasing my curious thoughts. I flinch at his touch, then lift my arm to better see what he's talking about.

"Oh. It's a hot air balloon." I respond nonchalantly, pulling my shirt up more to let him see the whole tattoo. The balloon is filled with intricately designed flowers ranging in hues of pinks and oranges. Clouds peek out from behind it and hearts hang off the basket. Six hearts, to be exact. One for each person who has a piece of my heart: my mom, my dad, Joe, Leila, Cora, and… Wes. I don't share that with him though. "I don't know if you remember but I've always liked hot air balloons."

"I remember," he confesses, and I can't help but wonder if he really does or if he forgot until right now. Did he think of me whenever he saw one over the last seven years?

I pull my shirt back down and pick at the strings stretched out over my skin in the holes of my jeans. I further explain why I got the tattoo, "The day, you know," I say, tripping over my words before I start over. "The day Joe died…he sent me a picture of a hot air balloon. He knew my love for them, and he always made me so happy when he sent those."

Wes looks over at me before eyeing the road again and I have a feeling he wants to reach over and touch me in some way. After a somewhat awkward silence, he does. He reaches over and squeezes my hand. "I love that you have that memory and your tattoo is…stunning, really. You rock your ink." He let's go of my hand before continuing, "And I'm glad you're choosing to have a more positive day than to spend it grieving, but I want you to know, Josie, there can be tears. There's nothing wrong with that."

This is the Wes I fell in love with. He's sweet and present, always listening to what I'm saying. He makes sure I'm happy and comfortable and safe. Always. The man will move mountains for me. He would have then, and I have a feeling he would now. Declining his advances and ignoring my cravings for him seem to get harder and harder every day.

"I know. Thank you," I reply as he drives me through the city and pulls into the tiny parking lot of my favorite local Thai restaurant, the one we picked up dinner from on our first date.

I look up to find him smirking at me. "Lunch time, birthday girl," he says with a wink. *This is going to be the longest birthday.*

Wes and I shared our lunch because we wanted to save room for dinner. After insisting that he wouldn't be imposing, he finally agreed to join us. I called my mom and had her add him to the reservation.

He really wanted to keep taking me out to do things for my special day, but I said I was tired and wanted to nap. I can't remember the last time I had a nap, and after sharing apps, an entrée, and a dessert, I was feeling full and sleepy.

Wes went to run some errands and promised to be back around five for the dinner at five-thirty. I set my alarm for four and had one of the best naps I'd ever had. I woke up with thoughts that slowly reminded me of the fact that I'm back in Tampa, living with Wes, and that it's my birthday.

And that Joe is dead. That's a hard one, waking up and forgetting he died, then remembering the twist of fate that came with it. Doesn't happen as often anymore but hurts just as bad each time.

I start up my daily playlist and jump in the shower. Now that I'm more awake, I have a little more of a pep in my step. I'd be lying if I said I wasn't excited to have Wes at dinner with my parents. I let the hot water run down my face and back through my hair while I imagine us walking into the restaurant. I try to keep thoughts of us as an *us* at bay, but I can see it clearly. I imagine myself holding onto the crook of his arm as he leads us to our table where he shakes my dad's hand and kisses my mom's cheek before he pulls my chair out for me. It all seems so real, I can almost smell him.

After the shower, I pad across the common area in my robe and notice that Wes isn't here. His room is how he left it: lights out and door wide open, and he's nowhere to be seen. I go back into my room and shut the door before I get dressed and start my hair routine. Having curly hair isn't always easy, but I'm lucky enough to have choices: straight, wavy, or curly. I know my big, natural curls used to drive Wes crazy—in a good way—so that's the look I'm going for. I pair some strappy sandals with my sundress and check myself out in the mirror. I look like summertime in September, but I'll blame that on Florida.

Checking the time, it's just a few minutes before five so I speed through my makeup, which is fine because I'm going for a natural look anyway. Once I finish up, I step into the living room and see that his door is still open with the lights off. I peek out the window only to find his truck missing from its usual spot. I decide to shoot a text off to him, but as soon as I open our messages, the three dots start dancing.

Wes: So sorry, running late.
Josie: No prob, everything ok?
Wes: Yea, something came up.
Wes: Let you know when I'm on the way.

My stomach drops and a sudden feeling of gloom takes over my previously cheery attitude. I wonder where he's at and what came up. Did they need him at work? I know Pump House runs twenty-four seven, but what could they need from him on his day off that another manager or trainer can't take care of. I shake my head in an attempt to shake any negative thoughts out. This is Wes. He wouldn't stand me up, whatever came up is something important.

I grab my purse and keys and head to my birthday dinner, party of three.

chapter twenty-one

that summer, 2015

wes

JOE IS GOING on and on about what it's like working at Home Depot, and how he spends more time directing customers where to go than actually doing his job. I'm only taking in about a quarter of what he's saying because my brain is not currently with me in the Rodriguez living room talking to Joe, it's in the kitchen with Cora and Josie.

And Josie's tiny jean shorts.

Their parents went to the casino for the night so it's just us four. We ordered pizza and the girls had us watch some shitty reality TV, but Joe and I did have a good time making fun of the contestants.

The smell of chocolate chip cookies has my eyes roaming to the kitchen. I'm hoping to get Josie alone soon, but I can't figure out how without making Joe or Cora suspicious. And if they're almost done baking, my time is running out. I need to tell Josie I have a plan for us to be on our own tonight. I won't lie though, I'm sweating some because I don't want her to be uncomfortable, and I also hope Joe doesn't catch us. But I'm dying to get her in her room and in my arms.

It's been two weeks since our night at the bridge, and I swear I'm losing my mind over this girl. Our nightly chats give me a connection I've never felt with anyone. She listens to me and asks me questions no one's ever asked. She makes me want to be a better person. It's just weird, I've never really cared. I would just get by. As long as Grams was happy and Joe and I were busy with parties and sports, I was good. But now the summer is here and if it weren't for Josie, I don't know how I would've been spending it. She's pushing me to go to school for sports medicine because I enjoy health and fitness, but for a little bit there, I wasn't even considering college. Josie makes me want to try though. I never cared to try before. Every night I give her a little more of myself. I hope she feels the same way.

Sneaking around is fun with stolen kisses and booty grabs when no one's looking but that's not often. Seriously, she grabs my butt when I least expect it and freaks me out. But it only makes it more fun when I finally get to sneak up on her.

I look up when I notice that Joe stopped talking halfway through his story and now I see why. Cora is cradled in his lap feeding him a cookie. They came out as an item soon after the day Josie came back, and I could tell it bothered her some. She expected them to hook up, but not label themselves as official. I talked to her about it and reminded her that they could be hiding it like we are.

I quietly get up and head to the kitchen. There's no need to tiptoe around because these lovebirds won't notice whether I'm in the room or not. Josie is transferring the cookies from the cookie sheet to the cooling rack when I come up behind her and slide one palm under her shirt, grabbing her waist, while my other hand reaches for a cookie. She jumps at my touch but quickly melts into my chest before she reprimands me. "You're supposed to wait until I bring the cookies out there for all of us."

"I'm impatient. Sue me," I say, lowering my voice before I kiss her shoulder. "Speaking of my lack of patience…I'm going to leave soon. Like really soon."

"What," she blurts and turns around, smacking me in the chest with the spatula on accident. She apologizes and brushes the crumbs off my shirt.

I cage her in, hands clutching the counter on either side of her. "Calm down, Betty Crocker." I reach up with one hand and move some hair out of her face. "Then you're going to make sure your window is open and unlocked for me. I'll park my car down the street, and you let me know when I can come to your room." I search her eyes for approval of my plan.

She gives me a mischievous smile and slowly turns around, getting back to her cookies. "Well, I don't know. Suddenly, I'm…" she fakes a yawn and finishes, "so tired."

I throw my head back and laugh. "Bull. Shit. I should be the one tired here considering last night I fell asleep on FaceTime and you startled me awake yelling my name because you wanted to tell me about the time you went to Battle of the Books in fourth grade."

"I won a trophy. I've never won a trophy before. That was a good story."

I ignore her elementary school tale and inhale her scent. Her hair always smells like vanilla and coconuts, and I better back up before my dick gets so hard she mistakes it for a fucking rolling pin in my pants.

We hear Joe's voice coming closer, and as if she's Wonder Woman, Josie shoves me away so hard I have to grab the island behind me to not fall on my ass.

"Dude, you making a move on my sister?" Joe grills me before Josie answers with a laugh, "He tried to take a cookie."

Joe looks at her like she's lost her mind. "For sure calm down, sis. Wes just has a crazy sweet tooth. His grandma is the best baker."

I don't miss Cora looking suspiciously between me and Josie.

"Alright," I say with a clap. "I am out of here because I'm tired as shit." I reach over and grab one cookie. Then I grab another one and Josie mean mugs me. I have to hold in a growl. I am so going to tear this girl up tonight.

Lord, please get me in that room.

I smile and wave on the way out, not wanting them to think I'm leaving because I'm annoyed with Josie beating me up over some cookies. I drive my car down the street and listen to music while I scroll on my phone, waiting for Josie to tell me she's ready. I send her a text to make sure we're on the same page once ten minutes pass, and she says she's still chatting with them but about to "go to bed." I lock my car and walk down the street to the house. As I walk up, she opens her window and leans out.

"Mr. Miller, to what do I owe the pleasure?" she says, all smiles and hair and coconuts. Fucking coconuts.

"Get the hell over here," I say as I grab her face and kiss her. She lets out a small gasp and opens up for me. Our tongues chase each other, and she grabs a hold of my shirt. I pull away and rest my forehead on hers.

"You gonna let me in or what, Miss Rodriguez?"

She giggles and lowers herself back into her room. I climb in behind her. It's dim in here with a lamp on, and for the first time it seems a little more picked up, aside from the pile of clothes on her computer chair and department store bags crowding her desk.

I hear faint music coming through the wall from Joe's room, and I give Josie a questioning look. "Is that Marilyn Manson's cover of 'Sweet Dreams'? What's your brother gonna do, fuck Cora then drink her blood?"

Josie laughs and fuck, it's beautiful. She covers her mouth because it's practically a cackle at this point. "I think it's a movie they're watching about this guy who reconciles his relationship with his son when he finds out he's dying of cancer."

"Really? That's morbid. And sad. You probably read about dark shit like that," I say this as I look over at her books. She's easily got more than a hundred here.

She sits on her bed and shrugs as a response. Then she smirks.

"You totally do," I say as I creep toward the bed. Her hands walk her back farther onto the bed until she's completely on it, laid back and holding herself up on her elbows.

"It's called dark romance. I may…dabble in it." She's biting her bottom lip and looking at me with wonder. She has no idea what I'm gonna do next because we have never been in this situation. On a bed. By ourselves.

I kneel on the bed, hovering over her, then lower myself to whisper in her ear, "You read some filthy shit, I bet."

She lets out a whimper and I feel her rub her legs together. *Fuck, this girl will be the death of me.*

"I don't know what the fuck dark romance is, and I'm not sure I wanna know, but there are a few things I want to know." I nibble on her neck.

I see the movement on her throat when she audibly swallows. She's nervous. I wonder how often she's been in this situation. I want to know who she's been with and how, but those aren't the questions I have for her.

"What do you want to know?" Her voice is shaky.

"I wanna know… is this okay?" I hook one finger in the front of her tank top to lower it some. She starts to nod senselessly so I continue to bring it farther down. Her eyes are fixed on her own cleavage, and when they meet mine, a "yes" slips from her lips. It's so low, I almost miss it.

I'm kneeling between her legs now with the back of

her thighs resting on the front of mine. I adjust myself to sit up more so I can use both hands to pull her top even farther down to the point that it brings some of her bra down with it, and now she's spilling out of the cups of her bra, rose-colored half-moons peeking out at me. My mouth waters at the sight before me. I've never seen anything more perfect than my girl in this vulnerable position, with her hair haloing around her head and her sweet parted mouth.

I clear my throat because let's be honest, I don't know who is more nervous here, me or her. I'm about to ask her if I can kiss her perfect nipples and completely free them, but I think I already know my answer as she bucks her hips up once, then twice, as I start to lower myself down.

"Is this okay?"

"Yes, please," she practically moans, and I can't help but lower my forehead to her neck and chuckle.

"What," she pleas, grabbing my head in her hands. "Why are you laughing?"

"I'm sorry, baby, you can't say yes if you don't even know what I'm asking yet."

"Wes, come on. I trust you to do whatever you want. Wherever you want." Her eyes are stuck on mine.

Down, boy! My head up here tells my head down there.

"Josie," I kiss her, first a peck then with tongue for a second because shit, she's driving me wild. "You have no idea, I would love—God, I feel like an idiot right now. I'd kill to go all the way with you tonight, but I don't want to rush things." I grab her hands and hold them up to kiss them.

She releases a hand and reaches down to cup my junk, pulling a groan from my throat.

"It's all I've thought about for weeks, Wes," she admits.

"You're killing me, babe."

Next thing, I know she is sitting up and tucking her amazing tits away.

No, no.. Come back! Damn, I'm an idiot.

"I have to tell you something."

"Anything, baby." I'll do anything she wants. Whatever makes her comfortable or whatever she's craving. I just want tonight to be special, whether we go all the way or not.

Being the good guy isn't always easy, I'll tell you that.

She grabs my hands, and this time she holds them in her lap, looking at me with tears in her eyes and a small smile. A smile that doesn't reach her eyes.

"I just...I need you to promise you won't freak out and you won't treat me differently." What the hell is she talking about?

"I'm not—" she puffs her cheeks out, then blows the air out. With the heels of her palms covering her eyes, she finally admits, "I'm not a virgin."

Okay. I am somewhat surprised, but it's not impossible.

"Okay. That's fine. We don't have to have sex, babe." I reach out and grab her hand, caressing it in hopes to ease the obvious stress she's harboring right now.

"I just—it was a mistake and stupid and it didn't matter. I wish it could've been you."

After looking everywhere but at me, she locks her eyes with mine. "I always imagined it would've been you."

I cut her off before she can continue, and I kiss her. I kiss her so slow it's almost painful. She places her hands on my shoulders so as to hold on and not let herself fall apart. I carefully come to a stand on my knees, not pulling away from her. I grip her waist and lift her up higher on the bed.

"Please, I want you tonight," she says with her hands tangled in my hair.

"Alright," I say as I straighten up and lift my shirt off and over my head, dropping it on the ground. "But we have rules."

"Okay." I can see the sadness dwindling down to nothing and that beautiful, bright face coming back. I need to make sure I come across clear though, I wouldn't doubt it if she regrets this asshole because he probably talked her into something she didn't want to do.

"Tell me the second you feel uncomfortable and need me to stop."

"Okay."

"If it hurts, tell me. If it reminds you of this asshole, tell me."

She nods.

"Last, I need you to know that you call the shots tonight, Josie. I need you to know that I did plan to sneak in and mess around, but I didn't plan for this."

A small smile forms on her lips and it's the sexiest thing I've seen all night.

"Tell me what you want."

Lying there, staring at me, she slowly reaches down to unbutton her jeans shorts. I help her shimmy out of them. I can't take my eyes off the dark boyshort underwear she has on. I blink when she sits up and removes her tank top, leaving her in her dark bra to match the panties. Did she know I'd catch sight of her underwear today? She lies back down and stares at me.

Then she asks a stupid question. Yes, there is a such thing as stupid questions, and here is hers: "Do you ever think of me like this?" *See, stupid.*

"Only every day since I was like fourteen," I admit while I grip my junk to ease the pressure in my raging hard-on.

She giggles and covers her face. I pull her arm away from her face, "Tell me what you want, Josie."

"I want you to do whatever it is you've dreamt of doing with me like this."

chapter twenty-two

that summer, 2015

josie

MY HEART IS BEATING against my chest at about a billion miles a minute. I knew this time was coming. I've been waiting for it. Craving it. Needing it. Needing him. My dream of having Wes as mine—in all the ways—is coming true more and more each day.

The dim lighting in my room shines on his face, masking some of my favorite features and accentuating others. Thick eyelashes blink at me while a shadow covers the chiseled jaw I know he sports.

His teeth dig into his bottom lip while his eyes watch me with hunger. I can tell he's still battling with himself about going this far, more so than before. Before he just wanted to take it slow. Now, I'm asking him to help repair me a little, only I asked in a roundabout way. I had planned to be honest with him, but I just couldn't. I don't think he would judge me, but I just feel like it'll change the mood if I tell him I was raped. I swear I will tell him one day. Just not yet.

I'm a fragile leaf under him, ready to crumble into pieces that are impossible to put back together. But I'm ready for him. He may not think so, but I know I am. I thought I'd never be ready to experience this the right way. But if anyone can put my impossible pieces back together, it's Wesley Miller. I know for me he can make the impossible possible.

His length tents the front of his basketball shorts, and for the second time tonight, I reach for him. This time he catches me by the wrist, then brings both of my hands up above my head, holding me there.

"You're a bad girl tonight, huh?"

"I want to touch you so bad," I admit.

"You'll have your turn, baby. Me first," he orders as he lowers himself, his weight crushing me in the most delicious way. His mouth finds itself back on mine, but only for a second before it's trailing down my jaw and to my neck. His hands leave mine and slide down my arms on their own separate journeys; one goes behind my head, gripping my hair, the other grasps my thigh and hikes my leg over his.

I feel him hot and hard against my center, and my hips take it upon themselves to grind against him. We both let out a moan, and his mouth frantically finds mine again.

"You locked the door?" he asks between kisses.

"Mmm, yeah," I can barely form the words.

"You gotta be quiet, alright, Josie?"

"Yes, I will," I oblige, barely taking in what he's asked.

He leaves my mouth and moves south again, kissing the swells of my breasts, igniting goosebumps in his wake. His eyes meet mine when he pulls the cup of my bra down and brings a nipple into his mouth, slightly tugging, then full-on sucking, and I almost come right then and there. My body twitches and he chuckles with his mouth full. He sucks again, letting go with a pop before moving to my other boob, as to not let her feel left out.

He leaves a trail of pecks down my stomach on his journey, and when he's level with my panties, I realize he is making himself comfortable there. I start to panic internally before I start to panic externally, quickly sitting up on my elbows. "Umm, what are you doing?"

Looking up at me for only half a second, he fingers the seam of my boyshorts and answers my question with a question, "What do you mean, what am I doing?" Now he's peppering kisses on my inner thigh. I've never gotten this far with anyone. Aside from that horrible night, I've had a few hookups, but nowhere past making out.

"Fuck, you smell good." *Oh my God, kill me now.* I'm in the most vulnerable position I've ever been, and my legs are trying to close on their own, but it's not so easy with Wes's big head in the way.

"You don't have to do this," I state, embarrassed as hell, and I'm sure he can hear the trembling in my voice.

Now, he settles himself on his elbows in between my parted legs and looks at me drunkenly, "What exactly did you think I dreamt about doing with you all these years?"

Oh.

With his hooded eyes still on mine, and his bottom lip tucked under his teeth, he presses the pad of his thumb to my underwear right over my clit and my breath hitches. He smirks and asks, "Is this okay?"

"What? Th-that you touch me?" His thumb is moving in the slowest, tiniest of circles, and *oh my God, please never let him stop.*

"That I taste you."

I respond with a moan that is completely involuntary and sounds nothing like me. A "yes" slips from my lips for the second time tonight. But this one I had no control over.

As if he were a magician, he removes my panties in no time and pockets them.

What the hell? Is he stealing my underwear? And before I know it, he spreads me with his thumbs and starts a work of sorcery down there that has my ass flying off the bed to the point that he has to hold me down. He's got one arm across my hips holding me down, one hand is busy spreading me apart while his mouth does the job of pleasing me.

I'll be honest, it feels like multiple hands are down there, but that tongue is the secret to his spell because abra-ca-fucking-dabra, I think I may actually be getting off tonight. I've heard all the horror stories of having a hard time orgasming in the hands of someone else. Hell, half the time I try to please myself I have a hard time reaching the big O. It's definitely a mental thing, too, not just the right touch. I know I usually have to be in the right mindset, and tonight there's so much on my mind, but I know Wes is experienced. He has a good idea of what to do down there. He's proving that right now as he laps me from the bottom of my slit to the top, making noises while he devours me before he flicks my little nub of nerves. I never imagined this could feel this good, and that I'd be unabashed to the point that I'm pulling my knees farther apart. And I definitely did not picture myself holding his head closer to my core—as if he could even get any closer.

Wes starts to change up his pace, slowing down right before I go over the edge. Part of me hates him for it, but the other part of me never wants this to end. I wouldn't want to experience these moments with anyone else for the first time. Hell, I only want him for all these moments at all.

Small moans escape me, and I nervously swallow when I realize I have my eyes set on the doorknob. What would I do if my brother tried to come in here? He usually doesn't, but my stomach is knotted up just thinking about it. How mad would he be at Wes? Is this something Joe would stop talking to his childhood best friend for? I shift my eyes to Wes and he's looking at me. His hand is no longer on me as his mouth is on a mission of its own, and he reaches up to hold my hand.

"Is this okay? I just want you to feel good and comfortable. And safe."

God, he's perfect. "Seriously? Um, yeah, it's good. Mmm-hmm." I'm so nervous he isn't enjoying it like I am. And why can't I stop imagining Joe barging in?

"You look worried," he says as he turns his head to face the door. "You said you locked it, right?" He gets up and I immediately feel cold and alone without him in my bed. He double checks the lock, then turns back toward me with a swagger he doesn't realize he has. He wipes his mouth with the back of his hand before climbing back on the bed and lays half his body on mine. All I can think about is the fact that his naked chest is plastered to my wet pussy.

"What's going on in that pretty head, baby?"

"I'm just nervous about my brother, but we've already had this conversation and I'm over these talks." I grab his head and pull him to me as I lean closer to kiss him. I can taste myself on him, and as weird as I imagined that would be, it's wildly erotic and has me kissing him harder. "Let's stop talking. I want you in all the ways I can have you, Wesley Miller."

He reaches down between us and slowly slides a finger down my slit and slips it in. "Goddamn, you're even wetter than you were when my mouth was on you."

He replaces one finger with two, and I'm practically riding his hand when I ask, "Please tell me you have condoms on you."

Hands on his shoulders, I feel his body shake when he chuckles and admits he's been carrying a condom around, explaining that he's never expected sex from me, but felt he couldn't leave home without one because he can't keep his hands off of me.

He withdraws his fingers and pulls himself off me again, now leaving me feeling empty. Wes drops his shorts, and holy magic wand, it's way bigger than his two fingers, that's for sure. I'm watching him in awe as he rips the foil wrapper and asks if I wanna cover him up. I do, and it's one of the sexiest things I've ever done.

This. This is the way a girl loses her virginity. This is the guy she loses it to. One she knew when he was a boy, who's now a man. A man who makes her feel beautiful and important. *And safe.*

Wes settles himself between my legs at my entrance. He leans down to kiss me while he slowly inches his way in. He stops kissing me and rests his forehead on mine.

"How is it? Are you okay? I can stop. Please tell me if you want me to stop."

"I'm good. It hurts a little but...in a good way." I open my legs wider as if to get him in farther. It burns some at first, but once he bottoms out and stays still for me, my hips start moving of their own accord.

"Okay, okay, wait." He's panting and reaches up to move hair out of my face. He kisses me, then chuckles, "I'm sorry. I just don't want to blow this. You're so tight, I can't think straight."

He takes a deep breath, then pulls himself out until it's just the tip before he slowly goes all the way in again. His eyes find mine for the millionth time tonight and I couldn't wish for anything else.

"Josie, I can't believe this. I've dreamt of having you for so long. Before it was just a fantasy. Something taboo. A girl who wasn't mine to have." With his eyes downcast on our most private parts, he slowly pumps himself in and out of me a few more times before he admits, "But now, it's different. These last few weeks have been amazing. I think about you in the morning after I wake up and I don't want to fall asleep without you on the phone. Fuck, I even think of you when I randomly wake up in the middle of the night. After dreaming about you."

I chuckle in-between moans.

"What?" he asks as he straightens one of my legs, resting my ankle on his shoulder. The position lets him hit deeper and my eyes roll back.

"I'm serious, baby. I'm fucking addicted to you. And the coconuts."

I eye him in confusion, and he starts to laugh while he fucks me. Which I've got to say is a sight to see.

"You always smell like coconuts. I gotta be careful about what scents I go for at Bath & Body Works unless I wanna sport a semi while I shop for candles."

I start to cackle, and he quickly reaches down and covers my mouth.

"Shhh! Before you get my ass kicked, gorgeous."

I calm down and he lowers my leg back to the mattress.

"Wes?"

"Baby?" he replies, and it takes a few seconds for him to tear his gaze from my boobs as they bounce with each thrust.

"Me, too. I'm addicted to you, too. I'm not surprised that I'm always on your mind because I can feel it. I'm up here on this pedestal you've placed me on, and I don't wanna get down from it."

He grasps one side of my waist and uses his other hand to rub my clit with his thumb. That coupled with his quick and even pace pushes me over the edge. The feeling takes over my whole body and I convulse underneath him. Our eyes are locked and nothing or no one could take this moment from me, from us. I don't know if it's how my nails dig into his ass, or my hips bucking, but he knows I'm coming and he joins me.

"Fuck, you're amazing," he pants. It's either a reply to what I said before or because I'm practically milking him, but his movements get jerkier and I feel him swell inside of me. The waves of ecstasy are still running through my veins, and it feels never-ending. I come down from the high with Wes's lips kissing my neck. I catch my breath and realize that was the best orgasm I've ever experienced. Better than anything I've ever given myself.

He slowly rocks into me for a little bit before he collapses on me. His sweaty body covers mine, and it's hot and cold at the same time, pebbling my arms with goosebumps. He kisses my mouth, then my cheek and my neck again before he rises off the bed and removes the condom, tying it into a knot before he tosses it into the tiny trash can in my room.

"When do you think your parents will get home?"

"I'm not sure." I check the time. "It's ten-thirty. Probably around midnight."

I get off the bed and grab pjs from my drawers and start to get dressed. "I'm gonna go to the bathroom real quick. I'll be right back."

Before letting me go, Wes comes up to me clad in his

boxers but still tenting a hard-on, and kisses me with both hands cupping my cheeks.

"Hurry back," he whispers against my lips.

I unlock the door and close it behind me, sneaking off to the bathroom wearing a smile the size of Texas on my face. I can see that the TV is still on in Joe's room from under his door. As quickly as I can, I take care of my business, (no UTIs, please) and head back to my room. I lock it again and turn to find Wes on my bed, hands behind his head, blanket up to his waist. His shirt is still off, and his gold chain shines in the moonlight.

"I can't stay long, but I wanted to cuddle some. If that's okay, I'm not ready to go yet."

I feel like a giddy schoolgirl on the inside. I crawl into bed beside him, and he molds himself into a big spoon behind me.

"You can stay on one condition."

"Anything."

"Leave after I'm asleep. Just make sure to unlock my door and shut the window."

"You got it."

We lie there and he tells me about his week, and how he submitted his applications to the university and the local community college. I tell him that I'm halfway through my reading goal for the summer. He absently caresses my shoulder and pauses in-between topics to kiss me, then goes back to drawing circles on my freckled skin. Finally, I drift to sleep and feel him whisper words I can't make out into my ear, and he ends them with a kiss to my temple.

chapter twenty-three

present day, 2022

wes

"FUCK! FUCK, FUCK, FUCKKKK!" I punch my steering wheel and yell at no one. Today has been great, amazing even. I'm pretty sure Josie liked the gifts I got her, then she accepted my request to take her out in the morning. That was the last thing I expected. She was pleasantly surprised when I took her to see Grams, and Grams was excited, too. Then we had lunch, and that brought me back to memories of our first date, but I didn't dare bring it up. We chatted throughout our time together, and I swear I'm getting through to her. *Finally!* I never imagined she'd be cool with me going to dinner with her family. Something about her was different today. She had a lighter air to her. And don't get me started on the little concert that woke me up this morning.

I even imagined I could kiss her or something tonight, but now this shit came up.

Leah Peters.

Leah and I were more acquaintances than friends in high school, but *after* high school, she and I were going down the same path, and let's just say it wasn't a path to paradise.

I was fucked up after losing Joe. For weeks Josie and I laid around mourning. Before he died, we partied a bit and I could tell the drinking was picking up, and Josie didn't love it when I'd take it too far and embarrass her or act like an idiot. After his death, Josie didn't say much about my frequent drunken state, but she never left my side. I could tell she was battling her own demons in a different way than I was.

We'd fuck all hours of the day, eat crap food, and never leave our houses, whether we were at her place or my Grams's condo at the time. Her parents picked up on the act pretty quickly, but all we did was stay at my place more. This went on for weeks, and I knew she didn't deserve it. She needed to get better, and I wasn't doing that for her.

After she left, I was really fucked up. I swore I'd clean up my act, but I continued trying to find the answers to my problems at the bottom of the bottle. Eventually, I stopped working and did nothing all day for months. I'd take Grams to whatever appointment, then drop her off at home and go out and get wasted.

One day I woke up on someone's couch to the smell of puke on my shirt. I didn't know if it was my own or not, but I'm sure it was. On my way home that morning I saw Leah walking down the street and remembered seeing her the night before at the house party. I pulled over and told her to get in. She was walking to her job at the smoothie joint, so I drove her there. She said she'd give me a free smoothie for the ride. We walked into the place, and since no customers were there, her boss started ripping her a new one before she even made it behind the counter.

She was late and he was over it. At first, he was loud, then he toned it down and you could tell he had a soft spot for her and was aware of her struggles. He told her to go to an AA meeting that morning. He told her if she kept her behavior up, he would have to fire her, but he didn't want to. Turning his focus to me and offering a sad smile, he then asked me to take her.

We got back in my car and she started to cry. I didn't know what the fuck to do. It was then that she told me she never imagined she'd be the girl who peaked in high school. I told her it wasn't true, to which she replied, "I hooked up with a guy last night just because I knew he'd have what I'd need to get me fucked up, Wes. Tell me my time didn't pass me by."

I couldn't believe it. I knew she wasn't that kind of girl, and she was just in a really dark place. Her parents had high hopes for her, and she had no idea what she wanted to do with her life. Everyone was getting scholarships to state universities, and she was rejected from her top choice and had a seat waiting for her at a community college. I didn't realize how much we had in common. This was something her parents told her they couldn't fathom as the start of a future for their daughter.

After she cried and wiped her tears, she asked how

I'd been holding up ever since Joe died, and then I broke down. It was my turn to cry. Something I rarely did. I told her how it happened and what that night was like, and how I let that night take away my best friend, and eventually, the love of my life.

After that initial AA meeting, we were going three times a week. Slowly, the classes decreased for us, going twice a week, then once a week. Finally, I was at once a month, while Leah was still attending weekly. Today, seven years later, she still goes on a regular basis. We promised we would always be each other's sponsors, and if anything ever came up, we had each other to call. I don't go as much anymore. Occasionally, I join Leah to support her, but it's been awhile. I've been sober over four years now.

I relapsed once. It had been one of those weeks where Grams was in the hospital from blowing out her knee, I was overworking myself and burning out, and I swear remnants of Joe and Josie were everywhere. A song on the radio brought me back to parties with Joe, and I'd run into Josie's coconut scent that would creep up out of nowhere at random times of the day. I just wanted to not feel the pain. I didn't want to reach out to Leah like I should have, I didn't want her to think I was weak when I was always so strong and present for her. One beer turned into two, which turned into another with a shot, and before I knew it I walked the two miles home and woke up feeling like shit. The hangover was nowhere near the guilt.

Leah has only been sober for two years now...she's relapsed more than once and has called me countless times. I don't mind being there for her, I never will. But of all the days, today is not the one.

I'm on my way to her apartment because she was overwhelmed at work this week and says she had a long phone conversation with her mom. I fucking hate her parents. They talk her down any chance they get, and never praise her when she's done a kick ass job these last couple years. She's kept her job, advancing in it even. She has her own apartment and car. She's doing great, but she'll never see it like that as long as her parents have anything to say.

My other issue is, I don't know what to expect. You see, when we hit two months of being sober, we decided to celebrate for the special occasion. We went out for a movie and then got some ice cream. The night gave off date vibes, but we were such good friends at that time, it was the last thing on my mind.

Until I drove her home.

Leah had just moved out to separate herself from her parents and had gotten herself set up in a little studio apartment. She invited me in because I thought about getting a similar place on my own once Grams went into her assisted living facility. She took me on a tour, showing me the pool and the lounge area that had a small theater and computers for guests to use. She unlocked her door and let me in. The place was small but livable for someone on their own. I sat on her Futon, and she plopped next to me with a bottle of water. Handing it to me, we unintentionally made eye contact. We didn't lose that eye contact. And before I knew it, the water bottle was nowhere to be seen and Leah was in my lap, straddling me.

My thoughts instantly went to Josie. And it was because of that face, those freckles, her big hair, the hitch in her breath whenever I'd kiss the spot under her ear—it was because of Josie herself that I grabbed Leah's face and kissed the hell out of her.

I had celebrated my first month sober on my own by going to see Josie. I wanted to apologize and tell her I was cleaning up my act when I saw her with her boyfriend at the time. The scene gutted me, and with Leah on my lap a month later, I knew I had to move on. I didn't feel like I was over Josie at all. I'd never be over Josie, but I'd do anything to ease the ache in my chest.

You can say Leah and I became fuck buddies except we weren't. It ended just as quickly as it started. Somehow the more we got sober, the more things started changing for us and we started drifting apart. Her boss saw the growth in her and gave her more hours and more responsibility, eventually promoting her to assistant manager. I started taking classes for my personal training certificate and getting promoted at Pump House as well. But we still see each other when we need to. It's rare now, but at first, those get-togethers, which were few and far between, only ended up with us bumping uglies and parting ways before the night was over a couple of times.

It's been years now since I slept with Leah, but for the first time I hope to God it's not what she's looking for tonight because it's not going to happen.

Not now, and especially not on Josie's birthday.

chapter twenty-four

present day, 2022

josie

I'M SITTING in my bed reading with a pile of used makeup wipes beside me and my childhood blanket in my lap. It's practically a rag now since it's over twenty years old. I keep it under my pillow and don't typically pull it out until moments like these. Somehow the familiar texture of the fabric brings me comfort and helps ease my anxiety. Otherwise, I just need to know it's under my pillow every night.

I drop the book in my lap and rub my temples. I've read the same damn page four times now. I can't stop thinking about Wes. And Joe. I tried to ignore thoughts about him all day, and it's like they've bottled themselves up. My parents even avoided bringing Joe up which breaks my heart. They shouldn't do that. It's wrong, but they know I never handled talks about him well. It doesn't mean they can't remember him. Even still, I didn't have the guts to bring him up.

My mind is spinning at the thought that something happened to Wes tonight. I'm almost convinced someone else I care for will be taken away sooner than they should be. Being unable to reach Wes is nerve-wracking. I have no idea what happened. I never heard from him again after those texts, and I even tried calling him in the car after dinner to make sure he was okay.

Nothing.

No answer, no reply.

Nothing.

So here I am trying to distract my sickening thoughts with a steamy romance, and it's not happening. As soon as I got home, I started to tiptoe to my room to avoid Cassie and Brandon. I don't want to have to explain my mood or the fact that it's even my birthday or anything. I know that as soon as she finds out she missed my birthday, she's going to feel guilty for not planning anything, even just a night out. But I don't want that. And it's not her fault I never informed her of my special day.

Luckily, the apartment was empty and I didn't need to sneak around. I changed into some leggings and an oversized tee before I crawled into bed with my book and wiped the makeup off my face. I pick my book back up to give it another try when a quick knock on my bedroom door is followed by Wes barging in.

"Josie! I'm sorry! I'm so fucking sorry," he pants with his hands on his hips and his head hanging low. His black Henley stretches across his chest and his dark jeans hug his thick thighs. It seems ridiculous, but he's gotta have a tailor because this outfit is molded to him.

He takes a few deep breaths before he continues, "I–I got a call from a friend who needed some help and then my phone died. I usually have a charger in my truck, but I left it at work last week. I even drove to the restaurant, and they said you had just left."

His heavy breathing has me thinking he sprinted up the stairs to the apartment just as fast as he sprinted through that story. "I wanted nothing more than to be at that dinner." His eyes are on me.

I toss the book and the blanket that covers my legs to the side and run to him. Throwing my arms around him, I breathe in his scent. Forever could separate us and I'd still be able to pick out his smell in a lineup.

He's wrapped up in my hug, but he holds a breath and doesn't move a bit. Like he's scared to touch me, like he's scared to breathe.

"I was so scared. I thought," I pull my head back and look up at him, "I thought something happened to you."

Wes finally releases that breath and pulls me back to him. He clutches me to his chest as if it's the first chance he's gotten to hold me after letting me go. As if he's in fear of losing me again.

"I'm here, baby. I'm so sorry."

"I'm just glad you're okay."

"You know I wanted to be with you and your parents, right?"

"I do."

"I'm so pissed my phone died and I didn't expect my friend to need me for that long."

I look up at him again. His ocean eyes peer back at me, and it breaks me. I remember they used to be brighter. A bright, light brown full of life would cut through the mix of blues and greens. Now, the brown is dark and dull and sad. I'm about to tell him to stop apologizing, that I don't care how long he was gone or that he had to choose his friend over me. That all that matters is that he is here and living and breathing. In my arms.

But before I get to tell him, he kisses me. *God, does he kiss me.*

His lips hold onto my own and I feel it zing through my body. I grip his biceps to hold myself steady, and he quickly steals my next breath when we open up at the same time and his tongue invades my mouth. He's still kissing me when he squats a little to grab me by the backs of my thighs and pick me up. As though it were second nature, I wrap my legs around his waist, feeling his hardness against me. A whimper I didn't mean to let out vibrates on his tongue and draws a deep groan out of his throat.

One hand grasps my ass, and the other reaches back to feel for the bed. Once he knows he's safe to sit, he does. He brings his hands to my hips, fingers pressing into me, and I pray they bruise me because I need proof of this later in case I think it's some sort of dream. I grind myself against his cock with too many layers between us. His lips leave mine aching and work their way to the spot below my ear that he knows I love.

His hands are all over my thighs when a finger slips into a hole in the inner thigh of my leggings.

Oh my God. No. My heart rate had increased as a result of that kiss, but now it's taken a turn feeling more like a heart attack. My face is heating up from the embarrassment. I forgot I was wearing these leggings. The hole appeared two washes ago, and damn my thunder thighs. I'm totally okay not having a thigh gap, but the fact that my girls are BFFs and constantly rubbing means there's always an end to the lifetime of my leggings or jeans.

He smiles against my neck before pulling away and fingering the tear. "I don't think this easy access is meant to be here, but I'm so okay with it."

I cover my face. "I keep meaning to toss these."

My clit pulses at his deep chuckle before he offers to help me with my problem. "I think I can lend a helping hand." Now he's got two fingers in the slit and he nips at my earlobe before he whispers, "May I?"

I bite my lip and nod my head.

He leans back, eyes between my legs. His focused look oozes sex off of him, and he pulls apart at the seam, tearing the hole across my entire inner thigh. Now, the rip goes up to my crotch, but he doesn't stop. He keeps pulling the fabric apart until my other thigh is completely bare. He narrows in on my (now wet) panties. They're black and lacy, and I hear him curse under his breath.

He rubs his hand across his jaw and looks between my face and my barely covered pussy. He is contemplating what to do next, and I am at a loss myself. I want to ride him, his face and his dick. I throb at the thought of it.

But then I also know I can't give in completely to Wes right now. It would be unhealthy for me. For us. I'll be obsessed with him. I'll practically move into his room, and we would be inseparable. But we aren't teenagers anymore. Everything is different now. We can't forget about the world the way we did last time.

"Alright, Josie. You gotta tell me what you want because I'm about to go nuts here. I don't want to cross any lines...at least ones I haven't already." He looks at me, almost terrified. "I can't lose you before I've even gotten you back."

"No sex," I blurt out faster than I mean to. "Believe me, I want to do more but...I, I don't know. Can we just continue what we were doing? Before you decided to shred my pants."

He laughs and grips my inner thighs before he leans in to kiss me again. Our tongues dance and his hands move all over my thighs and hips and ass before he starts to guide me, riding him at a steady rhythm. The friction between the lace and his jean-clad length feels like a dream. I'm somewhat embarrassed that I'm gonna soak through onto his pants, but I don't care because I know he loves it. At least the Wes I knew all those years ago loved it.

"Fuck, yeah. Ride me, baby," he orders. "Shit, I'm gonna be coming like a virgin soon, and I'm not even in you."

He releases his hold some to let me take over the grinding on my own. His eyes are glued to my bare skin, and when I start to lean down toward him, they shoot up to meet mine. His gaze takes me back. It brings a confidence over me that I'm not used to, but it's valid. I feel sexy and in control. I could ask him to fulfill my greatest fantasy and I know he'd do it on his knees.

My ex, Wyatt, could never make me feel this way. Wes worshiped me from day one. Wyatt was sweet and I know he was attracted to me, but it was nothing like Wes. He wouldn't lose control and need me. Wyatt had me as a convenience. Wes made it a point to appreciate me—every inch of me.

I whisper into his ear, giving in to the overwhelming confidence, "Won't be the first time." His laugh shudders between us. In a swift movement, he flips us so that he's on top and settles himself between my legs.

"That was one time." He holds up a finger, "One time!" Chuckling against my lips, he goes in for a kiss as I reminisce.

My parents had rented a beach condo for a week and Wes stayed with us. We couldn't spend much time together as we were sneaking around and there was no way my parents would ever allow the boys to room with the girls. We spent the morning out at the pool and in the sun. After we came in for sandwiches, my parents and Joe went back out to the water. I think Cora was with us that day, but she could have been working. I'm not sure. Either way, she would have gone back out with Joe. She was as infatuated with him as I was with Wes.

I told them I didn't want to go back out to the beach yet, and Wes said he had to call his grandma. He did, in fact, call her. He was sitting out on the balcony finishing up his phone call when I stepped out to join him. I sat on his lap, the heat from his bare chest on my back welcomed me. Before he hung up I started making small circles with my ass in his lap. I'd felt him harden up the second I sat down, and it only encouraged me to start moving. I remember he bit my shoulder as soon as he got off the phone call. He reached around and squeezed my boobs and told me he missed me. His roughness had me grinding harder, and as much as I was into the thrill of the fact that anyone could see us, I glanced over to look out to my family and make sure no one was looking this way. My dad carried around binoculars on the beach, and the sight of us would send him into cardiac arrest.

As I looked out, I bent over with my ass up in the air. Wes grabbed a handful, and to mess with him I started dancing in his lap, trying to be funny. Until I felt him hold me down with a hand on my hip and jerky thrusts, followed by a groan told me all I needed to know.

Wes snaps me out of my memory when he breaks the kiss. "I was eighteen and my smokeshow of a girlfriend, whom I had to hide from the world, was twerking against my dick. After I hadn't had her for days. And I knew we didn't have much time."

"It's okay, I get it. I was a smokeshow, huh?"

"Fuck, babe," he says with a single thrust against my wet heat. "You're still a smokeshow. You'll always be a smokeshow."

He sits up and his fingers curl over the waistband of my tattered leggings, pulling them down and off.

"No point in those anymore." He throws them over his shoulder.

chapter twenty-five

present day, 2022

wes

HER LEGS. *Fuck.* They kill me.

My weakness has always been Josie's legs, and her coconut scent. And now they're wrapped around my waist, her ankles locked against my lower back, and I groan at the feeling I've been missing for years. I took off her leggings that I'd ripped apart, and let me just say, that was the hottest thing I've ever done with a woman. Although, it wasn't so much the act that turned me on as the way she watched me do it in awe. Her mouth fell open, her eyes hooded, and I could smell the arousal she had pooling in her panties. Don't even get me started on the sight of her in those underwear. My new goal for the night is to steal them like I did the first night we were together.

The second I pulled off those leggings and got that familiar scent of my girl, I had to rush straight to the upper half of the bed and kiss her. If not, I knew I'd find myself ripping her panties, too, then tasting her, which would lead to fucking her because it's been too damn long.

She's kissing me back, our tongues chasing each other, and I'm grateful. I hoped she'd cave and take me back, but I would have never imagined it would be this soon.

And I have no idea what to think of what's going on. I can't tell myself that she's *taken me back* because she hasn't. For all I know she's going to regret it in the morning and never come near me again. I nuzzle myself into her neck, shaking away these thoughts, and her hands grasp the back of head, holding me there. I nibble on the delicate skin and follow it with light sucking while we dry hump like teenagers. I won't complain though, dry humping is like heaven when your cock is rubbing between the legs of Josie Rodriguez. Her hair tickling the side of my face, her scent surrounding me, the little whimpering sounds she's making, I could die a happy man right now.

"Okay, yeah. Don't stop," she cries, and I know she's close.

I keep rocking at the same rhythm for her, but push a little harder against her core to increase the pressure when I lift my head from her neck to watch her.

"Open your eyes, baby." Her eyes shoot open and her breaths become erratic.

The sexiest noise leaves her parted lips, and she even mixes my name in there. I'm on cloud fucking nine. Her jerky movements speak for themselves, and I can't take my eyes off of hers. I grasp her jaw with the free hand that's not gripping her bare hips and kiss her. Against her lips I whisper, "You're perfect. Better than I remember." I peck her on the nose while she looks at me like she used to. Like I hung the fucking moon, then named every star after her.

Crawling back off the bed and coming to a stand, I adjust my aching dick into the waistband of my jeans. I'm so hard right now that if I stood outside people would think I was directing traffic. Looking up, I catch her watching me with wonder.

"What?" I say with a smirk because I want to just jump back in and watch her orgasm again.

"Did you...you know?"

"Did I what?" Now I'm full-on grinning.

She giggles and sits up, curling her legs under herself with a cute little eye roll.

"Did I come?" I chuckle and lean over toward her. "I'm not that eighteen-year-old jerk anymore." The one who didn't know how lucky he was and how quick he could lose everything. I reach over and run a finger down her jaw. "When I come, you won't question it. And believe me when I say the next time I come won't be until this cock is back in that pussy where it belongs."

I'm scared I went too far, and I'm terrified of unintentionally pushing her away, but I'm not kidding with her. I won't take it back. I swear I won't even touch myself until I've fully won her back.

It's not until I'm almost at her door that I realize I just walked away. I turn around and come back, pulling at the back of my neck as I nervously clear the air. "Once again, I'm sorry about dinner tonight."

She shrugs and her somewhat frown I left her with turns into a smirk.

"But I have to run this by you because it's a special offer that won't last long." Her head tilts in confusion at my attempt to lighten the mood. "Tonight only, my bedroom door will be left open and welcome to anyone celebrating a birthday today. And if you decide to stop by within the next half hour, you can sleep in my bed." I hold a hand up by my mouth for show and whisper, "I have really good sheets."

Josie laughs and rolls her eyes at me.

"But wait, that's not all!" I continue in my best infomercial voice, "If you come in within the next ten minutes, I'll let you be little spoon so your ass cheeks can hug my–" A pillow flies at my head and I chuckle while she yells at me to leave.

I walk backward to exit the room with my hands up. "Remember, tonight only, and it has to still be your birthday." I wink before I turn and head to my room.

I clean myself up and brush my teeth before I get into bed in a pair of boxer-briefs.

I sit in bed, my room illuminated by the bedside lamp, hoping she'll come in. I feel like the biggest jerk for my decisions today. Granted, Leah did need me. I'm glad sex didn't come up, which isn't a surprise because it's been so long since we were together. But knowing I am finally on good terms with Josie has me nervous that the least little thing will mess that up.

I have to still tell Josie that I'm friends with Leah. I know they never got along, but that's high school shit that shouldn't matter anymore. I'm not ready to tell her yet, though. Everything between us is too sensitive and new.

A light knock at my door pulls me out of my thoughts, and I look over to see Josie standing at my door. Messy bun, same oversized shirt, but now she's in these tiny cotton shorts that have donuts all over them. I open up my arms. "You made it," I check the time on my phone, "Oh, no! It's been over ten minutes, but it's okay since it's still your birthday. I'll let it slide this time…you can be little spoon."

"You're an ass," she says with a smile on her face, walking toward my bed after she's shut my door.

I hold open my blanket and she climbs in, but instead of snuggling, she curls up on her side and faces me from the other side of the bed. I mirror her position.

"How was your birthday, gorgeous?"

She stares at me for a while before answering. I'm dying to know what's on her mind.

"I'd have to say…seven-point five out of ten."

"Not bad, not bad."

"I'm still glad you're okay."

I reach across the bed to tuck a lock of hair behind her ear.

"How was dinner?"

"Delicious, but awkward. They had no issue with you not making it, but it was as if they were walking on eggshells. They didn't mention Joe once, and it's pretty obvious that I've hurt them so much over the years."

"Don't look at it that way."

"They had to bury their son. Can you imagine? They were young when my mom was pregnant with us, and

I'm sure everything was scary and exciting, and having us was their greatest blessing. Almost the second we turn eighteen and ready to go out into the world he gets taken away from them. And they can't even grieve properly for him because of me."

"He was your twin, Josie. Of course, it's gonna be tough for you."

"Yeah…" she responds but I know she's not here.

"Are you okay…with what happened tonight?"

She looks up at me and a smile spreads over her face, "You mean what just happened like fifteen minutes ago?" I nod. "Yes, I'm okay with it. I missed it. I missed you."

"I know, I'm pretty good," I joke, earning me a punch to the shoulder from her. "I'm kidding, it reminded me of that summer. In the back of my truck."

She covers her face and laughs, "Oh no! I was so nervous. We ended up being so late to meet up with Joe and Cora. I don't know how they didn't figure us out by then." Before I correct her, she jolts up with her cute little serious-thinking face on, "Wait, do you mean the time you pulled the seat down and…you know?"

It's my turn to laugh. "Considering I didn't just devour you or fuck you, I was talking about our first date. But don't worry, babe, I think of all the times in my truck often."

A soft blush takes over her cheeks.

"How is Cora?" I ask because if we start talking about past sexcapades, I'm going to want to touch her again.

"She's good. She's doing great with the hotel, but I

know she still struggles sometimes, too. You seem like you've handled everything so well."

"That's not true, I still have my moments," I admit.

"I think everything was just so good. Then it was like the ground below me disappeared."

"That's how it was for all of us. I try to tell myself that Joe would be pissed if I dwelled on the fact that he's gone."

Then she looks up at me with tears in her eyes, threatening to spill but holding on.

"I feel like it should've been me."

I reach out and pry her hands from under her head and hold them between us. "You can't think like that, babe. I don't know what I would've done if it was you. Joe would never have let it be you."

A single tear spills out.

"You keep saying *babe* like I'm still yours."

You are.

"Will you hold me like I still am?"

I'm speechless and I can't take my eyes off of her. I don't understand how she thinks she's not my girl. She'll always be mine. She can shatter my heart and give hers to another man, and even though it would gut me, I'd still never deny she's mine.

I don't answer her with words, but I reach my arm out and adjust her position, pulling her close to me. I reach back to turn off my lamp, then spoon her, making it a point that we are touching in every way possible. I hold her as tight as I can while her body shakes in cries. I hold her until she calms down and her breathing evens out. I whisper a happy birthday in her ear and fall asleep minutes later.

josie

It's hot. So hot. Like I'm sleeping with a furnace against my back. I blink a few times, taking in Wes's dark room, and peer down to see his thick, inked forearm gripping my waist. He holds me in his sleep like he's scared I'll run away.

I have no idea what time it is, but it's pitch black out as I can see the moon watching us through his blinds. I want to reach out and grab his phone to check the time, but I don't want to wake him.

I stir a little with thoughts of our conversation before we fell asleep. I didn't mean to cry. He told me it was okay to cry earlier in the day, but I tried my best not to. I didn't cry after the awkward dinner with my parents, or even over the fact that Wes didn't make it.

I mentally facepalm because how could I forget Wes ripping my leggings apart and humping out one of the best orgasms I've had in a while. Just reminiscing about it has me rubbing my legs together. Wes thrusts once against my ass, and I'm not sure if he's awake or if it was in his sleep, but my nipples pucker in response.

Maybe waking him up won't be the worst idea.

I push my ass back against him. He already seems

harder than he was a second ago. His grip tightens around my waist, and a small moan leaves my throat. He responds with his own guttural sound that sings to my pussy. I turn around to face him, and his eyes are still closed but a smirk sits on his lips.

"What are you trying to do, baby?" His deep, throaty voice could have me coming from the sound alone.

"I can't sleep," I whisper.

He finally opens his eyes, but they go straight to my mouth.

"Want me to put you to sleep?" The hand that was around my waist travels down to my ass and he grabs a handful. I giggle and he interrupts my laugh with his strong arms adjusting us so I'm under him as he settles between my legs. His lips find mine and here we are, eighteen all over again.

"I promise I won't fuck you," he says between kisses, "but I need you."

He starts to work his way down my body, bunching up my shirt and kissing all over my stomach. My breathing is picking up, and inside I'm fist pumping because I know what's coming. Me. I'll be coming any–

I squeal when he grabs my ass, pulls me up to his face and growls, shaking his face against my covered pussy. "I miss this so much."

I can barely breathe. Part of me wonders if he is still asleep because I don't know where his mind is at, but I'm here for it.

He starts tugging my shorts and panties off, and once they're gone, he tells me, "You're going to sleep like a baby when I'm done with you, Josie."

He goes down on me, and it's just like he used to. He licks me from top to bottom, spending most of his time between flicking my clit and circling it slower than anything I could have ever imagined. My head thrashes from side to side, and it takes so much for me to keep quiet. All I need is for Cassie and Brandon to hear us.

Wes uses two fingers to fuck me, sending a gasp out of me when he first thrusts them in. And when he curls those expert digits of his, hitting the spot I swear he has a special map to, he looks up at me with hooded eyes. "I'm obsessed with your pussy, baby. It's been too long." He talks to me like I'm not clear on my way to heaven from his fingers and his tongue. Wes brings his head back down, then pulls his index and middle finger out, leaving me feeling empty yet still almost overstimulated by all the work his tongue is putting into rocking me to sleep. A wet trail from his hand works its way up my torso as he reaches up to tweak and pull on my right nipple. Looking down, I find his eyes on me while he devours me whole. I notice his other hand is gripping his cock, which is covered in athletic shorts. The craving to reach for him comes and goes just as quickly when he sucks on my clit, making me fall over the edge.

My head drops back on the pillow and my body convulses against him as I hold his head against me, unable to control my actions. The white hot heat runs through my whole body. No one has been able to do this to me that wasn't Wes. My arms fall to my sides, and I'm comatose as he trails kisses up my body and ends at my mouth where I taste myself on him and, once again, just like all those years ago, I don't even care.

"Sweet dreams, baby."

I fall asleep as he gets up and goes to his bathroom.

I wake up to the sun shining down on me and Wes spread out in his bed. We are both on our stomachs, and his arm is draped across my back. A smile creeps on my face as I remember last night. I'm giddy and stretch some, half of me wants to leave him asleep, and the other half thinks it won't be horrible if he wakes up with me again.

I reach over for his phone to check the time.

I'm surprised to see how late it is…it's after ten AM, but I don't care like I typically would at waking after nine in the morning. I'm more surprised to see the text notification, a text that has my stomach dropping. I quickly roll out from under his arm and look around, only finding my shorts. *Fuck it.* I decide I'll go commando and get out of his room as quickly as humanly possible while trying to forget what I just read on his phone screen.

Leah: Thanks for coming over last night.

chapter twenty-six

that summer, 2015

wes

JOSIE. She's all that's on my mind. Every fucking second of the day. Groceries with Grams: don't forget snacks for Josie when she comes over. Video games with Joe: is she around? Does she hear him cussing me out from the other room? Then, of course, there's during showers, I can't remember the last time I skipped one. Even now, working with Joe at Home Depot, I find any excuse to ask about her.

We are halfway through our fourth shift together since I started last week, and today they have us in the Garden Center moving around a shit ton of house plants. Without even realizing, I bring Josie up.

"You should get one of these for Josie."

"Why?"

"Isn't she into houseplants?"

"Hmm," he thinks about it and I'm nervous she's maybe only told me she wants to start getting into greenery. "Oh, my aunt Leila is into gardening and shit so it would make sense that she would be into plants and flowers." *Phew.*

"If her secret boyfriend doesn't buy her one first."

I shoot my attention toward him, worried he has an inkling I've been playing hide the salami with his twin sister.

"Oh, I uh," I pull at my neck, then quickly drop my hand trying to hide my obvious nerves. "I didn't know she had a boyfriend."

"Well, either that or she has a new hobby she's keeping from us. She's always running off to do secret shit, and sometimes she's lied about it. She tells me she's with Cora when…I'm with Cora. Doesn't add up."

Damn, we're being sloppy as hell.

"All I know is this asshole better be treating her right. Hey!" He smacks my arm and my stomach drops. It would be tough to tell who would win in a fight between me and Joe. He is taller but lankier than I am. I've got a broader chest and bulkier arms. But I'd let him kick my ass. It's the least I could do when I've been using Grams's "bingo night" as an excuse to actually be feasting in-between his sister's legs.

I snap out of my thoughts and wait for his fist to meet my face when he says, "We should follow her. She won't notice your car like she would mine."

"Nah, we don't have to do that."

"Why not, man? Watch it be someone we know who is fucking with her. She doesn't know these guys like we do."

"Your sister is smart."

"She is, but I don't know. I feel this need to take care of her. I'm guilty for not being the protective brother I should have been before."

"I think she forgives you, man." I hang the last basket of pothos and grab the now-empty cart to go back and grab more plants to bring out here. "She is cool with you dating Cora, and she seems better when we all hang out."

He follows me. "Yeah, you're right. I know what I'll do."

"You do?" This will be great.

"Yeah, I'll tell her to bring him to Sunday dinner. And you're coming. I need you to have my back if it's some douchebag we know."

Can't freaking wait.

josie

I told Wes not to worry about tonight's dinner. Joe insisted I invite my secret boyfriend, and we know that would be an interesting family meal so I turned down his request. But he's not buying it and he's brought it up every day this week.

Wes didn't like my original plan of paying one of my co-workers to come over and play fake boyfriend. He said something along the lines of, "I'd rip his arms off of his body if you two so much as bump shoulders."

Dramatic.

When Wes suggested I make up a new hobby that I'd gotten involved with, I didn't even waste time thinking of one because I'm a horrible liar.

And imagine Wes's face when I said, "Let's tell him the truth?"

He lifted his head from my neck where he was licking and nipping and quickening my pulse to say, "You've lost your mind, baby."

So, my "secret boyfriend" is going to piss my brother off even more because he's going to cancel at the last minute.

I'm sitting on the floor, flat ironing the last of my hair when my phone vibrates.

Wes: I'm here, in Joe's room. WYD?
Josie: You don't wanna know.
Wes: ?
Josie: I can't pick an outfit.
Josie: So…
Wes: So?
Josie: So…I'm not wearing anything yet…

It's a lie. I'm in a hunter green t-shirt dress. He says he loves the way the green complements my skin tone. I'm skipping panties, but not telling him about that just yet.

It sounds crazy but Wes has awakened my sexual soul. I went from nearing a panic attack when a guy was within three feet of me, to replaying the way my skin prickles every time he runs a finger up my thigh. I think

Wes being who he is made it that much easier to get physical with him. Now, we can't be in each other's vicinity without making contact, whether it's our pinkies touching in the backseat of Joe's car, a quick ass grab when we meet in the kitchen of my house, or when I practically climb him like a tree in the rare event that we are alone.

I'm waiting for him to reply to my text when I hear the click of my door. I see the brim of his hat first as he has it on backward and is facing the hall. He squeezes himself into my room, trying to be as sneaky as possible, and finally turns around and looks down at me. I'm hit with his ocean eyes, dimples, and a panty-dropping smile. Why is it like I'm seeing him for the first time every time?

"You little liar!" He squats behind me and practically tackles me from behind.

My straightener is off since I'm done with my hair, but it's still hot so I hold it up and away from us. "Careful, you're gonna burn yourself!" I say between giggles.

"Joe thinks I'm in the bathroom. He won't shut up about this boyfriend of yours." He talks to my reflection in the mirror.

"Oh, really? Well, *this boyfriend* just canceled on me. That fucker. I'll make him pay later."

"Oh, yeah?"

"Mm-hmm." I hum as I adjust the top of my dress. Completely unnecessary, but I love my power over him because his eyes are glued to my cleavage.

"What's he…" he trips on his words, "How're you gonna charge him?"

"I don't know. I'm thinking I'll have him take me out for dessert?" I turn around and flip his hat forward, pulling it down and practically covering his sight as I stand up and head to my makeup bag on my dresser across the room. "Or maybe I'll have him *have me* for dessert."

He almost knocks off his hat as he adjusts it, getting up and following me to my dresser. "He will most definitely pay up. And drop a fat tip." He chuckles into my neck as he grips my hips from behind.

I laugh and turn around, pushing him away, "Stop!"

He drops a peck on my lips and looks me up and down. "You look gorgeous, by the way. This dinner isn't going to be easy, is it?"

"You'll be fine. I've got it all taken care of."

"Says the girl who can't lie. Well, aside from that text, I've never run out to the bathroom so fast."

"I promise. We're good. Now get out. I'm almost ready, and my brother is gonna start looking for you." He kisses me again and heads toward the door.

"See you soon," he says before he opens the door.

I run up behind him, my nerves getting the best of me. "Let me make sure the coast is clear." I open the door and look up and down the hallway, Wes's hand resting on my lower back. No one is in sight, so I drop a peck on his right dimple and send him on his way.

I don't shut the door and hear my brother down the hallway as soon as Wes gets back to his room. "What'd you do? Drop a loaf in the bathroom?" *Gross.*

Josie: Good thing you got outta here quick. I

don't think I'm even gonna have time to put panties on.

Seconds later I hear Wes coughing from Joe's room and Joe asking if he's alright.

Wes: This will be the hardest—pun intended—dinner ever. Zero stars. Do not recommend.

wes

"He got called into work," Josie explains, her voice dripping in annoyance.

"Okay. Where does he work?" Joe says before he stuffs his mouth and gives her a closed-mouth smile.

Cora, who arrived right as we were sitting at the table for dinner, nudges Joe as if to say, knock it off.

Josie scoffs before she replies, "You know what I love about all this? I. Don't. Have. To. Tell. You."

"Does this guy not realize how rude it is to cancel on a dinner the first time he meets your family?" He mocks, then continues, "Piece of work."

"I already said it was a work emergency. And you know what? He's dating me, not my family, so get over it." Josie's face and chest is starting to grow red and blotchy, signs she is heated with her twin.

Their dad looks at me with raised eyebrows. I mirror

his look and reach over to take a drink of water. We've all been watching them go back and forth like a game of ping-pong.

"Enough, kids. Respect your mother's cooking. No need for this fighting," their dad demands with his elbows on the table, wiping his mouth with a napkin. Mario Rodriguez…the guy wouldn't kill a fly, but he scares the shit out of me. Always has. Looking at him, he isn't too intimidating. He and Isabel are a bit unusual as he's a little on the heavier side, and unlike Joe, who's over six foot, is shorter than his wife. Isabel, on the other hand, is obviously where Josie gets her looks from. For sure a babe in her day. Mario got lucky.

But piss the man off—like the time Joe and I added soap to the hot tub and invited girls over when they were gone one weekend visiting Josie—his eyebrows meet and his mustache seems to grow in those moments. Scary shit.

Mario pops the bubble I'm floating in and directs his focus to me. "Wes, how's your summer going? And your grandmother? Any secret girlfriends?"

I choke on my water while Josie looks over at me with wide eyes. Coughing into my fist, I answer him as best as I can, waving a hand around. "No. No, sir. All is well. My grandmother is fine. Thanks for asking."

"I personally think it would be great if Josie and Wes were the ones secretly dating," Isabel states, and now would be a good time for a meteor to hit the Rodriguez's dinner table.

"I second that," Cora mumbles to herself, but we

hear it plain as day. She yelps when, I assume, Josie kicks her under the table.

"Can we not have this conversation?" Josie pleas, trying to hide behind her blush. We make eye contact and break it just as fast.

Joe is seated next to me, so he uses our close proximity to his advantage and grasps my shoulder in warning. "My boy knows better than to do that."

I cringe and shoot him a tight-lipped smile. This dinner is going worse than I expected. I should've gone with the idea of Josie's co-worker playing her boyfriend.

Nah, just thinking about it makes me want to squeeze the asshole's throat until his eyes bulge out like those Panic Pete squeeze toys. I don't even know the guy.

Cora pipes up to my advantage this time by changing the subject and announces her dad's new position as a general manager of a hotel on the Las Vegas Strip where he lives. I finally let out a breath of relief as this causes an in-depth conversation of Cora's family (her parents are divorced, but she seems to have a healthy relationship with both of them). It also springs a memory of when Isabel and Mario went to Vegas during the winter in the 90s and he tried to drive her to the mountains, but they never made it due to the snow. Floridians, we don't snow well.

The outside of my left thigh rubs against the outside of Josie's right one, just enough for the hem of her dress to rise a little bit. I have to look away because her brother and his girlfriend sit on my other side, and the sight of her bare legs does weird shit to me.

Joe dropped the "secret boyfriend" stuff after Cora pulled him away while Josie and I helped clean up dinner. We made our way back to the living room where their dad was watching some action movie. Joe walked up to Josie, pointed at her collarbone, asking what she had there to then flick his pointer finger over the tip of her nose when she looked down. That earned him a shove from her, and within minutes, cheek-to-cheek kisses and hugs were dispersed with their parents before the four of us were out the door.

We ended up at a spot Josie calls Blue Water. It's like a small lagoon, and when you throw rocks in or disturb the water it splashes in a bright neon blue. She's obsessed with it. It's pretty cool and there's a scientific reason as to why it happens. I googled it and tried explaining it to her once, but before I could even finish she was turning up the radio where Shawn Mendes was singing about how he *bleeds until he can't breathe*.

"I can't wait for college, man. Parties. Booze. Girls…" Joe says, skipping a rock as we all watch the blue dance across the water but peering over at Cora, obviously messing with her.

"That's okay," she replies, flipping her hair to the side. "I can't wait to meet the history professor, I hear he's a—" Cora is cut off by Joe when he tackles her down and tickles her.

"You're lame, Joe," Josie chimes in, sitting up straighter. "I'm excited to try different classes and choose my major. I don't know what I want to be when I grow up. I feel like I'll never know."

"I can't wait to get all the pre-reqs out of the way and start some real business classes. Make Daddy proud," Cora says with a dreamy look on her face as she pulls away from Joe.

"Yeah, you will," Joe says, leaning back on his elbows, bouncing his eyebrows.

"Not you, moron. My dad. He'll show me the ropes to working the business side of his empire. I'll end up being your sugar mama instead." The girls high-five over Joe and his now sour face.

I keep quiet in my corner here. The truth is our little foursome has been the best part of my summer. Well, Josie has been the best part of my summer, but these nights when we drive around and shoot the shit make me forget the reality that when I look ahead at my future, I don't see much. An open road without an end. For one, I have no idea what I want to go to school for, like Josie. But I'm not worried about her at all, she'll figure it out. Two, they are under the impression my acceptance was deferred until the spring semester and my acceptance letter should be arriving any day now. I don't even think that's how it works, but they bought it. The truth is I was rejected from the university, but I did get accepted into the community college. I just haven't decided if I'm gonna go yet. Josie doesn't know this. It's been weighing on me, but each time it comes to a head and I want to bring it up, I find an excuse.

Joe is still going on about what he thinks college will be like while the girls correct him and pop his unrealistic bubbles one by one. He's seen too many movies.

Finally, Josie raises her hands above her head and yawns, asking me to give her a ride home. Joe has his car, his idea because he's probably going to try and fuck Cora here in the grass. Hopefully quietly since this is private property and I'd hate if we lost this little spot Josie loves. And well, I guess I don't want my friends getting arrested either.

We head back to my truck, my hand on Josie's lower back while she does this little whine to take her by Taco Bell. She knows I'll never say no, but that little beg from her makes the front of my pants tight.

I open the door for her and run around to the driver's side. I start my truck, then turn to her, "I'll get you Taco Bell, but I'm not getting anything for myself."

She pouts. "Why not?"

I reach over and tuck a lock of hair behind her ear. "Did you already forget you were gonna be my *fourth meal* tonight?"

She throws her head back and gifts me with the sweetest sound. I swear her laugh will haunt me forever. The sound zings straight through me. She catches me watching her, mesmerized. I blink and shake my head, mumbling and reminding her that she's beautiful and how I don't deserve her. Right as I put the truck in drive, she reaches over and makes small circles on the back of my neck. Quick glances her way validate that she's biting that plump bottom lip of hers.

I make it two blocks before I find myself parking on

the side of the road and begging her to cross the center console. I adjust the seat, adding more space between the steering wheel and myself as well as reclining all the way back. I'm almost completely horizontal when she straddles my lap.

I sit up some to get a better hold of her. My hands trickle up the backs of her thighs before I have two handfuls of her perfect ass. She yelps when I pull her cheeks apart and bring her down onto my hard-on.

"Yesss," she calls out when I do it again.

She grabs my face with both hands and pulls me in for a kiss. I massage her tongue with mine, deepening the kiss and swallowing her gasp. *Fuck.* I just remembered I never made it to the store today. I pull back and bring my hands to the front of her thighs, rubbing them before I admit, "I'm sorry, baby. I was with your brother all day and never made it to the store for more condoms."

She whines again. I swear the sound will put me six feet under.

"It's okay." I kiss the spot right under her ear. "I've got another idea."

She bites her lip. "You do?" Her eyes light up.

"Yeah. You trust me?"

I feel her heat surrounding my dick get even hotter. She's getting even wetter. *Christ.*

She hasn't answered me, so I ask again, "I need to know you trust me, babydoll. Last thing I'd ever want is for you to be uncomfortable."

She skips a beat before she finally answers, "Yes. I trust you, Wes."

"Alright." I pat her ass with my right hand before I lie back. "Come up here."

Her eyes widen and she looks around as if to see if we have any creepy voyeurs roaming around. "What do you mean, come up here?"

I chuckle. "Oh, hold up." I reach up to pull her panties off but find her bare under her dress. "Fuck, you weren't kidding." She slowly shakes her head, biting that bottom lip again.

After a few beats, she audibly swallows and looks around the truck again before gaining the confidence I know she harbors. She holds onto my shoulders and steadies herself as she crawls up my body. "Are you sure about this?"

"As a heart attack, baby."

She swats at my chest. "Wes! How am I supposed to do this—ooh!" She yelps when I adjust myself and lower my body into the seat. I shove my face into her pussy and nuzzle around like the dog I am, because let's face it, I'd let her walk me around on a leash if she wanted to. She braces herself on my shoulders and I maneuver us around so that she's got one knee on one side of my head and her other leg is stretched out, foot on the back floorboard. I grasp her thighs and bring her down, I want her literally sitting on my face, not hovering.

She's trying to tell me that we shouldn't do this, but when I get into the right position and start to caress her clit with the tip of my tongue, her pleas die out and turn into moans. I reach down and grasp my cock to settle the ache a little, then reach up and grab her ass cheeks.

Her breath hitches with a high-pitched sound. I don't know what to call it, but she makes it whenever I catch her off guard during a hookup. How I don't come from the noise alone is beyond me.

She's practically riding my face and fuck, I could die a happy man right now. Her taste heightens and I know she's about to come. She's got one hand up against the ceiling of my truck, and the other has my hair in a vise grip. I can feel her pulsing in my mouth and her movements become jerkier. I keep going at the same rhythm so she can ride the orgasm until she slows down her rocking on my face.

Josie is panting now and awkwardly adjusts her position so that she is straddling my stomach. She bends down and kisses me. I feel her hand traveling south knowing she wants to return the favor.

"It's okay. You don't have to do that."

"No," she replies. *Huh?*

"What do you mean, *no?*"

She reaches down and pulls the lever that sits my seat upright. The horn honks when Josie flies back against the steering wheel. She's a mess and we are laughing to the point of tears. I reach around underneath her and pull my seat back farther, holding her close to me so she doesn't fall again.

I'm attempting to give us more room, and my heart rate speeds up as I wonder what she plans to do.

"You don't have to do anything you don't want to."

Gripping my knees, she ignores my statement and makes herself at home, kneeling on the floorboard. *Shit.*

"Oh, I definitely want to do this. I just might need your help."

"Okay…" It dawns on me that this is probably a first for her.

Being that Josie and I are still hiding our relationship, some stuff has happened out of order. For example, we've had sex before a blowjob. I've gone down on her more times than I can count now, but that's because I'm a maniac for her pussy. I would never push her to blow me, and we typically are short for time. Just the thought of her mouth on me has my dick angry and throbbing down there.

Her hands skate up my athletic shorts and her fingers end in the waistband. I look away from her hands to look at her face and find her giddy. Giddy? She's excited? Maybe she doesn't plan to suck my dick like I thought. The girls I've been with didn't usually look this ready for it, especially if it was their first time.

Totally fine if she doesn't go for third base.

I'm good. She grips my shorts and I raise my ass to help her take them off.

It's cool. I'm cool.

My cock bobs back and forth as if he's beckoning Josie over. She strokes me a few times with her eyes on me, takes a deep breath and then, before I know it, all I see is the back of her head and I feel her warm, wet mouth. *Holy shit.*

Grasping my seat, I think about how this may not be my first BJ, but it's never felt like this before, and I know it's because Josie is the one pleasing me.

She goes between licking me all over and almost

taking me whole, retracting whenever she starts to gag. I barely care because she feels amazing. Reaching down and moving her hair out of her face, I encourage her, "Fuck. Yes, baby. Just. Like. That."

She stops and looks up at me, wiping her mouth, and I almost come from the sight alone.

"Is this…am I doing okay?"

I chuckle and admit, "You feel like heaven, babe. I promise you can't do anything wrong. Are you sure this is your first time?" I'm practically panting.

"Stop," she swats at my chest, "I don't believe you."

"You'll believe me when I get off faster than I ever have." Not a lie.

A smile erupts on her face, and before I can tell her how goddamn sexy she is, she's back down and giving me even more than before. All I feel is the wet heat of her mouth, and her suction has my balls coming together for a bro hug and slap on the back.

Seriously sooner than I thought possible, I start to feel that tingle in my spine and the heat traveling through my body. I tap her shoulder and uncontrollably mumble that I'm about to come so she may want to stop. I blink when I realize she isn't stopping.

"Josie, if you don't want me to come in your mouth, you better stop." I'm not even sure how I got that sentence out completely, but nothing can stop this girl at all.

I spill into her mouth and hope to God I'm the only person who will ever experience this from her. I love her. I love her so much, and I want to say it now but I know it's not the time. Not when she pulls back and looks up at me, wiping the corners of her mouth delicately with her fingertips. She looks shy and happy and perfect.

She climbs into my lap to snuggle afterwards and this is, hands down, the best summer ever. Through a yawn she tells me I'm perfect, but she has no clue that I'm not, and whatever she's seeing, it's all because of her. I drop her off at her place and go back home. It isn't until I'm face down in bed, surrounded by her scent, that I realize we forgot all about Taco Bell.

chapter twenty-seven

present day, 2022

josie

THE BELL at the front door of Loose Leafs tells me that the customer I just checked out has left. I'm looking through the trinkets that are kept up front by the register when Cassie comes out of nowhere and gives me a good ass smack.

"Hey, lady! Fancy seeing you here."

"Hey! What do you mean? You know I'm here most Saturdays."

"You are, and you're in *your* bed most nights, too, but not last night," she sings that last part and waggles her eyebrows at me. *Shit.* "Spill. I wanna know everything. Is he cute? Is he fit? What's he packin'?" She most definitely does not want to know.

While she starts to go through the books we have on hold for customers, she glances at me a couple times, waiting for an answer.

"Oh, right! About that…I stayed at my parents."

She stops and looks up at me, "Really?"

My "yeah" comes out as "why not" and I know she's not buying it.

"Are you okay? Did something happen?"

"No, I just had dinner with them and ended up at their house, and it was already too late to come home. Just didn't make sense." Avoid birthday talk.

"Hmm. Okay. Anyway, what are your plans tonight and tomorrow? I swear if you say you're going to your parents–"

"No," I cut her off. "I just plan to run some errands after I leave and just chill tomorrow. The receptionist at my job filled my schedule up some more, so I really should do some R&R before a busy week."

"Oh, yes, how exciting!"

"It is. I can't wait." And I really can't, meeting more new people with new stories. New struggles. Helping them find happiness, it makes me giddy thinking about it. "You can help me pick outfits for the week if you're not busy tomorrow."

"I'm there! I just have to work on a paper, but it won't take long. I really want to go to brunch though." She taps her chin. "Wanna go to this cute place in Hyde Park?"

"Yeah, I'll come! That sounds fun."

She stands up straight, placing her hands on her hips. "Hey, now that I think about it, I swore I saw your car last night."

"You did? Oh, yes. You did. They picked me up. And dropped me off. This morning. My parents." Each point comes out as new ideas just popping in my head. I'm a terrible liar.

Thankfully someone somewhere is watching me suffer and wants to put me out of my misery because Scotty comes out of nowhere to save the day. "Josie, you were supposed to leave ten minutes ago. I appreciate you still helping out when you don't have to, but no need to stay later than your shift. And Cassie, can you take some photos for the silent auction we're having next week? I've got the books set up in the backroom."

"Sure thing, boss." Cassie turns to me with squinted eyes as she walks away, "We're not done with this conversation."

I laugh and wave goodbye happily.

As soon as I'm in my car, I make sure to have the AC blasting the hair out of my face because it's hotter than a witch's tit out here. Plugging my phone in, the text I saw on Wes's phone this morning dawns on me. A knot sits at the bottom of my stomach. The knot has been there all day, but I've been doing a good job of keeping busy and forgetting about it. Yet every time I remember it, it seems larger than before.

Leah. The name leaves a bad taste in my mouth. For all I know, it's a different Leah. Either way, who is she and what was she thanking him for? He said he was helping a friend and, I mean, he can have friends who are girls.

Thanks for last night.

Dammit, Wesley. *I* should be the one texting him that right now. Just as that thought pops in my head, his name pops up on my phone with a new message. He sent me one this morning, but I've avoided it at all costs.

> **Wes:** Reached over for you this morning and you were gone. Sad Wes. Have fun at the bookstore.
> **Wes:** I've smelled you on my beard all morning, fighting boners like it's my job.
> **Wes:** Damn, if I could've grown facial hair back then, I never would've let you go.
> **Wes:** Fuck. Too soon.

I throw my phone into my passenger seat with several curse words. I'm not sure how to respond to that. Maybe I won't.

I don't have any errands to run like I may have told Cassie, but you won't catch me dead at the apartment right now. I can't face Wes. For all I know, I'm overreacting, but it's too fresh, and the idea of him being with someone right before he was with me last night hurts. The idea of him skipping my birthday dinner to be with some girl, quite possibly my high school nemesis, repulses me.

I end up at a Starbucks drive-thru and surprise myself when I order an extra espresso for my mom and head home for some much-needed motherly advice.

I find my mother in her Florida room, her sanctuary. It's basically a closed-in back porch with many windows and feels like you went outside, but you're still in the house. It's practically a forest, greenery surrounding a wicker outdoor patio set, a perfect chill spot. My dad renovated this room for her recently. Had it been like this when I lived here, I would have spent most of my time in here reading.

She looks up to find me walking in and holding out her espresso in the tiniest cup they have at Starbucks. "Aye, you're a saint, mi niña. What brings you here? I'm lucky enough to see you two days in a row now. I should have your dad take me to the casino later," she jokes and greets me with a kiss on the cheek.

"Ha-ha," I state sarcastically. "I can't come see my mom?"

"Oh, of course. I'm just surprised, that's all. Come sit, thanks for the coffee. Did you work today?"

"Yes, I did."

"You got a real job, you don't need one on the side. I swear you get that from your father."

"I promise, I'll leave the bookstore as soon as I'm more settled at the counselor's office."

We get comfortable in the opposite seats, she crosses her legs and I tuck mine underneath me.

"How's Wes? Did he get home okay last night?" Her concern is a casual one, not nearly compared to the anxiety I had last night when his phone was dead and I hadn't heard from him in hours.

"He's fine, got home about an hour after we left dinner. His phone had died, and he even went to the restaurant after we'd already gone."

She nods, taking an audible sip of her strong, dark

coffee. "How is it being around him again? I wanted to ask at dinner last night but knew you wouldn't want to talk about it in front of your dad."

"It's fine. We're fine. We're roommates. Friends."

"Josie, por favor, you're going to make me spit out my drink," she says, raising a brow at me. "I've seen him and what he's become. He was a cutie when you all were kids, and he's a man now. And you, you've grown up, too. You were so skinny back then. Now you've filled out. I won't believe for a minute that the attraction is gone."

I answer her in a grunt.

"I just don't want to get hurt again, Mom. I came back here knowing I'd eventually run into him, but I had no idea I'd be living with him."

"Is he treating you well?"

My eyes go to the fans on the ceiling, trying to keep the tears from spilling. "He's trying to make things right, he tiptoes around me, I can feel it. He doesn't want to mess up again. It's been so long, but my trust for him is still lacking."

"You're right, it's been a long time. Give him a chance. Take it slow. It doesn't have to be all or nothing."

"I know."

"I don't know what happened between you two. You left on such short notice, and after Joe passed, I knew it wasn't good. Neither of you ever said, but it's time you figure it out. He's a good man. He's always checked up on us. And he's never, not once, not asked about you. When he knew you were back, he respected you and kept his distance. You are different people than you were all those years ago. Explore that."

"I'm scared to push him away to a point that he won't give me another chance. I'm always running away from my problems."

"Josie," she pauses, setting down the empty cup on the small table between us. She sits on the edge of her seat with her hands in her lap, "I'm going to tell you something I've been wanting to say for a long time. And I don't want you to take it the wrong way."

Okay, great.

"Stop being so afraid of everything. I thought for sure my sister would have taught you this after all these years." She's referring to my aunt Leila I've lived with who still harbors a broken heart.

"Quit being scared. Look at yourself, you've graduated college and obtained the job you've always dreamt about. You found yourself a place soon after moving home, and I know the first chance you get, you'll be in your own place. You're a beautiful, independent, and smart woman.

"Your brother died unexpectedly and horrifically, and we have all been through hell for it, but you need to move on. Your father and I, we are not going to die unexpectedly like him, neither will Cora or Leila or any other people you're close to. *Wes* will not die before you're ready to let him go. And if we do, you're going to regret not being closer to any of us. Let us in. Enjoy us while we're here. Live your life. It's what your brother would want for you."

My face is wet from the tears, and I can't stop

nodding my head because I hear her. So damn loud and clear, I hear what she's saying, and I know this talk has been a long time coming. Our relationship hasn't been what it should be in years.

"And you can't be scared of Wes giving up on you. It's been over seven years and he's been waiting for you to come home this whole time. If I know anything about that man, it's that he regrets whatever happened between you two. He regrets letting you go and he won't let it happen again."

wes

Crouching down in the grass, I place a pack of Black & Milds in front of Joe's headstone. After rocking back and forth on the balls of my feet some, I decide to get comfortable and just sit on my ass. I pick at pieces of grass and wipe the sweat off my brow looking around. The day is gloomy, but the humidity still has me sweating my balls off. I usually come every few months to see Joe, catch him up on what's going on and boy, things have definitely been interesting.

"Remember when we were, what, thirteen? Fourteen?" I squint toward the sunset before I continue, "And you paid your cousin Diego to buy us Black & Milds? We both puked so bad that night. But the next week he brought them for us again and we ended up getting them almost every weekend after that. Man, those were good times." I tell the story out loud, probably to myself, but who knows…if my late best friend is listening, it'd be nice.

"Your sister says Cora's doing okay. She still has a hard time, though. You should send her a butterfly or randomly play a song you two loved on the radio or something. Don't do some spooky shit and flicker lights or turn something on like the TV or microwave." I laugh to myself. If anyone came back as a ghost to play tricks on the living, it would be Joe. "But yeah, you heard me right. Your sister. I talked to her. She's back, and sexier than ever. Erp, you probably don't want to hear that.

"She fucks me up, man. I don't know how to act around her. I don't know if she enjoys my company or if she wants me to leave her the fuck alone. But I can't. She's so different, yet the same. She finished school and got herself a real job. As a counselor, can you believe that shit? And she moved into my apartment, *my* apartment. Like, did it have to be mine? I don't mind it one bit, but it kind of shook everything up. Did you have a hand in that? You probably did, you asshole." I laugh again, tossing pieces of grass to the side.

"Anyway, things got a little…interesting last night. Nothing you need any details about, but fuck, it showed me how she is the same ol' Josie Rodriguez. She laughs at my jokes and her breath hitches whenever I get too close. And being with her, it felt just like it did all those years ago. I'm scared she's ignoring me today as she isn't replying to my texts. All I can think is that she regrets last night. I hope to God that isn't the case because I needed last night. I need her. Oh, and sorry I didn't come for your birthday like I usually do. I see Mama Isabel did." I pick up a fresh candle...she always leaves these tall, skinny candles with a religious figure on it. Putting it back down, I continue, "So, I thought of bringing her—Josie—here but I didn't want to bring her down or anything, so we grabbed lunch and saw my grams. She seemed to like it. I missed her dinner, but she said she was good with your parents. And then last night happened and, man, I don't know where her head's at, but I'm gonna make it right." I stand up and dust off my pants. Reaching down, I pat the headstone. "I'm gonna fuckin' make it right with her."

chapter twenty-eight

present day, 2022

josie

"HOW MANY?" The hostess at this cute *do it for the 'gram* brunch spot asks us. I hold up two fingers and Cassie calls out, "Four."

Four?

She catches my confused expression and decides to inform me that the guys will be joining us. Right away, my heart rate picks up and I can feel perspiration building on my hairline. The last thing in the world I want to do is face Wes, especially in front of our roommates after we haven't discussed the last forty-eight hours.

Once he realized I wasn't answering his texts, he sent more messages asking what happened and if he did something wrong. He asked if he went too far with me the previous night and apologized, stating that he couldn't control himself. After he knocked on my bedroom door and figured out it was locked and that I wasn't opening up, he sent another message stating: **I'm sorry, I don't know why yet but I promise I'll fix this.**

I silenced my phone and put it aside without responding, rolling over and going to sleep.

And now here I am, about to have brunch with–

"Hey, babe," Brandon greets Cassie and sits next to her, dropping a kiss on her temple, then nodding his head at me. I force a smile at him before my eyes meet Wes's, sporting a black hat on backward, a plain white tee which makes the ink on his arms pop, and gray sweats. It's loungewear, yet appropriate for brunch.

"You made it out of your dungeon, princess," Wes states.

"I did," I reply, avoiding eye contact.

The waitress comes at the perfect time to take our drink order, and when she asks if we're ready to order our food, I'm the only one who wants more time with the menu, but Wes decides to throw in his two cents.

"Oh, she'll have the chocolate chip pancakes with hash browns on the side. No whipped cream."

All eyes fall on him, including mine. The waitress smirks waiting for me to confirm the order. Embarrassed, I nod and hand her the menu. When I look up, Cassie has her eyes on me. She squints again just like she did at the bookstore yesterday. She's unraveling her napkin and pulling out the silverware.

"Spill," she demands, pointing her butterknife at me and Wes.

"That's what she's always ordered for breakfast," Wes informs them, earning himself a glare from me.

"Have you two been going on breakfast dates without us?"

"No." Comes from me.

Brandon chimes in, "What am I missing? I'm lost."

"We grew up together," Wes finally admits with a sigh, and I swear Cassie's eyes are going to fall out of her head onto the table and roll over to me.

"We were just friends!" I add in.

Wes shuts his eyes for two beats before he opens them and nods.

"Why didn't you guys tell us?"

Wes's jaw ticks, and without looking my way (he seems pissed), he confesses, "I was friends with her late brother."

Cassie's mouth makes an "O."

"Well, then you gotta tell us...was Mr. Miller here a dweeb or was he the dog he is now? Pullin' in the ladies like–" Brandon's attempt to lighten the mood earns him a kick under the table from his girlfriend, as well as a death glare from Wes.

"What, this is great ball bustin' material!" Poor Brandon defends his inquiry.

"Wes...ahem, Miller?" I take Brandon's bait, "He and my brother thought they ruled the school. Deep down they were dweebs. One hundred percent."

Wes whips his head in my direction, "That so?"

"Yup."

The waitress drops off our drinks and I take a sip of my iced coffee before I continue, "You guys thought you were *so cool*. My brother would drive you around and you guys would buy crap beer and cigarettes from my cousin who, to this day, still lives in his mom's basement."

Wes throws his head back in laughter. Lines form at the corner of his eyes and seriously, were his teeth always that white? Why don't I remember that?

Small talk takes over the table, and Brandon and Cassie bicker about how he doesn't want to visit his parents, but she's forcing him to go since he hasn't seen them in weeks. He says he prefers to watch football at our apartment rather than at his childhood home with his mom talking the whole time. Wes chimes in that he has absolutely no plans today, and has been looking forward to watching the games on our couch, all while offering to drive me back home so Cassie can join Brandon at his parents'. This guy, full of great ideas.

He turns to face me as if the conversation earlier never left his mind, and his knees bump mine. Our eyes shoot under the table and back up just as fast. "Alright, Dr. Rodriguez—"

"I'm not a doctor," I interrupt.

"Whatever. Who drove you around?" His eyebrows raise in question.

I roll my eyes and bring my gaze back across the table where Cassie and Brandon watch us in awe.

"I did end up getting my own truck, in case you don't recall."

The waitress—with impeccable timing again—drops off our food. Wes takes a bite of his omelet, points his fork at me and with a full mouth admits, "Actually, if memory serves me right, you knew that truck inside and out."

Cassie starts to choke on her breakfast and reaches over Brandon to chug his orange juice. Wes watches her, that muscle in his jaw is ticking away.

"What? I'm just sayin', I gave Josie here a lot of rides in that truck," he states with a wink for Cassie.

wes

"You're kidding." I break the silence, which has been going on for seven minutes now. Josie doesn't change her position in my passenger seat, facing out the window. I'm driving us home from brunch, which was awkward as fuck. She wants to keep our past a secret and I get it. Our history is…messy. But it's bound to come out. And I won't lie, not knowing why she's giving me the cold shoulder has me unhinged.

I know she didn't want to ride with me, but I had to get her to talk to me somehow, and luring Cassie to go with Brandon to visit his parents, I'll admit, was genius on my part.

"You're not going to say anything? I'm losing my fucking mind here, babe."

That has her shifting in her seat and shooting her gaze toward me. She always reacted when I called her *babe* or *baby*, whether it took her breath away or it pissed her off as it often has recently, but she always has some way of responding to the term of endearment.

"I saw your phone," she says it so softly I almost don't make out the words.

"What do you mean?"

She sighs and shifts herself toward me. "Yesterday morning, when I woke up in your bed." We make eye contact until I look back at the road. "I went to check the time. I grabbed your phone and there was a text...from a Leah."

Fuck. How did I not think of that?

"Okay, look. I can explain."

"No, there's no need to explain anything, Wes. This is my fault. I should have known better than to fall into your bed so quickly."

"Oh, no." I shake my head, gripping the wheel as tight as I can, knuckles losing their color. A sarcastic laugh escapes my throat. "That night, we may have moved faster than we anticipated. I get that. I see that. But there's obviously a chance," I say with a breath of relief to finally get this out in the open. "I obviously have a second chance with you and I'm not letting that go. I felt it, and I know you felt it, too. I swear to you that this is a misunderstanding and I'm not letting bullshit like this get in my way of you."

I don't hear a peep from her. As soon as I have the chance, I look over and see her just staring at me. "Then go on, Wes. Explain this *bullshit.*" Damn, she's pissed. I'm part terrified and part turned on. I have to be as honest as possible, show her I'm not playing around. I messed up once, resulting in a seven-year break. I park my truck at the apartment complex. Round two of spilling my guts to Josie in this damn parking lot.

I take off my hat and toss it on the dash, ready to explain. "I swear nothing happened. We have a history." Her eyes widen. "No, no. Not like that. Fuck. I mean, we do have a history like that–" I panic as she turns and reaches for the door handle, fast as fuck. Grabbing her arm, then quickly letting go and putting my hands up in surrender, I apologize, "I'm sorry, I'm sorry. Just let me be real and honest with you."

She crosses her arms with a *hmph* and keeps her attention forward.

"After Joe died, you know I started drinking more. And after you left, I got worse. I lost my best friend and my girlfriend all at the same time." She picks at her nails, refusing to look at me, so I keep going, "I ran into Leah Peters one day."

Her head whips to face me.

"What?" I ask.

"So, it is Leah Peters?"

"Yeah, I thought you knew that."

"No, I mean, I thought it could be but I wasn't sure." *Fuck*, I really made a mistake.

"Well, she was in a fucked-up state, too." I go on to tell her about how we started to help each other step away from our vices. I explain that it was harder for Leah than it was for me, but that we never lost touch. And when I tell her that I did sleep with Leah twice, I swear it was only two times, I look up to see her eyes brimming with tears. It hurts so fucking much. I grab her hands, and by some goddamn miracle, she lets me.

"Both those times, baby, I had you on my mind. I know that's fucked up to say, but it's true. I saw you with that…that guy." It takes a lot for me not to call him a douche or an asshole. "When I was with her, I imagined she was you. All I could see was nonexistent big hair. All I heard was your moans. I was surrounded by made-up coconuts. So I stopped that shit quick. It wasn't fair to me or her. It wasn't fucking fair to you."

All I can hear is the engine of my truck running and the AC going. I'm nervous to make eye contact with her. She doesn't have to believe me. Trust is my only hope, and with my track record, it's not on my side.

"Please say something, anything," I plead.

She sighs and starts to unbuckle her seatbelt, gathering her purse and phone.

Fuck. My heart rate increases, and I know I've fucked this up royally. There's no coming back from this. I just admitted to fucking her high school nemesis, and skipping her birthday dinner for the same girl. Why the hell did I ever think this would be okay?

"I get it," she interrupts my spiraling thoughts.

"What?"

"I said, I get it." She locks her gaze on mine. "I didn't know you came back and saw me with Wyatt." I cringe at his name, but not enough for her to notice. "I'm not a fan of it but I get it, Wes." She all but rolls her eyes at me. "So, what did you guys do?"

"What do you mean?" If she's asking me to give her details of when we hooked up, I don't think that I can do it. I barely remember it, anyway.

"On Friday, on my birthday. What was she thanking you for? Why did you miss my birthday dinner?" she asks with zero emotion on her face. Fuck a scary movie, this girl's death stare could keep me up all night with the lights on.

I rub the scruff on my jaw. "I'm basically her sponsor. She had a tough week and some family issues. Honestly, I thought about letting her figure it out on her own, but I thought it would be quick, so I ran over to her place. In the end, I'm glad I did because she sort of had a breakdown while I was there." The tiniest flash of concern crosses her face so quickly, there's no point to address it. When I got to Leah's on Friday night, she was practically burning a hole in her carpet pacing around. It was one thing after another this week, starting with a flat tire Monday morning, and her mom insisting she come over for Sunday family dinner. Leah always leaves those dinners early and doesn't talk to her parents for weeks afterwards. She admitted to heading to her car to go to a bar or the liquor store, but instead went back to her apartment to call me.

"But in your case, I wish I didn't go. It's just, I've seen her relapse and it's not pretty. She's different from the girl she was in high school."

Josie just nods.

"I promise we didn't do anything. I wish I could prove it somehow. We can meet up sometime if you want, she'd love to see you. She knows she was a bitch then."

She huffs, "I think I'm good. I'm not happy about it, but I believe you. Just try to tell me beforehand next time. It is going to take me a second to process though. So if I can go inside now, that'd be great."

"Of course, anything."

chapter twenty-nine

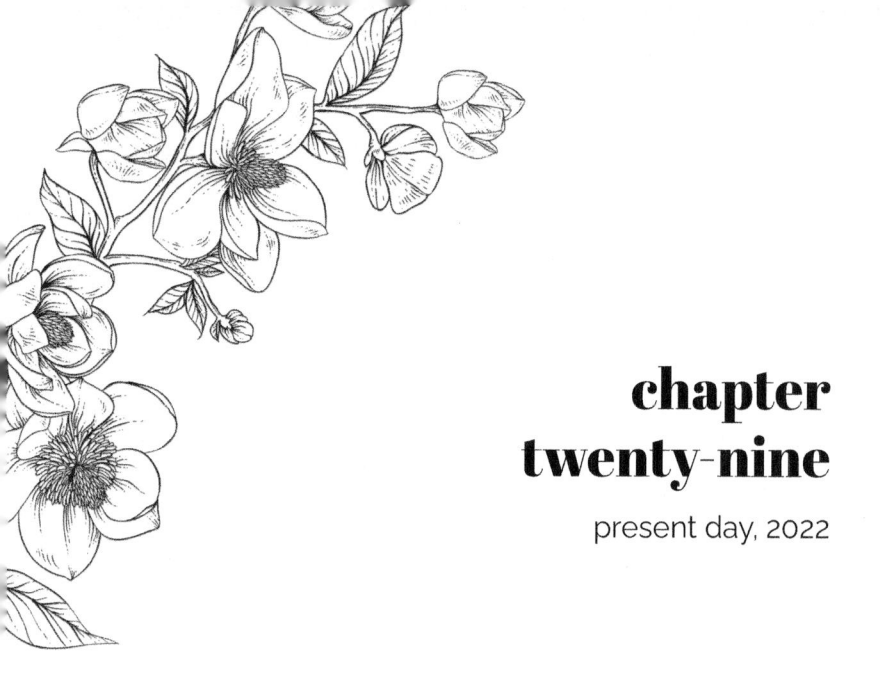

present day, 2022

josie

I SHUT the door to my room and back up against it, taking deep breaths. I even count the seconds to calm myself down. Breathe in for four, hold my breath for seven, and let it out for eight. After my third round, I'm already feeling calmer.

I can't believe he just admitted to that. Wes slept with Leah. The bile rises up to my throat and I push it back down. *And* I told him it was okay, that I get it. *Have I lost my mind?* No. The truth is, as much as I hate it, he did tell me it took him a long time for him to sober up, and when he came to tell me, I'd already started dating Wyatt.

This was seven years ago. We are different people than we were then, and as much as I don't want to admit it—I'm sure he's not wrong and that Leah has changed. Doesn't mean I'm gonna go get mani-pedis with her or anything, but if Wes thinks so highly of her, then I'm sure she's grown up some.

I spend the majority of the afternoon in my room cleaning and picking up. I'm not the cleanest apple in the bunch, but I've definitely gotten better with age. I'm organized with my work, but at home, the mess doesn't bother me. I just know that being prepared for this week will only help me. Plus, I need a reason to be cooped up in my room. I don't want to risk running into Wes. Or even Cassie or Brandon after that brunch.

To say that I want to wring Wes's neck for letting out the can of worms about our past would be an understatement. Yet, I'd be lying if I didn't feel a sense of relief that it is out. I'm nervous to talk to Cassie about our past, but I also feel like it's only fair to let her in.

Speaking of letting her in...

The blond bombshell barrels into my room. She looks out my door before quietly closing it like she's on the run and taking refuge in my bedroom.

"Okay. Let's do this. I want to know everything. I *have* to know everything. This has been the most exciting part of my day. Hell, the most exciting moment in months!" she whispers as she makes herself comfy on my bed.

Looking around, I ask, also whispering, "Why are we whispering?"

"Because Brandon's being lame and told me not to pry for info. But, like, what the hell? I feel like I just got a call from a cousin with the best tea, and you don't turn down a good tea sesh."

I roll my eyes at her, and when my mouth forms a

smirk, I tease her, "What's the tea?" She looks at me as though I've grown three heads.

"You," she points to me, then toward my door, "and Miller—Wes. Whatever his name is! You two, there's more to this."

"There's nothing to say. He was my brother's best friend growing up. Nothing happened."

I peek over at her from the closet where I'm hanging up clothes.

"You're a damn liar. You kept this a secret from us for a reason. And that wink! Did you see how he winked at me? About giving you rides in his truck!" She fans herself. "And he did it right in front of Brandon. That man is something else. Now, tell me or I'll ask him. His lips are looser than yours." Her eyes widen at the sexual innuendo she accidentally made there, which causes us both go into a fit of laughter.

I hang up my last few work shirts before I plop myself on the bed next to her with a sigh.

"Aww, babe," she runs her fingers through my hair. "This is deeper than I'm ready for, huh?"

I bite my lip and nod at her and start to give her the four-one-one, leaving out the assault that caused me to leave home the first time. My eyes practically turn into cartoon hearts when I reminisce about that summer. I tell her the truth about why I really left the last time, and how I'd just learned that Wes came to take me back, but it was too late. And Leah, I tell her about that because it's fresh and I need to vent. I never called Cora like I typically would because I didn't want to bother

her with it. Lord knows she's dried enough of my Wes-tears.

"Oof, that's brutal. So he slept with your high school bully?"

"I wouldn't say *bully*, but yeah, he did."

Cassie reaches over to hold my hand. "Okay, without getting too sappy, I want to say: I support you." A small smile creeps on my face and it must be contagious because now she's smiling, too.

"I'm serious. I'm not gonna be the friend that says, *fuck him! You deserve better! Blah, blah, blah!* Because I've known Wes for a few years now and he is the sweetest guy. I can't imagine him intentionally wanting to hurt you. He has reason behind his decisions. And yeah, he's made mistakes, but we're all human. I believe he's probably learned from these mistakes.

"And if you want nothing to do with him moving forward, I'll help you pack boxes. Or…I'll help him pack boxes because I'd love my own bathroom. Hmm." She taps her chin.

A laugh bubbles out of me and I don't even realize until now that I've got tears running down my face.

"But I'd say, you explore Wes as an adult. See what happens. Plus, I have this itty-bitty little feeling that he's packin' some heat, if you know what I mean." She wags her eyebrows at me and I throw a pillow at her. "I knew it was true! I just knew it!"

I sit up and look around to see my very loud and Hispanic family surrounding me at this...pool party? The sun beats down on my skin and I can already feel the straps on this lounge chair marking my body. How long have I been out here? And when did I get here?

My uncles at the domino table are slamming their drinks down and laughing with cigars hanging out of their mouths. My aunts walk around offering cake to all the guests.

"Josie, you want a piece? It's homemade. Your mamá made it, it has Wesley Toll House cookies in it."

"Wesley Toll House?" *What in the world? And my mom does not bake.*

"No, girl, I said Nestlé."

"Oh." *I'm so confused.*

I bounce in my seat only to look over and see—no. It can't be.

"Joe?"

"Hey, sis. You gotta try this cake Mom made. Why are you looking at me like that, you weirdo?"

"Joe, you're here! Oh my God, you're really here!" *I hug him and he stiffens. I feel like I'm crying, but when I reach up to wipe my face, it's completely dry.*

"Okay...anyway, try this." *He shoves a bite in my mouth, and it really is delicious.*

"See, told you." *I can't stop looking at him. He's bigger and older and just as I'd imagine him being at twenty-six. I reach out to touch the scruff on his face, but it's like I can't get close enough.*

"Wes, come get some cake," *Joe says, facing the pool.*

I look over and see Wes getting out of the pool. His tatted-

up and ripped body walks toward us slowly, water dripping down his chest.

"Hey, Josie," he says to me, ignoring my brother's plea for him to try the cake.

"Hi." I'm so nervous. It's as if I'm seeing him again for the first time after all those years.

"Come with me," he holds out his hand.

"Where?" I look at him, unsure what to do. I turn to Joe and he nods and says, "Give him a chance, sis."

When I look over to Wes, he is emerging from the pool again.

"Hey, Josie."

"Hi...?" What the hell?

"Come with me," he holds his hand out again.

"What?" I look at Joe and he does it again, nods and says, "Give him a chance, sis."

When I turn to see Wes getting out of the pool a third time, I freak the hell out. I stand up, tripping over the lounge chair.

"Josie! Give him a chance! Give him a chance, Josie! Josie, dammit, just give—"

My eyes fly open and I shoot up in bed. A layer of sweat covers me, and I can barely catch my breath. It isn't the first time Joe has made an appearance in my dreams, although it was a surprise to see him older. But it was the first time in years that Wes has shown up in my sleep. How bizarre.

I get out of bed and tiptoe to the bathroom. Once I'm in bed again with a bottle of water, I realize I'm wide awake and need to sleep soon. Tomorrow's my first full day at work and I want to feel well rested. Nothing more embarrassing than meeting with people to talk about their issues and have deep, personal conversations only to reward them with a yawn. A toilet flushes in the distance, and I know it's Wes. The main toilet is much closer.

I come to the realization that it's time I take my brother's advice. Cassie got in my head, too. The choice is mine. I can choose to believe Wes. I mean, why would he admit to being with Leah in the past if he were still doing it now. I could choose not to believe him and figure out how to be around him. But the truth is, being in his presence these last few weeks and spending most of my birthday with him, it felt good. A feeling that I hadn't had in a while. A feeling I'm not ready to let go of just yet.

Before I know it, I'm sneaking across the apartment to his room.

I'm quietly creeping into his room as he puts his phone on his nightstand. He makes himself comfortable, and I know he hasn't noticed my presence. It's dark, and now that the light from his phone is gone, I can barely make out anything in here. Right as I'm about to climb on his bed, I go to announce myself, but instead let out a yelp, "Ahh, fuckfuckfuck!"

Wes jumps up out of bed and runs to turn on the light. "Josie! Are you okay? What the hell!?"

He finds me on the floor with my leg bent into my lap, hand wrapped around my right foot. "I stubbed my toe!" It comes out as half a whine and half a laugh.

He squats down next to me, and I look back to find the culprit: a big ass dumbbell.

"What the hell, Wes? How much does that thing weigh?"

He chuckles and it's deep and sleepy, easily the sexiest sound in the world. I almost forget about my throbbing toe. "It's only forty pounds."

"There's no way. Look how big that thing is." I look up to find him smiling at me and I playfully smack his shoulder. He points to the "40" etched into the weight.

"Sometimes I lift before bed. Had I expected a creeper to come in, I would've shoved it under the bed."

He moves it under his bed effortlessly before he stands up, holding his hand out to me. "Is your toe better?" I nod and take his hand.

"What are you doing in here anyway?" He moves around the room, and I take in his bare chest and plaid sleeping pants that hang incredibly low on his hips. His muscles dance under his skin as he works his way around, turning on the lamp on his nightstand before shutting the bedroom light off.

"I couldn't sleep. I had an...interesting dream."

"Oh, yeah? What about?"

"Let's just say Joe was there trying to make me eat a cake that my mom would never make in real life."

"You underestimate Isabel," he says, shaking his head while he gets back in bed and pats the spot next to him.

"Oh, my Lorrrd. Isabelllll," I sing, sitting on his bed. He always defended my mom. Almost like a small crush, but I know it wasn't that. She was just another motherly figure aside from his Grams. "Why don't you just marry her, huh?"

"Whoa! Jealous of your mother, Dr. Rodriguez?"

"No," I roll my eyes at him. "You know what? Maybe I am. Maybe I'm jealous that they got to see you these last seven years. And you got to spend time with them, too. All while I was on the other side of the state."

He lies back with his hands behind his head and smiles with closed eyes.

"What, you don't believe that I feel I missed out on so much?"

"No, it's not that."

"What's that smirk, then?"

Without moving from his relaxed position, he opens his eyes and looks at me from the side. "I just like it when you get in your head and make a point. You get passionate about the small things. I kinda love it. You turn nothing into something in the best ways. Missed that about you." Welp. Didn't expect that to come out of his mouth.

He props himself up on one elbow and leans toward me, rubbing his fingers on his bottom lip. "I've never seen anything as sexy as you are when you're fired up."

With one strong arm, he reaches for my waist and turns me around, bringing me in front of him. And now, we're spooning. I'll admit, I didn't imagine what was going to happen once I came in here. Didn't think that far, to be honest. But this is good. I like it. The familiarity of being wrapped up by Wes takes over my body, and I can finally relax.

I push the thoughts of Leah out of my mind because

I'm getting out of my own head and choosing to trust him.

I feel his hand start moving around my stomach. When I look down to see what he's up to, he lifts himself up on his elbow. Uh-oh. His hand is cupping the bulge at the top of my sleep shorts. *Dammit, I forgot.*

Shock is written all over his face. Lifting my shirt and pulling my baby blanket out of my shorts, he holds it up and asks, "You're serious?"

Burying my face in the pillow—which smells delicious and so much like Wes—I let out a muffled and drawn out, "Stoppp!"

"I cannot believe you still have this thing," he says, unable to hold back his laughter.

"Shh! You'll wake up the others!" I grab it from his hand and cuddle it into my chest. "I forgot I even grabbed it. That dream shook me up, and I was also nervous coming in here."

He doesn't say anything, so I look up to see him peering down at me. At the slowest pace, he brushes the hair out of my face. "Don't be nervous to come into my room. I'll never turn you down or ask you to leave. Never."

His eyes flick back and forth between mine and jump down to my mouth before they close and he kisses me. He nips at my bottom lip before he opens my mouth with his, pushing his tongue in to meet mine. Heat pulls between my legs. A magnetic pull forces me to turn toward him, but his brawny hand stops me at my waist and he ends the kiss, peppering me with small ones on my neck and shoulder. "Seven fucking years I've waited to have you in my bed, so don't think for one second that I want you anywhere else but here."

I'm practically panting, and somehow having withdrawals from that kiss. And in a need to lighten the mood, I mention, "You know, you love my mom's yellow rice and chicken, but it's my Tía Elena who makes it best."

Shushing me, he reaches back and turns off the lamp, then brings his strong arm, which I can't get over how much bigger it is compared to when we were eighteen, back to its spot around my waist, pulling me even closer to his warm body. "It's one in the morning, and I have a client to meet at six. So go to sleep unless you want me to find another way to get you there."

I quickly shake my head, declining. Although his words make a beeline straight to my lady bits, I know we both need rest.

"Alright, goodnight." His deep voice could rock me to sleep on its own.

"Goodnight, Wes."

chapter thirty

that summer, 2015

josie

WES TUMBLES into the backseat of his truck after diving back there over the center console. His deep voice lets out an "Ow," followed by laughter.

"You're crazy!" I say, giggling and peering behind me, making sure he's okay.

His head pops up with his beautiful, cheesy grin, leaning toward me over the console, "I'm only crazy about you, baby." He plants a kiss on my lips. Once, twice, three times.

He backs away and sits in the backseat, his legs wide apart, eyes looking into mine. I swallow and take him in. He's got a bright tank top on opposite an even brighter pair of swim trunks. The colors pop over his tan skin, stretched over his lean yet muscular arms. He brings up his hands behind his head to hold onto the brim of his hat facing backward.

"Come back here," he nods all sexy and seductive

without even trying to be, and I can almost smell the sex oozing off him.

I crushed on him for years. His style and the way he carried himself, confident but not too cocky. A little mysterious, too, being the quieter one between him and my brother. Yet, I've never been as attracted to Wes Miller as I am now. This summer. He lets his confidence shine with me, showing that hidden cocky side. And the mystery is gone. He tells me everything.

I know what he's up to, moving to the back seat. We're supposed to be meeting Cora and Joe at the beach, but he took a detour, and now we're parked in an alley behind some of the local restaurants and shops that won't open until later this afternoon.

"Joe and Cora are waiting on us."

He replies, "Hey, this was your idea." Still wearing that goofy smile, his face suddenly turns somber, and he sits up moving closer to me again, "Seriously, we don't have to if you don't want to."

Umm, no. I am so here for this. Before he starts to climb over the console to get back into the driver's seat, I nervously turn my body to climb back there with him.

We haven't been able to take our hands off each other these last two months. And just last week I told him that I couldn't wait to give myself to him in the back seat of his truck. So here we are.

I settle my legs on either side of his and kiss him on the nose.

"I missed you this weekend. That was what, the most we've been apart in a while, huh?"

"Yeah," he replies, "Believe me, the only thing that

could keep me from you is Grams. It was fun, though, hanging out with her and her friends. They gambled and drank mimosas and laughed for hours on end." He took his Grams and some of her friends to a hotel on the other coast of Florida for the weekend. Something they do every summer. This was the second time Wes drove them. The way he takes care of his Grams makes my heart swell. It's not every day an almost nineteen-year-old guy drops everything for his grandmother.

"We talked about you. A lot," he says as he coyly avoids eye contact.

I bounce in his lap and almost squeal in awe, "You did?"

"Don't act all surprised. You're all I think about, Josie." His eyes find mine after looking at everything but me. "I couldn't stop if I wanted to." He takes a lock of hair and moves it behind my ear. "Which I don't want to."

I nip on my bottom lip, unable to take my eyes off his before he moves his hands to find my hips and thrusts himself up into my center. A moan escapes me before he reaches up to cup my jaw, bringing his mouth to mine. Our lips meet and it's slow and soft, like the first time we kissed. Lately, we are like hormone-raged teenagers. Our kisses rushed and chaotic and messy, not able to get enough of each other. This is different. He is taking his time, drinking me in. I dip my tongue in his mouth, finding his, and the feeling goes deep into my core.

His other hand comes up to cup the back of my head, fingers splayed into my hair. His lips leave mine and move down to my neck, slightly pulling my hair back to give him better access. I reach down, sliding my hands under his shirt, exploring the dips of his six-pack. Or is it an eight-pack? I swear there's so many of them. The obsession he has with the gym benefits me in more ways than one. His hands leave me, and he reaches behind to pull his shirt off over his head, tossing it to the side along with his hat revealing his military-like haircut.

My hands spread on his chest now, peppering kisses across his collarbone. One side, then the other. My eyes go to his, watching me in awe. Like he's still in shock of us and what we are. A feeling I also have most days.

He dips his head and plants his open mouth on one boob over the cloth of my bikini while his other hand palms my other boob. His mouth saturates the yellow triangle that covers me, and it takes everything in me to pry him off and let out the words, "My brother will notice a wet spot on my boobs."

He looks up at me with parted lips, "Well, we don't want that, do we?" I feel a zing shoot straight to my clit with that question. Before I get to answer him, he uses each index finger to pull the triangles down. He tips his head down to lick and then suck, *hard*, on one nipple enough to force me to grab his head and pull him off while I laugh at him acting like an animal. His eyes sparkle as he gives me his panty-dropping smile with a chuckle before he moves to my other boob, licking and sucking, *better this time*. I bathe in the pool of pleasure coursing through me, and lean back giving him better access while I hold onto his buzzed head. I watch as he devours me. Without even noticing that he removed it, he is tossing my bikini top to the side, joining his shirt and hat. I find myself grinding on him, feeling him hard as a rock now beneath me.

He unbuttons my jean shorts and tugs on them, "Off," he pants as if it's all he can manage to coherently come up with. Without wasting time, I climb off and sit beside him. Shimmying out of my shorts and matching yellow bikini bottoms, I keep my eyes on him. His gaze follows the shorts down my legs, then jumps back up to my face. My mouth. My breasts. My pussy.

"Fuck," he rubs his jaw and takes a deep breath, "I want to taste you so bad right now, but I know I won't be able to stop, and they are waiting on us. I just need inside, baby."

His eyes are hooded, and I nod my head. I reach over and tug on the string of his swim trunks, his turn to shimmy out of them, and his length springs out, bobbing, leaving my mouth watering. Growing up and seeing random, inappropriate joke memes or funny penis sculptures was always weird. Like how can someone be attracted or turned on by them? But now, seeing Wes's and how it's long and thick and perfect, it's the sexiest thing I've ever laid eyes on. I'll never get used to the sight of him.

I reach out to touch it and he grabs my hand, shaking his head. He pulls me by the wrist, leading me to get closer to him. I climb back on top as I was positioned before, straddling his lap.

"Shit. Let me grab a condom," he says and wraps one strong arm around my back so that I don't fall off his lap, and the other hand reaches into the center console, fishing out a condom that he holds up to show me with that grin again. Dimples on full display.

He tears the foil packet open and puts on the condom before reaching to touch the aching spot between my legs, "Fuck, you're so wet, Josie."

"You're to blame," I reply before kissing him again.

I reach down and wrap my fingers around him, stroking him once, twice, three times, then rise to my knees, guiding him to me. My face is positioned just a little above his head when he looks up at me as he buries himself right where he belongs, pulling a gasp from my throat. Even though we have sex often now, it always hurts a little the first time he penetrates me, widening my walls, making himself at home.

Once I'm completely sitting on him, the backs of my thighs against the front of his, I slowly bring myself up until it's just the tip of him in me. His eyes close, hands on my ass, fingers digging in, helping me rock as he pulls and pushes in and out of me. His grip on my hips tightens, and now he's gotten me bouncing in his lap. We keep up this changing of pace; slow, fast, slow, fast, oh so achingly slow, and then he's pounding into me from below. He brings one of my boobs back into his mouth and sucks, and with the friction he's causing on my clit, I can feel the euphoria. He releases my tit with a pop, and I bring a hand down to add more attention to my now-swollen nub, leaning back some more to give him a better view of me touching myself.

"Fuck," he lets out, eyes stuck to my hand.

"I'm gonna come," I practically scream.

He keeps us going at the same pace to keep me on the same path so I don't lose my climax. I can see his arms tense up, and I know he's trying to hold back and not let go before me. But as perfect as it can be, right as I feel him growing even bigger inside me, I burst into pieces. I'm looking at him, but the waves are crashing through me, and the feeling is utter satisfaction. My entire body heats up and my bones go limp. Time stops around us, and I'm overwhelmed with him and this summer and how I can picture having him just like this, whenever I want, *whenever he wants,* for the rest of my life.

Wes and I walk through the hot sand to meet up with my best friend and my brother. I'm a little nervous Joe will know something is up because we left not long after they did, but somehow made it here about forty-five minutes later.

The beach is packed with people. Different speakers blast music, and kids run around building and destroying sandcastles near the water. I push the fear of running into Drew Scott as far as I can to the back of my mind, but I can't help being aware of my surroundings the whole time.

I spot Cora's big floppy straw hat which is wrapped with a black band that matches her black bikini. Half her ass is hanging out, and my brother smacks it from his spot down on the towel, trying to get her to sit with him. Right before she does, she spots us and flails her hands around to get our attention.

Wes sets down a cooler and my beach bag as soon as we approach them. "Fuck, man, that traffic was ridiculous. You'd think it was spring break." He winks at me, and one wouldn't believe we just had sex minutes ago because I can already feel my bikini bottoms getting wet. Although it is true, the traffic to the beach is always crazy on any day that school is out. So, summer is prime time.

"Yeah, it was brutal, but how do you get here almost an hour after us?" My brother questions my secret boyfriend.

"Oh, well, I didn't realize I needed gas until after I picked up Josie." Wes and I played that we were running late when Joe was ready to pick up Cora, that way Wes had a reason to come get me. And just to make it a little more credible, I throw in, "And I made Wes drive me through a Starbucks."

"That line was also a killer," Wes says with a playful raise of his eyebrows.

I glance over at Joe, only to see him catch my smirk after Wes's look, but he looks away right after.

I lay out my beach towel next to Cora's, and she shows me her manicure she got yesterday. It's a candy apple red that complements her tan skin. I maintain my nails nice and short, only getting them done for special occasions. I don't think Cora's seen her natural nail beds for a couple years now, she's always sporting a fresh mani.

In the middle of our girl talk, where I'm telling Cora

that I want a book-related tattoo, Wes plops down in front of me and shoves the sunscreen in my face. "Lather me up?"

"Excuse you!" I playfully push him, and he laughs, looking between us. "Did I interrupt something?"

"Josie was just saying she wants a tattoo...on her ass."

Wes's eyes widen, "That's news to me."

"No," I roll my eyes at Cora's joke, obviously looking for a reaction from Wes. "I do want a tattoo, but not on my ass! I was thinking more like somewhere on my arm. Something like an open book with flowers coming out of it. Or maybe even a stack of books? I don't know."

"I dig it," Wes responds. "I don't know if I'll ever get a tattoo. They're cool, but it's like putting a sticker on a Mercedes, right?"

Cora swats at him now and gets up to go to the cooler. "You guys want a drink? Ooooh, Wesley coming through with the wine coolers," she sings.

"Yeah, I got that for you guys." Then he lowers his voice to me, "I know you don't always drink, but you can." I know he is offering me a drink, but secretly he's asking if *he* can drink so that I can drive us home. I've noticed him drinking more lately, but it doesn't bother me. Ever since he and Joe got fake IDs and don't need my cousin to vouch for them anymore, the drinking between all of us has increased some. The guys are pretty good about it. Joe won't drink if Cora's going to. "No, you go ahead, babe. I'll drive the truck." I make sure no one can hear me.

Within a couple hours, we pack up our stuff and go to the bar and grill right off the beach for a late lunch. Wes and Cora are buzzing from their alcohol, and Joe and I are having a good time badgering them.

"I'm serious," Joe says as we sit at a booth, him and Cora on one side, and Wes and I across from them. "Our dad would enter me and Josie in these domino tournaments in Cuba when we were five, and we would win all the time."

"I just…I don't know. I can't handle it."

"My mom keeps the trophies in the garage," I add into the fun.

Wes has a hard time believing us. He keeps shaking his head in disbelief. And he wouldn't be wrong to doubt this story. Joe and I have never entered any kind of domino tournaments, and we were born here in the states, not Cuba. My parents came to the U.S. when they were teens, and have yet to return.

"Well, handle it, my dude." Joe laughs at Wes and I shake my head at my brother, knowing he's having too much fun with this.

Cora is a sloppy drunk. She keeps flipping the menu. Until she finally sighs and places her elbow on the table, resting her chin in her hand. With a dreamy expression she finally pipes in and says, "I've never even been to Cuba."

Wes waves his hand in her face, "Not you, them!"

A few hours later, I'm driving to my house from Wes's place. We went there to grab some clothes for him because he's going to stay the night at my house. It doesn't come off suspicious or anything because Wes has been sleeping over since we were kids. Growing up, the guest room was practically his room. The sleepovers have lessened as the guys have grown up, but to say Joe is ecstatic for a buzzed Wes to come over and play Call of Duty until the wee hours of the morning is an understatement.

I check the rearview mirror and make a right out of his neighborhood when I realize he doesn't have his seatbelt on.

"Hey, boozy. Put your seatbelt on."

He replies with a frown. "But if I have my seatbelt on, then I can't do this." He maneuvers his head under my arms and rests it on my lap. His right hand comes down on my bare thigh in a smack.

"Are you serious right now?" I laugh, "What are you doing?"

"This is my favorite hangout spot." A blush creeps on my face, but thankfully it's dark out and he can't tell. He turns his head to face up and I flinch, not expecting it when his finger comes up and traces my lips.

"I've never been this fucking happy." Keeping my eyes on the road, I smile. We really have a lot of fun. Alone, and with Joe and Cora. I wish we could just tell them. I think she definitely has an inkling. She was quick to talk Joe into driving her home and me dropping Wes by his house instead of the other way around. I don't know if it was for my sake though, or for hers.

Nina Arada

"Explosions in the Sky" plays faintly in the background. It's soft instrumental music that I like, and I know Wes doesn't care for it, but lately he plays it on nighttime drives for me.

I've yet to say it out loud, but I can admit that I have fallen completely in love with Wes Miller. I thought I was in love with him in high school, but this is different. He does little things for me every day that I would never have expected in a real-life relationship. Book-boyfriend type stuff. He reads to me sometimes, orders extra food at the drive-thru when I say I just want fries, and just last week I realized he bought the multivitamins I take, as well as my sunscreen and makeup wipes, to keep at his house because I always forget to bring them with me. These aren't things he does super often as we don't have much time when we're sneaking around, but at the end of the day, it shows. I know he loves me, too.

"I'm happy, too. Really happy," I admit. He's still got alcohol flowing through his body, so I'm not completely engaging him in conversation. Let alone telling him my latest revelation on how I feel about him.

"You know what would have made you happier? Definitely would have made me happier."

"What's that?" I ask with curiosity.

"I regret not tasting you earlier." Electricity zaps its way between my legs, and he laughs when he feels my thighs clench together.

"You're a bad boy, Wes," I say when I bring my palm down to his mouth and run my fingers along his smooth jaw line. He replies with a chuckle and falls asleep within a few blocks.

I'm startled awake when the coolness hits me from my covers falling off my body. It takes a few blinks to realize my blanket didn't fall off on its own, but instead was pulled off by my boyfriend. My secret boyfriend. My secret boyfriend who's apparently sneaked into my room, in my house, where my parents and twin brother sleep.

"Wes!" I say in a harsh whisper. "What are you doing?"

"What? I can't come see my girlfriend? Tell her goodnight?" I don't need to see the smirk to know it's there. His voice also tells me that he's sobered up.

"You've lost your ever-loving mind!"

"Very possible." He's made himself comfortable with his chest resting between my legs where I'm covered in raggedy sleep pants. His chain glistens in the moonlight. He lifts my t-shirt and exposes my midriff, running his fingers over my belly.

"Is Joe asleep?"

"He is." His digits slowly crawl up my stomach and palm my breasts.

"Did you see my parents out there?"

"Nope." He pops the *p* and my body comes alive with chills when he uses each thumb to rub painfully slow circles over my hardened nipples.

I can barely catch my breath for the next question, "Did you–" I clear my throat, "Did you lock the door?"

"Of course." Now his hands crawl down my torso and stop at the waistline, fingering the band of my pants.

"What if someone wakes up and finds that you're not in the guest room?"

"I could have left." He hooks his fingers in the waistband and pulls my pants, along with my panties, off awkwardly in front of him, leaving me spread eagle, wet, and wanton. Ready for him.

"What if they try to come in? What if we get caught?"

He kisses the inside of my thigh before he dives in headfirst, "No regrets, baby."

chapter thirty-one

present day, 2022

wes

IT'S FINALLY THURSDAY. I've been looking forward to this day all damn week. Mostly because I love that Josie and I both share Fridays off, but also because we both need a down day. I've had a shit week, starting with my most popular CrossFit instructor coming down with the flu, leaving me having to train those classes along with my full schedule, and the sauna room is down, too. Pump House is most popular for its classes, including CrossFit and the sauna.

Josie's hasn't been much different. Her front desk girls, whom she kept calling *so cute and sweet* until this week, keep fucking up her schedule. First strike was when they failed to tell her that they scheduled her an earlier session on Monday morning. She had no clue until they called her asking where she was. Then they booked her during a time she didn't have a room available since she shares space with other therapists, resulting in her seeing a client at the local coffee shop. Against the rules, but she didn't want to lose the client.

She also came home fired up yesterday when someone ate her sandwich from the fridge. Although, it was fucking hot watching her walk into the apartment angrily putting her hair up in a ponytail and taking her heels off one by one before just chucking them into her room.

Needless to say, we are looking forward to a day off. We've both been coming home post-sunset. The good part of the week, the *best* part of the week, is the fact that she's slept in my bed every night. We haven't done more than cuddle or kiss here and there. I know I went a little overboard the night of her birthday, and I want her to know that I can control myself. I'm not that eighteen-year-old kid anymore. I want her to know this is real for me.

I mean, I do park my chub between her ass cheeks, and for now that's enough for me. I've kept my word and don't plan to get off until I'm inside of her.

I'm on my way to meet my roommates for dinner at BrickHouse. I'm craving this wind down and hopefully some normalcy with my girl. I know she spilled the beans to Cassie. And I'm glad because we are adults, we don't need to sneak around for anyone anymore. I'm willing to bet her parents would even be ecstatic if we got back together.

Walking into the packed restaurant, which is a sea of royal blue and white hockey jerseys, I spot Cassie and Brandon and head over to them. As I lower myself into the booth, I check my phone. "Where's Josie? I haven't heard from her."

"She was going to come but ran late at work and said she wanted to get some stuff done at the apartment."

I'm bummed she isn't here and hope nothing's wrong. There's no way I did something else, is there? Trepidation fills me as I wonder what the fuck I did now. The waitress shows up and takes our orders, and I'm relieved as soon as she walks away so I can shoot Josie a text.

> **Wes:** Hey, everything okay?
> **Josie:** Hi! I'm sorry. I just have laundry to do and I'm behind in dictations.
> **Josie:** I just want to chill tomorrow.
> **Wes:** I get it. You're missed though. Now I have to grab Brandon's thigh under the table.
> **Josie:** Better not.
> **Wes:** I like 'em hairy.
> **Josie:** Guess I'm not your type.
> **Wes:** Baby, I don't have a type.
> **Wes:** There's just you.
> **Josie:** So, you're saying you'll bring me food?
> **Wes:** Anything you want.
> **Josie:** Surprise me.

Fifty-two minutes later, I'm walking into the apartment clutching Josie's sweet potato tots and Philly cheesesteak in a paper bag with Brandon and Cassie following me. Josie's practically running across the apartment to her room, hiding behind her laundry basket when we arrive, and comes to an abrupt stop before awkwardly greeting us, "Oh, hi, guys..." We must have just missed her coming in from the community laundry room.

"Why are you being weird?" Cassie can be blunt in a not-so-rude way.

"Um, nothing. I'm just...uh, finishing laundry." She raises the laundry basket for show. "I had no clean clothes."

"Panthers?" Brandon questions, "Like the Plant Panthers? The high school?" I notice it right as he says it. *No shit.* She's wearing my high school football jersey. Now she walks, a little clumsy, backward into her room.

"Yep, that's the one," she answers Brandon.

"Whose jersey is that?" I call out, flashing her a shit-eating grin.

She glares at me, and Cassie looks between us, her eyes the size of saucers. Cassie takes off and chases after Josie, but she doesn't have to go far because Josie seems to start running on instinct, showing us the back of the jersey.

MILLER.

"This just gets better and better," Cassie says as if she's uncovering a mystery. I wink at Cassie before I go into Josie's room. I shut the door behind me and place her food on her desk. She's hunched over the laundry basket on her bed and slowly turns around, hands holding onto the basket behind her.

I take her in from top to bottom. Messy bun, pouty

lips, my jersey that swallows her up, but it does fit her a little shorter than it used to. Her legs are toned more than they were back then, too. My dick stirs in my pants.

"Care to explain?" I take slow, measured steps toward her.

"Like I said, all my clothes were dirty." Her chest rises higher now as she takes deeper breaths.

"When's the last time you wore this?" I ask as I finally reach her and finger the hem that sits on her mid-thigh.

"I never stopped." Now my cock wants to burst through the zipper like he's the Kool-Aid man.

"Do you remember the last time I fucked you in it?"

"I'll never forget."

"Damn, I kinda hoped you had." Her doe eyes wince in question.

I reach around her and grab two handfuls of her half-covered ass. "Because I want nothing more than to remind you right now." Not even an hour ago I told myself I'd take it slow. This old jersey determined…that was a lie.

In a blink, she's climbing me like a fucking tree. Her hands brace themselves on my shoulders and her legs wrap around my waist. Our lips meet, fast and sloppy and all over the place. I bring her down on the bed, beside the laundry basket and grind my hard as fuck cock against that sweet little spot between her legs.

We ignore the sound of the clothes-filled basket crashing to the floor. Josie uses the newfound vacant space to roll us over and straddle me. I cradle her face with both hands while I devour her mouth with mine. I stop and smile against her mouth, "Are you trying to tell me you wanna be on top for our second first time?"

She lifts herself up to a seated position and answers me by circling her hips over my dick. "Yes."

I reach behind her and palm her ass because, goddamn, I can't get enough of it. "If we fuck, this is over."

She flips her hair, a nervous tic she's always had. "What's over?"

"These games where you don't know what you want. Where you don't know if you can trust me. Where you let that summer get in the middle of us. I used to blame myself for what happened to Joe. I let that go a long time ago."

"Okay," she replies, and it sounds like she's admitting that she still blames herself.

"Okay." I thrust the ridge of my hard-on up against her, pushing a moan out of her. "Now, tell me you're mine."

She hesitates. I sit up and meet her face to face. "Just say what you already know is true, baby."

"These are mine." Her breath hitches when I grip her thighs.

I bring one hand up through her hair and grab a handful. "This is mine."

I pull back a little to give myself access to her neck, where I lick a line from the base of it up to her jaw, "My neck." She rubs herself against me, attempting to relieve the building pressure.

My other hand goes from her thigh and cups her

most intimate part. "My pussy." The sound that leaves her throat draws drops of cum out of my dick.

Bringing my hands to her waist, I keep my eyes on hers and plant a single kiss on her chest, where her heart is. "Tell me that every part of you is mine, Josie, and I'll let you ride my cock all you want."

She's practically writhing in my lap. "I'm yours."

My girl might as well have hit play on this little paused movie of ours because we become frantic again. Hands gripping, teeth clinking, panting breaths. I pull my jersey off her and revel in the sight of her dark curls falling against her full breasts, and her dusty rose nipples, a color that haunts me still, seven years later. I could probably pick it out of a paint swatch at Home Depot. I pull one nipple into my mouth and massage her other boob. Her hands grasp my hair against my scalp while my tongue plays with the hardened bud.

I pull myself off of her with a pop, and she rises up on her knees looking down at me. I lean back on my elbows and watch her, waiting for her next move. She tugs on the bottom of my shirt, and I raise my arms, allowing her to take it off. Her fingers run over my chest, over the lining of the tattoo I got in honor of her brother.

"You once said you'd never get tattoos. Some crap about not putting stickers on a Mercedes."

"A lot of shit changed after that."

"Hmm. Well, I like your stickers," she admits, tracing the beachy sleeve I got with her in mind. Palm trees with coconuts stand with the backdrop of waves and a sunset. I even got my old truck off to the side with my old license plate on it. We practically lived in my truck that summer, and I didn't have it for long but I loved all the memories it harbored. I also have the outline of the state of Florida filled with purple aster flowers, the flower for Josie's birth month of September. I don't know if she even recognizes it.

I wink at her, which rewards me with her infamous eye roll.

I'm about to smack her ass, an attempt to hit play on tonight again because I'm painfully hard at this point, but she climbs off the bed and grabs a condom out of her drawer.

I sit up higher, supporting myself with one elbow now. "Should I be concerned you keep condoms so readily available?" Another eye roll.

She tosses it on the bed next to me and reaches down to unbutton my pants and pull them off, I assist by raising my ass. She stands there in only a pair of yellow lace panties. I scoot to the edge of the bed and place a kiss on her navel before I pull her underwear down and let her step out of them.

I would marry this girl. In a heartbeat. She's everything I remember, yet different at the same time. Her hips are a little wider with faint stretch marks that prove she wasn't always as curvy, and I fucking love it.

I pull her onto my lap and scoot us farther back on the bed. My fist strokes my cock as I watch her adjust herself on top of me. She replaces my hand with hers and we both moan when she rubs my head up and down her wet slit.

Fuck, my balls are practically up to my throat with

anticipation. I've slept with several women since Josie, but no one even came close to comparing to her. I grab the condom and hand it to her. She rolls it on and wastes no time swallowing me into her tight sex. I'm so overwhelmed with the suction she has on me, I can barely see straight. Fuck, it's been a long time for me. Her palms hold onto my chest, and once she's filled with me and in a position she deems fit, she starts to ride me.

And fuck, does she ride me.

She lets herself go, and it's the most beautiful thing I've ever laid my eyes on. Her jaw hangs open, breaths short and barely there. Her hands move into her hair as she puts on this show. And I'm the lucky motherfucker she's putting the show on for. I can't even think about who else has been in this position. The thought makes me sick. No one else should experience the delicious weight of her on their hips, the sight of her soft breasts bouncing, the sounds our bodies make from where we're joined.

"Oh my God, I'm definitely coming tonight," she says, voice raspy and out of breath.

"Fuck, yeah, you are. Ride me all the way there, baby, don't stop."

"Mm-hmm," she hums and it's high pitched. "It's just," she pants and leans back, placing her hands on my legs behind her to hold herself up. She rolls her hips a few times before she finishes her statement, "I just don't want to be loud."

Is she serious? I want nothing more than to hear the sexy sounds that I've heard come out of her way too long ago. Aware that she's getting tired and losing energy on top as her movements slow down, I quickly flip us over without disconnecting us.

 I adjust myself between her legs and open her up wider, pumping in and out of her like I've been training years for this. I cup her jaw and kiss her, sweeping my tongue in her mouth to meet hers. Pulling away, I look down to see where my dick disappears inside of her as I hold her legs open. She watches me with flushed cheeks and parted lips, her face almost in pain as she tries to keep these sounds bottled up.

 "I'm tired of keeping you a secret. Let them hear you, baby."

 "Yeah?" she asks, like she never knew this was an option. I know in most situations it's embarrassing to be heard by friends, but maybe it can keep Cassie from snooping if we make her a little uncomfortable.

 I reach down to rub her clit with my thumb as I slow down my pumps but go as deep as possible. I'm pretty sure we both see stars each time I bottom out.

 "Yes," she says just above a whisper.

 "Louder, Josie," I order. I know she wants this.

 "Yes!" She brings it up some.

 "Fuck, good girl. Scream if you want to. Ride it out."

 As soon as I feel her pussy clenching around me, I pick up speed and grip her ass hard enough to know it'll show in the morning. She's chanting, "*YES!*" now and even throwing my name in there. They've got to be able to hear her.

 My orgasm hits me like a ton of bricks, and the pleasure radiates off me. I spill into the condom and thrust into her like never before. I come so hard I'm scared I broke the damn rubber.

I pull out and stand up, grateful that I did not break the condom. I lean over to kiss her before I dispose of it. Then I lie next to her.

"Think you can chant my name like that every time?"

She laughs and covers her face. I remove her hands, "What? That was the sexiest thing I've ever seen, Josie."

She leans over and kisses me. "I liked it when you flipped us over without warning."

"Oh, yeah? You like that, huh? I'll take notes."

Her eyes roam over to the bagged-up dinner I brought home for her. I jump out of bed and pull my pants on. I hold my hand out for her and pull her up to a standing position when she takes my offer.

Dropping a peck on her lips, and *another* squeeze of her ass, I smile against her mouth and tell her to get cleaned up while I warm up her dinner.

Cassie and Brandon don't emerge from their room the rest of the night, thankfully, and I put my girl to bed satisfied and with a full belly.

It suddenly feels like this has been the best week in a long time, and I can't wait for more of that.

chapter thirty-two

present day, 2022

josie

BLINKING, I slowly wake up but lie still, not wanting to wake him. The only part of me that's moving is my hand rubbing my childhood blanket under the pillow. I can feel his warm body behind me, his even breaths as he sleeps.

Two parts of my week have been unforgettable so far. I started off Monday with a Weekly Word I loved. It was unique and deep and all too relatable.

> **If you ever looked at me once with what I know is in you, I would be your slave. (Emily Brontë)**

This was one of the ones that really got to me. Right away, I copied and pasted it into my Notes app to keep. It's what I do with my favorite words. Later I'll open the app to reminisce about my favorites, I just love reading them and how they make me feel. If I'm ever bored, I'll play with the words in a graphic design app I have and post it on social media. I'll sit and write them out and put them in places as a pick-me-up. I've got some written on Post-it notes on my desk at work as they motivate me and help ground me when I have some clients with heavy issues that weigh on my heart. When it's a quote I really love and can't stop thinking about, I end up getting it as a tattoo.

I've got three of my favorites tattooed on my body, along with a lyric from a Billie Eilish song. Then I have my hot air balloon and an open book with flowers emerging from it. I've also got a couple tiny tats: a heart on my foot and the dainty script letter J on the side of my wrist. They're all small or easily hidden because although it's 2022, and we should express ourselves however we please, I enjoy the privacy and not having to explain myself to those who have different opinions regarding my tattoos.

The wonder of who sends me these anonymous texts always sits with me, especially when I receive ones like this that I spend the week thinking about. When I brought it up to Wes all those years ago, he had no idea what I was talking about, which crossed him off the list. I thought it was Joe at one point because the tone of these words and quotes were full of love and sorrow and guilt. We didn't have the typical relationship twins should have, but the messages didn't go away when he did. There was a slight pause in them, but it was no different than the random Mondays that came and went without a mystery message.

Thoughts stir in my mind and pull a sigh out of me. I

jump at my own sound and immediately feel Wes shift behind me. A deep, throaty moan comes out of him, and his arms tighten their grip around my waist. The second unforgettable part of my week.

Last night...it was perfect. I'm choosing to give this, us, a chance. A choice so difficult for me because he's broken my trust in the past. And although he never apologized for what he did, I know deep down it was something he didn't mean. He wasn't in the right headspace then. None of us were.

"This has to be a dream. My girl, still in bed the next morning." A smile forms at my lips and dammit, if those butterflies in my belly didn't just go through a pack of Red Bull.

"Good morning," I say quietly, then I turn around to face him. His eyes are still closed, and I take a moment to memorize what a twenty-six-year-old Wes looks like. A scruffy face, perfect lips—the bottom one slightly fuller than the top—and a scar on his eyebrow that I'll never forget tending to.

One of his eyes flies open and he grins at me, "What you lookin' at, gorgeous?"

"Remember when you busted your eyebrow in the Target parking lot that one night?" I run the tip of my finger over the scar.

"Of course, I do. You and Cora wanted to race in the shopping carts. And you got me the kale hat."

"Oh, yes! I forgot about that hat!"

"I still have it."

"Really, you do?"

"Yeah. It's in my locker at work. I use it when I work

out sometimes." I don't know why it means so much to me that he still has it and wears it, but it does.

I look over to see his fingers grazing my arm absentmindedly. I zero in on his sleeve tattoos, then rub his forearm and ask about them. "So, is there a meaning behind your tattoos?"

His lips pick up on one side, and he stretches his arm out to showcase it for me. "What do you think they mean?"

"I don't know, they definitely give off Florida vibes. This looks like your old truck," I say, tracing all around the intricate designs. "And I'm not sure what these purple daisies are, I know they aren't the state flower."

"No, it's called the aster flower." Now he smiles, showing his teeth and asks me, "You really don't know that flower?"

I give him a confused look, "No, am I supposed to know it?"

"It's the flower for the month of September." He gives me a knowing look, then continues, "Anyway, I have some errands to run today, you wanna go to the gym with me before? I need to get a workout in, but my ultimate goal is to get home to you as soon as I can." He nuzzles himself into the curve of my neck as if he didn't just tell me that he tattooed himself with flowers for my birth month. Maybe it was meant to honor Joe, even though he has the jersey tattooed on his chest. But knowing Wes, those flowers are for me.

I snap myself out of it and answer him, "Ultimate goal, huh?"

He looks up at me to explain, "I'd tell you my other goals, but if I remember correctly, you like surprises."

I do.

I stretch before I give him my answer. "Sure, we can work out, but we'll drive separately because I have stuff I gotta do, too."

"Sounds good. I thought you just wanted to chill today?"

"Ugh," I groan. "I know, but I forgot I have to pick up some stuff from my parents and get my check from the bookstore. I think I'm gonna quit." I sigh.

He sits up, holding himself up with his elbow. His pecs contract, which distracts me, and he tips my chin up to face his sly grin before he turns somber. "Why are you quitting? You love having the bookstore on the side."

"Yeah, I do. But I don't know," I groan. "This other job was just so exhausting this week, and I feel like all the mistakes the front desk girls make give me even more work. The last thing I want to do is work on the weekend, or turn Scotty down if he's expecting me."

"You think you'll stay at the office long? It's only been a few weeks and you seem miserable."

"I don't have anything else."

He starts to make a show of looking around the room, he lifts the blanket and turns around, dropping his head over the side of the bed to look underneath. I grab his arm and pull him back up here. "What are you doing, weirdo?"

"I'm looking for the old Josie. She was here last night," he says, playfully. "But she ain't here now because the old Josie I knew would not be so negative. You can look for something else. Or maybe something will come to you."

I roll my eyes. "You're right. I'm just annoyed because I was so set on getting this job and loving it."

"I get it, babe, but it doesn't always work like that. You'll figure it out."

I nod at him. "Thank you."

"Okay," he says and lifts the blanket again. "Where's last night's Josie? I wanna play with her again." He ducks under and brings himself between my legs, kissing my belly.

"Wes! No!" I say with a playful laugh, attempting to push him away.

He lifts the covers off his head and rests his chin on my stomach. "What." He deadpans. His face is serious, but I know it's an act. "I got things to do, Josie, places to go, orgasms to give."

Laughing, I grab him by the ears and pull for him to come up toward me. "Exactly, we've got places to go. We can get back to this later."

Wes climbs up my body, brings his mouth to my ear, and with his hands slowly running up the outsides of my legs, he says, "I bet I can have these pretty little legs quaking around my head in five minutes flat." Holy shit. That's tempting. That's more than tempting, that's enough to cancel all plans and never let him out of bed. I feel him hard and hot on my thigh, his eyes on my lips. God, it's getting awfully hot in here.

No. No! Be strong, Josie. Errands are to be run and Wes can have his way with you later.

"Later, we can do this later. Let's..." Oh, he's kissing my neck right in the spot that makes me weak all over. "Let's get done what needs to be done...and then...later you can...do all the things." I'm out of breath and it sounds like I'm trying to convince myself more than him at this point.

His head whips away from my neck, "All the things?"

"Oh, don't get carried away now, Miller."

He chuckles that sexy chuckle of his and gets himself out of bed, but not before he drops a kiss on my forehead. Without noticing, I bring the blanket up to my chest and watch him put his gray joggers on (commando, might I add). He changed into these last night after everything, but then got in bed naked.

His eyes are on me as he adjusts himself into his waistband. "See something you like, sweetie? I thought you had to go. Offer still stands."

I throw a pillow at him before I drag myself up and get out of bed. Ready for a productive day.

Hours later, I'm on the way to my parents' house where I plan to pick up more clothes—although last night's mishap wasn't the worst situation in the world—and eat.

Working out with Wes was really nice, actually. We started with a half hour of cardio, and then switched in-between reps on the weight machines. *Then*, the girls started coming out of the woodwork. Girls of all shapes and sizes and colors knew him. I swear everyone knew him. Which makes sense, he has worked there a while and worked himself up the management chain, causing him to spend lots of time at Pump House and often running classes. Yet, when I say that a green-eyed Josie came out, I'm not exaggerating.

Hey, Wes.

Haven't seen you in a minute, Wes.

Coach Wes, can't wait for our next sesh.

Loved that chicken and broccoli recipe you sent me, thanks!

Nice tan, Wes! (This guy was gay and even threw in a wink!)

And the one that really got me—*Still prioritizing those squats, huh, Coach?*

I was ready to piss on Wes and mark my territory. Although I wanted to give them all the stink eye, I settled on a fake smile. Even the gay guy, he was a catch. I'm sure Wes noticed I was threatened because at one point he ended up right behind me to whisper, "All I see is you, Josie."

That was enough to calm my ass down some.

Pulling into my parents' driveway where some classic games went down after-hours during family parties with our cousins and friends, I get out of my car and take in the nostalgia brought on by my family home.

"Mami? Papi I'm here!" I call out. "I hope lunch is ready because I'm starving. I had a good workout this morning." I smile to myself and quietly add, "And last night, too."

I turn the corner to find my dad and Wes.

WES? Jesus, save me a spot because I very well may be on my way.

My now...boyfriend? Lover? Whatever he is...has his KALE hat on backward, a sleeveless workout top paired with athletic shorts, not the same outfit from our workout this morning, but I'm aware this is his main attire. And a damn pencil is effortlessly placed between his ear and his hat. Let's not forget the smirk he's wearing. Did he hear what I said about *last night's* workout?

"What are you guys doing? What are *you* doing here?"

"Well, look at that." My mom coos from the hallway. "Both of you are here at the same time, how interesting." She may as well be rubbing her hands together like a nasty little villain whose plan was successfully executed.

I glare at her. "How interesting, huh?"

Wes clears his throat, "Your dad called and asked me to help him do some measuring."

My dad jumps in, talking with his hands, "Your mom wants these wire shelves out and wooden ones instead. Wes helps me with these kinds of projects often."

"That so?" I raise my eyebrows. Wes shifts his position and heads toward me in the kitchen. My eyes widen to the size of dinner plates because *is he about to kiss me in front of them*? They would go ballistic. Mom would start calling the caterers and Dad would be inviting friends we haven't seen in twenty years to attend our wedding.

Instead, Wes puts both hands on my hips and taps one side, nudging me to the left so he can reach into the cabinet above my head for a glass. I'm heady from his scent due to his close proximity and the way he winks at me when he leaves my side.

My mom walks over to my dad and plants herself next to him, his arm goes around her shoulders out of habit.

"So, how is it being roommates?" Wes and I instantly look at each other, unable to hide our smiles.

"What?" My mother panics.

"You didn't tell her?" He knows this just eggs her on. And me, too! Of course, I didn't tell her, it's barely been twenty-four hours!

"What! What is it? Are you two dating? What happened? You're pregnant?"

Wes spits out his water in surprise. Apologizing and half choking, he grabs the dish rag to wipe up his mess.

"Aye, mami. Cálmate." I attempt to calm her dramatic ass down. Although, she's not wrong. I mean it, she'll start planning a damn wedding.

"Then, what is it?"

"It's nothing. He's just messing with you."

Wes subtly shakes his head. He's basically calling me a wuss for not telling them, but it's so fresh. It doesn't feel right to say so soon.

"Well, don't try to sneak around on us like you did as kids. You guys aren't fooling anyone."

My jaw drops and Wes laughs, asking them, "How did you guys know?"

"Oh, Wes," my dad claps him on the back, "I know what a guy in love with my daughter looks like." Hearing my dad say that brings a blush to my cheeks. "That and her window always had a latch on the side that was loose."

Now, we are all out laughing. I realize everyone kind of zeroes in on me as the laughing dies down. I haven't let my walls down with my parents in a long time.

"I better go get what I need from my room," I say as an out.

A few minutes later, my mom is knocking on my door. She comes in and sits on the bed, looking over the clothes I'm stuffing into a duffle bag. "I know I embarrass you, and I don't mean to. He's done so much for us, especially your father ever since we lost your brother." She gets choked up. "We just love him so much, and we know he would treat you right, but I need you to know, mija, if you don't get together with him, we will be okay."

I smile at my mom. "Thanks, Mom. I know."

"Now, if you don't choose that boy and put him out of his misery. *He* may not be okay."

"Oh, here we go."

"I'm just saying. That boy. No, that *man* lights up when you're mentioned. And when you're in the same room, olvídate," *forget about it,* she says, with a swish of her hand, "you're the only one he sees."

A knock on the door startles us and my dad opens up. "Hey, are we gonna eat or are we gonna eat?

Everyone says they're hungry, but I don't see anyone eating." He points to himself, "I'm gonna eat." Then he walks back out, leaving me and my mom in a laughing fit.

"Is Wes going to be like that in twenty years?"

My mom backs up, appalled. "Have you seen Wes, Josephine? That man is nothing like your father. At this rate, he'll be bringing the food to you!"

We all eat lunch at the dining room table together and it feels good. Joe and Cora are missing in comparison to the old times, but this is nice, too. I don't miss how Wes nudges my foot any time my parents mispronounce a word, something we used to do as kids. We catch my parents up on the living situation and on Wes's grandmother. I update them on my attempt to quit the bookstore, but Scotty saw how my eyes got misty and said he'd take me off the schedule but not the payroll, so whenever I want a shift all I have to do is give him a call.

We make a date to do this again next Friday. Wes says he'd bring his grandmother to spend time with my mom, and he'll help my dad build and install the new pantry shelves.

He insists on leaving at the same time as I do so he can follow me home. Once we get to the apartment, we're reminded of the fact that Cassie and Brandon are staying at her mom's beach house, and we have the place to ourselves.

We move around each other so easily and comfortably, you'd think we started dating seven years ago and never stopped. We order pizza and watch Netflix while

Wes whispers in my ear that he didn't forget about this morning.

Before I know it, I've got one foot on the couch, and the other on the floor and my bottoms? Don't ask me where they are.

I swear Wes was put on this earth to go down on me. Michael Phelps was chosen to swim like a fish. Joanna Gaines, she's here to make houses all over America cozy and cute. Jim Carrey, to make us laugh. Wesley Miller—Grade A pussy eater. I typically wouldn't be so vulgar about it, but before the credits rolled at the end of the movie, he picked me up, wrapped my legs around his waist, then laid us down on the sofa. His mouth was on my neck, then down my chest. He didn't take his eyes off of mine while he pulled my shorts and panties off, and then broke eye contact only when he pulled his phone out of his pocket.

I'm wide open in front of him and he's kneeling between my legs. Nonchalantly, he has one hand rubbing his hard cock over his basketball shorts while the other messes with his phone. "Stopwatch or five-minute timer?"

"You don't–"

He cuts me off, "Timer. It'll be like a race to the buzzer."

Three-and-a-half minutes later, I'm coming on his tongue.

chapter thirty-three

present day, 2022

josie

MY PHONE BUZZES in the drawer as my client tells me about the panic attack she had when a specific song she heard brought her back to a night she'd never forget.

"And did you use any of the coping mechanisms we've discussed?" I ask, hoping that she used something I wholeheartedly believe in. Some people have a hard time accepting that they themselves can climb out of these holes we often fall into.

Hands in her lap, the young brunette sits up straight and a smile creeps on her lips before answering me. "Yes, I did. I tried to distract myself. I started to go through my teacher's names starting with first grade. At first I couldn't concentrate, but after a few deep breaths and some positive self-talk, I was able to ground myself and remember most teachers."

My hand goes to my heart, "Mia, I'm so impressed. You used several coping skills. That's amazing."

"I know and they really–"

My door opens loudly, and one of the front-desk girls sticks her head in, rudely interrupting my session. If looks could kill...

"Hey, Josie!"

"Yes, Lindsay? I'm with a client, what's going on?" I apologize to Mia, who gives me a shy nod. She's probably not bothered, but this is highly inappropriate in the psychotherapy world.

"Hey, sorry. It's just that your four o'clock wants to move to one, but I don't know if you have a long lunch or something." Lindsay picks at her teeth, then inspects her nail before looking at me for an answer.

"Do not interrupt my session for something that can wait. Take a message and give it to me between appointments, please." I cannot believe I have to explain this to her.

"So?"

"One o'clock is fine." I practically slam the door in her face. Maybe I'm being dramatic, but this isn't the first time. And it's not okay.

Once my client assures me she didn't mind the mishap and we finish up, I walk her out the front door and wish her a nice day, avoiding the secretaries.

"Josie?"

Irritated as hell, I answer her and turn around, "Yes?"

"These flowers were dropped off for you. There seems to be a note."

"Oh." I hold my head high and curiously turn the corner to see not flowers, but a gorgeous arrangement of colorful succulents and little cacti in a ceramic bowl. I already know this is Wes because he knows I prefer plants to flowers.

I quickly grab my plant assortment and card and scurry back to my room before the girls can ask any questions. They already had more to say than I'd been happy with when Wes came by last week to drop off my lunch.

I shut the door behind me and sit at my desk before opening the envelope that's tucked in-between the soft petals.

> **Can you believe you're mine and it's not a secret this time? Let me take you out and show you off to the world, gorgeous. I'll pick you up at 6 sharp.**
>
> **Yours,**
Wes
>
> **P.S. Don't worry about what to wear, I got you.**

My heart jumps into my throat. Is he asking me out on a proper date? I kind of love this, but now I'm nervous. Wes and I went on our first date all those years ago in the bed of his truck, but all of our "dates" since then were casual. We either lounged at his grandma's condo that summer, or now we go to the gym together and watch Netflix at the apartment. We don't go out very much. Working also holds us back from doing anything other than relaxing. And fucking. No more than three minutes go by without Wes tackling me anytime Cassie and Brandon leave the apartment. I barely have time to blink before I'm bent over the couch, on my back on the coffee table, or even spread eagle on the washer like he wanted to try the other day when I came three times while he fucked me.

Now, I'm more than ready for this workday to be over.

I pull my phone out of my desk drawer and see two unread messages.

Weekly Word: The sky looks different when you've got someone you love up there.
(Anonymous)

Wes: Don't let those bitch secretaries steal your succulents.

The quote goes straight to my Notes app. And Wes's text has me giggling like a schoolgirl.

At five o'clock, I'm barging into our apartment. Cassie dramatically makes a mess of popcorn on the couch when I startle her with my entrance.

"Was that really necessary? I thought you were breaking in!" Brandon snickers next to her while picking up stray popcorn bits.

Pulling off one heel at a time and stumbling all over, I manage to reply, "I have to be ready in less than an hour for a date with Wes."

"Is that so?" I can hear it in her voice. *She knows.*

I stop before I get to my room and slowly walk backward toward my non-conspicuous roommates, "What do you guys know?"

They both shove popcorn in their faces to keep from being able to answer me.

"Fine, let me stress out." I start fanning my underarms. "I have zero information on what's going down tonight. I'm fine. I'll be okay."

It's obvious I'm anything but okay.

"Really? Where are you going?" she asks with a smile on her face telling me she knows exactly where my date will be tonight, and that I have no clue about it. I answer her with a scowl. In mock horror she brings her hands to her chest, "Do you know what you'll wear?" Then she winks at me.

I turn and run toward my room as though I'll find a naked Wes waiting on my bed. Throwing the door open, I'm shocked to find a bag from Nordstrom next to a Tory Burch shoe box sitting at the end of my bed, which is oddly made. *I didn't make my bed.* I shake my head to myself because that's totally something Wes would do.

"Have you seen it yet?" Cassie asks, leaning on the doorframe to my room.

I glance at her for a second before slowly walking toward the new additions to my wardrobe. "No, I haven't." A smile that feels permanent sits on my lips. I look to her again before opening the bag. She seems just as excited as I am to see what's inside.

Under the tissue paper is black fabric, I pull it out to find a black chiffon maxi dress. Cassie shuts and locks my door for privacy then sits on my bed, chanting, *"Try it on, try it on!"*

I quickly and carefully wrap my hair in a bun at the top of my head knowing I'll be styling it soon. I undress while Cassie removes the tag from my new dress.

"This is so fun!" she exclaims.

"I'm so damn nervous, I don't even remember my drive home."

"What do you mean? You dated this guy years ago and now you guys move around each other like you've been married ever since."

I roll my eyes, "I wish it were that easy. We've known each other since we were kids, but only really dated a few months, and no one knew about it. We have such a complicated relationship. But you're right, we always just sort of…fall into this way of being. I don't know, it's hard to explain."

I slip the dress on and–

"Holy shit!" Cassie hoots, "Check out that slit!" The dress reaches the floor, but has a slit on the right side that goes up to my mid-thigh. The straps are thin, and the neckline falls low enough to show some cleavage, but not too much.

"He's gonna try to *get it in* before you guys even leave the apartment complex." I blush at that statement because I wouldn't put it past him to try.

I turn to the sides admiring how the dress perfectly clings to my curves. There's an elasticized waistline giving the illusion of a possible two-piece. *I'm in love with it.*

I feel comfy, but sexy, at the same time. The shoes turn out to be wedged espadrilles with black straps.

"Miller needs to teach Brandon a thing or two!"

"I had *no* clue he would be good at picking out an outfit for me, let alone get my sizes right."

Cassie slowly raises her hand. "I may have had a hand in that one. But that was it, sizing. Everything else is on him. He did well."

"Very well. Okay..." I grab her hand and pull her out my door toward the bathroom. "Time for hair and makeup!"

We both work like Cinderella's little mice, applying a natural look and styling a perfect half-updo with soft curls, in less than a half hour. A downside of curly hair, aside from the frizz and extra volume, is needing more than a day's notice for styling, but I'm lucky to be able to do anything with it after my session with the flat iron this morning.

"Honey, you've never looked better!" Cassie says to my reflection in the mirror.

I take a deep breath and smile back to Cassie just in time to hear a knock at the front door.

wes

My watch shows the time as 5:59 PM. Having known Josie most of my life, there's a real possibility she isn't ready, but I was getting a play by play from Brandon that told me she should be all set.

I hear footsteps and quickly hide my other surprise behind my back. Clad in jeans and a deep blue button-down, I bring myself to my full height. The door opens, showcasing my smokeshow girlfriend, or whatever she is. A few weeks ago we talked about labels and how there isn't one that really feels right for us.

I think she may have greeted me at the door, but I'm still stunned. The dress hugs her in all the right places. There's no way I just randomly picked out a dress that looks like it was made specifically for her perfect body. *Goddamn.* I can't tear my eyes off of her. I also have to keep myself from humping her leg like a damn mutt.

"Hi," I clear my throat and try again, "Hey, gorgeous. You look stunning. Is that a new dress?"

"Oh, stop." She plays with her hair, and I already know she's anxious. Her eyes then narrow to my arm, which is obviously keeping something out of sight. "What are you hiding?" Josie tries to look behind me.

Shrugging, I don't reveal the gift. "Just a little something."

"You already got me plants at my office and a whole outfit. *From Nordstrom.*"

"Oh," I lift the book, using it to point behind me. "Should I return it? Is it too much?" Her eyes light up. I had it wrapped at the local shop downtown, but it's no secret what it is.

Holding it up high and away from her grabby hands, I lean forward. "Kiss me if you want it."

She comes forward with her lips puckered, holding

back a smirk that would probably push me over the edge, and brings them to mine. My other arm curls around the small of her back, bringing her flush against me. It's a soft, chaste kiss. Smiling against my mouth, she says, "You smell good." Then, she pulls her shoulders back while I still hold her to me, "Where did you get ready?"

"Here. I left right before you got home and visited Grams."

"Aww, how is she?"

"Good, she said I better treat you right tonight."

"So far, so good." She smiles and puts her hand out.

I give in and place the book in her palm. We break apart, and I already feel desolate without her touching me.

She inspects the wrapping, then holds it up to her chest, her anticipation is cute as hell. "Do I open it now? Or should I wait?"

"Whatever you wanna do, baby. It's yours."

She takes another look at it, running her fingers along the edges. Treating it like a rare treasure before she turns into a psychopath and rips apart the wrapping. I flinch at the thought of her coming at my dick like that. *Jesus.*

"Oh! This is supposed to be a good one! Thank you so much!" She beams, running her hands over the brightly illustrated cover. I read something about a brother's best friend on the back and was sold. She comes back into my bubble and kisses my cheek twice. "I'll put this on my shelf, then we can go."

Once she's in her room, Brandon walks up to me and

drops his voice a few octaves, "Alright, son. Get her home by ten o'clock, not one minute later."

"Shut the fuck up, man."

chapter thirty-four

present day, 2022

wes

"YOU FEELING OKAY?" I ask Josie, as the room slowly rocks.

"Yes, I'm fine. We used to go on my uncle's boat in the summers. I never got seasick. Did you ever come with us?"

"No, I don't think I did. And I'm good, I never really get motion sickness." I take a sip of my water and watch her across the table. Her hair perfectly in place, eyes brighter than I've ever seen them, not a smudge on her lips. Although I can't stop imagining them making a mess all over my cock. I've been sporting a chub all night long, so much so that I'm regretting buying her the damn dress with the long ass slit in it. I didn't realize how high it went. She's oblivious to it, too. I don't think she's noticed the six guys I've wanted to knock out for just looking at her.

"So, tell me. Why are you doing all of this?" She

motions around us. "A dinner cruise, the gifts, the proper gentleman picking up his date. What are you trying to get out of me, Mr. Miller? Or shall I say, Coach Wes?" I roll my eyes at her. She's still hung up over all the clients we run into at work.

"What? I can't spoil my woman?" Her smirk makes my dick stir in my pants. "I just want you to know I'm serious about this. About us. We've been through a lot, together and apart. But through it all, you were always number one in my mind. Sometimes it seems unreal to me that you're even back, let alone the fact that you're giving me another chance."

"Don't fuck this one up."

I don't argue with her because she's right, and it hits me like a blow to the gut.

"I'm still working on your forgiveness, ya know."

"Oh, Wes," she says, blowing off how I fucking broke her heart during the hardest time in her life like it's nothing. "I forgave you already. You know that. I wouldn't be with you if I didn't."

"I think it'll be a long time before I can fully accept that."

I want to tell her I love her, that I never really stopped, but it's not the right moment. Not tonight. But soon.

A couple hours later, we're spending the end of the dinner cruise leaning against the railing of the boat, I've got my arms wrapped around Josie from behind. Her scent envelops me, and I can't help but brush the hair off her shoulder and drop kisses on her freckled skin.

The sky is cloudless, giving us a clear view of the

stars, and it's icing on the cake for my date night success. She turns around at the sound of people behind us and jumps in my hold.

"What?"

"Look! They're leaving, let's go!" She's been waiting all night for the shuffleboard table to open. We walk over and I begin arranging the pucks. I look up to see her sprinkling the sand all over the board. "You wanna make this interesting?"

"How? I'm not playing strip shuffleboard."

"Baby, you wouldn't be caught dead naked in front of these douchebags."

"Douchebags?" See what I mean? Oblivious.

"Never mind. Let's play a game. You get the puck past the line and onto my side without falling off the board, you get to ask a question. About anything."

"Okay," she answers, liking my idea. "And if we shoot and miss, then what?"

"If one of us misses, we have to..." I think about it for a second. "We have to compliment the other. Easy."

"Okay. Let's do this. I'll go first."

I grasp both sides of the board and nod for her to go ahead. She leans over and studies the board, I can't help but chuckle at her. I'm sure her first will be a miss just because she's gonna have to give it a few shots before she figures out the pressure she needs to shoot her puck.

Miss.

She groans. "Alright, a compliment," she says, tapping her chin. "Your eyes. They're my favorite. Always have been."

"Thank you. I love your eyes, too. They look beautiful tonight, in case I didn't already tell you. I don't know, something you did with your makeup that makes them different."

"Hey! You can't use that as a compliment now."

"I could never run out of things I love about you."

Her cheeks redden in the moonlight, and I clap my hands together, "My turn!"

I make it right onto her side without sliding off the board, causing her to roll her eyes. "First question," I say, rubbing the short hair on my jaw. "What did you like most about dinner?"

"The peanut butter pie we had for dessert." It *was* good, I let her have the last bite because I could tell she loved it.

Josie misses her second shot and gives her compliment right away, "Your tattoos." Nodding, I tongue the inside of my bottom lip, watching her attempt to hide her frustration is a fucking turn on. And the fact that she likes my ink. "If I'm being honest, I'm kind of sad I can't see them right now."

Damn, this woman is going to be the death of me.

"Your turn," she states.

I make it again. "Which tattoo of *yours* is your favorite?"

"I have this quote that means a lot to me on my side here. It's by F. Scott Fitzgerald." I'm unbuttoning my sleeves and rolling them up as she walks over and shows me the one I saw once when she first moved in. That damn quote almost cost me my life because I choked on a spoonful of chili at the sight of it.

I want to know you moved and breathed in the same world with me.

The script is delicate and dainty and perfect on her olive skin.

"I think that one might be my favorite, too." *Trust me.*

She adjusts her dress and goes to walk back, but first I grab her by the waist and pull her in for a quick kiss before I pat her ass, sending her back over to her side where she gets her first shot in.

"Yes!" She does the most adorable little dance. "Okay, I gotta think of a good one! Hmm... No, I can't," she contemplates her question.

"What? Just say it." I'm not sure if I should be excited or scared.

"When was the last time you masturbated?" Wow. I cock my head to the side, she's really going in for the kill.

"Today. When I showered. Getting ready for this date."

"Really?" She's surprised, but I had to unless I wanted to jump her bones during the date.

"Yep. You wanna know what got me over the edge?" I ask, my voice gravelly. She quickly nods her head. "I guess you'll have to get a good shot and ask me." She sucks her teeth in annoyance and urges me to shoot my next shot.

We go back and forth, learning more about who we are now and even more of *what* we like about each other as adults. She asks about my career goals, and I admit that I'm hoping to take over Pump House if it ever becomes available to me. Truth is, I wish I could just open up my own gym, but I don't have the funds to back me up.

I learn that she went years without reading. At first because she was overwhelmed with grief, and then because she was busy working and going to school. She tells me about how well she and Leila got along. I make a mental note to surprise her with a trip to Coral Springs soon to visit her aunt.

She strays away from any other dirty questions, and she never does ask what sent me over the edge. I wonder how she'd react to the answer.

Holding hands, we walk to my truck and she shifts herself into my side. "Thanks for everything. Perfect Monday to start the week. It's been a shit month with work, and I've come to hate Mondays."

"I told you to call Grams's friend." My grandmother's friend at her living facility has a daughter who's an assistant principal at the high school. While visiting the facility last week she mentioned the school having open positions, and had me bring it up to Josie knowing that Josie hasn't been loving her new job. But it's *our* high school, in particular. And I think that's what's keeping her from calling this woman. She never did return to that school after she left in the aftermath of that party sophomore year.

"I know, I will." I narrow my eyes at her.

She nudges me, "I promise."

The drive home is calm under the city lights. I think it's where I feel most at home with her. I drive with my hand on her thigh, it's the side with the slit, but I don't do more than rub circles onto her soft skin. I can feel her squirming in her seat.

We get to the apartment and it's quiet inside with some light from the TV shining under our roommate's door. I walk her to her bedroom, and she puts her arms around my neck.

"Are you real, Wes?"

"I am, baby." I kiss her and it's a slow, torturing one. "I'm waiting for you to ask me something else. I've been waiting all night," I whisper before dropping a peck below her ear.

"What?" She pulls back and tilts her head in question.

"Don't you wanna know what got me over the edge when I was in the shower?" I ask her this as I run my finger down her cheek to her chin, across her jaw, to that spot behind her ear. "You're not curious at all?"

"What was it?" she asks, all nervous and breathless.

I lean in to whisper in her ear, "I imagined that you showed up at my gym and locked us in my office." I drop a peck on her neck. "You slowly walked yourself over and acted like you were gonna sit on my lap, but instead, you threw everything off my desk and bent over it with your ass in the air." I watch her chest rise higher with deeper breaths. "You know what you were wearing in my little fantasy?"

I reach down and squeeze her ass with my right hand. She lets out a whimper, and I swear I can smell her arousal from up here. "You're in those little fucking shorts, that I swear will put me six feet under at some point, and you ask me to take you from behind, but before I reach up to pull them down," I thrust myself against her because reliving this daydream has me hard as fuck. "You stop me and just pull the stretchy ass shorts to the side, revealing your soaked pussy."

Josie pulls my face toward hers before I can finish the story, and starts devouring my mouth. I reciprocate the kiss and practically growl before I pull her off of me. "I told myself I'd hold back tonight."

"What! Seriously? After telling me all that?" I chuckle at her response.

"I want to be a gentleman. Prove I'm not in this for anything else."

She may as well be a four-year-old throwing a fit because I'm resisting myself. Then she holds her head high and pats my pecs before she turns around and opens her door. "It's fine, I'll just get myself out of this little number." She looks back at me with the thin black straps of her dress hanging off her shoulders and shuts the door after wishing me a good night.

I'm an idiot. I spin around and bite my knuckles the same way I did when I saw her months ago in the gym.

Fuck it. I turn right back around and nearly knock her door off its hinges, slamming it closed so hard, I'm sure the entire apartment complex felt it.

chapter thirty-five

that summer, 2015

josie

A POP SONG comes through my speakers as I clean my room. I need music when I pick up, or doing anything I don't enjoy, for that matter, I'd be paralyzed just staring at the mess around me without a familiar ballad in the background. But today's a special day, hence why I'm picking up at all. I usually thrive in my organized chaos, but I need to do something to keep me grounded for now. I'm a mix of emotions.

Wes and I plan to let the cat out of the bag.

We're going to come out as a couple to my family. Grams knows and has known for a while now. We never officially told her or announced it to her, but it was just an unspoken thing since I spend as much time at their house as I do.

I'm willing to bet Cora knows already. And my mom will be over the moon. My dad…I'm not so sure about him. I think Wes is more anxious about telling him than

I am. My dad has always loved Wes, to a point that I think he'd be okay with his daughter dating Plant High's former tight end. My dad never missed a game of theirs, his pride in their game wasn't a secret.

Then, there's Joe. Both Wes and I are most concerned about telling him. He's hinted before that he wouldn't be a fan of his best friend dating his twin sister, but we also feel like there's no way he hasn't figured it out. I'm holding onto faith that Cora has probably been warming up the idea to him.

The music quiets down for a few seconds, alerting me of an incoming message. *Speak of the devil,* my brother sent me a text. I open the message to find a picture of a hot air balloon. The sky is bright blue and barely littered with clouds. It's beautiful and automatically gives me goosebumps. He knows I love hot air balloons, and that riding on one is on my bucket list.

Joe: Thought of you, sis.
Josie: I love it. Thanks.
Josie: Hey, don't text and drive!
Joe: I'm a professional, Josephine. Look, I spelled out your whole name. LOL

Rolling my eyes, I decide I won't put him more at risk by not replying. I get back into cleaning mode and start a load of laundry, which consists mostly of clothes that were only briefly worn and didn't quite make it to the dirty laundry. The pile is so high now that it turns into a whole ass load for me to wash.

A light knock on my door pulls my attention to a

bright and beautiful burgundy-haired babe bearing iced coffee.

"Oooh, gimme gimme!" I reach out to Cora. "This is much needed."

"Apparently! Look, you have a floor!" That earns her a sarcastic laugh from me.

I take my coffee from her, thanking her between sips. "It's just that today's a special day."

"Same. It's a special day for me, too. After this I go wedding dress shopping with my mom," she explains with an exaggerated eye roll. Cora has never had an issue with her parents' divorce. They coparent like bosses, but I don't think she's a huge fan of her mom's fiancé. "How come it's a special day for you?" she asks, settling herself on the bed and scrolling through her phone, not completely focused on me.

"Wes and I are dating." The statement is followed up with a sigh because it feels like such a load off my shoulders.

"Mm-hmm," she hums while sipping her iced white mocha from the side of her mouth, eyes still on her phone.

"Yeah...and we have sex. Like, a lot of it."

"Oh, yeah. Cool." Like nothing, she replies as if I just told her I finished another book.

"Um, hello?!" She can't be serious.

Her eyes meet mine and she breaks out into a cackle. "I'm sorry, I had to." Her hand clutches her chest as she tries to catch her breath.

"You bitch," I say, throwing a pillow at her.

"The fact that you guys are dating is boooring. Old

353

news. But the fact that Wes Miller is hittin' that," she motions to my ass, then tosses her phone onto my bed giving me her undivided attention, "tell me more."

"It's good. Really good. We're just over hiding it," I explain as I pick at my nails, then I bring my attention up to her. "I love him. I'm so in love with him."

Her eyes practically turn into cartoon hearts. "I know, you have been for like three-hundred years. That's sweet, though, babe. And he loves you, too?"

"Well, we haven't actually said it out loud, but I'm going to tonight. There are so many times I want to, and I chicken out, but I believe he loves me, too."

"Joe and I said it like three days after we started hooking up."

"Yeah, because you guys are insane."

"So, when are you going to tell him? Your brother, I mean."

"Tonight. I'm not, Wes will. He's so nervous that Joe is going to be pissed."

"You do realize it's not that much of a secret, right?"

"What do you mean? He knows?" I ask and my heart rate increases tenfold.

"Yeah, girl. I mean, *we assumed*. Like when you show up late to stuff, or always find a way for you guys to ride together. It's not rocket science." She takes another sip of her coffee before she adds, "Plus, he never takes his eyes off you."

I feel my face heat up at that tidbit of info, then I remember she said Joe knows. "Are you serious? But he acts fine with Wes. He doesn't seem pissed or anything. Is he?"

"No, I mean, I think at first he was a little. And I do believe he won't be a huge fan of knowing you guys are sneaking around and lying, for real. But he loves Wes, and you know, Wes is a great guy."

"You're right. I gotta tell him! I have to text Wes and give him a heads up."

I go to reach for my phone and Cora stops me, "No! Don't tell him, it's just gonna make it more awkward for when he does tell Joe. Plus," she explains with a mischievous look on her face, "why not let him squirm a little?"

wes

One of the guys from our football team is throwing an end-of-the-summer party, but Jared is known to have sausage fests, so we didn't plan to bring the girls. Plus, Cora is with her mom today, and Josie wanted to stay home and read. She doesn't read nearly as much as she used to before she moved back. The four of us are always doing something, and when we aren't, she and I veg out at my place and binge watch TV.

The car seems quiet without the girls. That is until Joe starts, "So, the girls want to watch some movie that's a book. Paper Planes or Angry Towns or something."

"*Paper Towns*," I correct him.

"Yeah, that one. I want to watch the new *Mission*

Impossible." He flicks the blinker, turning us into our teammate's neighborhood.

"We can just go when the movies are playing at the same time and split up."

"What? No. Cora gets all hot and bothered every time we go to the theater. I ain't missing that."

"You're serious? We're with you guys at every movie. Do you do this when your sister and I are around?" I ask. I've never noticed more than some innocent making out on their end.

"It's 'cause you're paying attention to something else," he says as he pulls into the grassy area in front of the house to park. I hear the accusation in his voice, loud and clear. This is it. This is when I tell him about me and Josie.

I think what scares me the most is the fact that he's not an idiot, and he's gonna know right away that I'm fucking his sister. I'll take the hit. She's worth it. I audibly gulp without noticing, and go to explain myself, piggybacking off his comment when he's hit with an epiphany. Joe slugs me in the arm, as he tends to do on the regular.

"Hey! Maybe we can go to separate movies and then meet up in the bathroom sometime during the movie! Damn, bro. You're a genius." A huge smile covers his face and he gets out of the car, leaving me and my confession hanging out in here alone.

We've been here almost an hour now and we were right in expecting a sausage fest; I've only noticed two girls here out of the twenty-or-so guys. Joe and I just finished a couple games of beer pong where we played as a team and won. Both times. Obviously.

I'm starting to feel the alcohol as I drank for Joe and myself. He's driving tonight, which is fine with me because I need the liquid courage. We make our way out back for him to have a smoke, and I adjust my chain with the humidity bringing an instant sweat to my neck. Leaning against the railing of the deck we're on, I hit it harder than expected 'cause the beer has me feeling heavier than usual.

"You good there?" Joe asks before he lights his cigarette, caving it under his cupped hand.

"Yeah," I internally shake my head in an attempt to sober up some. Grabbing the back of my drenched neck again because I'm nervous as fuck, I start. "I, uh, I have something to tell you."

His eyes bore into mine and it scares the fuck out of me. I'm not scared he'll hurt me. I know he can, but that's not it. I'm scared I'll lose my best friend and our relationship. That's lame to say, and I'll probably never say it out loud, but Joe is my brother. We've lied for each other, been teammates, fought over girls, and practically lived together for years now.

Then, there's Josie. If coming out about us ends with losing her, I'd be left with nothing.

"What's up?" he asks before he releases a breath of smoke.

"It might not be the biggest surprise to you but–" I'm

interrupted when a group of girls come outside through the sliding glass door. They're laughing loudly and it seems like more females have arrived.

"You're fucking Josie."

My head whips to my best friend, and his lips pull up on the right side of his mouth. The motherfucker is smirking.

"Right?" Another drag of his cigarette.

Clearing my throat, I answer, "Y-Yeah. How'd you know?" I'm stunned he said it like that.

"You two aren't exactly..." He looks around, holding up his smoke between two fingers as he figures out how to complete his thought. "Sneaky. I mean, it probably took me a minute to figure it out, but you guys are both MIA often." Missing in action we are. I'm surprised we made it all summer without someone catching on and saying something.

"I love her, man. And I'm sorry we've kept this from you."

"Be thankful for Cora. She calmed me down when I first caught on. I didn't mind that you and my sister were together as much as the fact that you were both lying. To my face, like I'm an idiot." His face holds no emotion, and I can't grasp his reaction. "Honestly, man, I don't want to fight with you about that. At the end of the day, I love you like a brother, and I trust you'll never hurt her."

"Never," I confirm with the biggest sigh of relief.

"Then it is what it is. You prove me wrong, and I'll break your fucking neck. Alright?"

I smile, "I wouldn't expect anything less."

He flicks his cigarette off the deck and nudges his head toward the house. "Let's go pick her up."

"Yeah?"

"Yeah, why not? I'll give her a hard time."

I chuckle because she is going to shit, and she'll probably be pissed at me later.

We weave through the crowd which grew considerably in the last fifteen minutes, and Joe turns around and shouts to me, "You love her, huh?"

"Yeah, man. A lot!"

"Don't impregnate my sister! I'll kick your fucking ass!" We continue shouting over the crowd of partiers.

"Message received!" I call out, glad that the sex topic was buried just as quick as it came up.

"Hey, Joe! Wes!" One of the guys we've known since middle school calls us from the kitchen. We detour in there to find them fucking around with the keg. "We can't get it to work right." The evidence shows in the four lined-up plastic cups that are filled to the top with foam. "It's just head."

Joe and I turn to each other, and at the same time we say, "That's what she said!"

Joe pulls his phone out to check the time. "Hey, I'm gonna go get Josie," he says to me, then directs his focus to the guys trying to figure out the keg, "Wes knows these things better than I do. I'll be back." He claps me on the back and tells me not to let Josie know he's heading her way. He also doesn't want her to know I told him about us so he can mess with her some, and I don't mind it one bit.

I pump the keg and check the tubes feeling like I'm

359

on cloud nine. Admitting to my best friend that I am, in fact, fucking his twin sister went way easier than I could have ever imagined. I watch him walk out the front door and start counting the seconds to when I'll be holding my girl without having to keep what we have a secret.

chapter thirty-six

that summer, 2015

josie

NO ONE CAN PREPARE you for the worst moment of your life. It's not something you predict when you let a boy drive you home from a party. No one even tells you that you'll have multiple moments like these. You don't know the moment is coming until it's already here in the present time. One minute you're in bed, trying to read and focus on the pages, distracted with thoughts of the love of your life. The next minute your world is crashing all around you.

"Josie! Hurry! We have to go! It's Joe, the cops called and said there's been an accident."

I don't even remember getting into the backseat of my dad's SUV. I frantically call Wes. *He was with Joe, right?* They had planned to go to a party tonight. Wes's phone rings for what seems like forever, then goes to voicemail and I shoot him a quick text before trying my brother. His phone answers with the voicemail right away. I try Wes again. Voicemail. *Shit.*

My knee shakes uncontrollably, and I feel so cold back here as my dad nervously drives through town. Nausea sits in the pit of my stomach.

"Oh, Mario. He has to be okay. We can't lose our baby boy. We can't, we can't."

My eyes start to sting and fill with tears seeing my mom slowly lose control. Isabel handles everything in life so well. She makes it look like she gets through life effortlessly. But not now, or since she barged into my room. Right away I knew there was something wrong. She was in hysterics, shouting that the police had called and that there had been an accident, and we needed to get there as quickly as possible.

Blue and red lights come into view as my dad turns the corner, and my heart drops when I see an officer bending down, lighting flares to stop traffic. We halt to a stop and all rush out of the car to the scene.

The dark street is littered with all kinds of people and emergency vehicles including a fire truck, multiple ambulances, and cop cars. An officer stops us as we approach, and my dad tells him we're here for Joe. *And Wes.* The slight widening of his eyes tells me that whatever is going on is not good. I take in the chaos, my eyes searching desperately for Wes. I check my phone for word from him as we are pulled to one of the ambulances, but there are no new notifications. I realize no one's in the ambulance when another officer and paramedic come to us.

"Mr. and Mrs. Rodriguez, we've identified the driver from his ID as Jose Mario Rodriguez."

"Yes, yes. That's my son. Where is he? Is he okay?" Mom replies, full of panic.

"I'm so sorry, ma'am, your son was pronounced deceased when we arrived at the scene."

The most guttural sounds erupt from my mom and dad at this news.

"No! My baby!" My mom collapses into my dad.

No, no, no, no, no.

This can't be real. My hands clench my stomach, agony ripping through me. I squeeze my eyes shut when I hear a blood-curdling scream, only to realize the piercing cry is coming from myself. My dad pulls me into him, where my mom is already holding on for dear life.

It's just us now. Party of four, now three. Everyone who once knew me as Joe's sister will feel pity as I'm now an only child, just like that.

As his twin, wouldn't I have felt it? I should've felt the pang in my chest or the blow to my head. It makes no sense. Nothing makes sense. *And where the fuck is Wes?* My mind races a million miles a minute thinking about everything at once and nothing at the same time. How am I supposed to go on without Joe?

I want to wake up. This is a nightmare. This is a nightmare that I need to wake up from because this is going to break us all.

The officer must have done something to get my dad's attention because my dad lets go of us, and Officer

Matthews, according to his badge, continues talking. I only take in bits of what he says.

"The driver of the other vehicle has been airlifted to Tampa General."

"The driver was under the influence and ran the red light."

"Your son died on impact. He didn't feel anything."

My senses dissipate as I try to digest what's going on. Wails come from my mom again, but they seem far away. I can't feel the tears trailing down my face, I don't taste them as they end their journey on my lips. They blur my vision.

The last hour plays on repeat in my head.

"Josie! Hurry! We have to go! It's Joe, the cops called and said there's been an accident."

"Oh, Mario. He has to be okay. We can't lose our baby boy. We can't, we can't."

"Your son died on impact. He didn't feel anything."

I can't comprehend that my twin brother is gone.

It isn't until a mix of cologne and beer engulfs me and my senses rush back in full force. Wes.

Oh my God, Wes.

I smell him, I see him, I hear him, I feel him all around me.

His cries seem louder than mine as he wraps me in his arms. He holds me with such a strength it almost hurts, I welcome the pain.

"Josie, I'm sorry! I'm so sorry, baby," his voice cracks.

"Wes, he's dead!" I cry out.

"I know, baby. I was supposed to be with him, fuck!"

He yells as he steps back away from me and tugs his hair. Shaking his head, he's unable to stop moving around. I've never seen him like this in all the years I've known him. He grabs my face in his hands. "I should've been with him, but I had to help them with the keg and he didn't want to wait and *he knew*. Fuck, I told him, and he knew, baby. And he smiled and he seemed happy. For us." His voice is strained, and I'm consumed with his blotchy face and bloodshot eyes. He's barely holding himself together.

"I don't know if he was, he didn't say it, but I swear he was fucking okay with us."

I go to respond, to console him, because I hate seeing him hurt, and he's clearly in so much pain right now, but he continues before I can get a word in, "Trent got to Jared's and he came straight for me telling me there was a really bad accident. He swore it was Joe's car that he saw, and he rushed us outta there when he noticed Joe wasn't at the party. We left so fast I don't even know where I left my damn phone. I didn't believe it. It's the last thing I would've ever imagined, baby. What now? What the fuck now?"

He barrels through his explanation so quickly, slurring here and there, I can barely understand him. He pulls me to his body again and our cries continue.

Joe was my brother and his best friend, he was the glue that held us all together. I worked so hard on getting our relationship where it needed to be, and now he's gone. I feel empty and lost and overwhelmed with sympathy for everyone. I can only imagine Cora and how she feels. *Oh my God, Cora!*

"Cora! I have to call her!" I cry.

"Wesley! Oh, Wesley, I'm so glad you're okay!" My mother comes out of nowhere and takes him from us, pulling him into her. "Was he drinking? Please tell me he wasn't drinking."

Wes pulls away from her and places the palms of his hands in his eyes before answering her, "No, he wasn't. He didn't drink at all tonight, actually."

My mom's eyes well up with tears, it's obvious she's trying everything in her power to hold herself together. Thankfully, my dad comes over from talking with the officers and takes my mom into his arms.

"Why our baby, Mario? Why take him from us? How can someone choose to drive drunk?" Her cries turn to screams again, and my dad keeps her held against him as he grieves in his own silent way.

I look beyond them to finally see Joe's car, or what was his car. The metal and broken glass resemble anything but our ride to anywhere this summer. The sight brings tightness to my chest, and I'm finding it hard to breathe.

"Mom, we have to call Cora."

"I called her mom when I saw Wes first arrive while the paramedics were talking to us." She uses her pinkies to wipe under her eyes. "She's on the way, her mom is bringing her." She turns to my dad and says, "How are we supposed to handle this, and these kids? How are they supposed to go on like this, Mario? It's not fair. It's not fair!" She beats her fists against his chest and my dad takes it, tears streaming down his cheeks.

Time speeds up and people start leaving as if this is

all over. For them it's the end of another accident, it's time to go home and thank God it wasn't their son or brother or best friend, or even the love of their life for Cora's sake. The night might be over for them, but this will never be over for us. We aren't getting Joe back. This is our forever now.

The officers go over formalities with my parents and bring them to identify my brother, although they are sure he is who he is from his ID.

And when I think tonight can't get any worse, my eyes and ears betray me. Trent squints his eyes and looks beyond us. "Hey...isn't that Drew Scott's Jeep?"

My head turns so fast my hair whips into my face and my eyes find his Jeep. It's upside down, but sure enough, there's the *Scott's Landscaping* logo on the door. My stomach turns and I run to the grass and vomit. Wes runs up behind me and starts rubbing my back. I straighten myself up and look up at him. He pulls me to him, holding my head to his chest while I wail in his arms. "I'm so sorry, Josie," he apologizes. If he only knew what was going through my mind right now.

How can this be? Here I've been nervous to run into Drew all summer, and this is how he barges into my life? By taking my brother away from us. *Is this my fault?* All the times that Leila begged me to report Drew play on repeat in my head, but I didn't want to. I never wanted him to do what he did to me to anyone else, but I never wanted to have to deal with that again, or face him again, or break my family's heart.

Yet, here we are, broken beyond repair.

Cora arrives and we make a bee-line to each other

before silently hugging for what seems like forever. She doesn't say a word. Just hugs and nods to my parents and Wes. She's not here. She's so obviously heartbroken. Wes was supposed to be with Joe. If it were him, too, I wouldn't know what to do with myself.

The night continues on like a fever dream until eventually, Trent drives me, Wes, and Cora back to my house. Neither of us are okay to drive, and my parents have to go to the police department for paperwork.

We walk into the house and the silence is so loud, I realize I'm having a hard time catching my breath again. Like the start of a panic attack. It goes away just as quickly as it shows up.

"Cora, do you want to sleep in my room?" My throat feels funny as the words come out.

"Yeah, I can sleep on the floor and you can be in bed with Josie," Wes offers, defeat in his demeanor.

"Honestly," she starts to wipe her tears because they're coming again. "I just wanna be in his bed, if that's okay."

"Of course." She nods at me then walks toward Joe's room down the hall.

The door shuts and Wes grabs my hand. "Let's go, baby." He leads me to my room, and everything shifts when I see him take control. His movements are almost robotic, every action calculated and measured. He turns on my lamp instead of the bedroom light, and grabs a pair of cotton shorts and an oversized shirt from my pjs drawer. Without a word, he pulls my shirt over my head and unclasps my bra at the back, then dresses me in my sleep shirt. With a tug on my hands, he stands me up to pull my jeans off, unbuttoning them, unzipping them, dragging them down my legs and off my feet. I step into my shorts, and he comes to a stand, hugging me for the millionth time tonight.

We don't say a word, we stand here embraced in the dim room. We cling to each other in hopes we can keep everything, everyone, every part of us intact. This isn't the twist we imagined in our story. I expected the night to end with my brother pissed at me, or possibly be okay with my love for Wes. A tiny part of me expected Joe to try and take Wes from me, I never would have believed he'd be the one taken from us.

After what feels like forever of us holding on to each other, Wes slowly pulls me off of him and turns off the lamp, guiding me into bed. I curl up on my side while he undresses himself down to his boxers and climbs in behind me. His arm wraps around my waist, and he fuses me into him, his warmth the only comfort I know. My mind goes in and out everything that's happened, like I'm reliving this nightmare over and over until I feel sleep slowly pulling me in, then his grip tightens and he kisses my shoulder.

"I love you so much, Josie."

"I love you, too, Wes."

chapter thirty-seven

present day, 2022

josie

WES TRACES my lips with the tip of his finger. "I still can't believe you're here. In my bed. I dreamt about this for years. Fuck," he calls out as he pulls me in closer, turning me around and wrapping me in his arms. The embrace is so hard and strong, heat radiates off of him from just waking up.

I grasp his forearm and settle it right under my boobs. "This is my favorite. Always was. Waking up with you. Your smell. Your warmth. You're just so yummy in the morning." I almost whine my confession and snuggle into him as much as possible.

It's been a couple weeks since the dinner cruise and *Wosie 2.0*, as Cassie refers to us, has been like nothing I could've imagined.

We are a healthier, more grown-up version of ourselves. We work out regularly and do things that are more...*adult* now. We still catch up on our favorite TV shows before bed because I could never take TV time away from Wes or he'd act like a toddler whose iPad just died.

I started taking care of plants again, it's something I used to do at Leila's and I loved it, but I left all my babies behind. Now, I have a little nursery in the corner of my room which gets great sunlight for a good portion of the day. And surprisingly, Wes has a bit of a green thumb himself, adding to my collection as well as keeping me on my toes with watering. He even named some of my plants. My personal favorites being the dark pothos that sits higher, and the golden pothos below it. Wes named them Ben Affleck and Matt Damon. Catching Wes talking to my plants does things to my pulse that it probably shouldn't.

We've taken a few day trips to explore local shops, and now he's gotten into the hobby of collecting old posters or exercise equipment that he can one day have for his own gym. We stumbled upon an old Muhammad Ali fight announcement, and he's been on a treasure hunt ever since.

We're discovering these new things together, bringing us closer in ways I would've never imagined. It's a bond we didn't get to create the first time around. I find myself craving this time with him.

As teens, it was more than sex and hooking up, but we were exploring each other physically, and it was a unique experience considering we had to hide every-thing. Now we are discovering ourselves in other ways —and in front of everyone—and it's almost sexier.

Wes is supportive and in love with life and living in

a way I've yearned to be for years, it's contagious. He also pushed me to finally reach out to the woman from the high school, I'm just waiting to hear back. The idea of going back to my high school, let alone working there every day, is the last thing I want to do. But Wes is right, I'll be there under totally different circumstances, and it's been almost ten years. I love the idea of helping teens who are facing the same struggles I did then.

"How is it possible," his gravelly voice interrupts my thoughts. Clearing his throat and starting over, he says, "How is it possible that we were together for only three months? The way I miss you and think about you, it's like you were my wife of sixty years." He starts to chuckle at the end of his statement.

"At the rate we're going, I feel like I am your sixty-year-old wife. Did you still want to go to that flea market today?"

"Baby, I wanna do whatever you wanna do." It's a random Monday and we both decided to take off from work, but we never made any real plans. He adjusts us so that his chest rests between my legs and his chin sits on my belly. "You want to go to the moon? Let's go to the moon. You wanna grab a honey Cuban sandwich at the West Tampa Sandwich Shop? I'm there."

"Oooh! That sounds so good."

My phone dings from the nightstand, causing me to stretch to reach for it. Wes's fingers trickle up and down the outside of my thighs, "Your other boyfriend hitting you up?"

"Yeah, he took today off, too," I say cheekily.

"The fuck he did." I laugh at Wes feeling threatened,

and he starts to squeeze my sides. Now, I'm laughing *and* snorting. *Attractive.* He gets a kick out of this.

Once I'm calm, I explain, "It's those texts I get with the quotes."

His eyebrows shoot up. "You still get those?"

"Yeah."

"I really am going to have to kick this creep's ass, huh?"

I roll my eyes at him. "Please don't, I love them." He wasn't a fan of the messages back then, doesn't look like that will change.

"Alright, enlighten me with today's wise words," he requests, playing with the unnecessary untied strings at the front of my cotton shorts. It's then that I put my foot in my mouth because, unless this were Wes sending the messages himself, he wouldn't be happy with this. Wes had no clue about it when I brought it up years ago and he's right here with me, there's no way he could have sent the message. "It's alright, it's not a great one."

Weekly Word: It was always you. (F. Scott Fitzgerald)

And just in time, my belly grumbles.

Wes's head jerks back, "See. I know my girl. Let's go grub, then I'm taking you to a surprise and then the flea market." He speeds through our plans so fast that I almost don't catch what he did there. A *surprise* is a surprise to me. "But first," he says as his eyebrows bounce around and his fingers curl around the waistband of my shorts, but I stop him.

"What surprise?"

"That's what it is, a surprise. Now, let me…"

I practically push him off the bed, "No, Wes. There's no time. I have a surprise to get to!" I pull myself from under him and roll out of bed to get ready for the day, leaving him growling in defeat face down on the bed.

I'm buckling my seatbelt when Wes gets in the driver's side and hands me my medium café con leche to go. The Styrofoam is almost as hot as the coffee itself, but I'll risk a second-degree burn for this stuff. I lift the little plastic tab on top and blow into the coffee, steam hitting me right in the face.

"So, you gonna tell me yet?" I ask about the surprise he decided to torture me with by telling me about it right before we needed to leave. I'm freaking out inside.

"Nope."

"Figured." I lean back and push my belly out with a groan, "Ahhh, that was delicious. I'm so full, definitely rockin' a food baby right now."

He's got his right arm stretched, hand on the wheel, and his other arm is resting on his window. Backward hat and aviators. I'm not sure what's more delicious: this coffee or my boyfriend.

Definitely my boyfriend.

I catch his sideways glance and the subtle shake to his head. I turn to face him, knee bent now and foot tucked underneath me. "What? Why'd you shake your head?"

"Because you have no idea what it will be like when there's a baby in there for real."

"Oh, and you do?"

"I do." *Okaaay.*

"Do tell."

His eyes shoot up to the rearview mirror and I watch his every move. How he flicks the turn signal, the way his teeth graze over his bottom lip, the shift of his hips in the driver's seat. "When your belly is swollen, proof of what we mean to each other, proof of what you mean to me. I'll be the happiest man on earth. I'll make it known that you, and our unborn child, are the most important things to me. That I'll do everything in my power to protect you and make you happy. Whether it's grabbing you an ICEE in the middle of the night, or reminding you how exactly that belly came to be. I'll be waiting on you hand and foot, proving that you're my everything." He quickly glances my way, probably catching sight of my mouth wide open with drool spilling out before he brings his attention back to the road. "But we aren't there yet, so I don't plan to get you any late night ICEEs yet, and after last night, I'm closed for construction."

I bust out laughing and smack his rock-hard bicep. "Whatever, you'd pull over to get it in now if I offered."

He chuckles, "You're right."

We pull off the highway and I'm not familiar with this part of town. I know the exit well, passing it anytime we head to Orlando, but it's not an area I've been to many times in my life.

It isn't until familiar intersections bring images to my mind, flipping like a photo album. My grandmother's funeral and my grandfather's, too. *Joe's burial.*

My breaths come in short bursts all of a sudden, and I turn toward the window, about to roll it down, but instead pinch the AC vent to blow directly at me. I need air. I don't want Wes to worry, I don't want him to notice me freaking out right now.

He isn't an idiot, though, and his hand comes over the threshold between us, resting on my thigh. He pulls into the cemetery driving as slow as possible. I almost want him to go even slower, but we'd be going backward at that rate. Probably not a bad idea.

"I come here every few months. The last time I did wasn't too long ago. I came after y'all's birthday and kinda gave him an update on what was going on with us." I watch him as he talks and looks out his window, toward Joe's grave. I reach up to find my face wet with tears, and try to quickly wipe them away, but they keep coming.

"I usually bring something, but it's okay, today–" He looks over at me and stops mid-sentence. "Baby, please don't cry." He brings his hands up to the sides of my face and plants a kiss on my lips, lingering his face up close to mine. "It's healthy to come see him and talk to him." I nod with his hands still holding onto my cheeks. "I know your relationship was rocky, but he loved you so much, baby. He always talked about you when you were gone. He always felt guilty. He knew you left because of us and that party. Because of us and how we didn't stand up for you, and Leah was such a bitch then. We were all kids. We shouldn't have driven you away."

I shake my head because he has no clue. He's wrong. It wasn't because of them that I left. It was because my innocence was taken and there was nothing I could do about it. I couldn't bring myself back to that life. I had to leave. I had to leave my adolescence behind, only for it to haunt me for years to come.

"It wasn't your fault," I cry, shaking my head.

"Okay…" his reply is short, and I know he wants to know why I left the first time. "Why don't we go over there?"

He gets out of the truck, and right as I'm about to open the door to get out and join him at my brother's grave, the feeling consumes me.

It's time to tell Wes. He and Joe always swore they were the reason why I left, even though I told Wes that wasn't the reason.

He opens the passenger side door and stares back at me, concern etched all over his face.

"Are you coming out?"

Taking a deep breath, I turn in my seat, knees poking out toward him. I take his hands in my lap and confess, "It's time you know what happened the night of the party."

wes

Nervous for what she's about to say, I grip her hands tighter. Whatever it is, she's been keeping it from me for a long time. This is a big deal. She's playing with her hair, which only raises my blood pressure even more.

"When I left after that party sophomore year…" She looks up and blows out a breath, puffing her cheeks out, her tears really coming down now. I have no idea where this is going, and I'm scared shitless.

"I got a ride home from someone." I adjust my stance, trying to prepare myself for the biggest mystery of my life. I wrack my brain trying to remember who gave her a ride.

"Please don't get mad. No one knew besides Cora and my aunt."

I nod, waiting patiently, then flatten my hands on the tops of her thighs, rubbing up and down. She needs comfort right now.

"I don't, I don't know how to say it," she stutters.

"Baby, just say it because I'm about to lose my shit," I admit, unable to wait much longer.

"I was raped that night, Wes." My breath catches in my throat. I'm not sure if I heard her correctly, but she keeps going, "And that's why I left. It's why I was gone so quickly and without a goodbye. I wanted to forget that place and forget all the nightmares I associated with home."

All I see is red. This is not okay. The pain those words give me is indescribable. It's like a stab in the chest and there's no going back.

This can't be undone. It's the last thing I would have ever imagined she'd say.

I shake my head. "What you're saying right now is not making sense to me. It can't be possible. I don't understand." I back away, unsure what to do. Bringing my hands to my head, ready to pull my hair in frustration, I find my sunglasses. I clutch them and chuck them to the floor, one the lenses popping out. I want to slam my fist into something. Anything.

"But you—I can't—It's not," I mumble, barely making sense.

She covers her face and her body convulses while she cries. I rush back over and hold her in my arms.

"Baby, I'm sorry. I'm so sorry. How did this happen? I should've chased after you. I wanted to." And here I thought she left because Leah was teasing her.

She shakes her head and wipes her eyes, "No, Wes, please don't blame yourself. This is why I didn't tell you or anyone. I wanted to, but I never could."

I shake my head. "Who did this?"

She just shakes her head, "I can't."

"Josie, tell me who this sick fuck is." My words come out harsh, but it's not at her. It's my anger consuming me. This need to go back and protect her is all I feel, and I can't do that.

Shaking, she answers me, rocking my world, "Drew Scott."

I stare at her, speechless. I can't believe it. Drew Scott was the drunk driver who killed Joe. That nasty little shit. He didn't make it, but I never felt bad due to his choice to drive under the influence and murder my best friend. Now, I see that he really deserved it.

The guilt that I didn't follow her that night sits in my chest like a ton of bricks.

Her hands grasp my jaw, "Breathe, baby, please."

We share deep breaths together. I watch her inhale each breath I let out. Fuck, she's beautiful and she's comforting me when she's the victim here. Aside from the accident and losing her, nothing comes close to the pain I feel. She was so young and innocent, and I saw the changes when she came back that summer. Two years later, she had matured, and she was eager to be with me in every way, but I could tell she was damaged. Something wasn't right. And this is what it was all along. *I wish I would have known sooner.* I say it out loud without even noticing.

"That was something I dealt with for so long, Wes. Obviously losing my brother and my best friend and you, too. But for the longest time I blamed myself. I thought if I could go back in time and report him, maybe it wouldn't have happened. Maybe my brother would still be here if I would have had that asshole put away, or we'd moved or something. If I would have spoken up, I know you guys would have forced me to press charges, but I knew I couldn't have handled it."

"Josie," I cry, as we hold each other. "Nothing you could have done would have saved Joe's life."

She nods, "I know. I know that now."

"I used to blame myself, too. I thought if I hadn't told him about us, then he wouldn't have gone to get you, but we can't think like that."

I sense her tense up. *Fuck.*

"What do you mean, to get me?"

I bring my forehead to her shoulder and she backs away, letting me slip right off of her.

"You're not telling me. Why aren't you answering me?"

Her parents never told her the truth. It's been so long now, I figured they had to by now.

"I'm sorry," is all I can manage to get out.

"Wes, I need you to say it out loud because I'm confused and freaking out right now. You said he went to buy more beer since the kegs weren't working right. This was your story. Multiple times you told me that."

"I know."

"Do my parents know, or did you lie to them, too?"

I shut my eyes for a beat, then answer her, "Yes, they know the truth. They–" I correct myself, "*We* didn't know how you'd handle it."

"So, he wasn't on the way to get more beer. He was on the way to pick me up."

I bring my hands up, needing to grab onto something but knowing she's not going to let me touch her right now, and grab the bill of my hat behind my head. Our eyes meet and hers are filled with betrayal. Not only does she feel at fault that her rapist killed her brother, now she learns her brother was on his way to pick her up when he died.

"Yes, Josie. Please, th–"

"Because of us," she interrupts me.

I let out a growl, "Yes."

"I need you to take me home."

I go to grab her elbow, but she pulls away just as fast. "Babe, let's talk about this. He was happy for us and wanted to bring you to the party we were at and–"

"I want to go home," her voice breaks, cutting me off. She turns in her seat to face forward and shuts the door.

I have to fight myself not to slam my fist into my truck as I contemplate what this means for us. Are we not meant to be? Why is it that when things are good with us, something has to tear us apart.

My stomach turns when I remember what she told me. I want to go back in time and prevent that from happening. I want to go back in time and be the one to drive her home that night.

But I can't because we are long past getting a do over.

The drive to the apartment is quiet and awkward. I don't know what to say. She's so upset with me that she can't even bring herself to look at me.

Without a word we get to the apartment, and she takes off to our place without looking back. I stop in her room to find her shoving things into her pink duffle bag. What the hell is she doing?

"Let's just talk about this."

"I can't right now, Wes. You have no idea the bomb you just dropped on me."

"What about the bomb you dropped on me, Josie?"

"That is not fair," she says through clenched teeth and fuck, she's right. "What happened, happened to me. Not you. It took me years to heal. I struggled for so long blaming myself. I felt so much guilt that his death was because of me." She stops and looks me dead in the eye. "Hell, I had no idea it was because of us."

She walks past me, and I try to stop her to no avail. "What are you doing, Josie?"

"I'm doing what I'm good at, Wes. I'm leaving."

chapter thirty-eight

that summer, 2015

josie

"WES! My appointment is in an hour, I need you to get up soon," Grams calls through Wes's bedroom door. He groans and pulls me into him. I open my eyes to see the sun shining on the sheet that covers our tangled limbs.

It's been three weeks since Joe's accident, two weeks since the funeral, and we haven't spent a night apart. Losing my brother and learning who was at fault has turned my life upside down. I don't know that I'd be able to sleep without Wes. He's my lifeline right now.

My parents played oblivious until Wes left our house for the first time the morning of the funeral. They both sat me down and admitted to assuming Wes and I were a thing all summer. As expected, they approved of the boy who was like another son to them. Their *only* son now.

"Now, you're of age," my dad said. "But I need you

to promise to respect yourself and make sure that Wesley respects you, too."

"I know, Dad," I replied with a groan because this is the last conversation I want to have.

"Hey, you still live under our roof," he chuckled. "All we ask is that you don't come home pregnant or married for a few years, at least."

And that was the end of the "the talk."

Wes's hard length presses against the side of my thigh and intervenes my thoughts, but when he thrusts again, I turn to him with a smile. "Babe, we can't do anything right now. Grams has an appointment."

"I'll be quick," his deep voice says into my ear with a toe-curling vibration to it. His hand creeps down my stomach and into my panties, and I swear it takes everything in me to deny him, but I do.

"We can't, we have to take her. What's gotten into you? You drop anything for her."

"Yeah, and I'll drop these…"

Laughing, I push him away. "Will you stop?"

Defeated, he backs off and rolls onto his stomach with a groan, "Fiiine."

Lately, I feel like Wes and I are at our best when we have sex. It's the one time we can fall into each other and forget about everything else. We're both in a downward spiral right now. Sometimes I'm okay, but when I get in my head, it's like I can't get rid of the overwhelming guilt that weighs on my chest.

After having to drag Wes out of bed and both of us get ready, we take Grams to her appointment and grab breakfast after we drop her off, which is a nice change of pace to how things have been.

Everything has changed since Joe died. Cora withdrew from the University of South Florida. Instead, she enrolled in a college in Las Vegas and moved in with her dad there, something he'd been hoping she'd do after graduation. I dropped a few classes so that I'm not full time this semester. It'll be tough trying to concentrate on three classes, let alone five. The grief and guilt I've been carrying around has been crippling for my mental health.

As far as Wes, he's been dealing with his grief in other ways. He quit Home Depot and plans to start at the local community college in the spring. He's been a bum, for lack of better words. We spend most of our time together doing nothing. I know his grams sees it, my parents sure see it, but none of them have uttered a word. There are moments when we're lying in bed watching TV and he starts to fidget. His limbs become restless, he clears his throat a bunch of times until he finally can't handle it anymore and he'll go for a run. It's like his brain snaps. This is his only form of exercise right now. I think it's because Joe was his gym partner, and they rarely worked out apart.

I scheduled an appointment with a therapist because my anxiety is back in full force, and the accident brought me back to square one. In many ways, I feel like I'm back to who I was the first time I left Tampa.

I put the menu down after I decide what I plan to order and take a sip of coffee while Wes sits across from me clad in a hat and hoodie, looking down at his phone.

"Looks like the guys are having a small get together tonight."

A laugh bubbles out of my throat. "You mean a party? It's hardly ever a small get together."

"You know what I mean. Do you want to go?"

"If you want," I tell him truthfully, taking another sip. "Last one wasn't all that fun."

"It was a memorial for Joe," he says defensively.

"No one seemed that sad. Everyone was wasted. Including you."

"Not this again."

"What?" Now, I'm the defensive one.

"I'm sorry that I'm going through some shit and I just want to escape and have fun every now and then."

Is he serious? "Are you serious? And I'm not going through some shit, too?" I argue, pointing to myself. A fake smile covers my face while I shake my head. "I can't believe you just said that." I start to gather my bag when Wes reaches across the table to stop me.

"I'm sorry, Josie. I'm so sorry," he repeats as he comes around to my side of the booth and sits next to me, wrapping me in his arms. I'm crying now and embarrassed thinking people are watching us, hearing my sobs.

"Why would you say that to me like that?"

"I know, babe. I'm sorry, I just–I'm just taking it harder than I thought. I feel like I wish I knew or something and wouldn't have taken my time with him for granted." I nod, agreeing with him.

"Let's go home."

That night, and many nights over the next few weeks, we'd go to the "get togethers." And Wes would drink more than he'd promise. To the point where I'd stop going with him. Every night he'd go, we'd fight. Every time he'd apologize, and we'd end up having sex, falling asleep wrapped into each other. We'd spend the next morning with him praising me and apologizing, telling me everything he loves about me, how grateful he is that I'm alive. The way he loves me so much is overwhelming sometimes, but I bask in it like he's the sun on a perfect afternoon.

"I close my eyes and all I see is you, Josie. Your eyes and your hair. The way your skin stretches over your hips. A pair of lips that I hope our daughter doesn't get from you because I'd be in trouble. And I'm in love with your mind. Your kindness and smarts are no doubt what our kids will inherit someday. I can't get enough of you."

And by the time the sun went down, and the moon would take its turn lighting up the sky, he'd be gone again.

wes

I quietly shut the door behind me, locking it. I remove my shoes and leave them to the side, quietly trekking across the dark room only to stub my toe on the leg of a stool. *Fuck!* If I wake Grams at this hour, she will have my ass.

I pause, but don't hear anything from her room, which sits across the hall from mine. I continue the journey into my room, closing myself in when I hear movement from my bed.

"Wes?" Josie whispers, switching the lamp on.

"Josie? What are you doing here?" What the fuck, I thought she was at her house tonight. That must have been last night. *Shit.*

"What time is it?" She sits up and rubs her eyes. I'm caught up in her messy bun and the way the covers pile at her waist, her tiny tank top stealing the show.

"I, umm..," Stalling, I clear my throat. "It's four in the morning." Her eyes widen, taking up her whole face.

"What happened? Why did you come home so late? I must have fallen asleep, but you said you were on your way at midnight." Fuck, why do I do this to her? Hell, why am I doing this to myself? Feeling like an ass, I remember the beer that's in my pocket. I grabbed it as I walked out the door of the party in hopes I'd come home and just chill watching TV by myself.

"I passed out on Jared's couch." I really did, I wasn't doing anything shady. I'd never go out on Josie. I pull the can out of my pocket and place it on my desk next to me, behind a frame she gifted me on our one-month anniversary. I attempt to be sneaky, but I'm anything but as her eyes watch every move.

"Okay," she says because there's nothing else she can say. This is how I've been, and how I choose to spend my time ever since the accident. I mean, it's not like when you feel guilty forgetting to call a friend on their birthday. This is more like feeling guilty for letting your friend go on his own after you admit to dating his sister in secret and then he gets killed...it eats you from the inside out.

I should have been with him and I think about it every day. She knows it kills me and tells me every day that it's not my fault. She says we can't control what happened or the driver's choices. And I can't tell her that he was on his way to her, then she'd be in my shoes. I can't shake it. I can't shake any of it. And drinking makes me forget that this is our new reality.

All week I've been telling myself that I need to let her go. She doesn't deserve an asshole like me. She needs someone who'll take care of her, someone who chooses her first. Someone who can worry about her and protect her when everything has gone to shit. Right now, I'm not that someone. And keeping her to myself while doing whatever the hell I want to is selfish.

I rid myself of my shirt and pants and get under the blanket with her. *This is it.* This is when I tell her she's too good for me. Then I feel her shaking.

"Josie? What's wrong?" She answers me with a full-on sob. "Baby, please."

She takes a deep breath. "I just worry. I worry so much about you when you're gone at night. I told you I was here. You said you were already on your way. I let you do whatever you want. I don't care for the parties or the drinking, but I don't stop you. And now you lie?"

"I'm not lying, I swear."

"And I don't know if you have a plan for a ride. I'm terrified you're going to get in the car and drive. You're going to get yourself killed. You're going to kill someone like that asshole killed my brother. I just want it to stop."

"I know, babe, and–"

"I just love you so much. I don't think you understand. I feel like we were so in love the whole summer, and now Joe and Cora both left and-and I feel like you're not that in love anymore. I feel like I'm losing you, too."

In a move so quick I don't know how I did it with this much alcohol in my system, I get her underneath me and hold her hands above her head. Licking her across the lips and coming back to slip my tongue in, tangling it with hers, I ask, "You think I'm not *that* in love with you?" Her eyes are wide and a tear slowly rolls down her left cheek. I'm already hard because she does that to me, so I thrust into the warm apex of her thighs and lick the tear off her face.

"You think I'm not that in love with you." It's a statement this time. I kiss her neck, which she rewards me by opening her legs even more, spreading her warmth all over the ridge of my cock. She moans an apology and thrusts herself against me, trying to get me even closer to her core.

"If I weren't that in love with you, I wouldn't have gotten this hard the second I saw you were in my bed." There's too much clothes between us. "If I weren't that in love with you, I wouldn't think of you every minute," thrust, "of every day." I let go of her wrists and pull my boxers down at the same time as she tries to do something with her panties. "If I weren't that in love with you, then I wouldn't be able to admit that you're too good for me and I don't deserve you. Any of you." I pull the little bit of fabric that covers my favorite place in the world to the side and shove myself inside her. Thank fuck she got on the pill last month because I don't know that I would have had it in me to find a condom right now.

"I don't deserve this," I say more to myself than to her.

We fuck, and the whole time she tries to keep quiet for my grams' sake while I try not to think about where my head is at. When we finally come, I pull out and do it all over her belly. Panting, she watches me in wonder because it's the first time I've ever pulled out since she got on the pill, but I *really* can't have any accidents now.

Hours later, I wake up to a pounding headache. I need to go on a run but first, I make a decision and I do the hardest thing I've ever done. I watch her naked and beautiful, tangled in my sheets, soft breaths exhaling from her perfect lips for a beat or two before I find paper and a pen.

Josie,

Last night, I was an asshole. I never should have forgotten you were waiting for me in my bed. I've put everything above you lately in hopes you'd see the truth. I wasn't lying last night. I don't deserve you. You need someone who can protect you and hold you up on the pedestal you deserve to be on. You need someone who can give you the love that I can't give you right now.

So, go. Leave my room and leave my place and leave my mind. I can't do this anymore.

You're good at leaving, you've done it before. You'll be doing us both a favor...we can only go downhill from here.

Wes

chapter thirty-nine

present day, 2022

wes

I FUCKED THINGS UP. Big time.

My girl manages to bare her soul and share her biggest secret. A mystery I've wondered about for years, and I somehow let it slip that her brother died on his way to pick her up. I can't believe I let it slip like it was nothing. I can't believe what happened to her. I'm trying with all of my being not to think about it, but I can't stop. I want to know where he did this and how he managed to get away with it, but I also don't want to know anything about it. The thought sickens me, and if he weren't already dead, I'd have that motherfucker by the throat right about now.

And how could her family not have told her about the accident after all this time? I figured she'd know by now. Pissed off with myself, and frankly her parents, I get in a workout that I didn't plan to do today. It helps clear my head and sort the bullshit out.

Nina Arada

On my way to my truck, I pull out my phone and call Brandon. I want to know if he knows of Josie's whereabouts, and if he can talk because I'm at a loss of what to do. She packed a bag and got into an Uber, ignoring every text and call I send her way since. He responds by text that he's at a movie with Cassie and asks if I'm okay. *I'm far from okay.*

Before I know it, I'm pulling into the parking lot of Grams's assisted living facility. Three older women are walking out as I reach her door, each one of them practically undressing me with their eyes. *Jesus.*

"Okay, ladies, we'll meet again next week. And hands off my grandson! He's taken." *Huh, who knows anymore.*

She greets me with a tight hug, then admits, "I'm glad they're gone."

"Not a good sewing sesh?"

"Are you kidding? Dorothea there can't knit for shit. I bet she'll bring a hat next week that won't fit over the head of a newborn."

"Are you guys making baby clothes?"

"No, Wesley! Are you even listening to me? What are you here for anyway? You never come over unannounced."

She nags me as she walks into her kitchen, surely fixing a sweet tea and a snack for me.

I lift my hat and scratch my head. "I, uh, I fucked up, Grams."

She dramatically gasps, almost hitting her head on the fridge, and turns to me, "Don't tell me this is with Josie." My silence tells her she's not wrong. She slams the fridge door hard enough to make me jump in my seat. "What did you do this time?"

A sigh starts off my story and she listens intently while placing an ice cold tea, lemon slice floating at the top, and a plate of seven-layer bars in front of me. Of course, I leave out what happened to Josie the night of the party. That's her story to tell if she ever wants to.

"I just don't know what to do. I hate to break her heart, but she also needs to know the truth. That's not fair to her."

"Easy," she says, sitting at her dining room table and folding her napkin in her lap. "You know, Wes, I was lucky enough to step in as your parent. It wasn't hard because you weren't a dumbass often, though you had your moments." I chuckle and she goes on. "I let you make lots of mistakes knowing you'd learn from them. But not this time. I didn't raise a knucklehead, and I'll be damned if you let that girl get away again. Now get your ass on a plane and go to Vegas. Get your girl."

I fight the sting behind my eyes because she doesn't realize how lucky I am that she got to be more of a mother than my bio mom ever was. Then it hits me. "Wait... Vegas? What do you mean? Did she come here?"

"Here?" She points down, fingertip to her table mat. "No, she hasn't been here, but you said she packed a bag and left in an Uber. I'm sure she went where she can't drive to. Isn't her friend there? That sassy one?"

"Cora?"

"Yes, her. I always liked her. I'm sure she went to see her."

"God, I didn't even think of that." Grams watches me intently as I tap and swipe my phone screen trying to find someone, anyone, who can confirm she went to Vegas before I make plans that will only take up more time.

"You know, I have something for you. I've been meaning to give you for a little while now."

"Okay," I answer her absentmindedly as she pats my shoulder and goes to her room.

She emerges from the hallway with an envelope. My name is scribbled in the front. "What's this?"

She sits and nods for me to open it.

It's a check with *way* too many zeroes. My eyes quickly scan the light blue paper and find her name in the corner.

"I don't understand, what's this for?"

"This money has been sitting for too long now. It's your inheritance. It's from selling the condo and from when your grandfather passed. It was always going to go to you, and I figure…now is the time."

"I don't need this. I'm doing just fine. Our living situation and my pay at work gives me enough to set some aside."

"Wesley, my money is no good to me when I'm dead. I'd like to see what you do with it. Open up that dream gym of yours. And don't feel guilty when you spend an arm and a leg on that plane ticket." I watch her in awe.

"I can't take this," I admit.

"You can and you will." She smiles at me and wraps her hands around mine, holding the key to my dreams. "Now make this old lady happy. You gotta make up with Josie now if I have any chance of seeing some grandbabies before I kick the bucket."

Hugging her, I thank her profusely and keep making my calls as I walk out her door.

It's not until late that night that Cora gives me the response I've been waiting for: **She's here.**

chapter forty

present day, 2022

josie

DAN, the nice Uber guy who lifted my spirits when he told me all about his dog's birthday party he threw, drops me off in front of Cora's house. *Damn. I'm impressed.* Her house is a tan, two-story home with brown ceramic tiles on top. White rocks surround a cactus in the small area in front of her door, and a welcome mat reads *Hey, Good Lookin'* in a cute font. I ring her doorbell and look around the neighborhood where all the houses look very similar and brownish. I'm definitely in the desert.

I hear the door unlock right before my best friend comes into view. Only she looks like a different version of my best friend. This is my sexed-up best friend: hair disheveled, lipstick smeared, her shirt (which is not *her* shirt) has only a few buttons done unevenly and she's panting.

With wide eyes and a small wave, I greet her, "Hi.

Umm, are you okay? Do I..." I point back behind me toward the empty street since Dan left. "Do I need to come back?"

"Oh my God! What are you doing here?" She pulls me inside and shuts her door.

"Am I interrupting something? Is someone here? Oh no, is it the security guard guy? Is he here?"

She pulls me around again like a puppet and drops me on the sofa while she whisper-yells, "Shh! No!"

"Okay, well, this is interesting then," I say, motioning to her current wardrobe and I-just-got-fucked-and-need-a-cigarette state.

Right as she's about to explain herself, a half-naked guy slowly emerges from the hallway on the other side of the room. His hair is cropped short in a high fade, and he's cut, sporting a six-pack that feels wrong to look at.

The dreamboat flashes me a swoony smile and a wave, "Hi, sorry, but I, uh..." He motions to Cora who has her back facing him, and when I look up at her, I see that she's standing there with her eyes closed.

"I think he needs his shirt," I whisper and point at the mystery man who can obviously hear me.

What she does next, I shouldn't be surprised by, but I find myself speechless. Cora turns around and walks toward him while quickly unbuttoning the few buttons she had done and removes his shirt off her body, handing it over to him like no big deal. Covering her tits with one arm, my best friend clad in nothing but a pair of black lace panties sends the poor guy on his way.

Before he turns around to leave, he gives me an awkward wave goodbye and I return it.

"What was that?" I ask, pointing at the door.

"Let me get some clothes on and I'll explain."

Seconds later she returns in shorts and a tank top with her hair in a messy bun.

"Talk. Now." She demands.

"No! You first, what the hell was that whole show?"

"That's my friend, Ryder."

"Friend? I've never done stuff like this with a friend."

She laughs and finally starts to let her guard down some. "It's messy. I promise I'll give you the whole story later, but more importantly, what in the world are you doing here?"

I sigh. "Ugh. I had to get away." I melt into her couch. "I won't lie, traveling is exhausting."

"That's a long flight, too. Almost five hours. Are you feeling better?"

"Yes. No. I don't know, not really."

All these years I wondered. The scene of the accident put Joe on a route to our house, and I thought it was odd he was alone. But he was getting more beer. That's what Wes told me, that's what Wes told all of us. *Lies.* Except they weren't because that's what Wes was told to tell me. I was the only one who didn't know the truth.

She reaches over and puts her hand on mine, "I love you, babe. What's going on?"

Tears start to well in my eyes. "I don't want to cry again." I blow out a breath, then continue, "I'm sure you know since *everyone* knows but me." I look up to her big eyes that tell me she may know where this is going. "I didn't know that when Joe got in the accident, he was on his way to pick me up after learning about my relationship with Wes."

Her eyes shut and she rubs her face with both hands.

"Yeah, see. You knew." I shake my head and explain, "Wes said it on accident at Joe's grave this morning." Cora reaches over and hugs me.

"I know it wasn't right, although it felt right at the time. It would have broken you. And as soon as we found out about the driver, I really knew it was going to kill you even more," she admits, and I nod in understanding.

"It just hurts, you know, but honestly, I've made amends with the guilt. I know it wasn't my fault. I think now it's more about the fact that everyone knew but me. Like this big secret was being kept from me." I take a deep breath. "But I get it. I really do. I had a lot to think about on the plane. And I thought about Wes a lot, too."

"Yeah?" There's a smirk on her face.

"What? Why are you smiling?"

"Let's just say I had some texts from him when I went in the room to change just now." I nod with wide eyes, waiting for her to continue. "He was worried. *Really worried.* Earlier in the day, he asked if I'd heard from you, and I hadn't. I planned to check on you but it was…an interesting night."

"Did you tell him I was here?" Her lips form a flat line, and she answers me with a nod.

"Okay, that's fine. Okay." Trying to calm myself down with even breaths, I ask, "What should I do? I don't want to call him. I'm embarrassed. I'm constantly blowing up on him. I feel like a toxic girlfriend pulling him around, and he hasn't done anything wrong. And I told him today..."

"Told him what?" she asks.

"About Drew, sophomore year."

"Oh my, how did he react?" Her eyes are wide.

"He couldn't believe it, and I don't think he cried, but he almost did. I felt bad for him, I could tell it hurt him. But he deserves to know. He brought it up again thinking that it was because of them that I left. I just wish things could be easier for us. When it's good, it's easy, but then that goes away."

"You guys are dealing with some heavy shit, babe. You want to be with him, right? Before this, were you guys okay?"

"Yes, we had a hiccup, but yes. It's almost like we were never apart."

"Do you think he feels the same?"

"Yes. I do."

"Then you hold your head high. Trust each other. I know it's hard with how he ended it in the past, but you know he's always been in love with you. That was self-sabotage on his part."

"I know. My God, it hurt, seeing his face when I said it." Tears roll down my face. "I wish I never had to tell him. But I know it's important that he knows what really happened."

"We all have our secrets, Josie," she sighs and gives me a pointed look. "And sometimes they just gotta come out."

Confused, I tilt my head like a dog, trying to understand what she means. Her eyes fill with tears, and she takes a deep breath. "It took a long time to come to terms with this, but I don't regret it. A few weeks before Joe's accident, I found out I was pregnant."

It hits me like a punch to the gut.

She nods, wiping the corners of her eyes. "We had an abortion. And Joe, he was so good about it. He said it was my choice. If I wanted to keep the baby, he'd support me and be there, and if I didn't, he'd hold my hand through the process. And he was, he was there the whole time, well, not when it actually happened because they didn't let him. But he was there for me, and when he died, I just wished I could go back in time and take that back."

"Oh my God, Cora. I had no idea." I reach over and hug her.

The thought that we could have had a niece or nephew running around right now is wild, but that would have been so hard on her with or without Joe. I don't blame her one bit for the decision to terminate the pregnancy. Now, she's successful with her job and has a bright, beautiful future ahead of her. Raising a little one on her own would have taken her down a completely different path.

"Have we ever hugged this much before?" She laughs in my arms, and I pull back and look at her blotchy face.

"You could have told me, you know?"

"I know. And I almost did, so many times. But I just

felt like we could have had a part of him here, and we didn't because of my choice."

"No. You guys did the right thing. We were kids. Having a baby would have been so hard."

"I know." She takes a deep breath and smiles at me, pulling herself together. "Let's get to bed and finish this chat in the AM."

"Yes, I'm dead tired. Also, you gotta tell me more about the hot stuff who was here earlier. Don't think I forgot about that." She answers me with a groan.

Groggy and tired as hell, I walk into Cora's kitchen to find her in a pantsuit sipping some coffee.

"Good morning, sunshine. Aren't you a vision?"

"Ugh. I bet, if I look anything like how I feel," I reply, then motion to her. "This is a fun get up. Is this the type of stuff you wear to work every day?"

"Yep," she says right before rinsing her mug and placing it in the dishwasher. "I changed my schedule, so I'll only be gone a couple hours, and when I get back we can do whatever you want." Her eyes keep returning to the clock on the stove.

"Okay, that's fine. I'll shower and check my phone. I've been avoiding it since I got here."

"Yeah, Wes is probably freaking out."

"I'm scared to even look. But first, I want to know about last night. Don't leave me hanging," I whine.

"Fine. What do you want to know?"

"First off, why are you being so sassy about it?"

With an eye roll, she says, "Because we really are just friends. He's been a really good friend, and last night everything got messy."

"What happened to the security guard you were seeing?"

"Well, considering I went with him to last night's dinner and left with Ryder," she looks up at me before she continues, "I don't know."

The doorbell rings, scaring us half to death. "Saved by the bell," I comment, knowing I've gotten all I'm gonna get about Ryder for now.

Cora mumbles something to herself before she reaches the door, and right away hugs our visitor.

Wes is in a gray hoodie and black athletic pants, both which accentuate the fact that he is a personal trainer. I'm not sure why I expected it to be him, but I also can't believe it. *He flew all the way across the country at the drop of a dime like that?* Right away, I start fixing my hair and straightening my clothes trying to look as presentable as possible even though the guy has seen parts of me I've never even seen.

I overhear their greetings of: *'Hey, it's been too long"* from Cora and *"Hey, sweetheart, thank you for texting me back"* from him, which only makes me weak in the knees. They always got along well, and Cora has rooted for us since the beginning.

"You," Wes points to me across the room, "are in trouble."

My eyes widen at his entrance. I want to bark at him

like a little chihuahua for talking to me like that, but I won't lie, I love the assertiveness.

"I'm out," Cora says, throwing me a peace sign. "I'll be back in a few hours!" The door shuts.

My best friend is gone, and the love of my life stands there in the middle of her living room. With his hat on backward and his hands on his hips, he shakes his head at me, "Do you know the hell I went through to get here?"

"Yeah, I do. I went through it, too. Yesterday."

He chuckles and looks down before he drops his black backpack on the couch.

"Wes, I–"

"Nope. I want you to listen and I want you to listen good." I'm already heady from his scent and his tone alone. "I don't know the exact moment when you went from being like a sister to me, to being the girl of my dreams, but I'd say it was sometime in middle school when we stayed at Anna Maria Island with your cousins." I remember that trip, his chest had started to show the slightest definition and I had such a hard time not staring. "I always wanted to wait for you to be ready to head for the beach and my stomach would drop each time we split up from the girls. Suddenly, being close to my best friend didn't only bring video games, football, and shenanigans…spending time with Joe meant spending time with you. And dammit, if that didn't make me even more excited to spend weekends at your house.

"The second you came back after graduation, I swore to myself I wasn't going to let you get away again." I don't realize how close he is until he's moving a piece of hair behind my ear. "And then I fucked it up." A tear runs down his cheek. "This time it really was my fault, no one else was to blame. I lost myself in you. Our love and everything that we were overwhelmed me to the point that I couldn't see straight. And when we lost Joe, the glue that made us whole, I condemned myself for that.

"I know now that wasn't right. Writing that note to you, asking you, *begging you*, to leave was the worst mistake I've ever made. I'd take that back before I'd take back coming out to Joe about us, because we had no part in his death. But I know I killed us and everything we had, and there's no way to ask for your forgiveness for that dark moment of mine." He's grasping the sides of my face with both hands. "I never want you to forgive me for that, but I will ask you to learn to trust me again."

I'm nodding because I do. I do trust him. "I never stopped loving you, baby. Trust that I'll always love you and protect you and I'll always hold you as my first. You're my priority, and the respect I have for you has never been more important to me than it is right now.

"I can't live without you, Josie. I've tried several times now, and ten-out-of-ten, don't recommend." I let out a laugh that's mostly a cry. "I'm sorry that we all lied to you, there was a reason behind that, but it was still wrong. You should have known the truth from the beginning, but I hope you realize that the fact that Joe died driving to get you does not make it your fault."

I nod to him and my arms automatically go around

his neck. We kiss and he tastes like summers at the beach and a future so full it hurts when I think about it. When the saltiness of tears enters our kiss, he stops it to rest his forehead against mine. "I love you, too," I finally admit. "And I always have."

"I'm sorry I hurt you, and I know it's not my fault. It's clear we can't be blaming ourselves for things out of our control, but I can't go forward without telling you that I'm sorry I didn't follow you that night. I thought about it, but I was a coward and stayed back. If I had any inkling you left with someone, I wouldn't have let it happen."

He quickly wipes the tears that shed from his eyes.

"Wes, it's okay. I know it was hard to hear, and it never should have happened, but know that I am okay. I wasn't for a long time, but I promise I am now, and I continue to heal every day. Yeah, some days are harder than others. It wasn't right for me to go through that, but I survived and I moved on. I found love. Twice, now." His hands fall to my hips, and he drops kisses on my neck. "And to find out Joe was coming to me, it's more of a blessing to know he was happy for us and on his way to bring me to celebrate with you guys. I know this now."

"You know, for all you've been through, Dr. Rodriguez, you turned out pretty amazing."

I laugh through my tears. "Well, *Miller*, as long as I'm yours, I think I can be an even better version of myself."

wes

As soon as I found out she really was in Vegas, I booked the next flight. It was early in the morning so I was able to go to bed, but I didn't get a wink of sleep. I thought about what I was going to say. I had to apologize for keeping the truth from her, but most of all, I needed to apologize for the horrible way I broke her heart all those years ago.

I knew my girl was strong. I knew she suffered and battled on a field I couldn't even imagine fighting through, and now she proves herself to be even stronger than I thought. This scum of the earth took her innocence and her brother.

The last-minute trip to Las Vegas was good for us. As Josie says, it was *healing*. Learning that she was dealing with way more than I could comprehend, I know that these are going to be some feelings I'll have to work on for a long time to come.

I won over her heart again when she saw I brought her blanket that she forgot under my pillow. We got to gamble at the casinos, and Cora showed us some of the behind-the-scenes action of Sin City, although she was on edge most of the time. Josie mentioned something about sexual frustration, but I didn't ask any further questions. We planned to stay for five days, but it turned into four when Josie got a call to interview for the counselor position at the high school.

We get through security, arriving at our gate for our flight back home to Tampa. Josie sits reading her book while I go get us coffees when I come back to find her fidgety and distracted.

"Are you scared of flying?" I ask her.

"No, I mean, a little, but I'm nervous for that interview. In a good way!" She turns toward me. "I hope I get it. I didn't do well with high schoolers when I was one, but I think I'll fit in better in a position like this."

"You're going to do amazing, gorgeous. As long as you don't become a student-teacher scandal."

"Oh, no. I can't get into anything like that. Didn't you hear?" She looks around, then whispers in my ear, "I'm fucking my personal trainer."

"Damn right, you are!"

Then she kisses me in the middle of the airport thousands of miles away from home, ready to board the plane that'll fly us straight to our happy ever after. Finally.

epilogue

six months later

josie

WES NIBBLES ON MY NECK, causing me to turn away and snuggle my ass against him. Now, his fingertips trace my underboob. I can't help but whimper, half turned on and half exhausted, "Mmm, babe. I'm tired." It takes all my energy to blink my eyes open. "It's still dark. What time is it?" I ask, drifting off.

I'm startled awake when he kisses my cheek, hand flat on my stomach. "Oh my God, what time is it?"

His sexy chuckle makes a beeline all the way to my clit before he answers me, "I already said, it's four-forty-five." *Is he serious?* I'm a monster if I wake any earlier than seven in the morning.

"I was on top most of last night, babe, you can just get on top. I'll go back to sleep. It can be our secret."

"It'll be a cold day in hell before you fall asleep with me inside of you. Come on, I have somewhere to take you." He pecks a kiss on my nose. "Let's go."

Less than a half hour later, I climb into his truck, which feels about three stories high when I'm this tired. I huff and puff in my seat while I go through my makeup bag.

Wes laughs from the driver's seat as he cruises through the dark streets. "I never imagined you'd be so mean to me on the day I decide to surprise you with this."

I groan, "I can't possibly think of anything I want to wake up this early to do."

The sun is slowly making its appearance, and we are in a rural area I've never been to. I'm triggered anytime this guy drives me to unknown places.

My makeup is done, and earrings are in, when I see the huge basket in the field next to the largest colorful blanket I've ever seen. I sit up in my seat to get a better look.

Wes looks over at me with the biggest, sexiest grin, and grips my bare thigh. He got lucky the first dress I grabbed was this short floral number he loves.

"Is that...no. It is, isn't it? Are you?" I have to hold back the tears before I say it out loud, "Are we going on a hot air balloon ride?"

"We are."

I'm bouncing in my seat. "Oh my gosh! I'm so excited! Why didn't you tell me?"

"Because you love surprises."

"No, you're right, I would have been so mad if you didn't surprise me with this."

When he finally parks, I grab Wes's face and kiss him a million times. "This is the best day ever."

"Anything for you, gorgeous."

There's a few guys starting the motor and spreading the balloon, getting it ready for take-off.

Giddy, I fly out of the seat, and we meet up with Frank, the balloon guy. He explains how they get it ready and says we should be in the air within fifteen minutes. I take some selfies with and without Wes. I can't explain the feeling, it's bittersweet. Hot air balloons always remind me of my brother and are so special to me. It's no surprise that Wes would set this up for me, he's romantic in every way.

Since we moved into our own place a few months ago, that's walking distance from my job at the high school, I find flowers on a weekly basis. My favorite is when he gets a bath started for me with candles, salts, a book, and even candy every time. Of course, he's rewarded when I'm relaxed and ready for him to worship me in bed afterwards. Sometimes I blame his thoughtfulness on the possible guilt he harbors because he's so busy with running his own gym now, but I prefer to tell myself that he's just happy finally living his dream. Watching him buy the space and fill it with his favorite equipment, making it his own, has been everything. I'm so proud of him.

We climb into the basket and Frank has to yell over the motor explaining what he's going to do next. Wes nods at him in understanding and cages me in his arms from behind.

The panic starts to set in as soon as we lift-off, "Babe?"

"Yeah?" Wes answers.

"I'm scared. I don't think I can do this. I don't want to ride a hot air balloon anymore."

He laughs.

"Stop laughing! I'm serious. I don't think this is right. I don't even know Frank. What if he's a serial killer and he's gonna drop us off in those woods over there."

"Alright, crazy. We are fine. Besides, I've got you." He kisses my shoulder, and when I look out and see the view, I start to feel better already.

"This is beautiful."

"I love you, Josie."

"I love you, Wes. Thank you."

"Can you do me a favor?"

I look over at him, his three-day-old stubble doing things to me ever since he shaved his short beard. "I can't do anything naughty, babe. I'm borderline panicking and Frank is like, right there."

He shakes his head, "No, baby, do me a favor and check your phone."

Confused, I pull out my phone and see I have an unread message.

Weekly Word: Make me the happiest man, gorgeous. Marry Me.

I turn around so fast, I'm scared I'll fall out of the damn basket only to find Wes down on one knee holding open a tiny box with a beautiful, simple diamond being held by a gold band. My hands fly to my mouth.

"What in the world! Are you my weekly word?! It's been you this whole time?" I shove his shoulder, though he doesn't budge and comes to a stand. Tears fill my vision because I couldn't be happier it's him. A part of me fell in love with this mystery person.

"It wasn't always me. It was Joe."

Now, I'm hysterically crying. "No, I–I don't understand."

"I didn't know about it, only from what you'd told me. Weeks after the accident, your mom came to me with his phone. It was damaged in the accident, and she didn't know what to do with it."

I can't believe it.

"The phone was irreparable, but the SIM card was fine. I found this app on his phone where you send anonymous messages and can do all kinds of things like schedule messages, too. I recognized the ones you used to always talk about and realized it was him. I think it was a way for him to be close to you. Anyway, the first message I sent was this one." He rubs his fingers along my side, where my favorite quote sits just under my skin in black ink.

I want to know you moved and breathed in the same world with me.

"I found it was a way to be close to you when I pushed you so far away. "

I pull him up and get my fill of him, grasping onto him like I'm scared I'll lose him again. He pulls me away some, then continues, "I wanted to tell you, then got this idea. I've been planning this for months."

He brings the ring between us again. "So, Josie," he pauses until we lock eyes, "Will you be my wife?"

"I'm all yours, Wes."

THE END

Did you enjoy Wes and Josie's story? If you'd like an exclusive bonus scene from Because of Us, make sure to join my newsletter by scanning the QR code below!

Josie's tattoo

acknowledgments

I grew up with a library full of historical romance books in the living room, and I'll never forget trips to Almost New Books in South Tampa with my mom on a hunt for more paperbacks to fill up the shelves back home. I was always in love with love. And when I discovered falling in love with a book, I knew it was special and that nothing would compare. So, Mom and Dad, thanks for making romance novels a normal part of my childhood.

To my sisters, as a little girl there was nothing more I wanted than to be just like you two. If anyone knows me at all, they know I have two sisters. I'm lucky to have both of you there, backing me up in every way. Silvia, I've been obsessed with your words for as long as I can remember, and your advice never goes unnoticed. Mara, thanks for loving my characters and for reading even though it wasn't an audio-book, one day! I wouldn't be me without you hoochies. And Tuty, you're like a sister and have been my biggest Wes and Josie fan from the very beginning, reading with you is a pastime I'll always cherish.

A shout out to the OGs: Colleen Hoover, Jay McLean, Elle Kennedy and Sarah Dessen. These authors created stories and characters that made me fall in love with reading and gave me the courage to pull my ideas out of my head and try. Here I am over seven years later finally giving Wes and Josie their HEA.

To Bookstagram, and everyone giving their all to this little corner of the internet. If it weren't for this world, I probably would have stopped reading, which is so vital to this writing journey. I've made lifelong friends and met the most creative people from all parts of the world. And the fact that we live in a time where we can connect with authors as readers, I feel extremely grateful to be able to experience this. So, to the most positive community I've ever been a part of, thank you for accepting me and hyping me up on the daily.

Britt, the Christina to my Lauren, the mac to my cheese, the Cora to my Josie. You've been here every step of the way. You read Because of Us before it had a title. You asked for a snippet and now you're probably regretting it! You've read my story countless times and never ceased hyping it up. This book literally wouldn't be here without you as you demanded more after the "truck scene." I owe you so so much. My future PA - we did it!!!

To all my friends and family supporting me from the get go, THANK YOU. You know who you are. Keke, Wes may not be your type, let's hope Ryder will be ;) Thanks for being by my side this whole time, I know we've spent many minutes talking about that fist bite. Mari, you better read it. Haha!

To my beta readers: Kelsey G, Sydney, Jacqui, Vivi, Marian, and Madi - I appreciate you all taking the time to read my book and provide honest feedback. You laughed and cried and hyped it up, reminding me that I am not absolutely crazy for putting this story out there. I loved your kind words and your constructive criticism only helped push Because of Us to the finish line.

READERS! Wes and Josie are nothing without you guys. You are what brings this story to life and shines light on it. I can only hope I make you giggle from time to time, break your heart a little and my biggest goal: I hope you fall in love. I hope you feel it and I hope you close this book to start another and never ever stop reading. And I hope you love it enough to be excited for Cora and Ryder's book.

Elaine York at Allusion Graphics, thank you so much for being available at all times and polishing my story off to the shiniest finish. I have a feeling I'm going to learn so much with you by my side in this writing journey.

Sarah at OkayCreations, thank you for putting my cover together. I am absolutely in love with it and couldn't imagine another cover for Because of Us.

Last, and most certainly not least, to my boys. Leo you're headstrong and doing your best right now and rocking it. Cash, you're literally my number one supporter. You always tell me never to give up and how proud you are of me. You tell everyone about how your mom is a romance writer and it's no doubt you're my biggest fan. I do this for you. You're smart and curious and handsome, and I'm so excited for what you'll bring into the world - thank you for making me a mama. Mr. FancyPants, you never leave my side every single night. I'll make sure you'll have a cameo in the next one.

Cody, my first and only love. You're my real life book boyfriend and an amazing husband and dad. You believe in me in all the ways. Thirteen years and you still give me butterflies. You do so much for me and the boys and have given me this gift and opportunity to follow my dreams and put myself out there in a way I never thought I would. This writing journey is nothing without you. You hyped me up when I first came up with the idea all those years ago and you've never backed down since. You've never given up on me. Thank you for that. I love you to the moon.

Scan the QR below for the full Spotify playlist.

And you can scan this one below for my website:
www.ninaarada.com

about the author

Nina Arada is an Air Force wife and boy mom living in Montana missing the Florida sun (and the Cuban food). While away from family and friends, she keeps herself busy with her nose in a steamy romance and endless laundry. She's an early riser who tries to get her reading and writing in before the boys wake up and after they are tucked in bed, always with the cat by her side.

Printed in Great Britain
by Amazon